ONESTONIA
PURSUIT OF THE LIGHT CIPHER

EMORY FROST

Onestonia
Pursuit of the Light Cipher

© 2023 by Emory Frost

Cover Designer: Carlos Villas
Interior Formatting: Authortree

Publisher: Emory Frost
City of Publication: Benton, Arkansas
Author: Emory Frost

Library of Congress Control Number: 2023909038

ISBN: 979-8-9881827-7-1

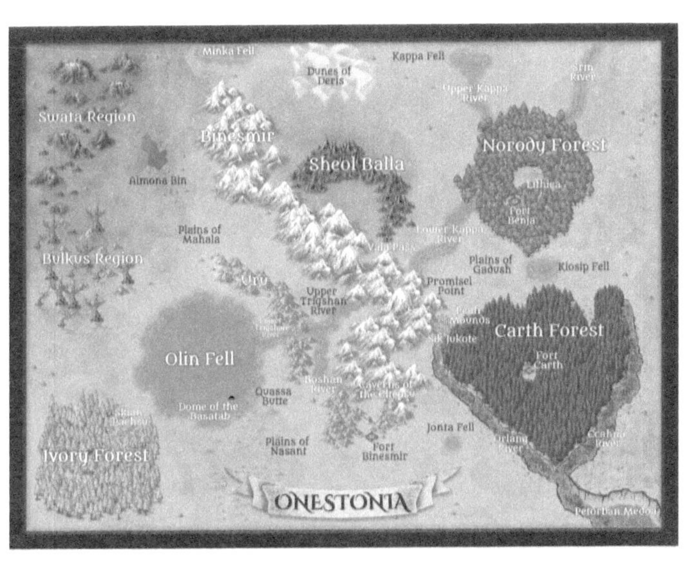

Swata Region
Minka Fell
Dunes of Deris
Kappa Fell
Upper Kappa River
Srin River
Binesmir
Almona Bin
Sheol Balla
Norody Forest
Lilhica
Fort Benja
Plains of Mahala
Lower Kappa River
Plains of Gadush
Kiosip Fell
Bulkus Region
Uru
Vala Pass
Promisel Point
Upper Trigshan River
Lower Trigshan River
Olin Fell
Posh Mounos
Sik Jukote
Carth Forest
Fort Carth
Quassa Butte
Roshan River
Caverns of The Clept
Dome of the Basatab
Plains of Nasant
Jonta Fell
Fort Binesmir
Orlang River
Ecahna River
Ivory Forest
Peforban Medon
ONESTONIA

Peah Mounds
Munda Ber
Cadox
Sik Jukote
Knafel Du Ply
Shwala Lands
Fort Carth
Akaretel Prison
Tughe Arena
Alenthe
Thrysal Cliffs
Byrre Syra
Davalit
Orlang River
Ecahna River

For mom and Tab

CHAPTER 1
CONTACT

Quiesce was upon them, the stirless time as most called it, when Onestonia was at its dark period of the tem-cycle. It was a rarity that Taukin had a seat near the circular wooden stage of the telling place, where only the most respected tribesmen were allowed to sit and speak, and Avent, Taukin's adoptive father, was reciting the story of the creation of their home planet Onestonia. "Our planet did not always exist. Many ulti-cycles ago, Hobaja Vael, the creator of all things, formed our world from dust swept up from the moons, and water and ice from the stars and fragments of rock that float overhead." Three fire pits jutted out from the stage separating the three groupings of wooden stump seats that fanned out into a great opening. Taukin, engrossed in the story, wasn't aware that a glowing ember found its way onto his favorite furry trochin blanket. Out of the corner of his large eyes, he noticed two young tribesmen scampering around the circle back to their stumps. One of which was Syonis, the future leader of the rintic tribe, and the source of most of Taukin's grief. The sight of

Syonis made Taukin's hairless head tingle with anxiety and filled his chest with fright, only he would never dare express his feelings outwardly for fear of physical punishment or worse…further isolation. A malevolent grin spread across Syonis's red face and Taukin's skin morphed to a golden hue matching the flames of the fire. Avent had only gotten to the part of the story where Hobaja Vael had placed the god stones at the Peah mounds when Taukin detected a hint of burning flesh, not his nor the rintic's, but a smell that he had remembered from his youth. Taukin opened his draped pelt cover and smoke rolled out, choking him as he stood, and he threw it from his back. The rintic in the circle burst out with laughter, all except for Soyha. She quickly covered the smoking blanket with a handful of cool dirt and tried to calm Taukin down so Avent could finish telling his story.

"Ignore them Taukin," whispered Soyha. "They want you to be angry; don't let them control you." Syonis sneered smugly at the anguish he caused. Taukin turned to the left and then to the right to make sure there were no more surprises before resting on his stump. Syonis hunched over and acted as if he was crawling on hands and feet. It was the derogatory gesture of the suvanth tribesmen, one to illustrate that Taukin was not fully rintic and that he was blood of both tribes and with that, neither pale blue like suvanth nor dark red like the rintic, but a unique violet color… most of the time, until his emotions drove his skin to a color of feeling. Unable to control his anger, his golden skin morphed dark orange with dark wavering stripes, and he yanked up his pelt blanket from the cold ground and shook the loose dirt from it. Avent continued telling the tale of how the Umgara came to protect the Eltepsu.

"Shortly after the creation of Onestonia, Hobaja Vael, the true light, created the Eltepsu. The Eltepsu were given the task of supplying the living things of Onestonia with agrum, the one substance all living things cannot survive without, so they became known as the sustainers. Upon doing so, there was a need to protect these essential beings. Hobaja Vael created the Umgara, giant beings that serve as protectors of the Eltepsu."

One of the younger rintic, in disbelief, asked, "How can twelve Eltepsu create enough agrum for all of Onestonia?"

Avent grinned and replied, "Agrum is constantly produced in the Eltepsu's bodies, and it's harvested and stored for when it's needed. We don't require much agrum between cycles. Some, like the Umgara, require more than others, but most Onestonians only require a few drops to replenish their need for nourishment."

Another young rintic quipped, "Captain, tell us more about the Umgara."

"Ah, the Umgara are spectacular giant beings, standing one and a half rintics tall. Their two legs are so massive they can crush a Doka shell with one fierce stomp." Avent arched his shoulders and put his arms out and continued, "They can twist their torso completely around to see what's creeping up behind them without effort. I've seen an Umgara soldier take up an ealtapa tree from the ground, using only two arms." The rintic youth stared in amazement as Avent reenacted the motion of pulling a tree out of the ground with his bare hands. "These beings are supremely strong and they gain their strength from the large quantities of agrum they consume."

Nelkum, youngest son of Avent, spoke up: "I'm going to be as strong as the Umgara when I grow up."

Avent laughed, "I'm sure you will be."

Avent was interrupted by an arrogant rintic youth who stood up and said loud enough for Taukin to hear, "If the Umgara are so strong and dominant, how did they allow one of the Eltepsu to be taken by the suvanth?" The youth shot Taukin a condescending look then sat down on the wooden stump between his counterparts.

Avent glanced at Taukin and then spoke up, "Quiesce consumes us. I'll continue my story another time. Go back to your huts and rest." A resounding sound of disappointment from the young rintic filled the stage. Avent glanced over to Taukin, whose blue-skinned face poured out melancholy.

Soyha squeezed Taukin's hand to elicit a response, but she received none. She slowly let go and said, "Rest well," then walked away to her hut.

Avent walked over to Taukin and said, "Let's go home."

Keel, Avent's oldest son, turned to Taukin, "Why don't you stand up for yourself?" Taukin kept his face down and shook his head.

Avent spoke, "Keel, Nelkum, leave him be, let's go."

Nelkum's squeaky voice faded as Taukin lingered alone on the trail. He kicked a lump of soil up in the quiesce air and fought back his tears until a loud snapping of dead limbs from the side of the trail at the last turn before Avent's hut caught his attention.

"Who's there?" demanded Taukin as he crept closer and scanned the trees with his large, amber-colored eyes. Taukin's quivering hand pushed down a sturdy limb and he moved his face closer to the edge of the forest. A silent shadowy figure stood hunched and perfectly motionless, not quite nine rintic away. It wasn't like the roaming rintic patrols to separate and go it alone, and the rintic youth never deviated from the safety of the trails cut through the mysterious forest. Taukin's skin turned a frightened golden hue, and his heart pounded so hard that it could leap out of his chest and run away to hide. In the silence, Taukin swallowed hard and tried to maintain his composure. He tried to call out, but his chattering teeth were uncontrollable and unable to form a single word. A gentle hand clenched Taukin's shoulder and he jumped almost a rintic high as he let out a nervous shriek.

"You scare so easy," said Taukin's adoptive mother. Taukin leaned his head back and shot out silvery plumes of breath into the chilled air and pushed down the branch again only to see the rigid silhouettes of the trees. "Are you spying on Soyha again?" asked Larnhi.

"What? No, I wouldn't do that. I don't do that. I saw something strange," replied Taukin.

"What was it?" asked Larnhi, with great interest.

Taukin shook his head, "I saw…nothing I guess. I thought I saw something, but it was just shadows."

"Come on," said Larnhi, and they both turned the corner and made their way to Avent's hut. "It's time to let go of that blanket of yours," said Larnhi.

"No, I'd like to keep it. Can you mend it?" asked Taukin.

"I can patch it, but this is the last time. Next tear, burn, rip, or any other mishap that befalls your cover, it's going away…for good. You're seventeen cycles old now," Larnhi sighed and pulled Taukin to her and embraced him like a mother would embrace her own young. The side of his violet face gently planted into her long, black hair that covered her chest. Larnhi hadn't realized how he had grown, although he would probably remain shorter than her. He seemed like he was still a youth, but not anymore, he was a young tribesman.

"Where do outcasts live?" asked Taukin with a twinge of defeat. She pushed back and gently shook his shoulders, "Never think that. You hear me. You belong here with us, your family, inside the protection of the forest," said Larnhi.

"I can do nothing without scorn from the elders and the young mock me. It has been this way throughout my life."

Larnhi lightened her skin, "Taukin, we all have trials that we go through, that we fight through; they are put before us to make us stronger, wiser."

"My birth mother…she," started Taukin before being interrupted.

"Your mother didn't want you and Avent and I took

you in and have raised you as our own. You are our son," demanded Larnhi, whose skin darkened with anger.

Taukin's face grew flustered and his skin darkened. He had heard these same words all his life, that he was unwanted by his mother. "You mean my suvanth mother," said Taukin, wanting her honesty.

Larnhi exhaled deeply, "What do you want in this life Taukin?"

"I want to be treated like the others. I want to be respected like they are, but I'm not like them, I'm short, I have a notch at the base of my neck, even my color and pattern are different," said Taukin facing the forest floor.

"You have two legs and two arms, you're no different than them. You think respect is given without any effort? Work harder than they do. Be better than they are, even when you want to be worse than them. You make the life you live. Embrace this if you want," said Larnhi with the sincerest of eyes and bright green hue.

Still angry, Taukin's face froze with a fixed scowl. "Leaving sounds better," said Taukin under his breath. They walked along the path that was dimly lit by Aebean, the closest moon and into the wooden, thatched-roof hut.

Taukin and Keel laid at an angle in their curved pelt slings, which hung perpendicular to each other in their drafty wooden sleeping room. "When are you getting rid of that ridiculous blanket?" asked Keel, as cold as the frigid waters of Olin Fell.

"It comforts me," replied Taukin, pulling the patched blanket over his shoulder as he faced the wooden wall.

"You look like a fool carrying it around with you."

Taukin pulled the blanket tighter around him feeling more secure now.

"Let me take care of it for you," said Keel fiendishly.

"When I'm ready I'll pack it away."

Keel stood, single short black braid and green eyes hovered over Taukin.

Taukin twisted his head, "What are you doing?"

Keel, quite larger and stronger than Taukin, ripped the blanket from his brother's body. Taukin yelled out, "No!" as he grabbed for his youth blanket. Keel pushed Taukin back into his pelt sling and proceeded to step on the blanket, tearing and shredding it to pieces. Tufts of trochin hair flew and floated about the scarcely lit room as Taukin yelled and cried out.

Avent, yellow-hued, appeared at the room's opening, "What's happening here?"

Through the tears and dark-blue skin Taukin said, "Keel destroyed my blanket!"

Avent's brown eyes went to Keel, "Is this true?"

Keel's skin morphed light green with fear, "Yes father."

"Taukin, it was time that you lost that blanket, it's kept you from growing," said Avent. Keel's hue went back to his normal orange-red color and his opalescent smile pierced Taukin more than the destruction of his blanket.

"Growing? It made me feel safe!" said Taukin,

unsure of whether or not he had crossed a line which he was careful never to do with Avent.

"Blankets don't keep you safe in battle, your weapon does," said a stern Avent.

"And what punishment will he be given?" asked a still-flustered Taukin.

Avent's skin darkened, "Hold your words, lest **you** want punishment for your brother's actions against you."

Taukin retreated to his pelt, still upright when Avent looked back to Keel and nodded with allowance. Taukin's skin went dark orange with anger, but he said nothing else the rest of the quiesce as he fell back into his sling with angry tears running above his ears and into the soft, pelt fur. All of the emotions had caught up to him and weighed down upon him and his heavy eyelids slowly lowered.

"It was time," said Keel.

Taukin's skin flittered with anger one more time before falling asleep.

The following lumeren, the time when the Eastern star's rays break over the horizon and lights Onestonia, Avent woke Taukin and Keel. "Rise up, it's time for your soldier training. Meet me at the Tughe arena for your first lesson. Eat on the way, get your strength, you'll need it." Keel and Taukin looked at each other equally surprised. They knew the time would come for their training, but they had no idea when that would be. They slid their coverings on and grabbed some kulee mush wrapped in ealtapa leaves and took up their blunt practice swords. Out the hut they ran while scraping the mush from the leaves with their teeth and tongues.

Light beams from the Eastern star broke through the trees in individual channels and warmed their bodies as they made their way down the trodden path to the Tughe practice arena. Keel swiped a mouthful of kulee mush and said in-between bites with mush bits falling out, "This is our chance to impress the officers." Taukin's violet lips pinched tight as he ate. "Maybe we'll get to throw kracklins," exclaimed Keel with excitement, being that he thought he would excel at the activity due to his physical prowess. Taukin continued facing forward without making a sound. Keel's skin darkened, "Go on, be angry with me, but you know that blanket held you back."

With their ealtapa leaves emptied and discarded the two young tribesmen found Avent in front of a squad of young rintic tribesmen. Towering trees that spanned what seemed to be the height of the Binesmir mountains surrounded the Tughe arena, but the wide opening in the middle allowed enough light in for combat training. Avent paced back and forth, his lone black braid whipped in front of his shoulders when he quickly turned his head to address the young soon-to-be soldiers. "Just in time, line up soldiers." He spoke even louder this time: "You will learn how to defend yourself and eliminate your enemy. This training is not to be taken lightly. It will help protect you and your combat brother. The suvanth have recently become more aggressive with the approaching alignment of the sister moons, the effergy is near, and we need to be diligent and observant, more so now than ever before. Look to the tribesman next to you and see who you protect… your brothers. Know they will never leave you. Know that they will die for you and you for them. This is the soldier's pledge!" A sideways smirk came from the young but tall tribesman next to Taukin. Taukin ignored the negative expression and focused on his Captain's words.

Avent ordered his subordinate-ranked soldiers to break up the soldiers into groups to begin their exercise. Taukin was grouped together along with seven other tribesmen. As they began their combat training, Meraco, the tall brawny general of the rintic army, short black hair, with tufts of gray behind his green eyes, assessed the young tribesmen's skills. He was particularly interested in Taukin's abilities being that Taukin was the only one that wasn't born of pure rintic blood, and he was physically smaller than his strapping rintic peers.

A brash and squatty sergeant named Blaiseph, whose belly protruded underneath his cold-weather covering, barked out orders in his gravelly voice, "Four by four line up across from each other now!" All soldiers scrambled across the dark dirt and Taukin found himself across from the large tribesman, who was at least a full head taller than the rest of the soldiers. "My job is to make you into agile killers. There is no sympathy given and none taken. All that stands between you and death is your actions. Now take up your weapons…fight!" ordered the sergeant. Taukin wanted to make a memorable impression on the General, who happened to be the father of Soyha, his most trusted friend, and in his mind, only friend among the rintic.

Taukin held his practice sword overhead as if he was ready to strike down upon his enemy.

Sergeant Blaiseph approached Taukin and ripped the wooden sword from his hands, "Soldier what are you doing? You must want to die! Do you think that the enemy is going to wait for you to strike down upon him with your fiery wrath?" All the soldiers laughed out loud at the comment and Taukin's skin morphed bright, yellowish green. Blaiseph continued, "Keep your weapon in front guard to defend and when you see the opportunity, then strike like this," and when the loud sergeant shouted, "Fight!" the large opposing soldier shuffled his pelt-covered feet in the dark dirt and aimed his wooden sword at the sergeant before launching his attack. Blaiseph deflected each thrust at him and retreated one step before lunging his wooden weapon at the neck of his opponent whose skin went violet and white with embarrassment. "Your size…or shape," Blaiseph patted his bulging belly, "doesn't matter. What matters is this," and he then pointed to his eyes. "Your focus…never lose sight of your enemy, or what you need to strike him down."

The Sergeant's words sunk into Taukin's core, renewing his belief in himself after focusing on his diminutive size his entire life. Sergeant Blaiseph sidled Taukin and his opponent, and gave the command to battle. Taukin's opponent came at him with his practice sword swinging erratically. Taukin's fear drove him backward, dodging the thrashing sword until he tripped over his own stumbling feet and crashed to the silty ground before getting the blunt sword at his neck.

Grumblings and laughter filled the arena before Avent silenced it with his eyes. His opponent's pompous smile drove Taukin to rise to his feet and reset his stance and his skin changed from yellow to dark orange.

"Fight!" came the command from the instructor. Taukin swiftly took three right steps to position himself to the back of his opponent, sword still at full guard. His opponent quickly turned around and stabbed at a surprised Taukin who narrowly escaped the straight wooden sword. Taukin, being smaller than the others and of suvanth blood, was quicker and more agile than his larger opponent. Taukin raised his sword high overhead for a straight, forceful blow. As his opponent readied his sword perpendicular to the incoming strike, Taukin, with great quickness, executed a foot sweep and put his opponent on his back. Taukin then put his blunt weapon against the soldier's violet throat to show he finished his opponent.

The other soldiers looked impressed, but remained silent, loyal to their rintic brethren—all but Sergeant Blaiseph who said, "And like that you're dead soldier. You must defend against any possibility. Your enemy will not follow any rules and will use any move possible to get at your neck." Taukin's opponent's skin morphed dark red, and he jumped up and came at Taukin with his sword coming down with a forceful blow, but a long metal sword cut the wooden practice sword at the pommel.

"Rid yourself of your emotion, lest it get you killed," said the commanding voice of red-skinned

General Meraco, who sheathed his long sword and turned to Taukin, "Come with me soldier."

General Meraco and Taukin walked side by side past the garando training area. One of the low and scaly garandos growled and snapped at Taukin, which startled him and made his skin flicker yellow briefly, but the garando trainer reigned in the creature before any damage was done. Meraco stared a short distance in front of them as they walked and said, "Do you know why the suvanth dwell in the caverns underground?"

Taukin contemplated this simple question that all rintic knew the answer to and proudly said, "Because the suvanth's misguided beliefs drove them to kill the rintic and they were banished to the pit by the Umgara."

"No," replied the General, then continued, "The reason they are there is because we didn't kill them."

"It's not the rintic way. We do not kill unless threatened," replied Taukin, hoping to impress the General with his tribal knowledge.

General Meraco continued, "Because we didn't kill them they have grown in number and require more agrum and have become more aggressive to meet their agrum needs. They know no restraint, even killing their own if needed…they are savages Taukin."

"I do not understand why you are telling me this General," replied Taukin, his hue morphing slightly yellow.

"You'll be presented an opportunity that will test your loyalty to your tribe. Succeed and you will secure your place with the upper echelon of Carth rintic."

"An opportunity?"

Taukin paused to absorb the words, causing his skin to flicker a multitude of colors with desire before morphing yellow with fear.

"And if I fail?"

They were far enough into the Carth forest that the towering green, moss-covered swaul trees hid any sign of the tughe training arena. The Eastern star had fallen below the tree line so that there were only enough shards of light to see a hazy view of the forest. They had walked farther than Meraco had intended and had followed one of the paths that led to Knafel Du Ply.

A rustling of tree limbs and crunching of dead leaves on the ground in the distance halted them in their tracks. Meraco raised his hand and motioned for Taukin to take cover behind the freshly fallen tree to the side of the trail. Meraco armed himself with his short saber, which he used for close battle. Taukin readied his wooden practice sword, it wasn't sharp, but it could still inflict damage. They both crouched down behind the fallen tree facing the path and Meraco edged his way to the splintered tree's base. The tree was still sticky from the resin that seeped out at the base and the pleasure of the aroma given off by the resin was short-lived by the impending threat of danger on the other side. A muffled moan came from behind their position and Meraco peeked his eyes over the rugged chunks of bark. "Soldier!" said Meraco as he leapt to his feet and scanned the surrounding area for danger. Meraco sheathed his sabre and knelt at the rintic soldier's side and asked, "What happened?"

"They came from nowhere. At least three of them. Suvanth warriors. They took Fesenius and left me to die." The struggling soldier raised his head to see his torso ripped open and dropped his head back in agony. "I won't live to see the quiesce," said the wounded soldier.

"Taukin get me two handfuls of moss now!" commanded Meraco. Taukin came to the bleeding soldier and handed the moss to the General, who carefully used the sterile strings to wedge the soldier's viscera into his body and keep more from falling out. General Meraco unraveled the blue armband from his arm and asked, "What's your name soldier?"

"Paero," losing his formality with the loss of blood and mind.

Meraco wrapped the armband around his waist, holding the moss in place. "Help me stand him up," said Meraco.

"I can't move," said the soldier.

"I'm not leaving you," said Meraco. "Open your hand here and press firmly," instructed Meraco to Taukin. One on each side, they lifted in tandem, with Taukin's hand keeping pressure on the moss. They took a step toward the path, but the wounded soldier had no strength and Meraco said, "Hold him steady."

Taukin lowered his head underneath the soldier's shoulder while keeping his hand pressed against his stomach. Meraco positioned himself in front of the soldier and squatted enough for Taukin to place him on the General's broad back. "Paero keep your wound against my back." Paero mustered his strength and pulled close to General Meraco. "Taukin go to Fort Carth and have a healer at the ready. Tell Major Zelzik what you've heard," said Meraco. With great speed, Taukin ran off over the rolling dirt hills under the dusky haze of the forest toward Fort Carth.

Taukin slowed his pace as he approached the rintic guards at the great wooden gate to Fort Carth and said, "Grant me entry by orders of General Meraco." Both guards looked at each other and burst out laughing. "I must speak to Major Zelzik now," said Taukin, gritting his teeth.

"You're not a soldier," said the older, lanky guard.

"He's not even rintic," said the plump, younger guard and continued, "Only soldiers and elders are allowed in the fort, now get home before you get lost in the quiesce."

Taukin moved his violet face nearer to the flame, "What's the worst duty in the army?"

The lanky guard examined Taukin then looked at his younger counterpart who raised, then dropped his shoulders, "There's nothing worse than cleaning the inobi stables," said the older guard through his helmet, and the young plump guard laughed in agreement and shook his helmed head.

"That's what you'll be doing next if you don't let me through!" said Taukin, and both guards looked at each other and their grins went straight and their color light-green.

The older guard motioned his head to the younger guard, "Open the gate."

Taukin scrambled inside, turned to the guards that

opened the gate and said, "Hold the gate open for General Meraco." But the direct order from their commander was to keep the massive gate shut and barred, and so it was. Once inside, Taukin ran around the torchlit parade ground asking of each passing soldier, "Where is Major Zelzik?" and being answered with shrugs, head shakes, or complete avoidance. Taukin focused in on a ranked soldier who stood near the wooden walkway leading to General Meraco's quarters. "Lieutenant, General Meraco needs a healer at the ready for when he and a wounded soldier arrive." Taukin held up his blood-stained hand, "His wounds are severe."

The Lieutenant called out, "Sergeant, find the healer and tell him to prepare his station." His sergeant ran off toward the North side of the fort where the healing stations were located.

"I need to find Major Zelzik," said Taukin, and no sooner had her name come from his mouth than Zelzik appeared behind Taukin.

In the torchlit courtyard, the Lieutenant motioned toward the Major with a head nod. "I'm here."

Taukin spun around to see the only female officer he was aware of, short-gray hair, two heads taller than himself and with an unchanging mark the shape of a garwelve right above her left eye, "Major, General Meraco and I were near Knafel Du Ply and found a soldier lying in the forest growth, critically wounded by the hands of the suvanth."

"Suvanth in the forest?"

"Those were his own words."

"Where are they now?"

"They'll be here soon. One more thing, a soldier named Fesenius was taken by the suvanth."

Zelzik looked sickly, as though some tribesman punched her in the abdomen. A ruckus started near the front gate and soldiers gathered around General Meraco who had carefully, and with the help of two healers, off-loaded the unconscious soldier onto a pelt stretcher, careful not to spill his innards. Both healers grabbed an end of the stretcher and moved swiftly toward the well-lit, covered healing stations.

Meraco spoke with intensity to Major Zelzik, "There's been a suvanth infiltration in the forest. Send two runners on inobi sleds to inform the Umgara of the suvanth attack. The Umgara should be at Jonta Fell by now." Zelzik whistled loudly and pointed her arm upward with two fingers and waved her arm in a circle, motioning for two inobi sled runners to come forth. Meraco continued, "I will inform Lord Hiko of the situation. Major Zelzik, put the fort on alert and increase the number of patrols from here out toward Munda Ber and Sik Jukote. Send three patrols to Cadox in a spread, we can't be blind as to where the suvanth are entering the forest. Have the soldiers report back to their camps every two par-cycles. Anything of interest, report back immediately. We must find out how they are getting past our patrols."

"Yes General," she said and made her way to the waiting officers to bark her orders. General Meraco clambered up the wooden ramp to his quarters, about half the height of the towering fort wall.

Zelzik turned to the two eager scouts she beckoned, "Inform the Umgara of the attack in the forest. Signal with your flute before you arrive…you don't want to surprise them."

"Yes Major," said the sled runners, then ran to the inobi sled stables to prepare their short-haired creatures for the arduous journey.

A pink illuminated signaling trisian was bound and sent up from the fort beyond the treetops to alert soldiers throughout the forest that the enemy was near. General Meraco and Taukin made their way through the fort gates right behind the prostrate inobi sled runners who lay waist-high to Avent on their porcine creatures and then disappeared behind a swirl of haze into the quiesce. The Carth forest was shadowed black by the colossal trees, but the light from the moon Aebean lit enough of a path to follow. They gauged the distance between the sled runners in front and themselves by the taking off of the sumoguls, whose large bone-like wings generated a substantial clamor and the floating of the luminescent trisians.

Soldiers ran along the trail, hauling gear and weapons from Byrre Syra down the trails. Taukin appeared first in the torch light along the trail near Byrre Syra.

"Taukin! Where have you been?" asked a dark-skinned Avent.

"With me," said General Meraco as he appeared in the light next to Taukin.

"General, are we at war?"

"Suvanth are in our forest Captain." Avent's skin lightened upon these words.

"Come with us to see Lord Hiko," said Meraco.

Two posted guards, outside of Lord Hiko and Lady Jusha's hut, halted all three of the quiesce wanderers before they were too close to the entrance that surrounded the leader's hut. As one of the guards called for them to identify themselves, Meraco said, "Take ease, it's General Meraco." The soldiers asked that he advance into the torchlight to verify his claim. Once the guards saw he was indeed their General, they allowed them to pass through the mud-hardened, arched entrance into the decorated, walled courtyard of their leader. Meraco rapidly approached the door that had a guard, Lord Hiko's intermediary and said, "Rouse our leader, it's imperative that we speak."

Taukin and Avent stayed outside the courtyard so as not to distract the General and Lord Hiko as they spoke. Hiko arrived at the opened door pulling his vestment across his chest. His eyes strained to see who was outside his hut in the darkness. "General Meraco, is that you?"

"Yes, my lord." Hiko waved his hand and ushered off the posted guard.

"What brings you here during the stirless time?" Hiko asked still trying to wake his senses.

"My lord there has been a suvanth attack in the forest. One soldier is badly wounded and another was taken by the suvanth."

At this Hiko gasped and woke up as if he had just jumped into the frigid upper Trigshan river. Hiko said,

"Impossible! The suvanth cannot enter the forest undetected."

"Our patrols are thick within the forest, we would know of any trace of the suvanth, except this attack…it was different. There were multiple suvanth, at least three, and they were deep in the forest, not near the borders." replied Meraco.

"Where?" asked Hiko, his tone of voice and color morphed in an unpleasant direction.

"My lord, between Knafel Du Ply and Fort Carth," replied Meraco, expressionless, careful not to react to Hiko's emotions.

"In all my cycles, the suvanth have never attacked inside the forest. They have tried, yes, but not one tribesman has been hurt and never has a rintic been taken. How could this happen General?" asked Hiko with disdain of tongue and skin.

General Meraco's rugged face leaned in close to Hiko, "My lord, we cannot rule out the possibility that there could be a traitor among us. How else could the suvanth get so close to Byrre Syra?"

"That is a serious insinuation that I scarce can comprehend." Hiko's auburn eyes traced the cracks on the stone pathway leading to his hut's entrance as he turned. Then silent, he paused with his back to Meraco.

"Nevertheless, it makes the most sense," said Hiko as he turned with suspicion in his eye and intensely stared at Taukin by the torchlight of the courtyard entrance. Hiko broke his gaze and redirected it toward Meraco and said, "This will be discussed with the Umgara when they arrive." Hiko, whose skin turned white, with slowly wavering, thin blue vertical lines stepped up to General Meraco and great intensity said, "I want the traitor found."

General Meraco replied, "Yes my lord," and started to exit, but Hiko spoke again, "And General, I want him to suffer." Meraco stared at Hiko's intense eyes and bright white skin before nodding, looking down, and turning away. Hiko stormed back inside his hut and the guard ushered the General back outside the courtyard.

Aebean's moonlight subsided, and the Eastern star revealed elongated dark ash-colored silhouettes on the black dirt and fallen leaves of the green forest floor as the soldiers made their way down the path past the circular telling place. Meraco proceeded with orders, "Captain make your way to Fort Carth, inform Major Zelzik to expand the search to cover the entire forest. If suvanth are found, capture them, else kill them. I'll be in my quarters making preparations for the Umgara right after I speak with Colonel Pella. Report back to me when you have something to report." Avent replied, "Yes, General." Meraco turned down the path that led towards the Byrre Syra armory and Avent made his way to Fort Carth. Taukin caught Avent and said, "I'm going with you."

"Go home."

"I helped General Meraco save the soldier attacked by the suvanth," said Taukin.

"And you've earned your rest, take it," said Avent stiffly.

"I can do more with my eyes open," pleaded Taukin, his skin turning orange.

"You can do more at home where you belong," said Avent firmly with darkened skin, causing other passing soldiers to take notice and Taukin's skin to morph white with shame.

"It's safe there. Stay with Larnhi until I call for you," said Avent after his skin returned to its normal hue.

Taukin followed his Captain's orders and did an about face toward Avent's hut, doing his best to hide his humiliation and avoid the slew of tribesmen scurrying about the brightly lit forest paths.

Taukin burst through the entrance right as Keel was reaching for his cold-weather covering. "Where are you going?" asked Taukin with twinge of contempt.

"Do you not know? Suvanth are in the forest!" said Keel with fear and excitement swirling in his voice.

"You can't go anywhere. Captain Avent wants us to stay here where it's safe," said Taukin.

"Father told me to report at Fort Carth," said Keel, questioning Taukin's words.

Larnhi stood right behind Keel and clung to her tan cloth covering, her skin scared light-green with large red circles, "I'd rather you stay here with your brothers and me."

Keel quipped, "Don't worry mother, father and I will return with a sack full of suvanth back bones!"

"I should be with you and Avent," replied Taukin, torn between Avent's orders and his own pride.

Keel said, "No youth are allowed outside their huts," cracking a wicked grin. Taukin's skin went deep orange and his face soured.

"You both do as your Captain has told you," said

Larnhi and she pulled Keel to her and said, "Be strong and observant." Then she relinquished her hold and sent Keel out into the forest.

Keel scampered down the worn trail and rounded the corner past the forest trees toward Fort Carth. As he turned, a shimmering object fell from his ruck on to the dark dirt and rolled to the edge of the path into the dead leaves. Taukin donned his cold coverings and went out to the trail's edge, busy with rintic soldiers marching toward Fort Carth, and others toward Davalit and beyond to the Thrysal cliffs. Taukin cautiously and covertly lifted the trinket and retreated back down his hut trail then examined the charoite-colored carving. Each detail of the miniature stone carving captured Taukin's attention, blocking out the noise and distractions of the passing tribesmen. This bauble was none like Taukin had ever seen. The markings and style were exquisite and the being itself was suvanth there was no doubt. Suvanth baubles were highly prized for their detail, scarcity, and composition from rare stones and elegant gems. He squeezed the bauble in his hand covering it completely with his fingers.

"What's that you're holding?"

Taukin's head jerked up and his eyes went wide and briefly changed skin color. "Soyha, you surprised me. Where are your guards?"

"They're on the other side of the trail past the marching soldiers. What's that you're hiding?" Soyha asked with great curiosity.

"Come with me," said Taukin and he grabbed her

hand and pulled her partway down the trace toward Avent's hut.

"After the last story gathering at the telling place, I was on my way to Avent's hut and heard a noise coming from the forest, so I peeked through the trees and saw something."

"What was it?"

"A suvanth. I'm sure of it. He saw me, but didn't move or make a sound. It's like he wanted me to know that he was there, and it was over there that he stood, not far from this path," said Taukin as he pointed to the wooded spot.

Soyha's skin turned light green and she said, "The suvanth could be here right now and we wouldn't know it…right underneath us," then she tucked her arms together against her chest and pulled close to Taukin whose skin turned a mild golden color from her proximity.

Soyha continued, "Together we're safe…aren't we?" Her gaze was entrancing and she leaned closer to Taukin.

Taukin's skin flurried with a burst of colors and he pulled back and said nervously, "Look what I found." Soyha lifted her head as Taukin brought his closed pulsing hand between them. Soyha's gray-green eyes widened as Taukin straightened his fingers revealing the colorful suvanth bauble.

"How did you…"

"It was over there by the trail's edge."

"It's remarkable. Do you think it came from the suvanth you saw?"

Taukin paused and tried to keep his hue from changing so as not to insinuate his thoughts, then replied, "I saw it fall from Keel's ruck."

"Keel? That's not possible," said Soyha, whose pattern of waving yellow lines and blue skin showed her disappointment.

"I found it…he might have as well."

"He would have told us if he found it," said Soyha with a knowing look. "I'll take it to the Elders," commanded Soyha as she held out her red hand.

"I'll keep it safe," said Taukin, turning and stepping back as he pocketed the bauble in his inner covering pocket.

Soyha stepped toward Taukin and said, "Taukin you're making a mistake, let me have it. I'll bring it to the Elders, they'll know what to do."

"They'll accuse me of treason. Somehow I'll be linked to the attack," said Taukin.

"Elders protect us, if this bauble can help with that, then they should know," and she moved her hand closer to Taukin.

"You want the recognition?" replied Taukin with a suspicious hue.

"Who are you talking to? The one with disdain for you? No, I'm the one that defends you when others rebuke you," said Soyha with such conviction that her skin went white with thin blue lines extending from head to toe.

His eyes dropped and his skin went bright yellow-green and he said, "I'm a fool five times over. At least let me talk with Keel before going to the council." Soyha's lips pursed in a mock smile and nodded with normal reddish hue.

"Taukin! Taukin! Come!" shouted Nelkum from the entrance to Avent's hut. Taukin reached for Soyha's hand, and he led her down the trail through the piercing light beams with her guards now in tow. As they approached the hut, Taukin patted his inner chest pocket and said, "Say nothing."

"What were you looking at?" asked Nelkum as they walked up the wooden stairs.

"Something from the forest floor," replied Taukin.

"Was it a suvanth weapon?" demanded Nelkum.

Taukin and Soyha's eyes widened at the question, but ignored young Nelkum and found Larnhi, "Solea Soyha," said Larnhi, which was the standard rintic greeting.

"Solea," replied Soyha as they made their way into the hut's comforting warmth and lingering scent of spiced foods. Larnhi motioned for Soyha to sit near the crackling fire.

Taukin's skin wavered with emotion and overtook his lips, "Our hut is surrounded by soldiers, there's no reason for me to stay here, I should be out there with Keel and Avent," then plopped down on a wooden stool that granted relief to his aching muscles and put him eye to eye with young Nelkum.

Larnhi responded, "What good are you to them in your state?"

"I can fight," replied Taukin.

Larnhi continued, "You have yet to wield a long sword."

"The same as Keel, but he's out there searching for suvanth," said Taukin allowing his skin to darken.

"Your father and I swore an oath to care for you. We won't break it now."

"An oath for a youth. Is that how you still see me?"

"Breaking a direct order carries great consequences," said Larnhi with white skin. "I'll hear no more of it, you'll remain here as you were ordered." With his focus now on the suvanth, Nelkum's lips had turned inward, his eyebrows were slightly raised, and his skin went light green.

Taukin put his hand on Nelkum's shoulder and said, "We are well protected here. Did you see all the rintic soldiers out there? Even Soyha's personal guards are here to protect you. The suvanth have all ran back to their hole in the ground." Nelkum could only manage a slight crooked smile at Taukin's words, but it was enough to reassure him as his skin turned rintic reddish-orange.

Taukin crossed his arms and tried to calm his mind, but his thoughts stirred him to move. Taukin grabbed his short saber and filled his pelt ruck with items for a journey. Still exhausted from his earlier adventure, he made his way toward the hut entrance. "Soyha should stay here with you. Her guards will provide protection. I'll return soon," said Taukin.

"Where are you going?" asked Larnhi in surprise.

"To find Keel. I can't sit here and do nothing knowing that my brother is searching the forest for suvanth. The tribe already considers me a coward." replied Taukin and his skin went golden. "This is a strange lumeren, full of questions and confusion. Because of this my Captain will understand fidelity over words…you'll see."

Larnhi exhaled deeply and focused on Taukin's bright, amber eyes, "Find them quickly and may Hobaja Vael guide you," she said.

Taukin threw his ruck over his coverings and rubbed Nelkum's fuzzy black hair. Taukin turned to Soyha, "Stay here with them. Your presence provides more security than I could." Soyha nodded in concurrence. Outside the hut, Taukin met Soyha's personal guards standing on the front porch with their pampa staffs at the ready. Taukin jumped over the worn wooden steps, foot coverings kicking up dirt, and turned around to Soyha twisting her cupped hands in front of her chest, which was the traditional rintic send off. He turned back and trotted to the trail where soldiers marched in both directions.

CHAPTER 2
IN SEARCH OF THE ENEMY

Taukin made his way past the great gray stone temple Woosan, where Hobaja Vael, the creator of all life and greatest of the gods, was worshipped, and on through the thatched-roof village towards Fort Carth to find Avent and Keel. Squads of soldiers patrolled the trails and two by two they scouted the wooded areas within Byrre Syra. Caustic glares from the tribesmen pelted Taukin, but he did his best to control his skin color and it only changed after a particularly spiteful older tribesman threw a rather large stick and struck Taukin in his upper back.

Taukin whipped around, unsure what just hit him. "My son Paero is dead because of your kind! He's gone!" he yelled at Taukin with skin so dark he looked like a shadow, then continued, "You don't belong with our tribe, you vile suvanth!" Taukin's skin went dark blue with this news and he rubbed his shoulder from the painful blow. Taukin shook his head wanting to pacify the discolored father, but instead hunkered over with his eyes tracing the dirt path, careful not to incite any more outbursts from the passing soldiers or awaiting tribesmen who began grumbling when Taukin appeared. They didn't know how he had helped Paero the tem-cycle before. They didn't know that he was on his way to join their ranks and help them search for the real enemy. All they knew was what they could see, which was an odd-colored being with a strange pattern that was neither rintic nor suvanth.

He walked at first, but eventually trotted on the trodden dirt and finally found himself outside the most populous village of the forest, Byrre Syra, where the marching soldiers had thinned. The safety of the forest blanketed Taukin, yet he couldn't quell the uncomfortable feeling that he wasn't alone. Dirt was compacted in the middle of the path and loosed on either side, a sign that many soldiers had passed through recently. He paid no attention to the brightly colored markers that denoted the route that led to Fort Carth, since he had most paths memorized from Fort Carth all the way to Sik Jukote. The straight stretch of path, midway between the village and the fort was the most recognizable of landmarks on the trail. Taukin passed the stretch and had just started making his way over the hill, when at the peak, two figures appeared. Relieved that he had caught up to Avent and Keel, Taukin slowed to a hasty walk.

The Eastern star's rays colored their faces vermillion and Taukin abruptly stopped when he made out Syonis's piercing sneer along with three other rintic tribesmen that appeared alongside their leader. Syonis drew closer and examined Taukin's packed ruck. The future rintic leader spoke, "Where are you going? Back to join your filthy suvanth mother in the pit?" Syonis's cronies laughed. Taukin's skin matched the golden rays of the Eastern star before going dark. "Look at that disgusting knot on your back, does it bother you that you'll never be considered rintic?" asked Syonis.

"I've always been rintic and now I'm a Carth soldier," said Taukin doubtfully.

Syonis quipped, "A Carth soldier? I bet you can't even wield a short saber," and laughed looking at his followers, who joined in the laughter. Taukin brandished his short blade and passed it from his left hand to his right with a short toss.

"Are you threatening me?" asked Syonis.

"I'm…" said Taukin.

Syonis's skin turned white with wavering blue stripes, a sign of intimidation, and he held his blue and yellow armband toward Taukin, "You dare attack the house of Lord Hiko?" and with that Syonis severed his armband with his own dagger allowing it to fall to the dirt-laden path. A band that touched the ground was a band to be destroyed. Taukin's skin blazed golden and it was all he could do to swallow.

All four rintic surrounded Taukin and he spun around and said, "Never!" as he sheathed his saber.

Syonis spoke, "You must pay for your betrayal."

"I did nothing!" said Taukin. Syonis motioned with his head and the tribesmen seized Taukin, holding his struggling arms steady. "Who'll believe you over me? You'll go to prison Akaretel for what you've done."

"Why are you doing this?" asked Taukin, squirming

and trying to shake free, but the more he moved the firmer the hold of the larger tribesmen became.

"Because you don't belong with us. You are unwanted by the tribe and they say that you're the reason the suvanth have made their way into the forest." Syonis paused, his skin went normal and he turned his back to Taukin, then continued, "There is a way out of this."

"Tell me," said Taukin, his voice riddled with desperation.

"You leave the forest…and never return." Syonis shrugged and continued, "And your crime will be forgiven."

Taukin winced and said, "I have no place to go. Death lingers outside the forest, you know that!"

Syonis's crony, Habik, who was short for a rintic yet still taller by a full hand than Taukin spoke with his head flinching to the side, a nervous side effect of losing the top of his right ear in a sparring incident, "It's a simple choice to me. Have you ever been inside Akare-tel? It's dark and reeks like the inside of a rotted trochin corpse. The smell alone has been known to drive prisoners insane." Taukin's skin went even brighter yellow.

"Do you choose freedom?" asked Syonis with his wicked grin. No sound came from Taukin, who looked to the ground and down the path in both directions.

"Help me!" screamed Taukin down the path. Habik plunged his solid fist into Taukin's gut, making him lurch over and cough as he landed on his side against the cold soil.

"Hold him," demanded Syonis. The tribesmen held

Taukin by his arms, but this time Taukin only struggled to catch his breath, his limp body could barely stand. "If you're waiting for others, they're not coming, we're alone here." Syonis pushed up Taukin's dangling head. "Touching your suvanth skin makes me sick," and Syonis's skin morphed a fierce color as he continued, "But I want you to see my face when you tell me that you're leaving the forest forever."

Taukin's skin went blue with a heap of sadness weighing on him and said, "I need some time, but you won't see me again."

A grin like that of Aebean's crescent blazed across Syonis's face and he dropped Taukin's heavy head. "So you don't forget…" and with that Syonis kicked Taukin in his gut with such force that his feet flew upward, and his head whipped forward as if he was pulled forcefully from his spine. His shoulders flew backward causing Taukin to land on his ruck, and his hairless head to slam against the hardened soil. Syonis squatted next to Taukin and ripped his band from his pelt-covered arm. Syonis studied the yellow crest and said, "House of Avent no more." Syonis balled up the armband and threw it on Taukin's curled-up body. Taukin, still dazed by the impact, slowly rolled over and looked toward his feet. Down the path Syonis and the others scampered away, back toward Byrre Syra.

Taukin gagged and carefully rolled onto his knees then paused. Tears dropped straight down from his eyes to the forest floor and he beat his fist against the cold soil, compressing the dirt more and more with each blow. Wearily, he staggered down the path muttering to himself, "They'll respect me," rage swelling inside him with every shaky step he took and his skin flashing with his emotions. The Eastern star began its descent below the tree line that surrounded the forest. He wound his way up and down the hilly paths that cut through the giant trees until the fort was in sight, then slowed his pace to a stumbling walk.

With his hand on his abdomen—careful to not inhale too deeply, for when he did, he winced—and squeezed his stomach muscles as he approached Fort Carth. Taukin stopped and rested on a flat rock to the side of the trail before entering so as not to appear unable to join a search party. It was unquestionably the most secure fort of all the rintic strongholds. The timber posts surrounding the fort were cut from swaul trees, which were as big around as a grown rintic male was tall, and were cut to stand at least twenty rintic high. The massive fort was constructed with help from the Umgara, whose strength, paired with rintic tools and technology, allowed for the placement of the enormous, pointed posts, driven deep into the forest ground. The fort's submerged base sits on top of the Carth forest's naturally occurring nionan crystal deposit, one of the hardest substances in all of Onestonia. Taukin said out loud, "The fort among forts."

Taukin crouched under the abatis of brush and trochin bone and received no grief as he was granted entrance through the South gate of the fort. He passed groups of soldiers marching towards the exit led by their superior-ranked soldier. The fort was abuzz with soldiers moving with purpose from one area to another, some carrying heavy equipment or weapons, and some steering carts pulled by strong trochin bulls. So many soldiers moved through the fort so quickly that they didn't have time to acknowledge Taukin's existence, which meant they couldn't show disapproval. This was a welcomed environment for Taukin…one of disregard, an invisible feeling. In the blur of running tribesmen was Dyant, one of the few tribesmen that treated Taukin fairly. Taukin went to the scout to get his attention, "Dyant."

Dyant replied, "You're hurt?"

"It's nothing. The wounded soldier Paero, he…?"

"He's gone. I know what you did, how you helped him."

Taukin nodded with blue skin and continued, "Have you seen Captain Avent, or Keel?"

"They left with the second search party headed towards Munda Ber. They could be as far as Knafel Du Ply by now." Taukin furrowed his brow, but didn't let it keep him down, he nodded and turned for the North gate when Dyant spoke, "Keep a watchful eye Taukin. The central trails of the forest shouldn't be traveled alone, especially in your condition." Taukin paused briefly, then continued towards the gate. The cross-hatched pattern on his yellow skin revealed his anxiety as he traversed the unfamiliar trails toward Knafel Du Ply.

Taukin hadn't traveled far before the rolling dirt trails took their toll on his weary legs. Each hill climbed felt as if Taukin was carrying an Umgara giant on his back. The thick dirt of the central trails and the lack of rest compounded the agony of his sore body. Knafel Du Ply was too far to reach before darkness fell, and his wobbly legs could carry him no farther. A tree with a forked trunk not far from the trail seemed like the ideal place to perch for the quiesce. It was known that a tribesman never lies on the forest floor due to venomous slithering garwelves, which were commonly known as leaping death for they lunged at their victims, fangs splayed and clawed tail open. The last beam of the Eastern star had completely disappeared and the stirless time was upon Taukin. Chromatic trisians descended to the forest floor to drink the sweet sap of the swaul trees captured in root bowls. At every leaf crunch or twig snap, Taukin turned and focused his eyes for signs of the suvanth. He scaled the forked tree and crawled into the pelt that was strung between the split trunks and scanned the forest all around his nest before settling down. He gently rubbed his bruised belly where Syonis kicked him and laid on his side, but no matter how he turned, the pain and Syonis's words reminded him of his place in the tribe, ever the outcast and now his pending exile. Eventually the lulling hum of the forest and exhaustion of his adventures overcame Taukin and he could no longer keep his eyelids from growing closer together, so he lifted a prayer to Hobaja Vael and then rested his eyes. Ascending sumoguls periodically awoke Taukin, and he would glance at the red-beaked and white-winged creatures, but he was in such a stupor that little attention was given before his heavy eyelids pulled tight again.

A drop of dew from the branch above landed

directly on top of Taukin's smooth violet dome. A few more drops fell along his right arm, which had worked its way on top of the encapsulating pelt, waking his groggy body. Light from the Eastern star penetrated the thinly covered area temporarily blinding Taukin. He slowly sat up and rubbed his eyes until he could squint around and see the outline of the forest. He noticed what looked like the silhouette of a tribesman settled in a tree across the trail. His eyes closed again to adjust to the brightness and reopened, focusing on the silhouette.

"The rintic are not far away now," said the shadowy figure. The unfamiliar dialect alarmed Taukin. He struggled to get out of his suspended pod in the forked tree and fell, bumping his head along the trunk on the way down. Taukin, woozy and wobbly, reached for his short saber to defend against this possible attacker. He got to his feet and looked up in the tree across from him, but the mysterious being was gone.

"Coward, where are you hiding? Reveal yourself," said Taukin in a brave front. The suvanth spy laughed at Taukin's foolishness.

"You don't know how to control your own flesh, I sssee your fear. If I meant you harm you would have not ssseen the lumeren'sss light."

The voice was coming from overhead in the forked tree, the enemy above him sitting in his pelt pod. His grayish-blue skin melded with the haze-covered limbs of the forest.

"Come down here so I can dispatch you to your resting place."

"I offer you what you ssseek. Ssset down your sssaber and let'sss talk calmly."

"I'll keep my blade ready," and Taukin kept the blade next to his side and stepped backward toward the trail, keeping an eye on the fleet-footed being. The suvanth hopped down from the forked tree and took a few steps toward Taukin. The mysterious being was a head taller than Taukin who raised his sabre again, hand shaking and golden-skinned.

"Like I sssaid, no harm will come to you," said the being.

The suvanth was close enough now that his thin-lined, onyx-colored, octagonal-shaped pattern could be made out. "That's close enough. You're the one attacking my tribe, aren't you?"

"I've only protected myssself from thossse who wish to harm me," said the suvanth lightheartedly.

"It was you that I saw the quiesce of the fire circle, wasn't it?" A nod came from the suvanth. "How have you made it through the forest undetected?" asked Taukin, slowly moving backward.

"An ally from your tribe hasss granted me accesss to thisss foressst. He getsss me where I need to be. A friend of mine…and of yoursss. Heeek, heeek, heeek, heek," said the mysterious suvanth with an odd laugh, much like he was choking and gasping for air.

"Tell me the traitor's name!"

"In time you will know, but I am here to offer help and hope for Taukin," said the suvanth in a more serious manner.

"Who are you?" demanded Taukin.

"I have watched you sssince you were a youth. I have waited a long time to ssspeak with you. I am the one who isss hidden anywhere. He who isss fassster than the godsss. I am Ssswinzal, ssspy for my massster Manisssta, the leader of the sssuvanth and he isss eager to meet you."

"What does he want with me? My house holds no sense of nobility, and I have no standing amongst those of prominence."

"That isss where you are wrong Taukin, you are of great sssignificance to the sssuvanth, but you have been misssled by the rintic. Come with me and you'll be given a gift, not of thisss world, from beyond…one from the godsss. You'll be powerful and all of Onessstonia will bow down and ressspect you." Taukin's skin unintentionally pulsed a variety of colors, revealing desire. "Yesss, Manisssta sssaid you would undersssstand. Come with me and find your place among the sssuvanth. Taukin paused, deep in thought, and his skin slowly went back yellow considering the words of Swinzal, but he shook his head, "The suvanth are my enemy."

"Taukin, the rintic dissspissse you and do not want you with them. I've ssseen thisss. You are a part of usss. Part of *my* tribe," said Swinzal with conviction.

Taukin's skin changed to stripes of anger. "I'm Carth rintic. Tell your leader I won't join the suvanth." Taukin said with a burst of fury.

Swinzal bowed his fuzzy, black-haired head to Taukin as if he was subservient to the young pariah. A pair of patrolling rintic soldiers crested the hill and instead of running, Swinzal quietly said, "Sssay nothing, I'll dissspatch them quickly," and hid behind a wide Swaul tree not three rintic away.

Taukin's skin went yellow, "No!"

"Soldier! Who are you talking to?" asked the burly soldier, who wore two slings across his chest holding two long swords.

"The trees," replied Taukin nervously.

"You're that half-breed soldier I heard about aren't you?" said the much smaller soldier who had squinty eyes and wore a foul grin.

"You both should leave now," said Taukin, skin blazing yellow.

"We don't take orders from you. That's your fear color, is it? You afraid of us half-breed?" asked the smaller soldier.

Taukin glanced at the swaul tree where Swinzal hid and faced the soldiers again.

"What's over there?" asked the larger soldier.

"Nothing. You really should go," said Taukin.

"Are you hiding something?" asked the shorter soldier as he moved toward the swaul tree. Taukin grabbed his cold-weather covering and said, "I beg you…don't." A forceful shove to the cold ground was his response and he continued toward the round tree. Taukin backed away onto the trail and watched the soldiers cautiously approach the tree, armed with their long swords. They both met each other around the base of the tree, and the larger of the two, with angry skin said, "You like tricks?"

"No, I just thought…"

"If we see you again, you'll be treated as a suvanth, now *you* go," said the larger soldier. Taukin hastily gathered his items, strapped them on his back, and headed towards Munda Ber all the while scanning the green forest for the pale-skinned suvanth known as Swinzal.

Green forest growth aligned the trail and it wasn't long before he was upon a smoldering pit of ashes thought to be left behind by Avent's search party. Taukin journeyed a little farther past a small creek that had a fresh muddy crossing. He wasn't sure exactly how to address the search party without startling them. Spears or kracklins being thrown at him wasn't the type of greeting he wanted. He knew that Avent would be angry with him for disobeying his command, but he thought one's anger for the favor of many, was a fair trade. Weakness was a scorned tribesman label that became their legacy. Suddenly the idea came to him and Taukin made a loud sumogul alert call that Keel would recognize, in hopes that he would respond and know who was approaching. No response. He made a louder call this time and it wasn't long before he received an identical call back from Keel. It was their own shibboleth.

Soldiers were flanked along the edge of the trail and squatted down like bulbous plants before bloom, all except for Avent whose now-crimson skin with yellow dash marks alerted Taukin that he was in serious trouble. When Taukin was in range, Avent spoke: "I told you to stay with Larnhi. You'll be dealt punishment later, now is not the time."

Taukin lowered his head in concession. There was

no need to argue the reasons why he left Byrre Syra. Keel smirked at Taukin's chagrin. "We're not far from the edge of the crystal deposit now," said Avent, speaking to the soldiers, "We'll camp there this quiesce and head back in the lumeren. Spread out and follow the trail." The trail was smooth and undisturbed with rich, black soil, and the surrounding foliage was thicker and greener than what Taukin was accustomed to. Taukin joined Keel on the East side of the undisturbed trail. They spread out two rintic-length apart and scoured the ground for any suspicious brush piles or openings large enough for a suvanth to fit through.

At first the search was exciting to Taukin, especially with the knowledge that Swinzal lurked in the forest, but as the Eastern star passed overhead and made its way toward the western horizon, the task became mundane and his mind drifted as he ducked and straddled wooden obstacles. They were on the outer edge of Munda Ber when one of the tribesmen on the opposite side of the trail from Taukin shouted, "Captain, I've found something." All of the other soldiers stopped and looked over to see what was discovered, making sure they did not lose their position in case it was a false alarm.

Avent quickly walked over to the where the commotion occurred. "What have you found soldier?" asked Avent.

"There is a stacked pile of brush and debris here. It looks like wildebush and splintered swaul limbs. How would wildebush get here?" asked the confused soldier.

"Only by placement," said Avent. "More importantly, how were the suvanth able to make a tunnel in the forest without detection from our patrols? Remove it, carefully, you don't know what lies beneath." The soldier slowly removed the foliage and wood from the pile, discarding each piece in different areas, so as not to create a similar-looking pile. After removing a few of the larger pieces of wildebush it was clear to Avent that this was indeed a tunnel used by the suvanth for access into the heart of the Carth forest. Avent drew his long sword from its sheath and prepared for whatever could spring forth from the dirt-laden portal. The last bit of covering was removed, revealing marks left by the burrowing tools on the outer edge of the opening. The tunnel slightly sloped downward, allowing in a parabolic light a short distance from the opening—beyond that nothing, complete darkness.

"I need a garando over here," said Avent. The message was relayed down the chain of soldiers toward the direction of the trail. Keel, too impatient to wait for word to come down the line, broke rank and notified the handler of his Captain's request. A yelp and pop of leash was all that was needed for the garando to lead in the direction of the Captain and crouching soldier. The garando's four powerful stubby legs effortlessly pulled the soldier along and Keel tagged right behind. The garando's low profile bodies were heavy and scaly, and their thick, extended tails dragged the ground crunching the leaves as they collected against each other. Avent never took his eyes off of the over-sized burrow, even when he heard Keel, who defiantly broke rank, talking to the handler.

"Release the garando," said the Captain. The handler unchained the creature and it quickly wriggled its way down the dark hole. Silence fell upon the squad, and the crouching handler moved closer to the hole, listening for screaming or yelling or any noise for that matter. For a long period there was no sign of the garando, and Avent lowered his sword.

Keel asked, "How do garandos know which tunnels to traverse?"

The handler spoke up, "The suvanth put off a distinct scent, like a fruit, which the garandos can easily track."

Avent spoke in both directions of the aligned soldiers, "Hold your positions, we will wait for the garando findings."

The handler said to Keel, "Garandos return with evidence of suvanth occupation of the tunnels shortly after dispatch, and on some occasions it drags back a squealing and hissing suvanth tribesman. The garandos don't have to travel far since the suvanth create nodes to link the tunnels together and store rations and supplies at the nodes." Some in the search party began to grow impatient, and with their short sabers, whittled make-shift spears out of the fallen swaul limbs, out of sight from Captain Avent of course. "Call the garando back," said Avent to the handler. His sumogul bone flute hung around his neck and the handler put the bones to his lips and played the rattling, high-pitched notes that the garando knew to be the comeback call. He waited a short time then initiated another call—nothing, no response, and no sign of the lumbering beast. "Captain, something's wrong. The garandos don't always return on the first call, but always with the second call, unless dead," said the handler. Avent responded to his squad, "Something troublesome is below us in our own forest." Avent turned to the scout behind him, "Send word to Major Zelzik that a tunnel has been discovered here and that the garando has not returned from its dispatch." The lone scout nodded and ran off toward Fort Carth. Avent continued, "Trap the hole."

"If we trap the hole, the garando will not be able to escape," said Keel, who had no experience with suvanth tunnels. The handler lowered the ruck from his back, removed the metal-chain suvanth trap from the pack and proceeded to set it up on the outside of the tunnel. The chains formed a taut web pattern with a large opening in the middle.

The handler pointed to the well-constructed trap, "See this thin strip hanging in the middle? It's the actuator. The garandos are too low to ever hit this, but once it's tied to a piece of hanging cover and the suvanth move it, they're caught. The sharpened chains dig into their flesh if they struggle to free themselves. I've returned to the tunnels to find severed limbs dangling from the center of the trap, other times trapped bodies. These traps work well against the underground scourge." Keel slightly rocked his head back as a rintic who was just made a bit more knowledgeable by the honesty and cruelty of the conflict. Avent sheathed his long sword and stepped back as the trapper put the last piece of limbs and brush on the trap to camouflage the tunnel.

"Where's your weapon?" Avent asked Keel.

"I used it to mark my location so that I wouldn't lose my position. It's safe with the other soldiers." replied Keel.

"A soldier never loses sight of his weapon, remember that," said Avent sternly.

Keel lowered his eyes and replied, "Yes Captain." Avent returned to the squad of soldiers along the trail.

The garando handler sketched the wooded area and took notes in a tablet. "What are you doing?" asked Keel.

The handler spoke as he continued drawing with the crude carbon tool, "I'm making note of all of the suvanth tunnel access points. Draw the nearby landmarks, like that parted faffal bush over there, so it's easily located. I also update the location on my map of tunnels, so we have an approximation of the underground connections and node points." The handler pulled out the folded map from his ruck. He handed it to Keel who unfolded the surprisingly neat and detailed map.

"This is incredible!" exclaimed Keel. All of the Carth forest was drawn with the outlying regions laid out, with dashes showing known tunnel paths and dots representing suspected paths, at least this is what he read from the legend. Keel's eyes squinted and his head slightly rotated, displaying a sense of confusion for a brief par-tem. "How do you know where the tunnels go?" quizzed Keel.

"We're tunnel trackers," said the garando handler. "We send in the garandos and if they return, we go into the tunnel and make note of where we believe they lead. We follow the tunnels to the node connection points then follow a different tunnel back out. Always go up from the nodes, never down. All downward tunnels lead to larger, more populated hubs and eventually to the pit. If we're detected, the garandos couldn't stave off a large number of suvanth. In the tunnels near the surface our weapons are of little use. You'll learn these skills." Keel's curiosity dissipated and the reality of the danger showed on his coquelicot-colored raised brow. "Still want to be a garando handler?" asked the cynical handler.

"Finish up here, then return to your position," said Avent. "We still have much ground to cover before quiesce is upon us." The handler stuffed his drawing tools back into his ruck and made his way back toward the trail. Keel trudged behind, still pondering what he just learned from the handler.

When Keel was in range, Taukin piped up, "What did you see?"

"It's an actual suvanth tunnel. The opening was only large enough for us to hunch through, well for me anyway." Keel smirked.

Taukin shot a piercing glance toward Keel at the crude comment. "What happened to the garando?"

"It was released down into the tunnel, but never returned. The handler set a trap in case the suvanth are close by. The garando won't trigger it, but a suvanth will."

Keel returned to his long sword position and retrieved it from the dried-leaf covered ground then sheathed it. He slid his cerulean-colored band back up his right arm so that the yellow tribe symbol was centered snugly on his covering sleeve. The handler took his position without the garando. Avent walked back to the trail and spoke loud enough for the soldiers to hear at the end of the squad, "Ready on the left?"

The group of soldiers replied: "Ready Captain," in unison.

Avent turned his head and faced Keel and Taukin, "Ready on the right?"

The soldiers, along with Keel and Taukin, replied: "Ready Captain."

"Forward!" yelled the Captain, and the squad moved forward to Munda Ber.

Munda Ber was a lavish open area of the Carth forest containing cold, freshwater springs, bountiful fruits from the sparse trees, and various exotic species of colorful flowers. If the area around Munda Ber was more secure and could have supported a fort nearby, the rintic would have established their main village there. As it was, the rintic rarely visited the scenic area, except for special occasions, which were few in the time close to the upcoming moon alignment.

The squad set up their camp on the outer edge of the forest while the last of the Eastern star's beams shone on the open oasis. It had been cycles since Taukin had visited Munda Ber, but it was as he remembered. He was tempted by the sweet aroma of the malpwa tree blossoms. Taukin turned to Keel and said, "Help me get some malpwa for the squad." Keel couldn't turn down an offer of malpwa.

He emptied his ruck onto his cot and said, "Let's go." They passed one of the posted guards on their way to where the tree line circled the open area. A trail, most likely made by wild garando, led through flowers and bushes to a small cluster of malpwa trees on the North side of the camp.

As they made their way to the patch of malpwa trees, Taukin presented the ornate suvanth bauble to Keel and asked, "Why do you have this?"

Keel's brow furrowed and his skin turned dark red, highlighted by yellow slivers, and he snatched the bauble from Taukin's hand. "You went through my ruck," said Keel with darkened skin.

"It fell from your ruck when you left for Fort Carth. Where did you get it?"

Keel grumbled and then with great intensity said, "I'll tell you, but you cannot tell any tribesman, not mother or father, not even Soyha." Taukin's skin fluttered briefly with a pattern of guilt, but not long enough for Keel to notice. Keel moved in closer to Taukin for fear of listening ears. "I was going home from training at the Tughe arena, the same quiesce that you and General Meraco found Paero wounded in the forest. A being, taller than an Umgara, and thin as a parabic, with sticks for fingers and covered in dead leaves and green moss and vines approached me while I was alone. I froze in fear."

"I'm not gullible," said Taukin as he smirked and turned away from Keel.

"You think I'm deceiving you? Where do you think

this bauble came from?" asked Keel, his skin flickered with anger.

"Ok, say I believe you, what happened next?"

"It stretched out its gangly, wooded arm and placed this suvanth bauble in my hand and said, 'A possessor young of an offering old. All you desire is yours if you but use this bauble.' Then it moved into the trees and fell face down into the leafy growth and became part of the forest."

"What does it mean?" asked Taukin, curious now and knowing that Keel wasn't known for his creativity or guile.

"I get what I want," said Keel, entranced by the glimmering bauble.

"This gift was meant for the suvanth, no good will come of it," said Taukin.

"We don't know that for certain," said Keel scowling at the thought.

"We better get back to camp. Are you climbing?" asked Taukin.

Keel's only reply was a trenchant look that gave his answer. "I'll climb," said Taukin reluctantly. Abrasive bark made for a difficult climb, but the far lean of the tree eased the burden on hands and feet. With his short saber in hand, Taukin hacked at the malpwa stems releasing the head-sized fruit. Keel caught the falling malpwa and quickly placed it in the ruck. When most of the reachable fruit was dropped, Keel cinched his ruck and raced back to the camp. "Wait, help me down." Keel was already gone. The stirless time had come quickly. "Keel…grrrr," growled Taukin.

He began his descent down the coarse tree when he noticed the brightly illuminated trisians launching closer and closer to the camp. "Suvanth!" Taukin said out loud, but no one could hear him. He descended faster now, his loose grip slipping on the rough bark. He was about two rintic high when he lost his grip and fell clumsily to the flowers below. Taukin stood, still a bit shaken, and allowed his eyes to adjust to the darkened area. His squatty legs moved quickly back down the trail. As soon as the campfire was in view he yelled to alarm the squad.

Something is rapidly approaching from the Northwest. I see trisians taking flight." The guard closest to Taukin prepared his pampa staff for defense against whatever was coming behind Taukin.

Avent stood and looked to the North, validating Taukin's claim. "Make fighting positions around the camp, two by two in each direction. Guards remain posted," Avent began. "This could be a distraction for a flank attack. Hold your positions throughout. I need a scout ready to decamp and report to General Meraco."

A strapping scout stepped up to Avent. "I'm ready Captain."

Avent pointed in the Southeast direction and said: "Take cover there, on my signal depart for Fort Carth, if you're in danger of being captured send up a signaling trisian."

"Understood Captain," said the scout and departed for the thick brush still observable from the firelight.

Avent looked to Keel and Taukin, "You both stay close to me, and put out this fire." Keel threw dirt on the fire then grabbed a trochin pelt and tossed it, skin side down, over the fire and quickly darkened the campsite. Avent, Keel, and Taukin squatted down next to the smoking pelt, long swords drawn, and watched the brightly colored trisians take flight closer and closer. Taukin's heart raced faster with the sight of each new illumination.

A young guard was positioned closest to the approaching danger. He hid behind a moss-covered boulder and peeked around to time his attack. He heard the crunching of leaves and snapping of twigs getting louder. He pulled his head back and silently began his countdown. He readied his pampa staff close to his rapidly expanding chest. The enemy was upon him. The young soldier swallowed hard, then stepped out from behind the mossy stone with his staff pointed out toward the charging being. Something crawled between the soldier's legs, which made him jump the height of a rintic youth. It wasn't a fierce suvanth warrior, but the missing garando. The raucous creature bumbled its way over to the handler who welcomed it with a slap on its scaly side. The soldier looked around to see if trisians were still ascending. The forest grew quiet and the last light of the trisians went out. Some of the younger soldiers laughed and mocked Taukin for alarming the camp when it was only the garando coming back to the handler.

Keel spoke up, "Quiet yourselves. You would have done the same thing." Taukin took this as a protective move from his older brother.

Avent intervened, "Guards stay posted, the rest of

you, as you were." Keel removed the smoking cover and blew on the smoldering embers, adding a dim light with each breath until the fire was rekindled.

The soldiers gathered their cots close to the source of heat. It was then that the handler noticed the end of the garando's tail was missing. Taukin spoke to the handler, "Did the garando get trapped?"

"Not likely. He must have been caught in something when I called him back," said the handler.

Avent joined in the conversation, "Have you encountered traps in the tunnels?"

"None," continued the handler, "It's possible that a suvanth injured the garando, but usually the garando would bring back a piece of a suvanth to prove its victory."

Avent faced the handler and said, "Have the healer look at the garando to see if he can do something about that nub of a tail. We'll need to map the tunnel then seal it. We will send out a mapping team when we make it back to Fort Carth." Avent looked to Keel. "I want you to join the team and assist with the tunnel mapping."

Keel paused and winced, "But father, I'll miss the Umgara arrival!"

Avent's brow furrowed, "You'll address me as Captain when we're on task," said Avent and continued, "Do you want to be a garando handler?" Keel's skin turned the color of Taukin's skin reflecting his embarrassment. "Yes Captain," said Keel under his breath.

"Sound off," demanded Avent.

"Yes Captain, I want to be a garando handler!" said

Keel, drawing the attention of the rest of the soldiers. Taukin read the apprehension across Keel's face, but somehow he had managed to maintain his color, or maybe the firelight disguised his anguish.

Then Avent spoke louder for all of the soldiers to hear, "We leave for Byrre Syra with the lumeren's light. Take your rest."

"Hwoop," replied the soldiers in unison.

Taukin set his cot next to Keel.

"Are you afraid?" asked Taukin.

"Of what?" asked Keel.

"Afraid of going down the tunnel," said Taukin.

"Tsssk," replied Keel, keeping his pride intact.

Taukin knew the danger involved and decided to stay quiet. He grabbed his trochin cover and pulled it on top of him, fur side down, then quietly offered praise to Hobaja Vael before falling asleep.

"Soldiers rise up," said Avent. The unkind beams of light blazed through the sparsely wooded area, stinging Taukin's eyes. He could only manage a sliver of a squint with his right eye. He wasn't used to waking to the extra light. A quick eye rub helped them adjust to the new lumeren. Some of the soldiers were already packing their rucks and a few were already packed and eating dried kulee cakes and fresh malpwa.

"Is there anymore malpwa?" Taukin asked Keel. Keel splashed his jacinth-tinted face with some fresh creek water from his pelt canteen, then pointed to the end of his cot. Taukin finished packing then grabbed one of the coarse, shelled fruits. He cracked open the tough shell against a flat rock that was embedded in the ground and ate enough of the juicy yellow meat to fill his belly.

Avent ordered the soldiers to form the search line. "You know what you're looking for now, so we can move faster. No games on the way back."

Keel and Taukin lined up with the squad and marched to the Western side of Knafel Du Ply where they began their sweep of the forest headed back toward Byrre Syra. The party searched in the same manner as before, checking odd bundles of bush and branch, but turned up no new signs of suvanth.

Fort Carth was a hazy wooden box from afar, such is the forest before the setting of the Eastern star. Major Zelzik met the soldiers along a secondary trail that led from Fort Carth to Sik Jukote. Major Zelzik spoke, "Report Captain."

"The lone tunnel was the only evidence found. The missing garando returned, but lost its tail…we assume due to suvanth works," said Captain Avent.

"Recommendation?"

"Send a mapping team with a pack of garandos to the tunnel after the Umgara arrive. The team can map, trap, and seal it. We don't want any surprises while the Umgara are here."

"I concur," said the Major.

"Major, any word from the other teams?" asked Avent.

"So far just the tunnel your squad discovered. There are still eight squads searching. Get that tunnel-mapping team ready Captain."

"Yes Major," said Avent, then led his troops to Fort Carth.

As the squad made their way into the fort, a commotion sprang up from the direction of the south gate, where large torches burned. It was the inobi sled runners who had returned from their journey to notify the Umgara of the suvanth presence in the forest. Sled runners escorted the exhausted knee-high inobis, sleds still attached, to their stable for recovery and rest. The sled runners wearily stood in front of Meraco to brief the General. "General, we met with Umgara General Reibo and informed him of the suvanth attack and capture of one of our own," said the higher-ranked inobi runner.

"What was his word?" asked Meraco.

"General Reibo plans to speak with you and lord Hiko directly. The Umgara will be here in the lumeren," replied the soldier.

"Well done soldiers, go recover," the General continued, "Captains, have your soldiers assist in preparation for the Umgara's arrival."

Avent's search party approached General Meraco. "General I have news to share with you," said Avent.

"Captain Avent, have your squad return to their dwellings then follow me to my quarters, we can talk there," said Meraco. Avent nodded with understanding.

"Soldiers, go home to your families. I want to see you here at the fort with the Eastern star's breach," said Avent and continued, "Keel, Taukin, remain here." Keel and Taukin looked to each other with confusion then approached their Captain. "Keel stay with me, I'll introduce you to the mapping team. Taukin go home and stay there until called upon. This time stay there. You can go see the Umgara, but then return home afterwards."

Taukin raced to the hut down the dark path guided by the moonlight, excited to share the news of the discovery of the suvanth tunnel. "Soyha, is that you?" asked Taukin as he approached her from behind with only the sister moons providing a source of light. The guards turned to defend against, or at least intimidate Soyha's pursuer with their pampa staffs.

"Guards stand down," said Soyha with authority. "Taukin!" she said with excitement and relief. "What did you find?"

"A suvanth tunnel," replied Taukin, "A garando went down, but came back missing his tail. We're not sure if it was caught in a trap, or was attacked by suvanth. Soyha, I need to tell you something," said Taukin glancing at her guards, whose darkened skin said everything. "In confidence," continued Taukin.

Soyha motioned her guards to back away and turned back to Taukin. "It's about the bauble, isn't it?"

"Keel said it was given to him by a being that was made up of the forest. He takes me for a fool."

"Was there a message given?" asked Soyha, whose skin went white.

"It said, 'A possessor young of an offering old. All you desire is yours if you but use this bauble."

"This sounds like an Unknown," said Soyha nervously.

"An Unknown?"

"Have you learned nothing from your lessons? The Unknowns are messengers of the gods. They have no body, so they take on the form of whatever is around them. They deliver messages from the gods and sometimes gifts or tokens. Depending on the god, their message can be cryptic or prophetic, or both."

"Why would a god gift Keel with a suvanth bauble?" asked Taukin, his skin showing confusion.

"The real question is *which* god gave the gift? Gifts from the dark gods lead to suffering," said Soyha.

Passing soldiers quieted Taukin who turned his back to them and edged closer to Soyha, whose guards moved in. "I'm fine, stand back," said Soyha firmly.

"Something else," said Taukin after a brief pause, then continued, "I spoke with a suvanth."

Soyha pulled back, her color showed her surprise. "How?"

"He found me. He said a Carth tribesman is helping him."

"Suvanth speak with twisted tongues," said Soyha fervently.

"That's what we've been told all our lives, but what if he's telling the truth?" said Taukin.

Soyha could only stare at Taukin, unsure of what to say.

"He wants me to go with him to the pit…to Sheol Balla," said Taukin.

"Why would a suvanth want you to go to the pit? That would be unwise Taukin. You don't even know how to defend yourself. I could put you on the forest floor," Soyha admitted.

"You couldn't…" and before Taukin could finish his words, Soyha swept his legs and he rolled to his side, dazed.

Her guards moved in, staffs aimed at Taukin's golden neck. "Stand down! He did nothing!" and when the guards moved back, Soyha continued, "And that's why you need to stay in the forest." Soyha helped Taukin up, brushing off the dirt from his coverings. "My father will ensure your protection."

"If you tell him, I'll be deemed a traitor like my father," whispered Taukin frantically.

"The bauble, now this…Taukin this is for the best."

"Who can I confide in if not you?" asked Taukin, whose skin went deep blue.

"Trust me."

"I always have. Grant me more time. I need to understand what's happening," said Taukin.

A guard stepped forward and said, "Soyha, the General requires us to get you home safely."

Soyha pulled Taukin away from the guards quickly, "The Needlesmith was found dead this lumeren."

"How?"

"Garwelve venom."

"It's garwelve season, they're plentiful with the cold," said Taukin.

"But there were no bite marks on her body," said Soyha half nervous half scared.

Taukin's eyes blazed with suspicion and anger.

"We must go," said the guard, this time demanding.

"Let's go," she said to the burly guard. She turned back to Taukin and said, "In the lumeren, meet me at the tanner's shop for the arrival of the Umgara. I'll be there early." Taukin ran off toward Byrre Syra, weaving in and out of the marching soldiers until he made it to Avent's hut.

Taukin quietly snuck into the hut and into his shared room, then silently collapsed into his pelt sling. Exhaustion drained his body, but not his mind and Taukin couldn't sleep. Thoughts swirled about Syonis, the Unknown and the bauble, Swinzal, Soyha, and the Umgara. It seemed that life had suddenly changed without warning. His feelings were amalgamated and stronger than before, those for Soyha and those against his own tribe who continued to push him out. Shadows stretched across the wooden floor from Aebean's light, moving from one side of the room to the other. Taukin focused on the ceiling and didn't blink his eyes until he couldn't resist closing them for much-needed rest.

It wasn't long before Larnhi stood over Taukin and gently nudged his side. "Taukin, it's time to wake. We must make our way to the village main to greet the Umgara," said Larnhi. Taukin rubbed his eyes to adjust to the bright beams of light coming in through the opening in the wall.

The smell of warmed kulee mush and fresh malpwa fruit made its way to Taukin. "Do I have time to eat?"

Larnhi laughed, "Not if you want to see the Umgara." Taukin rose and put on his best light-blue armband, reflecting his tribe's colors and Avent's house. He had hardly sat down when he realized that Larnhi was the only one with him.

"Where's Nelkum?" asked Taukin.

"He left to greet the Umgara," replied Larnhi. "It's almost mid-lumeren."

"Soyha!" piped Taukin. With that Taukin pushed as much of the food into his mouth as it would hold and ran out the opening to meet Soyha. Taukin bolted as quick as a sled runner ready to see the giants for the first time and to see Soyha again.

CHAPTER 3
THE ARRIVAL OF THE UMGARA

The main square of the village was full of coquelicot-colored rintic, so much so, that Taukin didn't know where to go since the huts and shops aligning the trails were simply a sea of tribesmen. The cerulean-base and yellow tribe-marked flags and banners lined the paths, swaying with the cool lumeren breeze. Forthcoming pride was an apparent characteristic observed by all beings who interacted with the rintic. Soyha grabbed his attention by flagging him from atop the tanner's porch across the central trail. Taukin was pushed and prodded as he made his way through the crowd over to Soyha; the rintic seemed exceptionally impeding for the young soldier. His politeness evaporated with each elbow and shove that his body took from the tribe, whether on purpose or not. His frustration level had almost peaked, and his skin was turning orange when he reached the ramp to where Soyha stood alone.

"Solea," said Soyha when Taukin made his way up to the porch. She smiled softly to Taukin.

"Solea," said Taukin in a grumbled voice. His orange-tinged skin slowly changed back to its dull violet hue. Taukin closed his eyes and leaned his head back to take in the heat given off by the Eastern star.

The cool air counterbalanced the strong light beams emitted from the Eastern star. "Better now?" asked Soyha. Taukin faced the rintic beauty and nodded. Glimmers in Soyha's gray-green eyes stole Taukin's attention away from the upcoming parade of Umgara.

He shook the gaze and asked, "Can I still trust you?"

"I've given you no reason to not trust me," replied Soyha. A rintic horn blared, announcing the upcoming caravan of Umgara and drew their attention to the parade. Loitering rintic scattered, making the already packed cells of tribesmen that aligned the trail even more compact. Taukin could feel the excitement all around and his skin bumped up. The tribesmen collectively changed hue and pattern to that of a soft yellow with small violet crescents. Some of the males opened their coverings for a more vivid display, a sign of respect. Taukin's skin didn't exactly coordinate with the rintic. His shade was off. The pattern matched closely, but instead of the soft-yellow color his skin hue was a dark auburn. He stuck out in the crowd of rintic like a brown leaf amid a field of yellow flowers.

The first of the Umgara appeared, standing on a massive brownish-gray, four-legged creature that had a slightly inverted black, tan shell, a thick neck, small brown eyes, and flat teeth. Melps were the only timid creatures strong enough to carry the colossal beings. The Umgara wore sleeveless pelt coverings and held weathered steering straps with their forward-facing arms while their backward-facing arms remained crossed against their lower back. As the first Umgara reached the shop where Taukin and Soyha stood, Soyha spoke to Taukin, "His name is Itil, he's an Umgara scout."

"They're giants," said Taukin, amazed. Itil looked over at Taukin, noticing his hairless head, similar to his own, but also Taukin's auburn hue and his shortened stature compared to his tribe. Soyha nodded with respect and prodded Taukin with her elbow to do the same. He followed Soyha's suggestion. The hairless Umgara nodded back, then faced forward. Taukin felt of a sense of awe and respect come over him. Two melps passed by, steered by Umgara, and a riderless third was in tow. The last and most eminent of the giant beings rode his rugged creature past them.

"General Reibo," Taukin muttered without any input from Soyha. He had more battle scars than the others, including one large mark running down his front ash-gray and black-speckled sinewy arm. The general, riding on his melp, stood at least a full rintic higher than Taukin did standing on the porch. The general's gaze penetrated Taukin's core, making him feel hollow and light, almost like the gaze alone could move his body where the Umgara wanted it to go. The stare continued past the tanner's hut, as the Umgara rotated his head and body completely around. Taukin finally blinked, then exhaled and relaxed his yellow tinged shoulders. Four youths followed behind the caravan hopping from one melp imprint to another. A trail of tribesmen fell in line behind the caravan and followed the Umgara toward Fort Carth. Some of the tribesmen's skin returned to normal, while others stayed yellow and patterned as they exited the village square.

They departed down the barren trail for Avent's hut. Alone Soyha asked, "Which god do you think sent the Unknown?"

"It's a suvanth bauble, and they dwell underground in the darkness, so it must be Cenro, the bringer of dark," said Taukin.

"We need to discover the purpose of the bauble," said Soyha. Taukin was about to respond when a lone, squatty Sergeant appeared, coming from Avent's hut.

"General Meraco has ordered Taukin report to Fort Carth immediately."

"You're welcome to go to Avent's hut if you'd like," said Taukin. Soyha bowed her head in gratitude, then Taukin trotted off down the dirt path toward Fort Carth with haste. Taukin had just passed the last of the crowd when he accidentally ran into a tall, slender rintic soldier whose covering sleeve drooped where his left arm used to be.

Taukin took a step back and abruptly went to attention, the patina-covered Colonel insignia on his collar and patch with a garando mouth agape on his shoulder standing out to Taukin. "I'd strip you of your rank, but you can't get any lower, half breed," said the Colonel with so much spite that spittle came from his lips." Taukin's skin darkened, and the Colonel spoke again, "Go on, say what you're thinking. Do my words sting?

Do they bite? There are worse things in this world than words soldier. Much worse." Taukin knew better than to utter a sound at these comments. "Where are you going in such a hurry?"

"Colonel, Fort Carth," said Taukin, looking straight ahead avoiding eye contact.

"On who's orders?"

"General Meraco's orders Colonel," said Taukin, expecting this to silence the wroth Colonel.

"Deliver this scroll to High Priest Kuxain at the temple Woosan."

"But Colonel, I am to go to…"

"That's a direct order…*soldier*," said Colonel Pella with a brief flicker of dark redness and swaying of drooped sleeve.

"Yes Colonel," ceded Taukin, and ran with great speed back to the Temple of Hobaja Vael and the gods of light.

Great arched wooden doors led into the decorative vestibule of the great stone structure. One single burning torch revealed articulate gold and silver traces outlining blue and white tiles along the walls and over-head. A place not for public worship, but for those of faith to genuflect if spiritually clean and humbled. Taukin's skin tingled when the exotic fragrance and warmth of the temple filled his senses. A true sense of holiness filled the temple. He opened the scarlet drapes leading to the holy place, viewing the ivory carvings of the gods when he was met by a young priest. He wore a green and violet robe and his head was completely bald like Taukin's, except for the single row of black braids surrounding his crown and whose crooked nose drew Taukin's attention.

"You are from the house of Avent, the one called Taukin," the priest said as he closed the drapes behind him, forcing Taukin back into the vestibule.

"I have a message for priest Kuxain," replied Taukin.

"Give it to me," said the young priest as he held out his red hand. Taukin went to move past him, but the young priest, a full head taller than Taukin placed his steady hand on Taukin's chest, "Only the purified may enter the holy place. Your message is sealed and will remain as such until it's in the hands of priest Kuxain. It's forbidden for priests to lie and certainly not in temple."

Taukin, under the pressure of time of command, hesitantly placed the scroll into the priest's hand and backed out of the temple, watching the expression of the young priest turn from a lenient smile to a look of disregard. An uneasy feeling blanketed Taukin, but the pressure of General Meraco's order got his feet moving promptly toward Fort Carth.

Taukin arrived in time for the lighting of the lookout perch torches, the signal that the quiesce would be upon them soon. The fort's four towers at the corners of the wooden walls flickered brightly, and the high perch, above the tree line, was viewable as dots of amber through the thick foliage between the dirt and perch. He passed through the South gate and entered the courtyard in search of General Meraco. The weary melps were being cared for by rintic soldiers near the North gate. Captain Avent stood with Dyant and other soldiers at the bottom of the ramp leading up to General Meraco's quarters.

"Taukin, you've kept the Umgara and Lord Hiko waiting, come with me," said Avent firmly.

Taukin trailed his Captain up the wide, winding wooden ramp to Meraco's quarters, which seemed high to Taukin, but was still far below the brave perch. The quarters were larger up close and the ceiling higher than typical rintic dwellings. There were groups of upper-ranked Carth soldiers scattered here and there including the single-armed Colonel, and on the left side of the room was a large oval-shaped table which was mostly covered by a pelt map of the same shape. The map on the table was of Onestonia, or at least what was the known terrain by the rintic and Umgara who helped create the map. It was exquisite, showing regions Taukin had never heard of before. The caverns of the Eltepsu were detailed, showing distances from the Carth forest and Sheol Balla, the pit of the suvanth, located north of the Binesmir mountains. Avent informed one of the two posted guards standing outside of the inner chamber within the quarters that Taukin had arrived. The guard nodded and parted the insignia-etched trochin tapestry as he walked into the inner chamber.

"That Colonel with the missing arm, who is he?" asked Taukin.

Avent replied, "Colonel Pella, avoid him."

Taukin was drawn to the case of numerous military medals hanging on the wall and in particular, the medal at the center, "The Nionan Star," said Taukin to himself. The badge had a blood-red ribbon, centered by a single vertical yellow stripe. The stripe led to a dull, gray metallic star and in the center of the star was fastened a rare nionan crystal shard, the size of a grain of kulee mush.

"The highest honor any rintic soldier can receive," said Avent. A few par-tems expired before the guard came back out.

"The General is ready," said the guard. Avent turned toward Taukin who was still analyzing the Nionan Star.

"Come," said the Captain as he held open one side of the pelt. Taukin stepped through into the inner chamber, which was surprisingly well lit by round, translucent trisian luminescence bulbs and oil lamps.

Five Umgara were seated in a half-circle on wide benches that would engulf even a considerable-sized rintic tribesman. The other half of the circle was made up of the tribal elders and Lord Hiko. Avent and Taukin sat next to the elders, who almost in unison, shifted away from Taukin on the bench.

Hiko stood and faced the Umgara. "General Reibo, the Carth rintic offer our gratitude and are pleased you have made the journey to our homeland. As you were made aware, there was a suvanth attack, a soldier died, and another was taken, presumably to Sheol Balla. We can no longer tolerate this defiant behavior by the suvanth. Never before has an attack breached the Carth forest. Their rebellion must be put to an end," said Hiko.

A low, bellowing voice came from the scarred Umgara General Reibo, "For too long have the suvanth violated the ordinance. They have invoked the wrath of the Umgara and will be dealt with in time, but our attention is given to the Eltepsu. The two moons will soon align in effergy and the trek of the Eltepsu will commence. The Umgara requests the Carth rintic pledge fidelity as they have for Ulti-cycles and join the Umgara to protect the Eltepsu during the journey," said Reibo.

Hiko's skin reddened beyond his normal hue and aureate dashes danced; he responded harshly, "And what of the protection of the Carth rintic?"

"General Meraco has increased rintic patrols until judgment is handed down to the suvanth. Umgara protect the sacred Eltepsu above anything else," said General Reibo in a calm manner. The frustration on Hiko's face was read across every wrinkle in his furrowed forehead and between his silver eyebrows.

General Meraco stood up and addressed Hiko, "My Lord, our military has significantly increased in number since the last trek of the Eltepsu. Perhaps we should continue the increased patrols within the forest until the trek has concluded," said Meraco in a respectful, but authoritative voice.

Hiko's tone changed, skin and voice, and aimed his gaze at the Umgara General and said, "Your focus is on the Eltepsu, my focus is on the Carth. How can my tribe offer support to the Umgara when they do not reciprocate? The Carth rintic will not pledge fidelity to the Umgara."

General Reibo stood, towering over Hiko, his massive arms folded behind and in front, a bauble wouldn't fit between Reibo's head and the ceiling. "Your assistance is not required for the Umgara, but for the protection of the Eltepsu, just as the Umgara protects the Carth Basatab retriever at Olin Fell. You see Lord Hiko, we are all here for a purpose, and we are all dependent on one another. The time for retribution is after the trek."

Hiko's skin remained reddened, and with a scathing glare he faced Taukin and gritted the words, "Why is *he* here?"

General Reibo continued, "Taukin is a critical piece of our next mission." All the rintic elders and Hiko turned to Taukin, whose skin flickered a nervous golden hue before settling back to his normal violet. Reibo continued, "We're going to rescue your soldier Fesenius and the captured Eltepsu Cuvsor. Hobaja Vael, we ask your protection over Cuvsor and Fesenius." Taukin saw the entire chamber lower their heads in respect of Hobaja Vael. After a pause, Hiko and the elders went white with the gravity of General Reibo's claim and Hiko raised the question, "How is such a thing possible?"

"We need a spy," responded Reibo in his low, drumming voice.

"Only suvanth can enter Sheol Balla," interjected one of the oldest elders, held steady by his wooden cane.

"Only those with suvanth blood in their veins," replied Captain Avent with a scowl as he moved closer to Meraco and pleaded, "General, he's still young. He's only started his training."

General Meraco spoke loud enough for all to hear, "Taukin is a Carth rintic soldier and I know he'll make the right decision," as he set his piercing green eyes on Taukin.

"The plan needs to be discussed in a more secure location," said Reibo.

"Carth is one of the most secure, if not the most secure fort that the rintic possess," said a proud Hiko.

"The suvanth have cut a tunnel into your forest, there is too much risk," replied Reibo. Hiko knew he couldn't speak against these words for they were the truth, so he lowered his silvery head.

Reibo continued, "The Umgara request General Meraco, Captain Avent, and Taukin join us at the Caverns of the Eltepsu." Taukin's skin morphed auburn just as it was when he first saw the Umgara, it was uncontrollable excitement. The giant general took this as Taukin's acceptance to the Umgara's invitation. All eyes went to Hiko who shot a distrustful look at Taukin, but nodded with approval of the mission. "We leave for Binesmir in the lumeren, we shall retire for the quiesce," said the towering Umgara as he unfolded all four arms and stepped toward the exit.

"Taukin, head home and pack for the journey. We'll meet at the village square in the lumeren. Do not be late," said Avent with a firm grip on Taukin's shoulder.

"Yes Captain," replied Taukin, then took the ramp down, and out the South gate he ran.

The farthest moon Febus supplied extra light along the path, allowing Taukin's pelt-covered feet to carry him swiftly over the smooth, compact soil. Shadow and moonlight alternated on the dirt below at a rapid pace. It was after he had passed the last squad of rintic soldiers when a sense of another being suddenly came over Taukin. To his right was something running at an angle alongside him at a distance. It was running faster than Taukin through the impeding brush and trees. Taukin ran full out, following the trail as it peaked and dipped and turned through the moonlit forest. Colorful bursts from the Trisians had become short-lived streaks in Taukin's peripheral vision. He knew he was faster than any of the tribesman. His chance to outrun the being was just ahead, the long, straight stretch midway between the fort and Byrre Syra, would provide enough distance for escape. He reached the straight path and dug up dirt that light hadn't touched in cycles. The being, no doubt suvanth, stood center, mid-way down the path. His moonlit-covered chest pumped massive quantities of air and splatters of bright luminescence covered his pelt-covered legs. Taukin looked on either side for more of the enemy and a way of escape. "You are quick Taukin. You have the agility of the sssuvanth," said the recognizable voice of Swinzal.

"Let me pass demon, or I'll send you to your master in pieces," said a winded Taukin, drawing his short sabre.

"I had hoped that you had reconsssidered my offer."

"I told you before, I'm rintic."

"I know your fealty to the rintic isss ssstrong, but I alssso know where the rintic'sss loyalty liesss and it'sss not with you. You ssstill have much to learn about the malice and dessseption of the rintic."

"The rintic accept me as I am," said Taukin,

knowing that Soyha was the only one that made that statement partially true.

"The onesss closssessst to you have influensssed you with their dessseitful wordsss. In time you will learn the truth. You have free will to choossse. Your kind isss sssuvanth. Join usss."

Taukin's brain raced faster than his breathing. "I…I must go now," said Taukin.

"I will find you again," said Swinzal. He slowly moved to the side of the path next to the tree line and allowed Taukin to pass. Taukin slowly walked the length to where Swinzal stood and turned his torso to watch the suvanth in case of a surprise attack. Swinzal turned as Taukin passed so that his face fell in the moonlight's shadow, and Taukin's face was completely revealed. Swinzal could read the uncertainty in Taukin's eyes, uncertainty of trust, and the uncertainty of his feelings. His task was complete, the seed of doubt had been planted. Swinzal turned and ran through the forest in the opposite direction of Byrre Syra.

Taukin returned to the hut and quietly filled his ruck with cold-weather coverings and some dried meats and fruit needed for the journey to Binesmir. Taukin reached into his coverings for the charm from his birth mother. He held the ivory bauble between the fingertips of both hands, like a bridge with the charm connecting both sides together, and ran his violet finger across the carved lines on the bottom of the stone figurine. Taukin lowered the bauble into his coverings pocket, and finished packing his gear. He sidled the stuffed pack next to his warm pelt sling. The heated cloth-wrapped rocks were placed directly underneath the sling providing warmth during the cold stirless darkness. Taukin lowered his body into the pelt and collapsed from the emotional and physical drain of the tem-cycle.

Faint conversation woke Taukin. Warm light filled the chilly room, the early-lumeren had arrived. Taukin adjusted his eyes and popped out of his pelt pod. Keel was fast asleep, no doubt the rigors of his tunnel-mapping proved wearisome. He covered his sinewy chest, grabbed his ruck, and started toward the main room of the hut, but stopped when he heard the conversation. "He's no longer a youth, he needs to know. If you don't tell him I will," said Larnhi. Avent nodded with concurrence. Taukin slowly walked into the main room acting like he hadn't heard anything. "Taukin," said Larnhi surprised by his sudden appearance.

"Solea, I'm ready," said Taukin.

"Eat. I need to wake Keel," said Avent as he left the room. Larnhi sat at the table.

"Get your strength," she said as she handed Taukin some wrapped kulee mush. The table was filled with fresh fruit and dried meats. "Do you have plenty of food for the journey?" asked Larnhi.

"Enough to get me to Binesmir," replied Taukin. Avent returned with a groggy Keel in tow. "Did you go in the tunnel?" asked Taukin.

"Not far," said Keel as he rubbed his swollen eyes.

"What if you see a suvanth in a tunnel?" asked Taukin, concerned for his brother. Keel didn't reply, his skin changed to light green with open red circles.

"He'll dispatch the hostile with the help of his garando," said Avent reassuringly. Larnhi's skin went darker than normal and yellow dashes appeared as she dropped a wooden bowl onto the table causing a loud THOK. "He's safe as long as he has his garando," said Avent.

"And what happens when his garando is killed and he's down there, then what?" asked Larnhi.

"Garando handlers are the best trained soldiers. They know what to do if that ever happens," said Avent.

"Not all soldiers desire to go down tunnels," said Larnhi.

"Those who want to be remembered do," said Avent arrogantly, "We leave soon, finish up," said Avent in his militarized voice.

"I'd rather travel to Binesmir than traverse a dirt tunnel," said Keel, frustrated with his position.

Avent replied, "You become a Handler and you'll get your opportunity." Keel shook his head and went to his room as Nelkum appeared and placed his shaggy black hair against Avent's back.

"Don't go," said Nelkum, his skin tan with black branches.

"I'll be home before you know it, and I'll have some new stories to tell you around the fire circle," said Avent. Nelkum's eyes opened wide and he grinned a closed-mouthed grin as he looked up at his father with tired eyes. "It's time," said Avent. Taukin stood and lifted his ruck to his back.

Larnhi faced Avent and said, "Protect him…and yourself." Avent squeezed Larnhi and whispered into her ear, causing her skin to morph bright green with yellow dots. Larnhi clenched Taukin's shoulders and said, "May Hobaja Vael keep you safe," and hugged him before they stepped out onto the black forest path.

Avent and Taukin traveled swiftly down the light-filled trail leading to Byrre Syra. The subtle heat from the Eastern star helped give the travelers' muscles some relief from the cold. They slowed as they arrived at a large crowd lined along the main trail near the village square. The tribesmen parted upon seeing the Captain with Taukin in tow. Among the crowd was Syonis, and as Taukin passed through, Syonis spewed directly to Taukin, "Don't come back or else I'll tell the tribe you attacked me, and we know what happens to traitors." Taukin shrank as he continued through the crowd toward the Umgara caravan. Hiko acknowledged Avent and rested an aged hand on his shoulder and moved close to Avent's ear.

Convince Taukin to be the spy we need," offered Hiko, and each made their way toward the vacant-shelled creature. With his hairless head, Taukin bowed to Hiko, but Hiko's response was simply a scowl with squinted eyes that cut through to Taukin's bones. General Meraco finished his discussion with Umgara General Reibo and joined Taukin and Avent on top of the bowl-shaped shell. Reibo gave the call for the caravan to proceed. Meraco, who normally seemed large to Taukin, looked miniaturized standing on the melp. The rintic general took the worn pelt reigns and gave them a shake to prompt the broad beast to move. The jolt made Taukin stumble backwards and he nearly fell off, but Avent grabbed his coverings and pulled him back toward the center.

As the creature lumbered forward, Taukin searched the crowd lining the trail for Soyha. They had nearly traveled to the edge of the main village square before Taukin spotted her long, ebony hair waving across her face as she stood on the crowded ramp of the sundry shop. She was twisting her cupped hands near her chest telling him goodbye. Taukin smiled and signaled back. He stood next to Avent, but remained facing Soyha until she was no longer in view. Taukin ran his hand along the rugged patterns etched into the shell of the melp. He used his finger to trace the connecting tributaries that seemed to widen at each connection point, as his finger got closer to the center of the shell where a constricting muscle opened and contracted leading to the inner part of the creature. Avent noticed Taukin's enlightenment and said, "Their shell catches the falling water. It's channeled internally so they don't have to find sources of water as often."

The Eastern star had breached the midpoint of the azure sky when the caravan reached the Orlang river, or stone river as some called it. The Umgara crossed at the widest stretch of the Orlang, which lay directly between Byrre Syra and the Umgara base at Binesmir. Taukin watched as the melps in front slowly descended into the rocky valley then quickly disappeared. "Hold on to the shell," said Meraco as he steered the creature toward the dry riverbed. Avent and Taukin went prone, latching onto the back and side of the shell as they turned and watched, with wide eyes, their General lean back almost completely and keep the reigns taut as they eclipsed the riverbank. The creature quickly made it to the smooth, stone riverbed below and went level again. Avent and Taukin released their grip on the thick shell.

"One more to go," said Meraco. Taukin and Avent looked at each other with anticipation and grinning faces. It was much farther between the Orlang riverbanks than Taukin ever imagined. The widest stretch of the stone river measured close to that of the distance between Byrre Syra and Fort Carth. It was a bumpy ride through the river valley and Taukin decided to lie with his back against the shell and admire the colorfully painted sky. Febus grew brighter as the Eastern star dipped closer to Binesmir in the western sky. Febus, the smaller of the two moons of Onestonia, seemed to bounce side to side with each step that the Melp took. Melps were relatively slow for their size, but because of their bulky size they covered a considerable distance with each stride.

"I suggest you move next to me," said General Meraco as they approached the opposite riverbank. Avent and Taukin did as the general suggested and suddenly, they were on the far side of the Orlang. Taukin had never ventured beyond the Orlang on the Southwest side of the Carth Forest. He saw herds of trochin grazing in the far distance and the hazy Binesmir mountains, which lay before them, easily fit in his curled-hand aperture. Taukin stood next to the General and gazed at the beauty of the flat landscape with the majestic mountains joining the ochre-colored fields with the pink and purple sky.

"Quite different than the forest, eh?" asked Avent.

"It's amazing," replied Taukin.

Avent continued, "Wait until you look out from atop Binesmir." An unimpeded blast of cool air blew over the trio causing Taukin's jaw to shiver.

"I, I th, th, think I'll enjoy the view from down here," said Taukin as he took a seat near the middle of the etched shell.

Avent joined him. "Most tribesmen never meet the Umgara, let alone the Eltepsu." Avent lowered his voice, "I don't know what will be asked of us, but know that you have a choice." Taukin gazed out into the dark openness of the field and considered this possibility.

"It's not much farther to Jonta Fell," said Meraco, "We'll set up camp there." The repetitive motion of the melp's movement on the flat land was like being gently rocked in a trochin pelt; paired with the darkened sky, it was nearly impossible for Taukin to stay awake.

Avent sidled up to Meraco and asked, "General, do you think that the suvanth will attempt an Eltepsu abduction during the trek to Lithica?"

"Manista's growing army demands more agrum and this can only be accomplished with a constant source."

"Or the agrum is the source of his godly ability," retorted Avent.

"We can't allow another abduction."

Luminescence lamps of various colors with floating larvae in the middle, hung from affixed rods that were mounted on the back of the melps' shells. Meraco steered his melp next to Itil and pulled back on the reigns. Taukin jostled and awoke with the sudden stop.

Itil took the reins and tied them to a large wooden stake that was driven deep into the flat, grassy land by the Umgara scout. Meraco and Avent dismounted, followed by Taukin who hopped down into the waist-high grass. Taukin instantly knew what he had jumped into. It was bayphea grass, which was prickly at the head and stuck to any woven cloth, generally armbands, and occasionally and most uncomfortably, it turned up in the undercloth. Light from both Aebean and Febus shone down and revealed the tethered melps expeditiously grazing on the bayphea grass. "They enjoy the bittersweet meat of the bayphea," said Itil, "Where they graze is where we will make camp this quiesce."

"Good idea," replied Taukin.

It wasn't long before the melps had cleared a large circular area around each of their stakes, which over-lapped in the middle and formed a cluster of barren land near the body of water known as Jonta Fell. The melps lay on the cool surface of bare field next to their wooden pins forming an incomplete circle, which from the sky would have looked like a circle made of six sepa-rated dots. Their bodies offered some shelter from the crisp wind, enough for Taukin to feel a sense of comfort. Heat from fire located in the middle of the melp circle, about the size of the melp's shell, added to Taukin's contentment. "It's not as comfortable as our hut, but it's not the upper Binesmir Mountains either," said Avent as he rested against one of the huge, calloused rear legs.

"It's cold," said Taukin as he leaned against the front

leg that was the size of a swaul tree trunk and rubbed his own legs over his coverings to generate some heat.

General Meraco approached his resting soldiers and addressed the Captain. "The Umgara have offered to stand watch this quiesce so that we can rest," the rintic General said.

"A welcomed gesture," responded Avent. Three Umgara positioned themselves between the melps, each with an open space between the sentries. Their body-length spears in hand rested on end against the stubs of grass below. Taukin covered himself with a thick flauva pelt and closed his eyes. Avent followed suit, except with a thinner trochin pelt instead.

The Umgara guard facing Binesmir stiffened and stood upright. He gripped his spear in both of his forward-facing hands and gave a low bellowing quip to alert the other Umgara of possible danger. His free hands facing the inner circle clapped quietly to supplement his low verbal alert. General Reibo and the other Umgara took up their armament and breached the makeshift fort of melps to investigate. General Meraco rose to his feet and quietly roused Avent and Taukin. "Take up your weapons," said Meraco. Taukin and Avent quickly and quietly rose to their feet and unsheathed their long swords, but remained within the confines of the makeshift camp looking outward into the darkness.

"Is it suvanth?" whispered Taukin. Avent turned his head slightly towards Taukin, but before he could answer, something from their right flank lurched out from the tall grass at one of the Umgara soldiers. Long, ivory canine teeth that seemed to almost glow in the moonlight sank into the Umgara's shoulder and his right leg buckled slightly. He released a fierce yell, one that chilled Taukin's bones. The Umgara twisted wildly and threw the creature aside. He turned and faced the furry four-legged beast, which was now held at bay by the protector's long spear. The Umgara's head turned completely back around facing General Reibo.

"Satupha!" said the soldier in what was a mixture of anger and pain.

Avent said, "Taukin, stay within the circle, do not leave it." Avent and Meraco joined the Umgara just as a wave of satupha attacked. General Reibo drew two long swords, one for each pair of hands forward and back. A large shadowy satupha, white teeth fully exposed, pounced at Avent, but Reibo's torso quickly twisted and his massive front hand grasped the beast by its fur-laden throat and with his rear sword, pierced through the underside of the creature's jaw until the crimson-covered tip protruded the top of the skull. Avent ran to Meraco who was caught between two satupha, his long sword and short saber brandished, holding them at bay. The beast turned its head just as Avent drove his sword into its side, which shocked the creature and caused it to jump sideways. Itil caught the injured beast mid-flight with his spear and spun around, hurling the creature into a rushing satupha. Blurs of action could be seen between the still melps, who had retreated into their protective shells.

Taukin climbed on top of a melp and offered shouts of warning to his tribesmen and Umgara. A satupha silently crept up next to the melp and launched at Taukin's front, but Taukin being small and having the quickness of the suvanth, fell to his back and with his powerful legs propelled the ravenous creature over himself and into the fire. Taukin turned and watched as the creature, tangled in the thick brush, instantly ignited, its fur, acting as a crude accelerant, melted and dripped from the pelt like drops of fiery rain. There was a loud roar and then the creature went still and slumped, wilting as it burned. Taukin's heart raced and he turned back to see the other satupha withdraw and retreat into the darkness. Itil and the other Umgara, facing the field with weapons ready, slowly walked backward to the camp.

Avent went directly to Taukin, "Are you hurt?" asked Avent.

"I'm fine," responded Taukin as he jumped down from the melp's shell.

Meraco turned to Reibo, "I have never encountered satupha this far from the Mahala plains," said the Rintic General.

"This is peculiar," said General Reibo in his deep, body-permeating voice. "Something has driven them here," continued Reibo, "This anomaly will be presented to Gosin-Tare." Itil made a muddy, grassy paste and applied it to the wounded Umgara's shoulder. The soldier was expressionless even though the laceration was tender to the touch. "The satupha have retreated. Be at ease," said Reibo.

General Meraco turned to Avent and Taukin and said, "The forest stands firm." Avent nodded and all three rintic sat down on the cool ground and rested against the melps as the Umgara once again took their positions between the still creatures, but kept their eyes open wide.

As the Eastern star broke over the horizon, Taukin saw that the Umgara had not moved. They were still enough to pass for stone statues, except that every so often one would rotate his head completely around. Jonta Fell provided a refreshingly cold bath by hand. Taukin cupped the chilled water up to his face and back of his neck, instantly waking himself up. His face and neck discolored uncontrollably to a shade of dark gray and Avent laughed, familiar with this color freeze effect. Taukin smirked, but was somewhat embarrassed because he couldn't change his skin back to its normal, dull violet hue. Taukin made his way over to the white and black embers still able to garner some heat. His skin returned to normal as he stared at the ashes, and the skeleton of the satupha that was as long as Meraco was tall.

General Reibo gathered the Umgara and rintic inside the melp circle. They feasted on strips of dried trochin meat and carried with them a translucent tear-shaped vial of green agrum. The vial easily fit into the hand of Reibo, who pierced the tough, but flexible clear organic skin with a pointed stone plug. Other Umgara followed Reibo's lead, drinking their share of the essential substance. Reibo passed his vial to Meraco, which contained enough agrum for Meraco, Avent, and Taukin to partake in the ritual. A smidgen of agrum remained, but it was more than Taukin had ever received. Taukin took the vial from Avent and raised it to his bright, amber-colored eyes and examined the liquid. He removed the smooth, polished stone plug, no doubt handled many times, and allowed the somewhat viscous fluid to drip into his upward turned mouth. A feeling of heightened senses and great strength came over him. All soreness and weariness evaporated. He felt like he awoke from the longest slumber completely rejuvenated and stronger than ever.

"I could battle a satupha with only my hands," said Taukin.

Reibo spoke, "Such is the effect of agrum, life-sustaining and life-valorizing." The same rush of strength and ability came over Avent and Meraco. "Are we ready to proceed?" asked General Reibo.

"Ready," replied Meraco. The group mounted their melps and continued their journey to the mountains of Binesmir.

Bayphea grass rolled in waves across the great golden plain. Taukin watched as the Carth forest disappeared from sight with each long step the melp took. With the disappearance of the forest came the magnification of Binesmir. The Eastern star had arched through the sky and was now resting at the tip of Binesmir. Taukin pivoted around and focused on the massive mountain range they were approaching. Agrum still pulsed through Taukin and this time the repetitive swaying of the creature didn't faze him. Febus and Aebean moons appeared, but the god Haalek hadn't allowed the Eastern star to relinquish control of lighting the planet. The troupe carried on toward the home of the Umgara and the Eltepsu as the light faded.

Swinging luminescence lamps dotted the way to Binesmir. Umgara poured out from the village at the base of Binesmir once the horn blew announcing their arrival. Their huts were integrated into the mountain and the lights randomly splattered either side of the mountain inlet. Pale-skinned Umgara easily descended the preface of the mountainside on a combination of ramps and swinging ropes, which couldn't be seen, even by Taukin. Their steady lateral movements mixed with quick descents intrigued Taukin. Once the Umgara tribesmen made it to the ground, they quickly lit pools of torches posted along the village base and made their way to Taukin, lining up alongside the path leading to the center of the village. Firelight revealed the number of gray-colored giants to the trio of rintic, which brought about a tinge of anxiety in Taukin, causing a cross-hatched pattern on his now-golden skin. It was his turn to be the focus of attention now.

General Reibo steered the caravan of melps toward Fort Binesmir, which lay at the bottom of the village on the Eastern side of the mountain inlet. General Meraco followed the caravan along the thick line of Umgara lighting the way with burning torches aligned on both sides of the pathway. The Umgara lowered their heads, and some offered their upward-turned palms at the passing of their fearless General and nodded with the passing of the rintic. Taukin followed Avent's lead and lowered his head, peeking occasionally until they arrived at the well-lit fort.

Fort Binesmir was four times as long as Fort Carth and much wider, but surprisingly not tall. From what Taukin could see with the torch light, it was one long wooden box structure that ran along the mountain base and was built off the ground, just high enough for the Umgara to walk under. There were cavernous firelit lookout towers built along the rock face that led down to the fort and to each other, but there wasn't much else to the village, at least from what could be seen in the dark.

The trio dismounted and waited by the gathering group of Umgara while General Reibo visited his quarters. Some soldiers were dispatched from the quarters to prepare the fire circle and their meal for the quiesce. Umgara youth made their way to the inner crescent to see the rintic visitors. One youth, a female, approached Taukin with two hands extended, palms up. Her ebony hair, short and fuzzy, indicated her gender. She was slightly taller than Taukin, but much younger. Taukin took the palms up gesture as a friendly greeting and politely offered the same gesture. The Umgara tribe laughed, especially the youth.

"In their culture, only females greet others with their front-facing palms up," said Avent. Taukin smirked, unfamiliar with this gesture, and in the torchlight, his now bright yellowish-green skin could be seen. This fascinated the Umgara, who normally didn't interact with color changers, and their unified gasp filled the air. Reibo, stripped of his weapons and gear, rejoined the rintic and his tribe and led them to the warmth of the fire circle.

Gosin-Tare, leader of the Umgara, and his life mate Subian, joined the gathering around the fire circle. Gosin-Tare was hairless on top like all male Umgara, and his dark eyes matched those of Subian. A white, furry covering draped over Subian and Gosin-Tare and he moved, slow and careful, with his walking stick that was as tall as General Meraco. By firelight, judging by the wrinkled skin, it looked as though Gosin-Tare was quite possibly the eldest of the Umgara, "Tribe, make welcome our guests," said Gosin-Tare with a deep voice similar to Reibo, but not as loud and much gentler with a slight crackle at the end. The Umgara cleared out and left an area of large swaul stumps for the rintic to sit. Meraco sat next to Reibo and shared smoke from a curled, carved pipe filled with hannes leaf found only in the Ivory woods. The Generals and Umgara elders were the only ones who shared this rare indulgence. The leaves were difficult to come by and usually were offered by the Parabics when it was time to gather for agrum distribution as a gift of gratitude for the agrum.

Gosin-Tare removed his furry covering and walked around the dirt path between the center fire and the crowd looking at the Umgara. "My tribe, as you know, the effergy of the moons Febus and Aebean will soon take place. It is almost time for the Eltepsu trek to Lithica for the decegen process to proceed. Our sole purpose is to protect the Eltepsu, this responsibility given to us by Hobaja Vael our creator. We have reason to believe that there will be another attempt by the Suvanth to abduct more Eltepsu during this journey. If there is an agrum shortfall, life will cease to exist. We failed to save Cuvsor, let us remember our lost sustainer," said Gosin-Tare as he continued walking the circle. All tribesmen bowed their heads, including Taukin, for a short period, offering crackling firewood the chance to break the silence.

"My tribe, we are strong, we are Umgara! Let us never fail again!" said Gosin-Tare with as much vigor as his wrinkled and worn body could muster, bringing the tribe out of quiet remembrance and to their feet with shouts of concurrence and pride. Taukin stood, silent at first as he looked around, but let his voice ring out in unison. Gosin-Tare raised his four arms to silence the crowd and motioned for them to sit once more, then continued, "We ask that Hobaja Vael keep us strong and wise in all things. We lift shouts of acclimation to the creator for our blessings. Let us start our feast and build our strength and sharpen our minds for the journey ahead!" Umgara soldiers brought pallets full of delectable, cooked meat, fruits, and various-colored leafy plants and set them upon the swaul stumps. Taukin took up a long, flat wooden bowl, slightly smaller than a rintic shield, and placed some meats and fruits in it. Taukin stepped down to some pots of clear liquid containing red swimming creatures with three flailing appendages that the Umgara skewered with a forked wooden stick. Taukin's face contorted in repugnance and he quickly set his forked stick down.

"Their ways are different than ours," said Avent with a grin, and he and Taukin filled their bellies then retired to their cliff cavern hut for much-needed rest.

Taukin awoke to find he was alone. Light penetrated around the cloth covering over the entrance to the cavern hut. Taukin stood and pulled back the covering, shielding his eyes from the light. Avent looked back from the covered wooden deck. "I was about to come rouse you," said Avent.

Taukin's eyes widened as he looked out over the valley. The Eastern star had just painted the top of the mountain peaks on the Western side with golden rays and Umgara were scaling up and down the rock face and were busy about below. "The only view that's better is where the Eltepsu are. You ready to meet them?"

Taukin awoke with excitement. "Now?"

"Soon. General Reibo requested we join him."

Taukin raced back into the cave and dressed in his best pelt coverings and grabbed his short sabre and ruck, then darted back onto the overhang. "I'm ready!" exclaimed Taukin.

Avent nodded and they started their way down the series of suspension bridges, knotted ropes, and rope nets to the deck of General Reibo's quarters. Avent asked, "Do you know why the Umgara use a combination of bridges and ropes for accessing their huts?"

"To strengthen themselves?" answered Taukin.

"Mmm, the main reason is to prevent ease of access to the tribe by invaders. The enemy cannot easily carry weapons while climbing ropes," said Avent.

"No being can touch the Umgara," said Taukin.

"How do you think General Reibo got that scar? The Umgara are incredible beings and certainly most dominant, but they are not without limitations. Every being has a point of weakness."

Generals Reibo and Meraco stood on the edge of the fort deck awaiting Avent and Taukin's arrival in the early lumeren light. The architecture of Fort Binesmir was similar to that of Fort Carth except everything was proportionally larger, even the planks of wood that held the structure together were cut wider and longer. The guarded entryway dwarfed Taukin and even Avent and Meraco. Towering Umgara soldiers stood on both sides of the entry, and came to a stiff attention before Reibo gave the command to ease their stance. Taukin stood as tall as he could while entering the General's quarters and measured his height at the soldiers' waist. Feeling less significant, he looked forward, relaxed his stance, and lowered his head slightly then went into the General's quarters.

A wide, tan pelt map covered a wooden table in the middle of the quarters, much like the map in General Meraco's quarters, but on a larger scale. White light filtered through the portals in the sidewalls and light blue luminescence lamps hung from the tall ceiling over the map showing the plot of Onestonia.

Meraco motioned for Avent and Taukin to join him next to General Reibo. "This is the route that we will follow for the trek to Lithica," Reibo used a long whittled Ealtapa stick to trace the black dashed line from the Caverns of the Eltepsu alongside the Eastern side of Binesmir up through Sik Jukote over the plains of Gadush, and finally to the Norody Forest which surrounds the rocky dome of Lithica. "We believe that the suvanth could attack here between Sik Jukote and the Norody Forest. We will stay away from the areas of concealment, such as the Carth Forest, as we have done in the past. We will send scouts before the caravan to scan for tunnels and traps, we request assistance from the rintic army for this task," said Reibo.

"The rintic will assist the Umgara in any way necessary," replied Meraco.

"You speak for Lord Hiko?"

"I speak for the Carth rintic," said Meraco with whitened skin.

"General Meraco, what is your plan for the retrieval of the Basatab," asked Reibo.

"The retriever has been chosen, my daughter Soyha. She will retrieve the Light Cipher and will present it to the Umgara at Olin Fell three tem-cycles before the journey to Lithica," said Meraco. Upon hearing this Taukin's skin darkened and drew the attention of Meraco.

The Umgara General Reibo said, "As you plan to present the Basatab to the Umgara at Olin Fell, the Umgara will escort your party to and from Olin Fell." Meraco nodded in concurrence. Reibo turned to Avent, "Captain, have you and young Taukin eaten this lumeren?"

"No General, we came directly to your quarters," replied Avent. Reibo gave a low bellow to signal one of his guards that was posted outside the wooden structure. The guard quickly appeared in front of the Umgara General and stood attentively.

"Take Captain Avent and young Taukin deck-side for sustenance," said Reibo.

"At once," replied the guard as he lowered his head

to the General, turned, and awaited Avent and Taukin to join him with three arms aimed at the exit. Taukin and Avent followed the mighty Umgara out the wooden opening and onto the deck that supported the General's quarters. The Umgara guard led them to a large wooden table with a smooth wooden bench to sit. Upon the table was a modest feast of cooked meats, fruits, kulee cakes, and to finish it off, they had partially filled hulls of agrum. Taukin looked to Avent, who had just lowered his head in appreciation to the Umgara guard. Taukin quickly bowed his violet, hairless head and then tore into the meat. The table was positioned near the edge of the deck to see the happenings of the Umgara. The large beings were busy carrying materials, conducting weaponry practice, and trading goods with tribesmen from diverse regions of Onestonia. Avent took a swig of agrum, which quickened his senses. He looked out upon the field and something in the distance caught his attention. A hooded figure, wearing a black and white armband, signifying the rintic Sugot tribe, carried a woven basket of goods across the grassy field. Avent quickly stood and stepped over the bench like he was preparing for battle.

"What is it?" asked Taukin, who stood up to look over the wood railing. Taukin could see the lone, hooded figure and could tell he was who Avent's gaze was fixed upon. "Do you know him?" asked Taukin. Avent stood silent analyzing the being from the deck. The unidentified tribesman slowed, then looked up toward the deck at Avent. Half of the outsider's face was shown under the hood, revealing his vermillion nose and jaw. Avent cocked his head slightly and lowered it showing respect, but Taukin saw that his suspicious eyes never broke their fixation upon the stranger. The figure lowered his head in response, but was more formal than Avent, with a full forward lowering of his head. After the brief acknowledgement of Avent, the stranger carried on with his business with the Umgara. Avent lowered his head, deep in thought, then resumed eating his meal.

"Who is he?" asked Taukin.

"He looks like someone I once knew, but he…" Avent trailed off.

One of General Reibo's guards appeared next to Avent at the table. "Captain, General Reibo is ready to meet with the Eltepsu," said the lofty being. Taukin quickly grabbed a handful of vittles and the vial of agrum from the table and crammed the morsels in his mouth, washing it down with the agrum. He could feel himself strengthen as the agrum flowed through his veins. Taukin stood and followed behind Avent and the sentinel.

Meraco and Reibo, both with packs ready, stood on the worn dirt path that led into the mountainous valley to the Caverns of the Eltepsu. Reibo carried a full cloth sack larger than Taukin slung over his shoulder and held firm by his scarred arm. Avent and Taukin joined the Generals and as they walked, Taukin focused on the sack and his curiosity grew, but he knew not to say a word until he knew General Reibo couldn't hear him. "We'll walk the path to the Eltepsu," said Reibo, his head turned completely around facing Taukin and

Avent. Taukin's eyes followed the dirt path past the distraction of busy Umgara into the mouth of the valley until it wound around the inner mountain face. The Eastern star hung in the mid-lumeren sky and its rays clipped Binesmir, casting a shadow on the trail. Reibo hauled the sack over his back and led the foursome down the path along the Eastern side of the valley, past Umgara and other Onestonians as they conducted business and training.

They walked far enough to reach the narrowest part of the canyon, which was gated and guarded. In the middle of the fence four Umgara stood in front of a tall, weathered wood and metal gate, two at the hinged sides and two at the latched opening. The fence looked to be ten rintic high and made of thick Swaul wood. From what Taukin could tell, these were a different type of Umgara soldiers. Not only was their uniform more decorative with gold trim and crimson swirls, but they held Latris staffs, each end of the staff was mounted with a curved blade that came to a curled point and each had several large kracklins hanging from a belt strapped across their thick chests. Swirled translucent Doka shells, used for seeing far distances, hung on the left side of each guard. Reibo halted the group and approached the sentinels.

Taukin could no longer hold back. He leaned toward Avent and asked, "What does he carry in that sack?"

Avent replied, "Honor offerings to the Eltepsu." Reibo leaned in to the guards and spoke quietly, as quietly as an Umgara can speak, and the inner guards grasped the creaky metallic rings and slowly pulled open the wide gate. The rigid guards looked forward toward the direction of the Umgara village, their onyx irises fixed on the horizon as the group passed through the gate and into the realm of the Eltepsu.

CHAPTER 4
CLIMB OF BINESMIR

The mere passage into the land of the Eltepsu gave Taukin a slight feeling of significance and in a strange way, a feeling of belonging. Warm beams penetrated through the widened gorge and illuminated the green grassy field that stretched between the rock faces on either side of the worn path. The foursome trekked along silently with Reibo leading and the others following inline by order of rank. Except for some random trickles of water falling from some low rocky overhangs, life in the valley was quiet and seemed motionless. When Taukin rounded the Eastern rock wall, the chasm opened up to a vast flat grassy field with an object protruding from the rock face in the far distance. As they got closer to the object, Taukin peeked around the leaders to see the carved stone stairs that ran next to the left side of a smooth stone crag, leading up a steep incline into a small opening in the mountain. The stairs followed the crag up until they merged with the mountainside, where they twisted and ascended up to a cliff high above the valley.

A pair of decoratively dressed Umgara sentries stood

at the bottom of the stairs and next to a circular stone wall that the polished rock channel disappeared into. Taukin lagged behind and allowed the party members to get ahead and around the curved wall. He jumped up to get a peek inside of the stone surrounding, but wasn't quite tall enough to see over the wall. Taukin caught up to the rest of the party just as General Reibo had the guards move aside. Avent turned around to check on Taukin right as he stepped in behind the Captain. Taukin flashed a mischievous smirk. Avent shot him a look of suspicion, but turned back around regardless. "Follow me, but be cautious of where you step," said Reibo, with his head rotated back towards the rintic.

The group of four ascended up the steep stone steps. They had climbed up beyond the height of the circular wall, and Taukin paused to peer into what was a pool filled with clear-skinned, teardrop-shaped vials of agrum. Taukin's large eyes grew even larger. It was a tremendous amount of agrum; more than he had ever seen before and he estimated it was enough to last his entire tribe throughout his lifetime. Avent turned around, "Taukin come on," he said in a hushed tone. Taukin, still looking at the agrum, slowly took a few steps, then looked up at Avent and caught up with the group. They followed the twisting stairs and now traced the mountain face up to the cliff. It was easy to see that the Umgara had constructed the stairs due to the width, which was enough for three rintic to walk side-by-side. It seemed the air was getting thinner and colder with each step taken.

Taukin followed inline, but glanced over the outer

edge and was instantly hit by a strong sense of dizziness and scurried backward until his back hit the cold stone of the mountain. Seized with fear, Taukin slowly slid one foot to the side and then the other until he was following behind Avent again. The group undulated in and out along the mountain face. What couldn't be seen from the ground were the cavernous passageways cut from the steps into the mountain. Reibo passed the first passageway, which piqued Taukin's curiosity. Taukin closed in on Avent. "Where does that lead?" asked Taukin.

"Not to the Eltepsu," replied Avent firmly. It wasn't long before they reached another cut in the mountain, and like before, Reibo continued past it. The party ascended the stairs and with each step Taukin's body moved closer to the chilled rock face, his right hand never lost contact until they reached the next side passage.

Before they entered, Reibo turned his head and torso back to the tribesmen, "Follow close behind me." The passage wound left and right and continued inward toward the heart of the mountain. Reibo carried a luminescence lamp, the yellow light was enough to allow the group to see which way to go, but not enough to see which way they came, no doubt done on purpose. The location of the Eltepsu was only known by the Umgara, and within their tribe, only a select few knew the clandestine route. At times the lamp disappeared behind rock walls, which slowed Avent and Taukin's progress. Wind passed through the caves creating a deep chant, ominous and rattling. Taukin found himself paired with

Avent and separated from the Generals. Their light source was thinned to the point of blindness.

"I can't see anything," said Taukin.

"Don't worry, Meraco is right around the next turn. Once he realizes we aren't with them he'll come back to find us, but let us continue so he doesn't think we stopped," said Avent. With outstretched arms they slowly walked around, feeling their way down the blackened path. Avent knew they could only travel to the next fork and then they could go no farther. "Taukin, run your hand along the left wall. I will run mine along the right wall, but stay with me," said Avent. Avent took a few steps and suddenly went down, slipping on an outlying algae bed that stretched out from a thin creek that ran across their path. "I'm down," said Avent. The slickness of the algae and the rushing of the water was enough to pull him into the creek leading down to an opening in the wall next to Taukin. Taukin dropped to his hands and knees and started feeling around for Avent. Taukin's hands found the coolness of the water, which gave him a shock. He reached farther in and felt Avent slipping by. With his right arm Taukin hooked Avent underneath his shoulder and with his left arm braced himself against the wall where the creek ran into an eroded opening. Avent, using Taukin as leverage, pulled his right leg out of the opening and kicked against the cave wall until his torso was free from the swift current. Taukin kept pulling until Avent was completely out of the flowing water.

Winded, Taukin asked "Are you alright?"

Avent, mostly shocked, but also out of breath

replied, "I'm wet, that's all," Taukin rested his back against the cave wall while Avent lay on the cold cave floor. Suddenly a glimpse of light came creeping around the curved path. The cave brightened and the lamp was suddenly in front of them.

"Captain Avent, you'll have to stay closer," said Reibo, as his deep voice reverberated down the portal, and he extended his massive hand. Avent grasped Reibo's branch of a finger and was pulled upright without effort.

"Where does this creek lead?" asked Avent.

"Through Binesmir and into the Boshan river," said Reibo. Taukin was up and following behind Avent again, trying to avoid the slick tracks left behind by his Captain. They met up with Meraco, who had been waiting in place a few turns ahead of the creek. Reibo took lead of the party again. This time they huddled closer to each other as they maneuvered the rises and falls and twists and turns. Avent slowed and Taukin was suddenly upon him. Taukin saw the luminescence lamp slightly swaying as it rose upward. They happened upon more stone stairs. Taukin moved closer to Avent as they climbed stairs within the passage. The steps were wide and the duo reached a level spot where they were stopped short by Meraco, who lagged behind at Reibo's request. A thin line of light could be seen outlining a large, circular rock. A sound like stone slowly grinding against stone emitted from Reibo's direction and echoed against the walls of the silent cave. The cut boulder slowly receded into a wide cut in the side of the cavern. Light engulfed the passage, Taukin shielded his eyes with his forearm and squinted before raising his arm to see the others moving toward the opening. He gradually approached the exit, his eyes slowly adjusting to the excess of light. Reibo waited for them on the other side with two more well-armed Umgara guards on either side of the circular passageway.

Taukin stepped through the stone portal into the open, frigid landscape. They welcomed the open sky, but at that altitude the Eastern star provided light only, the warmth that could be felt at the lower level was nonexistent in this desolate, rock-filled space. Gray and black stone formations and paths laid before them leading to other openings in the mountain. From what Taukin could make out, this was just another way to keep uninvited visitors from reaching the Eltepsu, or they were simply paths to other areas inside Binesmir. Reibo took the lead again, winding around the stone formations that came up to his chest. Avent and Taukin stayed closer to Meraco as they wound through the pointed mineral structures. Not far off, Taukin could hear a gentle rustling and talk in an unfamiliar and unique tongue, one that was difficult to understand. They moved through the stone forest a little farther until it opened to a wide-mouthed, cavernous portal with a wide gray stone overhang to match. It was there that they were stirring about under the covered opening —the Eltepsu, the sustainers of Onestonia.

CHAPTER 5
DISCOVERY

Lantia, the second youngest of the Eltepsu and most energetic, scurried over to greet them. It was a peculiar looking creature, about half the height of its kin and Avent. It was covered in shaggy brown hair, matted and drooping over its hunched body almost touching the stone floor and covering its limbs so that it appeared as a moving ball of fuzzy hair. Its flat, hairless oblong face, which was the only part of its body that allowed Taukin to distinguish it from some of the common bush in the Carth forest, revealed large bright, yellow and green eyes nearly as round as the moon Aebean, and minuscule holes for its nose and mouth.

"Welcome General Reibo, we have made preparations for your visit," said the Eltepsu in a squeaky voice that didn't seem to match its brown, bulbous body.

Reibo lowered his towering body to one knee and bent his head down paying respect to the young Eltepsu. "We are most grateful," replied Reibo. The rest of the party took a knee and bowed except for Taukin, who just stared in disbelief that he was actually standing in front of the Eltepsu. Lantia's round eyes made contact with Taukin, who thought he detected a smile on the Eltepsu's face, but the tiny opening of a mouth was the size of a malpwa seed, and could scarcely stretch enough to speak. Taukin then realized he was the only one in the party standing; he quickly went to his knee.

"Come, we will meet after our quiesce prayer," said Lantia. The Eltepsu shuffled into the cavern and briefly disappeared from sight. The foursome arose and followed Lantia into the tunnel. As they walked further into the cavern their eyes slowly adjusted to the flickering of the fiery torches mounted on the winding cave walls that filled the Eltepsu's dwelling with golden light. The rintic followed Reibo, who was familiar with the Eltepsu paths. Harmonious chanting echoed down the passage. The tunnel opened to a great sanctuary with carvings embossed around each tunnel entrance. The domed room smelled both musty and fragrant, and looked ancient. Taukin knew this was a sacred place and felt a sense of respect pass over him. In between tunnel openings were long torches that lit the sanctuary enough to see completely around to the opposite side. Above was an oculus focusing light upon the centered segmented circular stone bench, which was populated with ten Eltepsu of various sizes.

Lantia joined the rest of the Eltepsu in their melodic chant. The Umgara guardians that were assigned to watch over the Eltepsu greeted Reibo, who then suggested Meraco show Avent and Taukin the story floor while they waited. Taukin stood on his toes and whispered to Meraco, "What are they saying?"

Meraco cocked his head and whispered back,

"'Praise be to Hobaja Vael, our creator, who works through us to sustain all life on Onestonia.' They pray in their native tongue."

Taukin looked on with admiration. "It's…serene," said Taukin as he stared at the Eltepsu who slowly and in unison, rocked side to side with their smooth, pale faces skyward and held their three-digit hands palm-side up.

Meraco turned to his tribesmen, "Follow me." Taukin and Avent quietly moved further inside the dome, following close behind Meraco, but staying far enough away from the sustainers so as not to disturb their genuflection. Taukin couldn't read the inscriptions, but could make sense of the vibrant swirled drawings on the cavern floor. He stood over a tile that showed a tall mountain, which breached the thick, white Onestonian clouds. At the peak of the tall mountain was a bright blue light, like the flickering light emanating from the stars surrounding Onestonia. On a smaller mountain, below the clouds, stood twelve auburn Eltepsu arranged in a circle facing upward toward the bright light. Surrounding the lower mountain were the Umgara, the protectors of the Eltepsu. Their massive pale-gray bodies spread along the base of Binesmir looking up at the Eltepsu.

Meraco quietly asked Taukin, "Do you recognize them?" as he pointed to the tile that Taukin stood over.

"I can tell there are Umgara around Binesmir and the Eltepsu are at their dwellings on Binesmir. But is the light at the top of the tallest mountain Hobaja Vael?" asked Taukin. Meraco nodded his head in affirmation.

They followed the drawings around the outer circle of the majestic room, closest to the torch light, reading the drawings like a colorful story brought to life. The next tile reflected a member of the rintic tribe wearing something that looked like a black ruck on her shoulders, but with straps covering her mouth. Umgara stood on both sides of her, dwarfing her rintic body. She stood next to a large body of water and in her hand was a cylindrical crystal and stone baton with symbols etched in each of the five sections. Taukin's eyes widened and at once he knew what it was that the rintic was holding. He turned to Meraco, "It's the Light Cipher, isn't it?" asked an excited Taukin, who forgot to muffle his voice.

"The Eltepsu call it the Basatab," answered Meraco in a hushed tone and continued, "Shortly before the trek to Lithica, a rintic tribesman, escorted by the Umgara, journeys to Olin Fell, the largest body of water in all of Onestonia. The retriever blows the horn of Cerona to announce their arrival. The Staleans are our ally and they provide the retriever with a sherob, an aquatic creature that breaths for and allows the retriever to remain underwater until the Basatab is safely with the Umgara. While in the water, the Staleans protect the retriever from the deadly creatures lurking in the dark waters. The retriever swims down and into the underwater crystal tube that leads up to the black crystal dome in Olin Fell.

"Many Ulti-cycles ago after the suvanth were banished to the pit, fears arose that it would be possible for the expelled demons to obtain the Light Cipher and control the Eltepsu and therefore control Onestonia.

After much deliberation between the Eltepsu, Umgara, and rintic, the leaders decided the dome was the one place that would be impossible for the suvanth to access. Suvanth have evolved such that their bodies cannot survive in colder climates like that of the peaks of Binesmir or frigid waters of Olin Fell. The Staleans agreed to guard the Light Cipher, and in return for their part in the security of the life cycle, each cycle the Umgara provide an offering of agrum to their Chief. Another offering happens prior to the effergy but supplied by the rintic. We must do what we can to protect this process." The singing tone of the Eltepsu became deeper and softer.

"Their prayer time is ending," said Meraco and he quickened his pace along the story tiles, to show as many as he could to Taukin and Avent before the prayers were complete. They passed a tile painted with Eltepsu on their journey to the gray dome of Lithica, then another tile showing the Umgara holding a pointed staff, banishing the suvanth out of the Carth Forest and to the solitude of the desolate Sheol Balla. Taukin could have spent an entire tem-cycle looking over the tiles, but time was limited. However the next tile could have been avoided entirely and Taukin would have been the better for it. He stopped and examined this particular tile. It had a rintic tribesman pointing toward the caravan of Eltepsu, the suvanth attacking the Umgara, and an Eltepsu being dragged down a tunnel by the suvanth. Taukin knew the captured Eltepsu was Cuvsor and the tribesman that committed the treason was his father Ethius. In the far upper-right corner of the tile, behind Ethius and away from the others was a small being, a female Suvanth, who was hiding behind a tree. Taukin's skin tone deepened to a dark blue and his heart grew heavy.

"Is that my mother?" asked Taukin, burdened by the representation.

Meraco looked to Avent to provide the answer. "She is Luspa, your mother," replied Avent. Taukin lowered his head either with respect or sadness, or both. Just then silence fell upon the great room. The harmonious chants were gone. Prayer time was over and the Eltepsu stood and turned to face their guests.

Taliph, the eldest of the Eltepsu, slowly hobbled over to Meraco, who stood two heads taller than the Eltepsu. His long gray hair hung low enough to drag over the story tiles, which he did to hide the tile that Taukin was fixated upon. Meraco lowered his head and went to his knee. Avent reached up and tugged on Taukin's arm to pull him out of his stupor. Taukin quickly dipped down.

"Arise friends of the Eltepsu. We are most grateful that you agreed to meet with us. Come with me," said Taliph in his high-pitched voice. The trio followed Taliph across the great room and through another tunnel that led to a room that was centered around a raised stone slab covered with what looked like maps. Taukin squinted upon entering the well-lit room for the light was blinding at first, but shortly afterward, Taukin's eyes adjusted. General Reibo and the other ten

Eltepsu were already gathered around the fixed platform discussing their plans. Taukin noticed that one of the Eltepsu in particular needed more space than its kin due to its width. Judging by the even mixture of gray and brown in its hair, Taukin guessed that this Eltepsu was close to middle age for an Eltepsu and probably an expectant female. Taliph sat next to Reibo, who loomed over the Eltepsu even though he was seated.

Taliph addressed the guests, "Please take a seat and join us." The Eltepsu looked up at the entrance, staring mostly at Taukin, who was unique in all of Onestonia. The only being that was of both rintic and suvanth lineage. Taukin's skin changed to a mild golden color and his bashfulness shone through his brown, cross-hatched pattern. He followed Avent to the table and took seat nearby Reibo and Meraco. Taliph turned toward the Umgara, "General Reibo if you will." The General stood, his bald dome nearly touching the stone ceiling, and in his low and echoing voice addressed the members around the table.

"Sustainers of Onestonia, the moons Febus and Aebean are almost in perfect alignment with Onestonia and the time is near for the trek to Lithica. General Meraco's own daughter, Soyha, has been selected as the retriever of the Basatab, which we will protect and carry with us to Lithica. Suvanth attacks upon Onestonians have increased in the last cycle and we believe the reason is that they need extra agrum in order to strengthen their army for an attack on the Eltepsu caravan during your journey between Binesmir and the Norody Forest. We believe they will expect an extra defensive strategy this trek and will pull their soldiers from the garrison in order to fortify their offensive front."

Taliph spoke, "General Reibo, with the loss of Cuvsor, our kind has suffered greatly. Cuvsor must partake in the decegen ritual or else lose the ability to produce agrum and die. Our planet's agrum supply is already lacking. Onestonia cannot survive losing another Eltepsu. With the expected increase in the suvanth army, do you plan to increase the rintic presence during the trek?"

"There will be an increase in rintic presence during the trek, but there is another objective. This increase of suvanth above ground will provide us the best opportunity to rescue your captured kin, Cuvsor." There was a loud gasp by the Eltepsu as their eyes widened and there was a commotion of squeaky voices that sounded more like chirping sumogul chicks than anything understandable by Taukin. The Eltepsu's discussion went back and forth across the table and side-to-side to their kind.

Taliph stood and quieted down the piping Eltepsu then asked, "General Reibo, if soldiers are pulled from your ranks it will leave the Eltepsu more exposed, and the suvanth are unorthodox in their actions. Is this wise?"

"The rescue squad will be few in number. The impact to our forces will be unnoticed. This plan offers the best chance for an underground rescue. The rintic have trained ceaselessly. You will be protected."

"Surely you understand the risks involved with such a mission? Who is willing to attempt this rescue?"

"The Umgara have drawn up a plan that, along with

the help of the rintic, will have a squad of highly trained rintic soldiers infiltrate the Sheol Balla and rescue Cuvsor and the captured rintic, Fesenius. The squad will follow a predetermined tunnel out of the pit to a safe zone, where the Umgara will then escort Cuvsor and Fesenius back to the safety of Binesmir," said Reibo.

"Suvanth are the only Onestonians that have knowledge of the tunnel structure leading to the heart of the pit," replied Taliph.

General Meraco stood and addressed the sustainers, "The rintic have been mapping the suvanth tunnels since Cuvsor was abducted and can predict some underground interconnection locations since the general vicinity of the heart of Sheol Balla is known. We cannot predict new tunnel locations, and we can only map within a set proximity to the pit, but we feel we have enough mapping to get our soldiers access to the main tunnel hubs of the pit."

"General, you need precise mapping to have any hope of rescuing our kind and yours and making it out alive," replied Taliph.

"There is a way that we can locate them and escape, but the danger and difficulty involved is significant," said Meraco.

"How can this be done?" asked a confused Taliph.

"Spy craft, which is why Taukin is here with us now," said Meraco.

Taukin faced Meraco, a puzzled look on his face. Meraco looked at Taukin's slivered eyes, "Taukin, what we ask of you is something that could not be asked of any other Onestonian. Because suvanth blood runs in your veins they will take you in as one of their own. Because you have knowledge of the rintic ways, they will hold you in high regard and you will be put in the higher class of suvanth, which allows you access to areas and information that lower classes do not have. We must know the exact location of Cuvsor and Fesenius through the maze of tunnels that makes up the pit. You can help us rescue them and restore the order of the Eltepsu. If Cuvsor is not rescued then the future of all of Onestonia is uncertain. This is our best option for a successful rescue, but also the one that carries the most risk. Once pledged, the suvanth will test your allegiance. You have to prove that you are suvanth, even if it means going against your principles. Taukin, this is your choice alone, it is a dangerous mission, but one that I know you can accomplish."

Taukin, deep in thought, looked down upon the painted map that covered the table. His large eyes ran back and forth between the Carth forest and the gray, finger-shaped area close to the Northern tip of Binesmir labeled Sheol Balla.

Meraco faced the Eltepsu, "The only other option is to lead an all-out attack at Sheol Balla, but this could give the suvanth enough time to move Cuvsor and Fesenius to a hidden location. The Umgara could only assist in the areas they can access. The potential loss of rintic and Umgara in this attack could be immense," said Meraco to the council of Eltepsu and General Reibo.

"Who will lead this squad of rintic soldiers on this rescue mission?" asked Taliph.

"Captain Avent has courageously agreed to lead this

mission, with your council's approval of course," said Meraco.

Avent stood, removed his cover exposing his chest, arms, and neck, then faced forward forcing his skin to alternate pattern and color, showing his devotion to his tribe and Eltepsu. Taukin focused on Avent, surprised by his decision to lead the squad into the pit. He detected a sense of rintic pride in Avent's fiery eyes.

Taukin stared around the table at the Eltepsu who were fixated upon Avent's brilliant display. His mind drifted to thoughts of his future with the rintic and their acceptance of him if he was their spy.

Taukin disrobed his top cover, exposing his stalwart upper body and sinewy shoulders and arms, and stood as tall and straight as possible. He forced his pattern and color to match Avent's as closely as possible. "I'll do it. I'll be your spy," said a proud Taukin.

Meraco gave an approving nod.

With wonder, the Eltepsu stared at such a rare creature who pledged fealty to unfamiliar beings.

Avent's skin blazed his pride, but his expression was one of concern, not for himself, but for Taukin.

The Eltepsu began praising Hobaja Vael in their harmonious tone. Their praise was the council's agreement with the plan.

"We depart in the lumeren and will plan logistics as soon as possible. Taukin, this mission is known only to those who need to know and no others, keep it that way," said Meraco.

"Yes General," replied Taukin.

Avent and Taukin followed Lantia through the

dimly lit, winding stone corridors to their quarters for the quiesce. Lantia pulled back the red cloth drape that separated the room from the tunnel and motioned for the tribesmen to enter.

"I hope these accommodations please you," said the young Eltepsu in a trill voice.

The tribesmen fixed both torches in sockets on opposite sides of the quarters. Taukin scanned the dome-shaped room that contained two raised platforms of cloth and pelt coverings, which looked soft and inviting. It was quite spacious and there was an area far across the room where cool running water was accessible through a hole carved in the wall.

"Lantia, we are most thankful for the invitation to stay here with the Eltepsu," said Avent.

"If you will excuse me, I must retire to the Eltepsu chamber. We will talk again in the lumeren," said Lantia, as the drapery was released and hung straight again.

Taukin went to the thin stream and rinsed his face, then ran a handful of cool water across the back of his dry, gritty neck. He dried off and took a seat on the pelt-covered platform in the middle of the room. After a period of silence Avent looked his way. "Taukin, this is no game, the suvanth are vicious, they're more beast than being. I agreed to lead this mission after much thought. You weren't afforded the same opportunity, are you sure you want to do this? It will never be mentioned to the tribe if you change your mind," said Avent with concern in his voice.

"There is no other way, even with a full-on attack,

the risk of losing Cuvsor is too great. Cuvsor will die if not rescued and we don't know what condition Fesenius is in, or if he's even still alive. I must do this," said Taukin, his face a mixture of mettle and fear.

"There is still the obstacle of gaining access to the pit. I don't believe this to be a trivial task."

Taukin's mind raced. He wanted to tell Avent about his encounters with Swinzal and how Swinzal had twice tried to recruit Taukin to meet Manista. His thoughts swirled in his head and his tongue almost betrayed his feelings when he said, "I know how." Avent squared his look and Taukin panicked, but calmly continued, "I know how…difficult it will be to gain entry, but there must be a way I can enter undetected," said Taukin, trying to conceal his near blunder.

"We can discuss this further with Meraco. We should get some rest," said Avent as he stood and made his way to the nearest torch.

He put out the torch flame and went to put out the other torch when Taukin asked, "I heard you and Larnhi talking before we left Byrre Syra. What is it that you need to tell me?"

Avent's hand stopped before the metal snuffer reached the top of the crackling orange flame. He lowered the snuffer into his other hand and slowly faced the stone floor. "The truth about your mother," replied Avent.

"I know the truth. She died when I was young and you and Larnhi took me as your own," said Taukin with complete innocence and ignorance.

"She didn't die," said Avent.

"What?" asked Taukin, his skin light red with blue dots. "Where is she?"

Avent, still unable to face Taukin, "That, I do not know. She disappeared shortly after you were born. There have been rumors that she is back with the suvanth, and some say that she is beyond the cinder vents of the Swata region. You deserve to know the story of how you came to be with us, you are owed that much."

Avent sat on the raised, cloth-covered pad directly across from Taukin. The sole torchlight flickered and colored Avent, highlighting the vermillion peaks of his long rintic face. He looked off to the side of Taukin in deep remembrance.

"Your father Ethius and I were friends. As young tribesmen, we were inseparable. After our soldier training, and before our second mission to assist with the trek of the Eltepsu, he was assigned to Fort Benja in the Norody Forest, near Lithica, to patrol and scout for suvanth tunnels and traps. One tem-cycle, while patrolling between the upper and lower Kappa Rivers on the far western side of the Norody forest, he discovered a tunnel and started to install a spring trap when she happened upon him. Luspa, the suvanth mother who bore you life, showed no aggression toward Ethius. He lowered his weapon, removed the trap, and allowed her safe passage into the dark, muddy tunnel. A bond was forged, and they continued to secretly meet each other at the tunnel near the river for many cycles. Both believed that peace between the suvanth and rintic was possible, but not as long as Manista was leader of the suvanth. They planned to repeal the banishment by the Umgara, under the condition that Manista be imprisoned, but Luspa had conceived and their plans changed. Luspa continued her trips to the Norody forest to meet with Ethius throughout her growing term. She was near due and Manista grew suspicious as to what lured her to the forest in such a state and on one particular trip, he had her followed by a suvanth spy."

Taukin's skin quickly switched to a light-golden hue, and he pushed down a difficult gulp. Avent took note of Taukin's change of emotion, but didn't comment. Taukin's color returned when Avent continued.

"That trip, Luspa gave birth—it wasn't a pure suvanth youth, but both rintic and suvanth, it was you. They were joyous and their love for you poured forth. It was then the spy was discovered watching them from the branches above. Ethius gave chase, but the swift demon entered the tunnel unscathed. Luspa knew she could never return once Manista learned of her betrayal. Ethius tried persuading the rintic to allow you and Luspa entry into Fort Benja, but the tribe refused to allow your mother shelter within the fort walls in accordance with the law. A nurse from the fort cared for you while Ethius helped your mother during her recovery. It wasn't long before suvanth began searching for Luspa. Your parents moved about, setting up temporary shelters in the Norody forest, close to Fort Benja. Rintic patrols increased in the forest. Signs appeared that the suvanth were close to discovering their location. Then

Luspa disappeared. There was no sign of foul play, no sign of injury, she simply vanished, leaving behind that ivory bauble that you keep with you. Ethius returned to Fort Benja to care for you, but searched for Luspa every chance he could. Many tem-cycles passed and it was when the moons were in alignment that something happened, his anguish suddenly grew. At times he was distant, other times inconsolable. He asked that I watch over you if anything ever happened to him and I swore an oath. He became more and more critical of the rintic leadership and Umgara—even the Eltepsu—and his extreme views were seen as radical and he was banished from the tribe. The tribe was outraged over your allowance in the Carth forest, and had it not been for Lady Jusha persuading Lord Hiko to let you stay with us, you would have been banished as well."

Taukin took it all in. His face was blank as if in a trance. Taukin breathed in deep and exhaled, the anticipation of disgrace grew over Taukin's face, "Is it true what they say? Did my father betray his tribe and help the suvanth abduct Cuvsor?" Taukin's watery gaze focused on the smooth, stone floor.

"Those were the words of those who feared your father. He lost himself; he became wild and irrational, acting more like a suvanth than a rintic. I don't know what transpired after he left the forest," said Avent, careful not to unsettle his adopted son.

"Why are you telling me this now?"

"Lord Hiko has wanted you banished since you were brought to the forest. The tribe doesn't consider you one of their own and Larnhi and I thought if you grew up with this knowledge that you would do something outside your character. We only wanted to protect you and that's why we kept the truth from you until now. Taukin, we have no way of knowing what will happen with this rescue mission, but you needed to know the truth."

Silence pushed out the ambient noise as if all the air was sucked from the room. Taukin's head dropped straight down, and with his skin slowly darkened blue, he murmured, "I'm ready to sleep now."

Avent obliged his request and snuffed the lone torch before laying to rest for the quiesce. Taukin's thoughts drifted to the disloyalty of his father and as he drifted to sleep, the whereabouts of his mother.

Taukin woke to the sound of soft, peaceful chanting. It was the Eltepsu offering their early lumeren prayers to the omnipotent one, Hobaja Vael. Avent rose along with Taukin. Taukin slid on his coverings and packed his gear, and he and Avent made their way down the dimly lit tunnel to the dome prayer chamber. The Eltepsu swayed gently back and forth with their thin hairless arms interlocked, occasionally looking upward at the oculus from which light shone down upon their shaggy tufts of brown hair. Taukin and Avent made their way around the center, following the vividly colored tiles on the floor to Meraco and Reibo, who stood near a tunnel entrance.

"It's time we go back to Byrre Syra," said Meraco to both Avent and Taukin. Both nodded, trying not to disturb the praying Eltepsu. Shortly after, the chanting quieted and the Eltepsu stilled their bodies. The group of sustainers broke their circle and Taliph approached the foursome.

"General Reibo, I trust you will keep the Eltepsu informed of the development of the rescue plan," said Taliph. Reibo bowed with his upper arms against his chest, and back lower arms similarly following suit against his back. "We are most interested in receiving word about young Taukin's progress," said the elder Eltepsu and with that comment, Taliph trotted over to Taukin. Their eyes aligned and Taukin, nervous, but determined, kept his color mostly violet even though flecks of his exposed skin went golden. Taukin's eyes were large like a suvanth's eyes, but even he was entranced by the Eltepsu's larger, piercing yellow and green eyes.

"Young Taukin, you undertake a task that no other Onestonian could attempt. Learn from your instructors, they will guide your hands as well as your thoughts," Taliph continued, "Most importantly, listen to your heart, the suvanth can be especially persuasive, there is no doubt that they will try to convert you to their suvanth ways."

Taukin conjured a slight nervous smile, weighing the uncertainty of the mission and the wisdom of the Eltepsu. Taliph grasped Taukin's shoulder, "Do not be troubled young Taukin, your strength is great and your heart is pure. Hobaja Vael will watch over you," and then Taliph turned and went with General Reibo toward the largest of the tunnels. Taukin's skin returned to its normal white specks and soft violet hue, feeling comforted by the Eltepsu's encouraging words. Taliph walked ahead to lead the visitors out of the busy sanctuary.

As Taukin turned to exit, Lantia, the most colloquial of the Eltepsu, gripped Taukin's hand. Taukin flinched and quickly turned and looked down upon the young Eltepsu's expressionless face. "Taukin, I wish we could have talked more, I would enjoy hearing what life outside of Binesmir is like."

Taukin smiled gently, "As do I about life here at Binesmir," and carefully enclosed Lantia's soft, three-fingered hand with his other violet hand.

Lantia released from Taukin's hands and said, "I want to show my appreciation for your dedication to Cuvsor's return," Lantia reached into the matted folds of auburn hair and removed a brown wooden bauble of an Eltepsu. "It was given to me by one most special and I present it to you as capethica, so you promise to return it to me when your quest is complete."

Taukin was moved that a being such as an Eltepsu would present a capethica request to him. His round amber eyes glistened in the torchlight. Taukin turned the bauble over and ran his finger over the engraved marking on the underneath. "What does this mean?" asked Taukin.

Lantia wriggled nervously and quickly spoke, "Perhaps when we have more time, I will tell you." A quiet pause lingered as Taukin processed Lantia's deflection.

Taukin broke the silence, "I have something for you as well." Then he quickly reached into his inner pocket and removed the white stone charm that was his lone gift from Luspa. "I think of this as my mother's capethica to me," said Taukin as he reached out for Lantia's hand. He placed the white stone carving in Lantia's tan palm and it seemed larger in such a narrow hand. Looking down, the Eltepsu's circular mouth stretched into a dark crescent, surprised by the primitive bauble.

"Do you know its origin?" asked Taukin.

"It symbolizes peace through Hobaja Vael. The craftwork is that of the suvanth, I have no doubt. The suvanth belief in Hobaja Vael diminished once they were banished from the Carth forest, so this predates the banishment. I will know more when we meet again," said Lantia. Taukin turned to look for Avent and Meraco, who had already passed out of sight. "It seems that I've kept you longer than I should have," said Lantia. Taukin anxiously started backing away and moved toward the light of the cavern exit. Lantia bowed and Taukin respectfully bowed back, then dashed off into the gaping tunnel.

Taukin caught up with Meraco and Avent who followed Reibo through the largest of the caverns toward the stone garden. The group came upon Umgara soldiers patrolling the caverns. Their impressively decorated bodies went taut with the sight of General Reibo. "As you were," said Reibo and the soldiers relaxed their stiff torsos and continued their patrol. The group made their way through the maze of stone and tunnels and the open field back to Fort Binesmir.

The smoky scent of cooked meats and sweet aroma of cut fruits filled the air as the foursome arrived at Fort Binesmir. They made their way through the busy clusters of Onestonians, who were busy bartering with the Umgara. The diverse crowd filtered into what appeared to be an open-air Umgara market outside the fence line of the fort. Taukin recognized some of the visitors from tales that Avent told during the gatherings around the fire circles. The beings traded their local wares for Umgara-crafted tools and goods and agrum. Among them were the tall, slender, tan-colored Parabics of the Ivory forest region who brought hannes leaf from the bordering fields of the Ivory Forest. Not to mention the Pugotals, native to the dangerous Swata region, a somewhat primitive, dark-colored, hunched and confrontational sort, that herded and trained the diminutive inobi, which were used for rapid transport. Greetings toward the Umgara General poured forth from the beings in the Umgara manner of bowing the head as the group waded through the mass of Onestonians. Reibo's massive body dominated the crowd and as he walked through, a path formed with walls of traders of various sizes and colors. Taukin and Avent followed Meraco up the wooden stairs to the entrance of General Reibo's quarters. Meraco turned to Avent and Taukin. "Prepare our transportation," said their General.

Avent nodded his head in concurrence. As the two walked across the wide planks of the deck, Avent noticed the same hooded figure that he saw earlier standing out in the field near the roped-off Umgara feasting area. Avent stopped and gripped the railing of the deck, his shoulders squared with the mysterious figure who was dealing with Umgara at a distance. Blazing light from the Eastern star shone straight down on his gray woven hood, casting a shadow over his face and concealing his identity. Avent kept his eyes fixed on the being and slightly twisted his head toward Taukin. "Find Itil and prepare our transport. I'll meet you in the field by the melp stable," said Avent in a solemn voice.

"Yes Captain," said Taukin, and off he ran toward the stairs to find the Umgara scout. The hooded figure tipped his head up, revealing the lower portion of his bearded crimson face. The stranger noticed Avent staring at him from the deck of the Umgara General's quarters and hurriedly finished his transaction. Avent made his way toward the stairs, keeping his eyes fixed on the hooded being as he descended the oversized steps. The crowd suddenly seemed to thicken between Avent and the mysterious being. Avent pushed through, receiving crude stares and surly remarks. He made it to the border rope of the feasting area, but the hooded being was gone. Avent looked around, making a complete circle, but the bustling crowd of Onestonians made it impossible to locate the cloaked figure. Frustrated, Avent made his way to the melp stable to prepare for the journey back to Byrre Syra.

As Avent neared the melp stable, Taukin met him on the path. Umgara were within earshot, so Taukin addressed Avent by his rank, "Captain, the hooded stranger departed shortly before you arrived."

"Did he speak?" asked Avent.

"No, he hurriedly mounted his Flauva, turned the creature, looked behind, and then departed at full gallop."

"What of his identity?"

"His Flauva was tethered on the far end of the stables."

"Flauva?" Avent squinted in deep thought then continued, "No matter, we need to make our way back to Byrre Syra. Are the Melps ready?"

At that par-tem, Itil arrived with two snorting melps in tow, one behind the other. "Captain Avent, I will escort your party back to Byrre Syra. The journey is more dangerous with the discovery of satupha roaming the plains," said the ash-colored Itil.

"Your presence is most welcomed," replied Avent with a gracious grin. Taukin lifted the hefty pack belonging to Meraco and placed it near the steering straps close to the rim of the melp's shell. He followed with his own pack, which weighed less and smelled worse than the General's. Taukin climbed onto the concave shell and opened his ruck. At the bottom of the ruck, squished and partially fermented, he discovered the fruit he had packed. He cupped his hand and scooped it out, tossing it behind and overhead toward the stable, near the base of the mountain. *Plop* the stench-filled pulp landed directly on the right cheek and neck of Itil who was tightening the steering straps of the second melp. Taukin, not knowing his blunder, continued scooping and tossing in the same manner until his ruck was free of fermented fruit.

"Are you finished with your purging, young Taukin?" asked an austere Itil. Confused, Taukin stood and turned to face the giant. Avent came from the front of the first melp as well to see what Itil meant. Taukin's eyes widened with surprise. He immediately recognized the random patterns of yellow mush strewn across Itil's neck.

"Many apologies my protector! Had I known what I was doing, I would have ceased after the first toss, which would have maybe covered an area the size of a malpwa seed, which happens to be on your cheek there," said a contrite Taukin as he pointed at his own cheek.

"Be not troubled young Taukin. The smell of spoiled malpwa is better than the smell of a freshly scrubbed melp," exclaimed Itil and with that quip, Avent and Taukin burst out in laughter. Even the quiet Itil managed a smile and a short-lived chuckle. Soon after, Generals Reibo and Meraco arrived. Meraco had rolled maps tucked under his arm, the trochin skin looked fresh with nary a mark, so they must have been newly made. The riders mounted their transports, Itil on a lone melp, and the three members of the rintic tribe on the other.

Reibo leaned over to Taukin, who was still a bit shorter than the Umgara General even with the extra height of the melp. "Young Taukin, I will see you during the trek of the Eltepsu, but know that you will have the full support of the Umgara in the meantime," said the General in his low pulsating verbal tone that slightly dizzied Taukin. Reibo nodded to Itil to lead the melps back to Byrre Syra. The still melp, with Meraco at the control, slightly reared and began moving its legs in an alternating fashion. Reibo's words lingered in Taukin's head; he was speechless, partially due to the paralyzing effect of the Umgara's voice, but also because he started to feel that he was of significance if he could call upon the Umgara for help.

In the same way as they arrived, a corridor of ash-gray Umgara formed, comprised of all sizes and ages, and bowed their heads as Itil and the rintic passed. Umgara poured out of the hut caverns on the side of the mountain and effortlessly scaled the nets and ropes for a better view of the departing foursome. Once the party made it past the first jutted spur of Binesmir, the signaling horn sounded three steady blows, announcing their departure.

The air grew colder and large silvery puffs of breath from the melp wrapped around Meraco's torso as a soft embrace. Taukin lay on his back and stared up at the blue flickering stars, which rocked back and forth with each stride the melp took. Aebean and Febus grew round and bright against the black sky and seemed close enough to touch. Taukin stretched out his moonlit hand pretending that he held the Febus moon between his thumb and forefinger. Letting go of the captured moon, he pulled the wooden Eltepsu carving from the interior pocket closest to his heart and held it up in front of the larger of the two moons. The rounded brown bauble eclipsed the white space of Febus, and Taukin's mind drifted to the Eltepsu and the story tiles covering the floor of the sanctuary, in partic-ular the drawing of his mother and father. The rhythmic motion of the melp suddenly ceased. Taukin sat up and looked around, confused by the lack of movement. It was still dark and the moons had sneaked by Taukin's watchful eye and were mid-sky. "What's happened?" asked Taukin in a half-awake half-asleep manner.

"We've arrived at our camp for the quiesce," replied Avent.

"Did I fall asleep?" asked Taukin.

"You've slept the better part of the quiesce. Go back to sleep if you can," said Avent. Taukin lowered himself to his elbows and then relaxed his back against the sturdy shell. Sleep came back to him quickly. Meraco dismounted and tied the steering straps to a post that Itil had driven deep into the dirt. Avent joined Itil and Meraco. The melps made quick work of the bayphea grass, creating a grassless circle that became the spot for bivouac.

"I will stand guard for the quiesce," said Itil in his deep, guttural voice.

"I will join you also if you do not mind," said Avent.

"Very well, we should build the fire near the melps. We can keep watch from atop the shells on the dark side. Satupha will not approach from the fire side," said Itil. Meraco climbed on the sleeping melp, laid next to Taukin, then rested his eyes. Avent sat, legs dangling, on the cold side of the shell peering out into the darkness. A gentle whisper came from the tall bayphea grass as each chilly gust of wind passed through the spiny heads, causing the grass to sway back and forth. Avent's eyes grew heavy and his head began falling to the side. He suddenly awoke, startled and surprised as if there was an attack. Itil spoke, "I believe you fell asleep Captain."

"Yes…I must have, perhaps I should chew on a

bayphea stalk to wake up," replied Avent, this of course was in jest. Just then Itil quickly stood and looked south over the head of the resting melp.

"Something hastily approaches," said Itil as he drew his long sword.

Avent shook Taukin and quietly roused Meraco. "My General, something approaches from the south," said Avent. Meraco was up with his sword drawn before Taukin even got to his knee.

"Satupha?" asked Meraco excitedly. The shadow of the creature grew larger with each passing par-tem.

"Larger, it stands at least one rintic above the grass," replied Itil.

"Taukin, scan the flanks," said Meraco and the wide-eyed Taukin turned to check the north for the savage creatures. Taukin stood and peered out into the swaying grass and darkness. "I see nothing on either side General," said Taukin. Itil jumped into the cleared circle and with his backward facing arms unsheathed his short sabre, and with his arms facing the approaching crea-ture, steadied his primary sword.

"Prepare to fight," said Itil.

Taukin spun and focused on the advancing shadow. "It's a tribesman…and I believe he's riding a Flauva," continued Taukin, "His spear is raised!"

That was all Taukin could get out before the weapon was launched. Taukin watched as the tribesman released the spear with force and accuracy, aimed directly at Itil, who was a well-lit target against the blackened quiesce horizon. Itil bent backwards supporting his weight with his back arms to avoid the speeding dart just as a large satupha, mouth agape and white teeth protruding, jumped for the Umgara's neck and into the path of the hurled spear. Three more satupha appeared, one on Itil's flank, but the Umgara soldier quickly spun on his anchored hand and delivered a bone-crushing kick to the ribs of the attacking beast, which made a horrendous whimper and fled into the tall grass. Avent jumped from the shell, blade raised and hacked into the midsection of the nearest satupha, eviscerating the creature. The beast ran toward the tall grass, but fell dead before reaching the cover of the field.

Taukin made for the fight, but Meraco stopped him. "Stay up here and keep lookout," said the General. The last satupha faced Avent and Itil with its rear toward the field of grass. It roared wildly, flashing its long canines while it slowly crept backward. Just then the mysterious tribesman appeared next to Itil, long sword drawn, adding to the defense. The savage creature, alone and outnumbered, growled lowly then turned and ran into the shadowy cover of the tall, prickly grass. The soldiers and unknown tribesmen surveyed the surrounding area for hidden satupha, weapons drawn.

"They're gone now. My Flauva can sense when satupha are nearby," said the unknown ally as he sheathed his sword. Itil quickly placed his weapons into the sheaths and bowed his head to show gratitude to the tribesman.

"You have tremendous accuracy with your spear, and for that I am indebted," said Itil. The tribesman returned the bow, revealing his woven gray hood. It was the same hooded tribesman that was seen near Fort Binesmir. Taukin recognized him immediately and looked over to Avent whose body straightened with the discovery.

Meraco stepped over to the tribesman. "I am Meraco, General of the rintic army of the Carth Forest. It might be safer for you to join us for the quiesce, we can offer some protection against the dangers lurking in these fields."

The tribesman nodded his head, "My Flauva and I accept your offer." Avent approached the tribesman. Firelight reflected off half of his mysterious bearded face, revealing deep scars that ran along the side of his carnelian neck. The tribesman, aware of Avent's stare, pulled his cloak up over his neck.

"I'm Avent, Captain of the Third Rank of the Carth army."

"My name is Okos, from the Sugot rintic tribe of Skian Packsu," said the tribesman, and he turned his arm toward the fire revealing his ebony armband bearing the white Sugot symbol. Avent continued to stare as if he were passing judgement on the truth of Okos's words.

"You were at Fort Binesmir dealing with Umgara, correct?" asked Avent.

"Trading for Umgara-forged tools, the best you can find, and a ration of agrum for my tribe."

Avent slightly raised his chin toward Okos and said, "You gather tools and agrum for your tribe, yet you travel alone. Carrying agrum poses great risks."

"I'm a gatherer and am capable of doing what's needed without assistance."

"You have your supplies, but why do you travel away from your home instead of toward it?" asked Avent.

"I plan to meet with the leader of your tribe, Lord Hiko, and offer my allegiance and support during the trek to Lithica."

"A lone Sugot tribesman appears in the Carth forest on his Flauva, with supplies for *his* tribe, and requests to journey with the Eltepsu, is that it?"

Okos replied, "That's an accurate assessment."

"The Sugot are not known for their benevolence, why haven't they offered their services before now?"

Meraco stepped in between the tribesmen. "We have plenty to eat and drink, and some for your Flauva too," said the General to the outlander.

Okos's voice changed to a calmer tone, "Both have been hard to come by lately, we can offer safety from satupha." General Meraco nodded in acceptance. With that, Okos grabbed the reigns of the Flauva and ran his hand down the long furry neck of the creature until he got to its back and began rubbing the underbelly of the creature. The Flauva bucked and snorted making a gargling sound, then produced a bubble of saliva that grew larger the longer the tribesmen rubbed its underside. It grew the width of a melp shell and was as tall as an Umgara. Okos grabbed a wooden paddle that was tipped with Flauva hair and slapped the sticky ball loose from the Flauva's mouth. The thick mucus ball slowly rolled forward toward the field of bayphea collecting loose bits of chewed grass and loose particles of dirt so that it gained texture. Okos continued rubbing the furry Flauva generating ten more large, slobbery balls that were incredibly thick and elastic. With the furry paddle, Okos herded the sticky balls together forming an adhesive wall of saliva bubbles around the camp, leaving a wide gap between the fire and the wall.

"This'll suffice," said Okos and he placed the paddle back into its holder on the side of the Flauva. He fed some bayphea heads to the weary Flauva.

Taukin jumped down from the resting melp and approached the nearest saliva ball. Firelight reflected off of the translucent bubble and Taukin could see his shadow cast upon the tough exterior amongst the tuffs of Flauva hair and bits of debris picked up from the ground. He first poked it with the pommel of his sword and amazingly it stayed just as he had touched it. It was horizontal and didn't waver. He grabbed the grip and pulled, but the sword didn't come loose. He placed his covered foot on the translucent sphere to gain leverage and pulled with all his strength only to have his foot covering stick to the ball as well. Laughter arose from the rest of the party including Meraco, but Avent merely smiled. Okos grabbed the hairy paddle and walked over to where the wriggling outcast struggled to keep his balance on one foot. Taukin loosed his grip and Okos wedged the hairy paddle in between Taukin's foot and the thick skin of saliva and drove the wooden plank down until the hair separated the trochin covering from the sticky sphere. Taukin fell backwards due to the force of the release and landed near the leg of a melp and well within the light of the flames. A Flauva hair footprint was left on the sticky ball where Taukin's foot used to be. The soldier's laughter erupted even louder than before. Okos grabbed Taukin's sword by the grip and wedged the mangy paddle down releasing the weapon. Okos held the sword, point side down, and turned back to return it to Taukin.

"In my tribe, soldiers do not lose their weapons, especially on a Flauva ball," said Okos facetiously. Taukin stood and leaned against the melp shell while he adjusted his twisted foot covering. Okos stood before him and Taukin sensed his presence, but continued looking down, embarrassed by his ignorance and actions with the Flauva ball. Okos lowered his voice, "What's your name?" Taukin slowly raised his head, the firelight revealed his skin color as much as it could in the darkness.

"My name is Taukin," Okos's eyes widened as his skin went light green and his breath was stolen. Silence filled the space between them. Okos could only stare, speechless.

Avent broke the uncomfortable silence, "You act as if you've seen a wandering spirit."

Okos blinked and broke his gaze and stuttered to Taukin, "You're…you're not rintic."

"I'm Carth rintic!" demanded Taukin.

"But your skin…it's not like…and yet you're a Carth tribesman?" asked Okos.

"I'm a Carth soldier," replied Taukin proudly. Okos's skin went normal and his face contorted with confusion.

Meraco stepped over to the melp where they were and said, "Let's eat our rations, we still have plenty of quiesce before us," and the group dispersed.

The scent of cooked meat ascended and attracted curious creatures around the camp. Their eyes glowed orange through the bayphea grass and were distorted by the translucent spheres, making them seem larger than they actually were. Fear of the unknown sticky fortress kept the beasts at bay. Itil sat with his back to the linked Flauva balls and the rest of the party joined him in a circle encompassing the crackling fire. General Meraco passed Okos some victuals and his pelt canteen. "This is no ordinary drink," said Meraco, "the water that flows through the caverns of the Eltepsu is unequalled." Okos smiled at the statement but was in disbelief after swigging the frosty water.

As Okos ate, Taukin focused on the scars that ran along Okos's neck. Thin shadows formed underneath the raised scars revealing the severity of the wounds. "How did you get those scars?" asked Taukin. Avent, Meraco, and Itil turned their attention to the outlander.

Okos continued chewing his food then swallowed. His eyes fixed upon the leaping orange flames. "It was many cycles ago, maybe when you were a small youth, I was on a mission that took me North of the Uru mountains headed toward Almona Bin, when I came across a squad of suvanth that had just opened a new tunnel. Most were still behind their tunneling device, but three had gotten around the tunneling suvanth called Paptifs, and they spotted me. I rode my Flauva west toward the Swata region, but the scourges were too fast and caught up to me. The first one pounced from the rear and I was able to dispatch him while riding full stride. The second jumped on me from the rear as well and sank his claws into my neck and pulled me from my Flauva. We spun off and as we landed, I drove my short sabre into his chest. I sat up and the last suvanth was on me before I had a chance to stand upright. He struck me with a strong blow to my chest. My vision went blurry and I couldn't catch my breath. Fortunately for me, my Flauva returned and drove him back long enough for me to regain my focus. He came at me again with great speed across the rocky terrain. I was on one knee, blood was spurting from my neck and running down my arm, stopping at my tribal band. He sidestepped and spun around lashing out with his bone weapon, but I was able to bring my long sword up just high enough to meet his barbed bone. His backbone splintered and was useless to him. He remained on all fours like a satupha and I raised my sword, but he was outmatched and weaponless, and quickly strode back to the freshly dug tunnel. I was able to escape on my Flauva before any more suvanth arrived," said Okos and he took another bite of his meal.

"Did you need healing from the cut?" asked Taukin, who didn't really know any form of verbal restraint.

"Indeed," muffled Okos, "I had lost plenty of blood and I eventually fell from my Flauva into a patch of wildebush just South of the Swata region. I scarcely remember anything, only flashes of Pugotals and inobis and staring up at the darkened sky covered in stars that spun around. I wasn't sure that I was going to make it through, but Hobaja Vael was watching over me. He has a purpose for me and it's to help the Eltepsu and my fellow rintic during the trek to Lithica." Avent let out a cynical guffaw and Okos glared briefly, then looked back at Taukin. Okos reached up and pulled on the trochin strap releasing his long black hair that fell well past his shoulders. "But that doesn't answer your question. The Pugotals are allies with the rintic, and they took me to their healer. They fed me and cleaned me and I healed enough to continue on my mission shortly thereafter," said Okos.

"I'm curious," said Avent with disdain, "What exactly was your mission?" Okos's eyes went down and it was difficult to tell through the flames and vapors of the fire, but it looked as if his eyes were glistening.

Meraco intervened, "We should rest while the moons are still above us." Seeing the protection offered by the Flauva balls, Itil agreed and took his spot on the chilled ground and folded his rear arms behind his back while he placed one hand on his short sabre. He took a deep breath, closed his dark round eyes, and relaxed against his sleeping melp.

Avent pulled Meraco to the side away from the fire and others and close to the protective balls of saliva. In a quiet voice Avent asked, "My General, do you think we can trust this outlander while we sleep?"

Meraco looked over at Okos who was preparing his resting spot against his lying Flauva near Taukin. "I have no reason not to trust him. He came to our aid when we needed it," said Meraco.

Avent replied in a low voice, "General, he travels alone. How many rintic, Sugot or otherwise, do so?"

Meraco teetered on this statement, then said, "I agree it's unusual, but not unheard of."

Avent leaned in closer to Meraco, "I have no proof, but my gut says he's not who he says he is."

"Captain, let's see what he can offer our tribe before passing judgement. You should try and rest, but if your instinct makes it impossible for you to do so, I suggest you stay on guard this quiesce and rest on the way to Byrre Syra. I myself, intend to sleep," replied Meraco chidingly. Avent, pride intact, agreed and they made their way back to the fireside of the melps, and Meraco prepared his spot for rest. Avent leaned against the rough exterior of the melp's leg and stared at the smoldering fire. Okos was covered with a trochin pelt, feet near the head of Taukin, who had been lulled to sleep by the fire's comfort and the tem-cycle's exhausting events.

Okos looked up one last time to check his surroundings as any trained rintic soldier would do. As he scanned he noticed Avent sitting upright against the tree-trunk-sized leg. Okos propped himself on one arm and said, "Captain, I assure you between the senses of my Flauva and the barrier it created, we are safe for the quiesce."

"I have no doubt you are correct, but thoughts other than the threat of satupha keep me from sleep," said the Captain.

Okos nodded, "I find it's best to give those concerns

over to Hobaja Vael so you can find rest. He will lead you down the right path."

Avent smirked with contempt, but remained upright, his back resting against the rugged leg of the melp. Sleep fell upon the soldiers and Itil, even Avent dozed in and out of sleep from time to time, but mostly stayed awake by tracking moons Febus and Aebean as they passed overhead and behind the translucent barrier of bubbles that had thinned and shrunk in size.

Okos woke at the first sign of the Eastern star's light, and he looked around to see if the others had awoken. Shades of pink and purple sky peeked through the ominous gray and orange-bellied clouds. Thin gray smokestacks writhed upward from the embers of the fire. Meraco was up and about packing his gear into his pelt ruck. Avent nudged Taukin who slowly lowered the cover below his squinting amber eyes. "It's time to go," said Avent. Taukin popped up and quickly dressed, then packed his ruck. He didn't want to be the last one ready to go. A smile stretched across his scarcely stubbled face as he thought about the tribe's reaction to his journey to meet the Eltepsu and Umgara, but mostly his thoughts dwelt on Soyha. Okos loaded his gear on the crouching Flauva and took up his fur-covered paddle and placed the fur end in the smoking embers. He crouched down and blew a steady stream of air across the embers causing them to glow orange and light the fur on fire. The hair on the paddle burned like a torch; he held it away from him and ran over to the nearest ball of saliva. He held the fiery paddle to the ball's surface and in a par-tem the bubble burst, sending bits of white foamy spittle around the camp. He did this to all of the translucent spherical shields until they were gone. All of the fur had burned up, leaving a bare and charred wooden paddle that Okos brought to the Flauva along with a handful of bayphea heads. Meraco, Avent, and Taukin stared on as Okos fed the heads of grass to his Flauva, and midway through chewing stuck the wood into the side of its mouth layering the paddle with pulverized grass particles and sticky slobber. Okos ran the paddle along the sides of the Flauva, pulling long strands of loose tan-and-white hair. Winding it around as he rolled it along the side of the creature's protruding belly.

The party made their way to Byrre Syra, eating rations from their rucks and telling stories of battle and adventures that they had lived. Okos's Flauva moved at a faster click than what it was used to, but Okos had off-loaded most of his gear onto the melp that Itil steered so as to offset the pace. Avent was more curious than before and instead of resting, asked, "Okos, do you have family?" Okos's response was a serious one, but the trotting of the Flauva made it seem a little humorous, Taukin thought before he heard the words.

"I did…but my son and lifemate are lost to me," said Okos without expression and looking straight ahead.

"I'm sorry," said Avent sincerely. Few words were spoken between the travelers from that point on. Taukin pondered what Okos's words truly meant until he spotted the rocky edge of the dry Orlang river ahead.

Taukin stood and squinted. "I see the stone river ahead," he said excitedly.

Itil faced Meraco and said, "I will cross the Orlang with you then return. You'll be safe once inside the Carth forest."

Meraco nodded and said, "Agreed."

Gray stones protruded through the dry grass more and more as they approached the bank of the Orlang. Itil led his melp headfirst down the steep embankment, quickly disappearing from the group. Next into the river was Meraco, Avent, and Taukin who had already braced themselves, clinging to the tan and onyx shell as they descended. Okos halted the Flauva at the edge of the barren river. Flauvas were not the nimblest of creatures and Okos had to walk the hairy beast down the rocky slope. When the river rock leveled out, Okos mounted his Flauva and made his way across the sand and stone riverbed. Itil made it to the top of the other side, where the Carth forest merged with the rocky rim of the river. Taukin dismounted after Meraco steered the melp to the top of the riverbank. Okos slowly made his way across the Orlang. The Flauva cautiously crossed the dry river and made it to the embankment. Once again Okos descended from the beast and led the hesitant Flauva up the coarse rocks to where Taukin was waiting. "Sand and dirt are the preferred terrains to travel with Flauvas," said a winded Okos. Taukin smiled at this statement. Itil still on his melp turned, shielding his eyes from the stinging beams of the Eastern star with his fleshy shield of an arm and approached the others at the forest edge.

Meraco spoke first, "Itil, you're most welcome to join us at Byrre Syra."

Itil's gutteral voice pierced the quiet of the forest and emptiness of the Orlang, "My time with the rintic is done for now. I must return to Fort Binesmir. The Umgara will be in contact soon." Meraco nodded and the pale protector and his melp disappeared down into the rocky river and into blinding light.

"Let's make it to Byrre Syra before Aebean lights our path," said Meraco. The three rintic on the melp and Okos on the Flauva made their way into the dark foliage of the Carth forest. Sudden loud swooshes from sumoguls surprised Okos as he passed around the bends in the dirt path right behind the ponderous melp. As they traveled farther into the forest the path seemed to darken, not only from the sinking of the Eastern star, but the soil grew darker in nutrients as they approached their destination. Glowing blue and yellow trisians slowly ascended against the blackened sky. Their rippled reflection converged on the riders as they crossed a shallow but wide creek, and were greeted with a chilly breeze before making it to the outer edge of Byrre Syra. The realization of Syonis's threat weighed on Taukin the closer he got to the village.

Avent placed a glowing malachite-colored luminescence lamp on the holding rod attached to the melp to alert the rintic of their presence. The swinging lamp could be seen from quite a distance, even in the thick cover of the forest. They were met by armed guards at the entrance to Byrre Syra. "Halt!" said one of the guards as he lowered his pointed staff toward the melp and near Avent. Just then the melp and Flauva were surrounded by rintic soldiers. Their silhouettes outlined by the white light of the moons.

"As you were soldiers," said Meraco as he lifted the lamp closer to his face, revealing his identity.

"General Meraco," said the highest-ranked guard, then he turned and ordered the others to stand down. Some of the guards around Okos and his Flauva were slow to lower their weapons.

"We can walk from here. Captain Avent take Taukin home and recoup. In the lumeren we begin mission preparation," said General Meraco.

"General, what about Okos?" asked Avent in a tone that was out of earshot of the wanderer.

"Send word to Lord Hiko that Okos, of the Sugot rintic, wants to meet with him and vow allegiance to the Carth rintic during the trek to Lithica," Meraco said in a lowered voice so that only he and Avent could hear. "Keep a watchful eye on Okos. We'll see if your suspicion has merit."

"Yes General," replied Captain Avent. Taukin lowered all of the rucks to the nearest rintic soldier then planted one hand on the rugged shell and jumped off of the side of the still melp. Avent dispatched a scout to inform Hiko of the request of Okos and another to tend to the melp and Flauva. Meraco, Okos, and a troop of soldiers departed for Fort Carth with the lumbering melp and graceful Flauva in tow.

"Taukin, let's return home," said Avent, and with renewed energy Taukin moved toward their hut.

Frigid wind blew down the paths of the forest and

the ground was chilled, Taukin removed his foot coverings and ran the cool, moist dirt through his toes. It was a relief to feel the soil of the Carth forest on the bottoms of his calloused feet, cold or not. Aebean and Febus lit their way down the trails that led to their hut. Avent pulled the heavy portal covering back and entered the hut, startling Nelkum and Larnhi. Nelkum ran and hugged his father, pressing his vermillion cheek against Avent's hairy pelt covering, "Solea, father!" Nelkum then went to Taukin. "Tell me about your adventure!" said Nelkum in an excited squeaky voice, reminding Taukin of the Eltepsu. Larnhi smiled and started walking by, but Avent grabbed her and squeezed her against his body and kissed her directly and with subtle force on her cerise lips. She slowly pulled back and smiled, still captured in his strong arms.

Keel came through the front portal behind Avent and Taukin, "Solea father…Taukin."

"Solea, son," said Avent with a smile.

"Solea," said Taukin, and he made his way to their shared room with Nelkum along his side, but not before Larnhi placed her hand on Taukin's shoulder.

"Solea Taukin."

"Solea," he said quietly facing downward, then entered the shared room.

Larnhi looked at Avent, "He knows," said Avent. Larnhi nodded with understanding and relief, but her skin went tan with sprawling black branch patterns showing sadness, for she knew that he might not ever think of his adoptive family the same. Taukin unpacked his ruck, lit the small oil lamp opposite the pelt slings, and told Keel and Nelkum of all of the experiences with the Umgara, satupha, and the Eltepsu. All except for the secret mission, which was to remain strictly between those involved. Nelkum had a question waiting at the end of each response Taukin gave. The quiesce went on like this until Nelkum could no longer keep his eyes open and went to his room for rest. Taukin had receded into the warmth of his hanging pelt sling, but sat up and turned to Keel.

"You arrived after we did. Where were you?" asked Taukin.

"Garando training," said Keel, but Taukin took notice of his brief skin flicker revealing deceit.

"By now you should know well how to manage the creatures," said Taukin in a supportive fashion.

"You find humor in my failed attempts with the garandos?" asked Keel as dark as blood mud.

"I thought with all your training that…"

Keel cut him off, "Focus on your own shortcomings."

"No, at least let me explain," pleaded Taukin.

"I'm done talking."

"I didn't know," said Taukin.

Keel was still for a long while and said, "I'm going to sleep," and Keel snuffed the lamp and huffed and tossed about in his pelt sling, battling the words and thoughts that filled his head.

Taukin awoke to the aroma of cooked trochin meat and slivers of light penetrating through cracks in the pelt portal covering to the room. The entire house was gathered together and was preparing their lumeren meal. "So you finally decided to join us?" said Larnhi humorously. Taukin rubbed his heavy eyes and slowly cracked them open, for the eating area was well lit.

"I can't believe you were attacked twice by satupha!" said a rambunctious Nelkum. Larhni gasped and her skin turned light green with large red rings with fear.

Avent, surprised by the statement, asked, "Who told you that?" in a gruff manner. Nelkum quickly shoved a handful of meat into his mouth then aimed his brown eyes at Taukin, whose skin yellowed and sleepy eyes quickly widened.

Avent's skin darkened and he said, "No more talks of satupha or tunnels or suvanth at the table," to put a stop to the discussion due to Larnhi's worrisome nature. Eyes moved around the table, but words were not spoken. Only the sounds of slurping and chewing. "We should finish and make our way to Fort Carth," said Avent, whose skin was lighter than before.

Avent, Keel, and Taukin set out at mid-lumeren and the Eastern star warmed their way along the busy walkways. Four other soldiers under Avent's command joined with them on their way to Fort Carth. Paths were full with rintic carrying on their normal activities in Byrre Syra. Soldiers walked through the forest, rustling and crunching the large dried swaul leaves while they searched for signs of suvanth. Taukin's pride from his trip to Binesmir was short-lived after spotting Syonis and his band of followers just ahead of them walking in the same direction. There was no time to be berated by the son of the rintic leader, but it was inevitable. Taukin could sense the anxiety building inside him and his skin disobeyed his wish to remain unchanged. A brilliant golden fleshy display contrasted the brown background of the wood buildings and trees that lined the dirt path. A tall, silver-haired tribesman who was sweeping the leaves from the wooden porch of a sundry hut, obviously made aware of Taukin, quipped loudly, "Solea Captain, you and that suvanth back from Binesmir already? He's got some color about him that's for sure." This made Syonis turn around abruptly, his face grimaced at the word, "suvanth".

He faced Taukin and in a loud voice said, "Tribe, look! The outcast has returned! My prayers to Hobaja Vael have gone unheard!" The tribesmen formed a semi-circle around both groups. Taukin's brow furrowed and his skin went orange. Avent's skin went blood red and yellow dashes flashed vibrantly.

The Captain moved directly in front of Syonis's face and replied furiously, "Your father's wisdom was lost upon you."

"You dare speak to me as a commoner? I could have you and your family in Akaretel before the Eastern star passes midpoint!" screamed Syonis. "Did you know this suvanth Taukin attacked me?" said Syonis turning to the crowd holding his tattered armband. Gasps and mumurs came from the crowd which turned to jeers and cursing aimed at Taukin. Avent looked at Taukin and he shook his head denying the words of Syonis. Syonis continued as he scanned the crowd landing his eyes upon Taukin, "You know the law, Carth shall not harm their kind!"

"Prison!" shouted one boisterous tribesman, "Send

him to Akaretel!" yelled another and the crowd joined in with the shouts of proclamation for imprisonment. Syonis's guards moved in to secure Taukin with chains outstretched. Avent drew his long sword and his soldiers followed suit, forming a barrier around Taukin.

"Step away lest you lose your hands," warned Avent with pure white skin. Keel's eyes widened at the verbal threat and he turned to Taukin who was equally as surprised.

Syonis's skin went dark with anger, "Captain, do you really want to protect this traitor?"

"I'll protect him with my life," said Avent with fervor.

"We'll see," said Syonis, then continued to his guard, "Send word to my father of this betrayal."

The guard nodded and ran off toward Fort Carth. "I'll tell him myself," said Avent as he sheathed his sword and made his way toward Fort Carth with Taukin and his soldiers in tow, careful to avoid Syonis's antsy guards.

Fort Carth was busier than usual. Toward the stable area, two soldiers struggled to scrub the sensitive underbelly of the lurching melp. Okos nodded to Taukin and Avent, his black and white armband stood out as he carried multiple wooden paddles like the one used on his Flauva. Keel departed for the garando training area outside the fort's walls near the Tughe training area. Avent and Taukin made their way to General Meraco's quarters. They slowly ascended up the wooden ramp and passing them on the way down was Syonis's guard. Eyes locked, but words stayed caged inside as their hands rested on their sword pommels. Taukin and Avent were granted entry into the quarters by the posted guards. The rugged scent of freshly tanned trochin hide lingered in the General's quarters and beams of light poured into the room through the transparent portal openings. The inviting feeling of the quarters was short-lived after Hiko spoke, "Approach Captain."

There on the large, map-covered oval table in the middle of the meeting area were Meraco and Hiko leaned over, with hands resting on various parts of the pelt map and in a sense, Onestonia itself. Avent moved with apprehension and skin pure white to show his sincerity, "My Lord I…"

"Silence!" said Hiko, his skin now dark with anger. Hiko stood square to Avent, "I have never doubted your fealty to me, but your actions against my son require judgement."

Avent replied, "Yes my Lord."

Hiko continued with normal color, "However should you succeed in this mission, you will suffer no consequences for this act of treason." Hiko turned back to the map and Avent looked at Taukin, whose skin showed his concern.

"My Lord, Taukin will be pardoned as well?"

Hiko examined the tribal outcast, "Upon his show of loyalty and successful execution." Avent and Taukin nodded toward their leader. "What matters at this time is this rescue plan. Stand at our side." And with that, Taukin approached and Hiko turned back to the map and nodded for General Meraco to speak.

"Taukin, keep this mission to yourself. When the suvanth ask about the journey to Lithica, tell them that you are not made privy to such information, but you have overheard soldiers talking about the displeasure of traveling through Sik Jukote."

"General, that *is* the path the Eltepsu will travel, has your thinking become obscured?" asked Hiko, back to his usual displeased self.

"Lord Hiko, revealing the actual route serves two purposes. It verifies what Taukin tells them, so trust can be established. They will surely have scouts reporting our maneuvers. It's critical that trust is maintained until Cuvsor and Fesenius are back with us again. Also, the suvanth will focus their numbers at and around Sik Jukote. The more suvanth removed from Sheol Balla, the better our chances of rescue," said General Meraco.

"General, that is true, but it also increases the chances of another Eltepsu abduction which puts us back in the position we're in now!" said Hiko, skin angry.

General Meraco replied calmly but firmly, "My Lord, the Umgara will increase their presence around Sik Jukote, and our army will as well. We've increased our strength with the addition of the Fourth Infantry Brigade and the Norody rintic have strengthened their forces as well. If we can discover the suvanth tunnels before the trek, then we can seal them off and prevent the suvanth from surfacing."

"How do you plan to locate the suvanth tunnels?" asked Hiko.

Meraco turned his sobering green eyes to Taukin

and said, "Taukin will lead us to the tunnel nearest Sik Jukote and then to Cuvsor and Fesenius."

Taukin's back stiffened and his skin went bright yellow before he forced it normal again and after a diffi-cult swallow asked, "How?"

"With this," said Meraco, handing Taukin a rugged brown cloth pouch that easily fit in the palm of his violet hand.

CHAPTER 6
THE MISSION

"This is the gateway to Cuvsor and Fesenius," said Meraco. Taukin tugged on the braided string, opening the sack, and pulled out a short wiry tan root. Meraco continued, "Sassa root. Keep it out of sight and plant it by tossing it ahead and stomping on it as you pass. The scent is undetectable by rintic and suvanth, but the garandos are trained to pick up even subtle hints of the root at long distances. The trail you make is what the garandos will follow to the Sheol Balla. There is no doubt that you will be met near the tunnel entrance and taken as a prisoner, but you will not be harmed since you have suvanth blood running through your veins."

Avent's face went taut, "General…Manista…" Avent crimped his lips and his eyes went to the wooden floor wanting to say more, but knowing his place.

"What of Manista?" asked Meraco stolidly.

Avent looked up at the General and piped, "Is Taukin the right choice?" concern strewn across his face.

Hiko spoke firmly, "He is the *only* choice Captain.

Continue General." Avent acquiescently nodded and kept his eyes down on the map.

Meraco turned his attention back to Taukin, "When you find Cuvsor and Fesenius, plant the remaining sassa root nearby, but discreetly. If the root is discovered it could disrupt this entire mission. This will attract the garandos to the captured Eltepsu and our tribal brother."

"General, what happens after I plant the sassa root?" asked Taukin his skin showing his worry.

"You gather as much information as possible about significant locations, military size, weapons, personnel, battle plans, weaknesses, anything that would lessen or prevent harm to the Eltepsu and rintic," said Meraco.

Taukin nodded with understanding and asked, "General, when will my mission begin?"

"You will be told when it's time for you to leave for your mission. Once you leave there will be no communication or support from the rintic. You will be on your own once you step outside the forest," said Meraco and then asked Taukin, "Do you understand your mission?"

Taukin, whose head still swirled with doubt about the true intentions for his role in the rescue mission, stoically responded, "Yes General."

Hiko spoke, "The elders are ready to speak with you General Meraco."

"Yes my Lord. Captain, Taukin, finish your preparations for the mission. Carry on," said the General, and with that Avent and Taukin made their way out of the spacious quarters and down the wide winding wooden ramp to the bustling fort.

Avent looked to Taukin, "I sense the mission will start soon, but you must learn to throw kracklins. It's the best weapon from a distance. I'll join you shortly," Avent steered Taukin toward the East where a band of soldiers hauled sacks of kracklins on their backs toward the South gate. Avent pushed on Taukin's shoulder, nudging him toward the fort's South gate and turned and walked toward the Northern side of the fort. Taukin stumbled forward, taking in the words given by his commanders and the commotion of soldiers preparing for a possible battle. At the Western side of the fort, Okos demonstrated the process for Flauva-ball generation as he slowly rubbed a hairy paddle on the Flauva's soft underbelly.

Taukin stumbled and fell into a soldier, "Watch it filthy crawler," said a disgruntled Corporal who dropped one of the pristine polished doka shells onto the compact dirt. Taukin picked up the long clear shell, brushed off the soil, and handed it to the Corporal who snatched it from his violet hands and shot a flustered look at him. Taukin ignored the comment as he had done his entire life, and moved toward the gate following the kracklin instructors.

Taukin made his way to the tughe arena, staying well behind the other soldiers, all the while looking around through the dense forest of swaul trees for any sign of Swinzal, but there were only patrols of rintic soldiers searching for signs of suvanth. Right outside the metallic rod and wooden arena, Avent caught Taukin with Keel and Okos in tow. When they arrived at the tughe training arena, a group of scouts welcomed them, purposely ignoring Taukin, all except Dyant who spoke, "Solea, Avent, Taukin, Keel, and I haven't met this tribesman yet."

Okos lowered his head and said, "I am Okos of the Sugot tribe."

Dyant nodded in approval, "Dyant," replied the scout, but Dyant already knew who Okos was from his black armband, noticeable scar, and long scruffy onyx beard. Dyant stepped back to the larger crowd and spoke up, "Soldiers we will conduct kracklin training for the rest of the tem-cycle. Before the quiesce comes, you'll know how to carry and launch a kracklin to hit your target at varying distances. Break up into squads, each with a trained kracklin instructor."

Avent, qualified to handle kracklins, chose Okos, Taukin, Keel, and two young scouts to be in his squad. "We don't have as much time as I'd like to train, so I'm just going to show you what you need to know. Kracklins are a potent weapon, and if they are used properly, they are deadly," said Avent. The Captain reached down into a rough cloth sack and drew the cold round disc, careful to not shake or spin it in his hands. He continued, "This is the way you handle a kracklin. Keep a tight grip on it, and do not spin or swing it until you are ready to launch it." Avent fit the thin disc in the cradle made by his curled, crimson fingers. With his other hand he pulled an empty translucent doka shell from the same ruck. The elongated spiral shell was then pressed into cool ground by the pointed end so that the wider opening was exposed and essentially became the stopping point for the kracklin thrower.

"You might not have much time to plant your doka, so you need grip your kracklin, then plant. If the enemy is close, you do your best without the planted shell. Now, if you do have time and your enemy is at a far enough distance, this is how you launch your kracklin." Avent pointed down-range at the far end of the tughe training arena. Targets in the form of suvanth, stood at varying distances from the squads. Avent continued, "Gauge the distance and your enemy's speed, if they're approaching, then plant the shell to stop your spin. Once your doka shell is planted take two long steps backward, like this," Avent planted his shell and took two lengthy strides to the rear. Avent continued his instruction, "Kracklins are harmless if left alone. What activates the springing action inside is the spinning and once it's activated, the barbs extend out. When the target is hit, two barbs will depress slightly, triggering the spring mechanism in the kracklin, which then opens and rips into the enemy's flesh. If the hit is square and happens between bone, it will break the bones causing serious injury. I will now demonstrate." Avent looked down-range on the empty dirt-covered arena and judged the distance to the nearest target in their squad's lane. He dropped a leaf to check the wind direction and speed. He gripped the kracklin and spread his arms, and then in a fast-spinning motion twisted around twice, stopping at the planted doka shell. The metallic kracklin flew swiftly down the range over the dusty ground and harshly struck its target, a few par-tems later a THUD! was heard. Dust from the split target rose, which contrasted the colors of the emerald swaul trees, signaling that the Captain hit his mark.

"You will all get a chance to throw, Taukin will go first," said Avent. The Captain nodded to Taukin, who stepped up to his ruck and removed a kracklin. It was surprisingly light for a metallic weapon, comparable in weight to a short sabre. Taukin's hands shook, but he was careful not to spin it or make sudden movements that might activate the sharp barbs. Blazing light rays reflected through the planted doka shell, briefly blinding Taukin, who blocked the light with his forearm. Avent chimed in, "Do not look directly at the shell, or you could temporarily lose your sight, like Taukin just exemplified. Remember, you will only have a few par-tems to get set and launch." Taukin closed his round amber eyes and lowered his arm. He gently kicked the crystalline doka hull sending dust and dirt down the long spiraling shell, then took two long strides backward. He let the cold kracklin rest in his cupped hand and smoothly rocked it back and forth across his stout body. Suddenly he spun, fast, faster than Avent, and stopped at the partially buried shell, but continued past the doka stopper hopping on one foot due to the intense momentum. The kracklin flew over the first target, then the second and third and finally out of the arena. It was difficult to see, except for the bright reflection of the mid-cycle beams off its shiny exterior. A thick swaul tree stopped the flying weapon, and if it hadn't, Avent guessed it would have traveled the length of three arenas. "Well done, you have the technique, you just need to judge your strength against the distance," said Avent.

Keel grimaced and in a pompous tone said, "It doesn't look too difficult, let me try." Avent agreed and Keel followed the same instructions as Taukin did. He spun quickly, but not quite as fast as Taukin and during his pivot, his foot hung on the protruding doka shell, which caused him to fall forward while still spinning. Keel released the kracklin straight up into the air. The Eastern star's blinding light gobbled up the activated weapon and Avent yelled, "Take cover!" All squads ducked underneath reinforced shelters. A quiet thud came from behind the shelters as the kracklin landed on its side and kicked up dirt as the device actuated upon hitting the ground. The soldiers turned and looked toward Avent who stood and waved both arms over his head and said, "All clear!" Soldiers evacuated the safe zones and went back to their launch spots to continue their kracklin training. Keel couldn't keep his skin from changing violet and speckled with small white leaf-like shapes as some of the soldiers pointed and laughed.

Avent spoke to Keel, "Watch your step, one more misthrow and you'll be kicked off the range." Keel was strong, but clumsy, his strength would help make him a fine garando handler. Taukin smiled at his brother's folly, but didn't go as far as to join the others in laughter.

"Bumbling brawn," said Taukin, smiling wildly at the common term describing those whose strength overcast their dexterity. Keel's embarrassment turned to anger, and his skin changed to a blood-red and flashed with yellow lines. "Calm down, it was only a joke," whispered Taukin to Keel. Keel kicked some of the black dirt up away from the launch spot and away from the soldiers until his fiery emotions were assuaged.

Each soldier took their turn throwing the flying kracklins and most hit at least one target throughout the tem-cycle, but Okos had an extraordinary ability to hit every target no matter the distance. Avent's focus went to Okos's throwing technique, it seemed similar to his own, but kracklins were not a weapon used by the Sugot tribe.

Avent's suspicion grew and he said, "Well Okos, either you have an uncanny ability to master weaponry with your first try, or you have been trained in the art of kracklin throwing." Okos sneered. Avent continued, "I wasn't aware that Sugot employed kracklins. May I ask who trained you?" said Avent.

"It wasn't any Sugot tribesman. I've learned many things in my dealings with others over the cycles. Once I learned of these weapons, I taught myself. Our tribes might have different cultures, but we have the same abilities," said Okos. Not satisfied with the answer, Avent prepared to dig deeper with his interrogation when Dyant called for the discs to be retrieved signifying that the training had ended.

Dyant rounded up the soldiers, "Most did well, some still need practice. We'll pick back up in the lumeren. I need volunteers to go down-range and retrieve the kracklins."

Taukin stepped forward, but Avent called him back. "Taukin, you're with me. Keel can get the discs," said

Avent turning in search of Keel. "Where is he?" asked Avent inquisitively.

"He's probably already shoving trochin noses down his gullet," said Taukin jokingly.

"We should do the same," said Avent with a half-smile. A youthful spryness came over Avent. "You know I used to be the fastest tribesman in the forest when I was your age. I'll race you home," said Avent.

"You should start now," replied Taukin. Avent grinned, knowing this to be true, so he secured his sheathed sword in his left hand and raced off, his shoulder-blade-length black braid swayed in wiggly jumps from side to side, but disappeared quickly into the darkness of the forest. Thinking it only fair, Taukin started a countdown to thirty par-tems then jetted off. The forest seemed particularly active as the Eastern star filtered through the trees. Maybe it was the storied odd effects that the alignment of the two moons and the pending perigee could have on living things of Onestonia. A loud Swoosh! on the right side of the winding path came from a rather large sumogul taking flight. Taukin rapidly happened upon an unusual brood of slithering garwelves that were midway across the path. Tock! Tock! Upon hearing the warning sound, Taukin instinctively leaped up and far over the venomous creatures. Taukin looked ahead for signs of Avent along the path. He could see the early, floating iridescent glow not far off in the distance.

An unmarked path created by some of the younger tribesmen was Taukin's chance to gain ground, knowing that the two trails would come together across the creek.

Taukin veered off of the scarcely lit path onto a darker, uncleared trail that was full of crisscrossing branches and thick vines that hung low enough for Taukin to jump over. Some of what he gained in distance, he lost in time, but he was gaining on Avent. Forest creatures stirred, displaying bright flashes of color to the left and right, some small and some not so small. It was as if tiny orange and yellow moons turned on and off while ascending and descending throughout the thick forest. This path was still relatively new to Taukin, but he knew the widest point of a crossing forest creek enveloped a section of the passage, and that was the best part of the shortcut.

Taukin took a sharp curve bending around a small cluster of Ealtapa trees then, no more than ten rintic away, was a suvanth more beautiful than any being Taukin had ever seen and he kicked up dirt in an effort to stop his momentum. Her pale skin contrasted the green foliage and her cerulean eyes seemingly glowed with the last bit of the Eastern star's light as she noticed Taukin before disappearing into the ground, but she wasn't alone. A hooded figure stood over her and turned toward Taukin. A shadow was cast over the tribesman's face, but Taukin's skin turned bright yellow when he made out the symbol for Avent's house on the sleeve.

"Keel?" said Taukin just loud enough for his own ears to hear. The hooded figure turned away and ran into the thick of the trees toward Byrre Syra. Taukin ran too, faster than before along the unmarked trail to cut off his brother, over the dirt hills, jumping felled trees. He happened upon the creek's cliff that was at least three rintic high. Taukin took a few steps back focusing on the group of vines that hung low, out from the cliff, and over the creek bed below. With the help of the new moonlight Taukin chose a thick vine that hung closest to the large swaul tree, but far enough away from the gnarly roots. In a burst of suvanth-like speed, Taukin leapt off the cliff, grasped the low hanging vine, and swung across the wide creek, his coverings skirted across the cool rushing water. He had all but reached the silty embankment when the vine pulled loose from the tree and caused him to crash, face-first, midway down the grainy soil cliff. The vine fell into the flowing creek in a long, noisy splashing succession. Taukin, still dazed from the impact, spit out the mouthful of wet dirt, wiped the excess from his squinted eyes, and walked backward to the water's edge to gain enough momentum to run up the cliff.

The tem-cycle's tiresome effects wore on Taukin, but he knew he had to make it home before Keel. With a hop, then sprint, he planted one foot then another into the damp soil, quickly ascending and pulling on the exposed dangling roots along the edge of the cliff. Taukin slowed, but managed to latch onto a draped root that was stretched out as if the tree had grown a wooden arm with which he could pull himself up from the deep creek bed. His head had almost crested when a firm grip grasped his wrist, as though a satupha had latched on to him and he was pulled up and continued forward due to the momentum until he stumbled and tripped over a knotty root. On his knees and with his head dropped toward the capillary-like roots covering the ground, Taukin fell to his back, completely void of energy.

His lungs rapidly pumped plumes of breath straight up, making it difficult to speak, "I saw…something… Keel." Out of the corner of his left eye the glow of trisians ascended and descended and Taukin slowly raised his head toward the main path. He could see gleams of the reflection of Aebean coming from the pommel of the sword that was carried by the passing soldier; it was Avent.

Taukin stiffened in shock, but he quickly sat up and faced the shadowy figure, whose head was outlined by Aebean. "You sssaw nothing other than the ssside of that cliff," said Swinzal in his unique hissing dialect. "That vine besssted you. Heeek heeek heek," laughed Swinzal, but quickly quelled his jubilance. "You have been given ample time to consssider my offer. Time isss running out, have you made your desssisssion?" The moonlight accentuated the short, muscular frame of the suvanth, but the shadows hid the dagger that Swinzal held close to his waist, partially covered by his clawed hand.

Taukin stood and wiped the loamy soil from his smooth crown. This was Taukin's chance to gain access to the pit. His already racing heart pumped faster at the thought of fulfilling his duty as a rintic spy. He could feel blood sensitizing his skin, but did his best not to show his anxiety to Swinzal. "What you told me is true. I've been lied to my entire life. I see this now," said Taukin more assuredly.

"Yessss, Manissssta will be pleasssed. Traveling too

far a distanssse in the tight tunnelsss under the Carth foressst will prove too much for you. We ssshall enter through the tunnelsss outsssside the Carth foressst. You've caught your breath, we leave now. Here isss a tassste of agrum, it will give you enduranssse for the journey home." Swinzal held out the small organic vial, and the effluent rays of Aebean colored the contents bright green like a luminescence bulb.

Taukin's eyes widened from the desire for more agrum, a natural feeling for any living being. Taukin turned his head away to the side and responded, "No, I'll go with you to the pit, but after I leave for a mission. I can separate from my squad while traveling through the forest. If I leave now, they will no doubt search for me and will increase patrols making it more difficult for us. I could use a taste of agrum to make it back to Byrre Syra this quiesce." Swinzal gritted his pointed teeth and slowly moved his hand behind his back to sheath the dagger underneath his coverings, unbeknownst to Taukin. Swinzal was to kill Taukin if he denied the request for a third time. His other hand raised the vial of agrum to his pale lips and with his head gently tilted back the agrum quickly disappeared down the spy's throat before handing the remaining smidge over to Taukin, who downed every last bit.

Dissatisfied with Taukin's answer, but obedient to his master, Swinzal said, "I will find you at that time. Run home now, your rintic family will wonder what isss keeping you." Taukin's skin pulsed with the intake of agrum and he immediately felt the energizing effects as he walked away backward, stumbling over the small loops of root running along the ground. Swinzal lowered his body to the cold silty ground, and on all fours scurried over the cliff, back down to the creek and out of sight. Taukin ran down the fresh path as fast as he could, knowing that Keel had a lead that would be hard to overcome.

A mixture of smoke from swaul wood and cooked meat surrounded the hut as Taukin arrived. He removed his sweaty coverings and hung them above the crackling hearth. "Here he is now. Oh look at you, filth and dirt everywhere!" said Larnhi as Taukin entered still breathing deeply. As he walked past his rintic mother, she leaned her head over and whispered, "It was kind of you to let your father win."

Taukin smirked at the remark. "Where's Keel?" asked Taukin in between breaths looking for his brother. Larnhi handed him a warm damp cloth and Taukin wiped the silt from his head and face.

"I suspect he's still looking for that first kracklin you threw," said Avent making a long sailing motion with his hand.

"Hand me that stirring spoon," said Larnhi to Taukin. Taukin stretched his arm, but was unable to reach the spoon set upon the top shelf. Avent nudged Taukin aside and grabbed the spoon for Larnhi.

"Taukin, sit next to me," said Nelkum. Taukin took his seat next to his younger sibling. All except Keel were seated at the rectangular wooden table and Avent recited the giving of thanks for the abundance of food they had. "Is it true you threw a kracklin outside the tughe arena?" asked Nelkum excitedly.

All eyes went to Taukin whose eyes turned to Larnhi, "Not on purpose. Can you pass me the trochin noses?" asked Taukin quietly.

Larnhi obliged by handing the steaming plate of noses over to Taukin and also by changing the subject. "Your father told me that you're leaving again. When?" Taukin glanced at Avent who gave a knowing look for Taukin to remain reticent about the mission.

"Soon," was all he said.

Larnhi spoke again, her voice starting to crack, "That young soldier Paero…he died, and another was taken by the suvanth. And now you want to take their place?"

"I'm a soldier now, I have no choice," said Taukin.

"As my son, you do," said Larnhi, her skin darkening.

"Larnhi…" started Avent before being cut off.

"We swore to protect him and that's what I plan to do," said Larnhi, her brow deeply furrowed and with the darkest of skin, continued, "Stay here…with your family, both of you."

A brief bit of silence conquered the room until Avent spoke gentle but firm, "It's not enough to stay here in this hut, or this forest. Lack of action will bring about our end." Tears filled Larnhi's eyes and her lips parted, but she could only look away to keep from breaking down for her promise was fracturing. For a period of time the only noises heard were the squishing of rubbery trochin cartilage and slurping of stew.

Taukin decided to break the awkward silence. He looked at Avent, "When we were at the caverns of the

Eltepsu, Meraco mentioned that Soyha would be the retriever of the light cipher. Why was she chosen?"

Avent replied, "She's a strong swimmer, and passed the sherob test."

"Sherob test?" questioned Taukin.

"Groups of rintic test their ability to use a sherob to breathe underwater. Some cannot adapt to the sherob breathing for them, be it a mental or physical challenge. The ones that do pass become candidates for retrievers of the light cipher."

"Are there dangers in retrieving the light cipher?" asked Taukin.

Avent answered, "If the retriever's body rejects the sherob, yes. I've also heard about attacks by predatory creatures from the deepest parts of Olin Fell, the shadow waters, as it is called by the Staleans. The underwater Stalean escort protects the retriever from such attacks."

"She shouldn't be the retriever," said Taukin.

"That's not our decision to make," said Avent matter-of-factly.

A quiet rustle of cloth came from the front entrance as Keel hung up his covering by its hood and tried sneaking into the hut unnoticed. "Keel join us," said Larnhi.

"I'm too tired to eat," said Keel, wiping sweat from his brow.

"Since when are you not hungry after a tem-cycle's worth of training? The last fire circle before the moon perigee is this quiesce and I know you don't want to go hungry," said Larnhi knowing this to be an oddity for her son. "Come in here and eat. There's a spot here across from Taukin. Come on now," she continued. Keel dragged himself to the table and plopped down next to Larnhi. "Here, have this," said Larnhi as she slopped down some kulee mush on Keel's wooden plate. Keel kept his eyes down as he raised the mush to his mouth.

"Did you throw your kracklins as far as Taukin?" asked Nelkum.

"Not quite," said Keel under his breath.

Taukin glared at Keel and asked, "What took you so long to get home?"

Keel's skin turned a hint of green before saying, "Dyant had us clean the kracklins before storing them away."

"Is that right?" asked Taukin, with enough contempt that even Nelkum took notice.

Keel faced Taukin, "Yeah that's right. See the dirt on my hands? Where do you think it came from? Looking for *your* kracklins, that's where," said Keel flashing an angry skin at Taukin.

"Settle down and wash your face and hands with this," said Larnhi as she handed a warm wet cloth over to Keel. Taukin stood abruptly and returned his angry skin briefly before turning for the exit. "Where are you going?" asked Larnhi.

"The fire circle," said Taukin.

"Don't forget your youth blanket," said Keel just to add more color to Taukin's angry orange skin. Taukin yanked his cold-weather covering from the hook above the fire and in doing so tore a gash in the collar.

Avent went after Taukin, "Taukin stay here. Get back here soldier." demanded his Captain. Taukin looked at Avent then ran outside. As he ran his skin whirled a colorful mixture of anger, fear, and pain and his disobedience to Avent would surely come with a hefty toll.

Taukin's body was exhausted, but his mind was wide awake. He envisioned holding Soyha, her long ebony hair draping over her soft carnelian back. She was the only sense of comfort he had in this oppressive life and they were both about to be farther apart than ever before.

Moonlit smoke lifted up from the fire at the telling place, and yellow flickering flames could be seen from the path. As he neared the circle, Taukin slowed down so as not to startle the unsuspecting tribesmen. A priest spoke loudly of Hobaja Vael, but Taukin was not interested in what the rintic had to say. He passed the trees that stood like wooden guards surrounding the large circle and searched for Soyha by firelight. Taukin's eyes quickly adjusted, and he walked along the trees holding his right arm out touching each tree to keep his bearings while he peered across the circle.

He was halfway around the circle when he spotted Soyha. His skin went violet before a shade of affectionate green appeared. She was the only one who made him feel like he belonged. She sat forward and listened intently, hanging on every word the wise elder spoke and never noticed Taukin behind the circle of seated tribesmen. Taukin leaned against a young swaul tree, crossed his arms and listened, but Soyha's beauty commanded his attention. When the speaker paused, Soyha leaned back on the stump revealing Syonis, who was sitting next to her. Taukin stood erect, which caught Syonis's attention. He smiled his devious grin and placed a trochin blanket over Soyha's shoulder so he could squeeze her and infuriate Taukin.

Syonis moved in closer and whispered something to Soyha who quickly glanced over at Taukin. He smiled at her, his skin showing his feeling of pleasure, which was lost in the dim light of the fire. The look on her face was not of joy, or adoration, but one of alarm, a look of guilt as her eyes moved from Taukin toward the forest floor. Taukin instantly felt betrayed and his skin darkened so much that he blended with the darkness of the forest behind him. Taukin stepped back and around, disappearing into the blend of thick forest trees. He found the grassy path leading to Davalit, a rocky refuge away from Byrre Syra, and raced toward it as tears of anger and distrust ran down his darkened face.

How could she betray me? Taukin's scattered thoughts paced through his mind faster than his legs moved on the scarcely traveled trail. Davalit was thick with towering swaul trees, and a canopy of branches and foliage hung overhead blocking almost all light from the moons. There, it was dark and there it was quiet. Not even trisians landed in this part of the forest. The only sound was the gentle bubbling of the stream that ran underneath the stone overhang. Taukin crawled up the stone protrusion from the moss-covered slope and walked out onto the narrow crag. He sat on the rocky ledge with his legs dangling lifelessly. This was Taukin's place of solitude, a place where he could think without the distraction of the rintic. Taukin's fingernails dug into his palms and a low growl grew into a fierce roar, which he couldn't contain. The quiet finally surrounded him again, but it was short-lived. Behind him, off the path and in the forest, something moved, a fallen limb snapped against the forest floor.

"Swinzal," said Taukin under his breath and he wondered, *Have his orders changed?* Taukin's body remained still as if he hadn't detected the tribesman, but under the cover of darkness he slowly slid his right hand to the pelt-covered grip of his short sabre. This time Swinzal wasn't as stealthy and when the crackling of leaves and snapping of twigs quieted, Taukin knew he had reached the moss cover of the stone. Fine hairs rose on Taukin's neck, his senses were heightened, and he readied himself for the worst. With the quickness of a suvanth, he spun around and drew his short sabre in preparation for an attack. The being was far enough away that Taukin wasn't immediately threatened. "Reveal yourself!" said Taukin.

"Okos," said the bearded sugot tribesmen in his proper voice.

"Okos?" said Taukin as his skin lightened and he took a single step backward, more afraid than if it had been Swinzal.

"You can lower your blade now." Taukin lowered his sabre, but kept it in hand. Okos continued, "You're fast. I lost you on the way to this place, if I hadn't heard you cry out I would have gone down the wrong path. I thought you were attacked."

Taukin replied, "I'm fine."

"I'll join you on this rock." A self-induced shocking jolt shot through Taukin's body and a feeling of discomfort guided his thoughts and words.

"I'm going home," replied Taukin in hopes that he might cross paths with rintic along the way in case Okos meant him harm.

"Very well," replied the outlander. They made their way, side by side, along the dark path, which gradually became a moon-speckled path. "Taukin, this might be my only chance to talk to you alone." Taukin's skin pulsed in the moonlight. Okos paused, "My real name is Ethius." Taukin stopped abruptly, lurched backwards, and drew his long sword, its blade reflected Aebean's glow among darkened trees that lined the path. "There's no need for weapons, I won't harm you," replied Ethius in a calm, reassuring tone as he showed Taukin the palms of his hands.

Uncertain, Taukin asked, "Why do you reveal yourself to me?"

"Because Taukin, you are my flesh, and I'm your blood."

"You're a traitor. I know my father…the rintic who raised me as one of his own."

"And he's done better than I could have, of that I'm certain," continued Ethius, "Allow me to tell you our history."

"I know *our* history. You betrayed my tribe," said Taukin as he regripped and pointed his sword.

"Lower your weapon. If the rintic discover my true identity, I'll be imprisoned."

"I should alert the others," said Taukin, his sword shaking.

"Do it and you'll be praised, but you'll never know about your mother," said Ethius bluntly.

"I know about her," said Taukin, and he inhaled deeply.

"Wait!" blurted out Ethius.

"Do you know why I came back to the Carth forest?" asked Ethius. "I'm searching for your mother."

"In the forest?" asked a confused and flustered Taukin.

"When I saw you at Fort Binesmir I knew I should come back to the forest. We can find her together."

"Together?" said Taukin with disdain.

"Do you feel the same for her as you do me?"

"She didn't choose to leave me," replied Taukin.

Ethius's skin darkened, "I chose to find her so we could live together. I've spent half of my life searching for the one thing I love most. You can't understand the toll of such an act," said Ethius.

Aebean's light flecked Ethius's skin and his normal crimson color returned. "The life I've led has hardened me," continued Ethius, "I risk my life by revealing my identity to you." Taukin hesitantly sheathed his sword.

Ethius slowly reached to touch his son's shoulder, Taukin swatted his muscular arm away and his furrowed brow shadowed his large eyes. "You betrayed our tribe, and now you wish to embrace me?"

"You need to know the truth. You need to know who I am and who your mother is."

"Tell me about her," said Taukin as he began

walking slowly along the trail. Ethius walked with him, but at an arm's distance, this was Taukin's unspoken rule, and Ethius abided by it.

"She's beautiful. Her heart is full of compassion and love for all living things. How she was born a suvanth, I will never understand. She desires peace between the rintic and suvanth. Knowing her heart, the most difficult thing she has ever endured is being apart from you, of that I'm certain." Ethius looked ahead and quietly chortled in warm remembrance, "She would gently rock you back and forth in her arms, you were swaddled in the softest pelt wrap and not a single word would come from her, she would just stare into your eyes. You have her eyes you know."

Taukin grinned, forgetful of his distrust of Ethius and fond of the idea of knowing he shared her features.

"The color and size." Ethius stopped abruptly and said, "We're close to Byrre Syra, you'll learn more later, our focus should be on your mother." Taukin, now frustrated with himself for not trusting Ethius earlier, agreed with his father.

"Keep walking, if the rintic find us stopped along this grown path talking alone during the stirless time, they will suspect something treasonous, if for no other reason than you being with me," said Taukin.

The wanderers had made their way through the densely wooded area of the trail and moonlight shot through the towering swaul trees enough to highlight Taukin and Ethius against the darkened forest. "How do we find her?" asked Taukin.

"I have a plan, but we'll have to be most careful. If

the rintic discover who I am, or any of what we've discussed, they will imprison us both, do you understand?" asked Ethius in a serious manner. Taukin paused and then nodded, his fear of imprisonment rivaling his fear of being labeled a traitor.

"Avent is suspicious of me, so my time here with the rintic will be brief. If you join me, the rintic will not allow you back in the forest, it will be a final decision." Taukin slowed his pace and the coolness of the soil through his foot coverings seemed warmer.

Ethius continued, "Fourteen tem-cycles from now the Eltepsu will make their pilgrimage to Lithica. When the scouts are sent out ahead of the ranks, I'll separate from the rest of the tribe and continue my journey to find your mother. I'll wait three tem-cycles for you on the Western side of the Uru mountains where the lower Trigshan river meets Olin Fell. After which I'll continue on my mission with or without you."

"How will I get there?" asked Taukin.

"You'll find a way," said Ethius.

Taukin's trust in Ethius grew and he understood that they had a common objective of finding Luspa.

They came to an area where bright white light fully illuminated the grassy path and Taukin firmly embraced his blood father who hesitantly patted Taukin's back when Keel happened upon them.

"What are you doing?" asked Keel, breathing heavily.

Okos slapped at Taukin's back then pushed Taukin away and said, "Blasted stinging whits. Taukin got into a nest of them. I think we got 'em all."

"Many thanks," said Taukin acting indebted to Okos.

"Where have you been?" asked Keel breathing heavily.

"I was at Davalit. Why are you here?" asked Taukin defiantly.

Keel glared at his adopted brother, "You weren't at the fire circle and we have been looking everywhere for you. Father is furious. You'd better return home," replied Keel. Taukin looked at Okos nervously. Keel then changed his focus to Okos. "You were at Davalit as well?" asked Keel, his suspicion queued up.

"I was scouting the forest for suvanth and was drawn to the area by young Taukin's shout. I thought a tribesman was in trouble and needed aid. That's when I stumbled upon a distressed Taukin."

"Stinging whits?" asked Keel.

"Much worse, it was pain of the heart," said Okos who knowingly looked to Taukin, who caught on and shot a frustrated scowl at Okos.

"My relationship with Soyha is my business alone."

Okos backtracked, "Forgive me. I've said too much." Keel's pretentious smirk signaled that his focus had now shifted to Taukin's pain and was no longer on the fact that Taukin was alone with Okos at Davalit. "I had better continue my patrol," said Okos who glanced at Taukin, then quickly disappeared into the shadowy forest.

Taukin turned to Keel and said, "I know what you're doing during the stirless time. Why you're getting home late, and how your hands get dirty. It's not from kracklins!"

Keel's skin darkened and he moved so close to Taukin's body that a grain of kulee couldn't pass between them. "You know nothing and you'll speak to no tribesman," said Keel doing his best to intimidate Taukin.

"The bauble is changing you, why?" asked Taukin.

"You're jealous that I was given this gift and you weren't," Keel rolled the ornate suvanth bauble in his palm. "There's something…about it, some great power, I can feel it."

"Who was she?" asked Taukin.

"Who?"

"The suvanth that you were with a few par-cycles ago," said Taukin with disdain.

"The only suvanth you'd see would be under my feet after I slay the creature!" said Keel fervently.

"Avent must know," said Taukin vehemently then took three steps away from Keel and turned and rushed down the path, sending trisians upward.

Keel yelled out, "No!" Keel followed as quickly as he could, but he couldn't keep pace with his younger sibling. Avent was out in front of the hut smoking his short stone pipe when Taukin arrived out of breath and rested his hands on his shaky knees.

"I should strip you of your rank and let you spend your tem-cycles wallowing in your self-pity," said Avent quietly, but with conviction.

"I know…I'm sorry…but…Keel is…helping…the

suvanth," said Taukin, barely able to speak in between breaths.

"First you disobey me, then you accuse your brother of treason? What proof do you have?" asked Avent with greater intensity, moving closer to Taukin as if he would strike him.

Taukin's hand went up halting Avent. "Wait…I saw him…with a suvanth. That's why…he's been…out late…during quiesce…just three…par-cycles ago…he was…with a suvanth…on a side trail. I saw his armband…it was your house!"

Avent stepped back, unsure of Taukin's words. "Are you certain of this?" asked Avent.

"Without doubt," said Taukin, firm in his statement.

"Where is Keel now?" asked Avent, his skin dark with anger.

"Right behind me," said Taukin. Keel arrived par-tems later panting heavily, sending plumes of breath into the air surrounding his head.

"Where have you been?" asked Avent, skin still dark.

"Looking for…Taukin. I found…him on…the trail…to Davalit," said Keel, trying to force the words out between the deep breaths.

Avent looked to Taukin who nodded in concurrence.

"Taukin says he saw you with a suvanth, not long ago."

Keel squirmed and his skin morphed light green, "I was training."

"Are you in league with the suvanth?" asked Avent flippantly.

Keel stood erect and with his skin white, "Father… never," said Keel with so much honesty that Avent's skin lightened.

"Liar!" said Taukin, raising his voice. Avent raised his hand to halt Taukin.

"Why does Taukin accuse you of such acts?"

Keel's skin went dark red with anger.

"Maybe *he* is the one in league with the suvanth. I found him wandering the forest with the outsider Okos."

"Okos?" said Avent inquisitively as he turned to Taukin.

Taukin shrunk away from the comment, and did his best to prevent his skin from going golden.

"He found me at Davalit and came to my aid after I yelled out in anger."

"Alone?"

"He said he was scouting for suvanth," said Taukin.

"Scouts patrol in pairs…always," said Avent with furrowed brow and turned to Keel and Taukin, "His actions spur my suspicion. His purpose here has been hidden from us."

Avent looked back and forth between Keel and Taukin and said, "This feuding between you and Keel stops now. You're both feeling the effects of the stress placed upon you. Hit your pelts…in the lumeren we depart before the rising of the Eastern star."

Taukin quickly hung his coverings up on the eye-level spikes wedged in the wall and slipped off his foot coverings. He fell into his broken-in pelt sling, and rolled to his side facing the wall and pretended to be asleep. Keel stumbled into the room and Taukin did his best to keep his skin from changing color in the ambient lamp light. Keel's skin went dark red with anger and he turned to say something to Taukin, but Taukin lay still as a fallen swaul tree. Keel turned back to his pelt and stripped down into his undercloth, leaving his musty pelt coverings in a pile on the cool, wooden floor. The wooden planks supporting Keel's pelt sling creaked as he slowly climbed in. The last sound heard in the room came from Keel as he blew out the lone flickering lamp flame. Taukin did his best to remain still and Keel tried, but his anger drove him to speak out to himself and caused his body to toss about. Taukin quietly rolled over to his back in the darkness and lay still, but his mind rolled with thoughts of Soyha's true feelings for him and of Keel's doings during the quiesce, and how the relationships with two of the only tribesmen he trusted were now broken.

"…Keel, Taukin, wake up," said Larnhi firmly. "Your father is preparing for your mission." Taukin heard the words, but didn't register them. Something seemed amiss, was he dreaming? He cracked open his eyes, but the room was filled with darkness. Larnhi spoke again, this time hovering over Keel, "Rise up, you leave soon," and she placed the lone lamp on the small table next to Keel's head. Taukin sat up. Had he even slept? It felt like he had just laid down to rest. Keel groaned and rolled over in his sling and covered his head with his pelt blanket.

As Larnhi left the room, Taukin quietly made his way past Keel and took the suvanth bauble from Keel's coverings, placing a similarly sized rock in its place. Taukin slid on his cold-weather coverings and placed the bauble in his inner pocket, then made his way to the eating table. Avent raised his metal mug and drank the last of his steaming herba linka drink, then said, "We'll head to Fort Carth shortly, eat, pack your gear, and make sure Keel is ready."

Taukin followed his adoptive father's orders and was outside the hut with Keel before the sumoguls ascended to their nests to shelter themselves from the Eastern star's light. The three faced an emotional Larnhi, who wasn't privy to the details of the missions, but perceived the peril of their tasks. She embraced each one individually, giving her full affection and love to each tribesman. The last was Taukin, and she looked into his large amber eyes, which, in the darkness, were simply orange reflections of the nearby torchlight, and said, "My son, you have made me proud. You have Hobaja Vael's favor, I hope you find comfort in that. Watch over your brother." Taukin politely smirked and he squeezed her tightly, not knowing if that would be the last time they would embrace, then left and followed Keel and Avent down the cold, dark path.

Through the thickness of their pelt foot coverings, the chill of the compacted soil could be felt on the traveler's calloused feet as they made their way toward Fort Carth. The path was empty of tribesmen; the darkness slowly lifted and Cenro, the god of darkness relinquished control of the sky allowing Levic, the goddess of light a turn at filling the planet with illumination. Taukin couldn't remember a time when Byrre Syra was as peaceful and still as this moment. Even with the heavy stuffed rucks on Keel and Taukin's backs, they were nearly silent as they walked through the lifeless forest, a skill learned from their Captain.

Keel wouldn't look at Taukin and Taukin understood, but could sense the anger from Keel's seemingly permanent scowl. Neither dared cause a ruckus on such an important mission. Avent broke the silence, "Now that we're together, Taukin tell us what you thought you saw last quiesce."

Taukin glanced at Keel, whose skin flickered a warning, but he wasn't intimidated with Avent there by his side. "On the way back from kracklin training, when you and I were racing home, I cut through a path off the main trail. Partway down, near the creek, there was a female suvanth entering a tunnel, and a hooded rintic helping her down. The armband worn by the tribesman was that of your house. No tribesman dare wear another's house on their sleeve, it's forbidden," said Taukin as he looked at Keel.

"It wasn't me!" exclaimed Keel.

"Lower your voice," said Avent then continued, "And was the hooded tribesman's face that of your brother?" asked Avent knowingly.

Taukin murmured, "I couldn't tell."

"Speak up," said Avent with impatience.

"I couldn't see who it was," said Taukin, louder and with impudence.

"Then there's no evidence against Keel," said Avent.

Keel boasted an arrogant smirk. Avent turned to Keel, "This still doesn't explain where you have been during the stirless time," said Avent, verbally wiping away Keel's smile. "What keeps you out so late?"

Keel fidgeted with his ruck straps and fumbled with his words until he fessed up, "I…have…I've been practicing with garandos during the quiesce. I can't control them yet, and I want to prove that I can do it."

Taukin quipped, "You don't believe that do you?" toward Avent.

Avent's face contorted to discontent and faced Keel. "I had a feeling that it would be too challenging for you," said Avent whose disappointment cut to Keel's heart but angered Taukin.

Keel pleaded to his father, "I want to make you proud, I just need more practice."

"I'll grant you more time, but if you're unable to control the beasts, then you'll be a common infantry tribesman," said Avent. Keel solemnly nodded in concurrence.

"Keel is one of the strongest soldiers in our tribe, how can he not control a garando? It's obviously a lie," said Taukin imploring Avent.

"I believe Keel, I suggest you do the same Taukin," replied Avent allowing his dark-red skin to reinforce his stance. Distant orange glows of torchlight marked the lookout towers high above the forest floor that signified they were near Fort Carth. "Two acts are wearing heavy on me. Okos scouting alone and the mysterious hooded tribesmen that you saw. Could they be one in the same?" asked Avent as they arrived at the fort.

The soldiers made their way through the thick brush and bone abatis, the early rays of lumeren light penetrated through the white haze and drew a golden crown on top of the wooden fort wall. Only the tower lookouts and guards were stirring this early, but Avent knew it wouldn't be long before the fort was busy making preparations for the trek to Lithica. Avent passed the verbal challenge the guards presented at the South gate and once inside the fort, he sent Keel to gather the squad of garando handlers from their barracks within the fort. Avent and Taukin made their way through the thick veil of mist that filled the fort and spotted the yellow glows of torchlight leading up the ramp.

"Taukin," said a voice in the mist.

"Who's there?" asked Taukin, squinting and waving the fog from his face. Soyha appeared in front of them. "Soyha? Why are you here?" asked Taukin.

"I'm preparing for the retrieval of the light cipher. You won't see me for some time. And when I return it won't be the same for either of us," Soyha paused to see if a response would come, but there was nothing so she said, "Taukin what you saw…it's not…Syonis asked…*demanded* I join him at the fire circle." Taukin's orange skin displayed his anger at Soyha and she replied, "Are you never going to speak to me again?" Avent sighed and stood over Taukin, pressuring him for his response, but Taukin didn't say a word, he just stared down at the ground intently, biting his lip. "So be it, enjoy the journey to Binesmir or wherever you're going. Maybe one tem-cycle you'll have a reason to talk to me again," said Soyha as she trudged off toward the western side of the fort.

"Come," said Avent, gripping Taukin's shoulder.

A mysterious hooded figure whose face was wrapped completely in a dull, green cloth except for the thin opening revealing piercing gray eyes, descended the ramp and quickly disappeared toward the North gate leaving a swirl of fog in his wake. Taukin asked Avent, "Who *was* that?"

Avent shook his head and replied, "I have a feeling we'll find out." The pair quickly ascended the back-and-forth winding wooden ramp to General Meraco's quarters. Taukin winced at the sudden beam of light that spilled over the top of the pointed fort wall. "General," said Avent as he passed through the tall, arched opening into the quarters where their General was hunched over the oval table looking intently at the pelt map of Onestonia.

"Captain, are the garando handlers ready?" asked Meraco.

"They have been requested General, and should arrive shortly," replied Captain Avent, who knew the question was more of a formality to break up the ominous feeling surrounding the mission that Taukin was about to undertake.

"Taukin, come over here," said Meraco, whose skin had become ivory colored with a thin blue line slowly coursing down from head to toe underneath his pelt coverings…a sign of grave seriousness. Avent took notice, for it was rare that General Meraco ever displayed emotions through his skin. Taukin quickly approached the table where Avent and Meraco stood. "Taukin, your mission starts now. You'll travel with the garando squad until you receive instruction from Captain Avent to depart. There you will separate from the squad without their knowing it. Depart during the most opportune time. There is an abandoned suvanth tunnel in the middle of the Peah mounds that you'll follow to the pit. The tunnel at the Peah mounds is where you start planting the sassa root. Plant some at all junctions that lead to the pit. If the suvanth detect any presence of the rintic, a battle will ensue and the plan will fail, this is why you must go alone. The garando handlers will map the tunnel paths as much as possible before the rescue mission, but only after you descend and plant the root."

Near the bottom of the ramp, Keel stood at attention with the squad of six weapon-clad soldiers, equally as rigid, adjacent to him and each tethered to a poised, scaley, dark-green garando. "Taukin, join them," said the General. Meraco placed his arms behind his back, interlocking his rugged hands, and paced back and forth in front of the soldiers. "You have been briefed on your mission. The need for mapped suvanth tunnels is critical to the successful rescue of the Eltepsu Cuvsor and your brother in arms Fesenius. This mission is grave in nature. There is a chance that you will not return. Your best weapon stands in front of you. Be quick in your decisions. There's no need to battle the suvanth in the tunnels if you can avoid it. High ground is where we have the advantage. Do not disclose any information about this mission. If you are captured do not make mention of Cuvsor, Fesenius, or mapping of the tunnels. Tell the suvanth only your name and rank. Let Captain Avent's instruction guide you. You are the best at what you do. The forest stands firm!"

General Meraco took a step back, which signaled Captain Avent to take command of the squad. Avent methodically walked in between General Meraco and the attentive squad, all linked to garandos except for Taukin, and commanded them to move out. The inline squad marched out spaciously, garandos wiggling in between each soldier. Warm light filled the gaps between the towering Swaul trees along the path between Fort Carth and Akaretel and all fog dissipated. Along the way, Taukin paid attention to the sides of the path, looking far off into the gray distance of the woods, taking in all movement, searching for a sign of Swinzal. He knew the ashen-skinned demon would keep his word and find him again, but he didn't know when. Keel's garando dragged him in and out of alignment with the rest of the squad.

Avent looked back and barked, "Take control of your garando soldier." The powerful beast pulled Keel back and forth until, using both arms, Keel pulled back on the tether with enough force to get the garando back in line.

The discipline that the garando handlers maintained in the presence of General Meraco disappeared once outside the fort. With Avent out of earshot, the soldiers in back of the squad decided to rile Taukin and Keel. The soldier nearest Keel and Taukin, smug and proud, spoke up loud enough for other soldiers to hear,

"Keel, that garando is getting the best of you. You'll have to stay on the surface until you can actually control it."

"I can control my garando," replied Keel, skin dark red and spitting out his words.

"This squad knows that you're no garando handler, you're too scared to go in the tunnels. If you weren't Captain Avent's son, you'd be slinging mush back at the fort," said another handler, full of spite. Keel's skin morphed to violet, and white splotches appeared.

"Better keep a tight grip so it doesn't attack Taukin." Laughter erupted within the squad and Taukin's skin went orange with anger.

Taukin's blood boiled and his desire to tell his fellow tribesmen about his mission grew to a point that his lips parted and the words formed, but Keel spoke up first, "Taukin wasn't ordered to join us on this mapping mission, he volunteered for this mission. I don't know a single soldier that is as brave as he is to do this. You might want to keep your words to yourself, lest I turn my garando loose on you!"

All laughter quieted down and Taukin, surprised at Keel's response, nodded to him in approval. Keel looked forward and didn't acknowledge Taukin, but was satisfied knowing he did what was right even if it did take away his credibility amongst the squad.

The Eastern star positioned itself directly above and hid the tree's long shadows that usually covered the green forest floor. Avent halted the squad partway to Akaretel prison. The soldiers kept their positions, with Taukin and Keel to the rear. "Where are the patrols?

Something's out of place," said Avent looking around for anomalies.

"Yeah, it's this poor excuse for a garando handler and his suvanth brother," quipped the same handler as before, just loud enough for the targeted tribesmen to hear.

Keel lurched at him, but Taukin did his best to restrain him. "Quiet back there. I want three groups of two to check the perimeter for signs of tunnels or suvanth remnants. If you happen upon rintic scouts, our mission is to search for and trap new tunnels within the forest. Remember, make no mention of breaching the forest boundary or of mapping tunnels outside the forest. Be back in one par-cycle and sweep the open distance between each other on your return." Avent blocked Taukin and Keel from stepping forward by holding his left arm out. The brothers stepped back in concession. Pulled by their eager garandos, the three groups of rintic soldiers spread out in equidistant directions. When the handlers were far enough away Avent quickly turned to Taukin and said, "It's time for you to set out on your own." Taukin was taken aback.

"Now?" asked Taukin, shocked and suddenly nervous. His exposed neck, head, and hands turned golden.

Avent gripped Taukin's shoulder and said, "I promised your father I would watch over you. But now it's time for you to be who you were meant to be, a Carth soldier. The next time we see each other, it'll be below ground. Stay sharp."

"I can't do this," said Taukin, his hands quivering.

"Remember take the path to Akaretel then turn North for the Peah mounds. You can follow the trail at the base of Binesmir to the mounds. If you encounter rintic, run and hide. They can't catch you, now GO!"

Taukin slowly took two steps backward, while tightening his ruck on his back. His eyes were locked with Keel's surprised stare. He slowly turned and started through the forest on his way toward Sik Jukote, but stopped five rintic away and turned back. High above in the trees, a shadowy figure fluidly descended from branch to branch until between Taukin, Keel and Avent, Swinzal dropped to the rugged forest floor. Avent and Keel drew their long swords and approached Swinzal cautiously.

"Taukin run!" ordered Avent, but Taukin instead moved toward Swinzal with urgency.

Swinzal faced Avent, "Where are you sssending Manisssta'sss new pupil off to?"

"What does he mean?" asked Avent his words aimed at Taukin.

"I don't know," yelled Taukin.

"Come now Taukin, be honessst with him. You agreed to learn from Manisssta and you're going with me," said Swinzal.

Avent looked at Taukin full of disappointment and said, "You're the one helping the suvanth in the forest?"

"No, I…I swear it!" said Taukin, his skin bursting with emotion. Taukin turned to Swinzal and said, "I'm not going anywhere with you demon."

Swinzal grinned, "Then, they die. We have the advantage," Swinzal looked to his sides and multiple suvanth warriors appeared from behind the swollen swaul trees, surrounding them. "Or go with me and they live."

Taukin looked back to Avent and Keel still shocked by Swinzal's words then moved between them and Swinzal and said, "I'll go."

Swinzal looked at Taukin with his pointed grin and nodded. *THIWP!* came from Swinzal's lips as he motioned with his hand to his kind to leave. All of the suvanth ran off through the thick of the forest in a burst of speed back toward Binesmir. Taukin lowered his head and went in front of Swinzal toward Akaretel. Avent and Keel were nearly to Swinzal and Taukin when Avent told Keel, "Alarm call." Keel raised his sumogul flute to his lips and placed his fingers over the holes to make the loudest alarm call possible. He breathed in deeply and with a strong force, blew the call loud enough that it echoed throughout the forest trees, a dagger entered Keel's upper chest and the alarm was quelled as he fell into the green overgrowth of the forest floor.

"Keel!" yelled Taukin as he ran to his brother, but Avent's sword kept Taukin at bay.

"Get back!" Taukin backed away, stunned and stung by Avent's reaction, his skin went deep blue. Avent quickly removed the dagger from Keel's pulsating chest and applied a handful of green moss to help with the bleeding. Keel squirmed in agony.

"I'm sorry," said Taukin whose eyes flooded with tears.

Keel's suffering eyes locked on Taukin's tears and he gurgled out, "Traitor, like your father."

Taukin shook his head, "Not me," said Taukin as he backed away. Taukin looked back at Swinzal who had another dagger in hand. Taukin raised his hand in objection toward Swinzal. "No more! I'll go with you," said Taukin, torn between the destruction he caused within his house and the direction given by those who despised him.

"I'll kill you both," said Avent. Taukin's skin went so blue that he blended with the dark forest behind him. A distant alarm sounded acknowledging Keel's warning and the garando handlers were making their way back to Avent. Taukin was in shock, and Swinzal pulled at his rintic coverings to follow him.

Down the trail, Swinzal said, "Quickly now, drink thisss," and he handed Taukin a small green vial of agrum. Taukin didn't hesitate; he grabbed the life-sustaining sustenance from Swinzal's clawed hand, bit off the squishy top of the ampule, and gulped it down. A surge from the liquid pulsed through Taukin's body, instantly boosting his strength and awareness and his focus shifted to now being an enemy of his house and tribe. "Give me your gear and follow me before the rintic come back with reinforsssementsss," said Swinzal.

Taukin held up his ruck to Swinzal who strapped it tightly to his pelt-covered back. Taukin's blade went to Swinzal's neck, "I should slit your suvanth throat," spit out Taukin.

"Make it fassst. You won't make it out of the foressst before they catch you. You are their enemy now jussst like I am." Taukin lowered his blade and Swinzal's eyes squinted before he continued, "Follow clossse behind me. If I ssstop, you ssstop. Be asss quiet asss posssible. We need to avoid rintic patrolsss. Breathe deep." And on the third breath, Swinzal took off as quick as the blowing wind.

Taukin looked back one last time. Avent was carrying a limp-bodied Keel back to Byrre Syra and with the ample amount of agrum feeding his body and senses, Taukin took off and ran faster than he could ever remember catching up with the suvanth spy. Swinzal followed the dirt path as much as he could to cut out noise from the crackling leaves that covered the forest floor. A euphoric feeling overcame Taukin as he ran, as if nothing could impede or harm him. He felt the speed at which he ran was unmatched and he scarcely made a sound. Far off in the distance the prison Akaretel was a small gray dot, alerting Taukin to the possibility of discovery by the rintic. It was as if Taukin merely blinked and was upon the outskirts near the prison. Swinzal slowed then quietly jumped up onto the lowest branch of a swaul tree. Taukin followed suit, but wasn't quite as nimble. He jumped, but only managed to noisily grasp the branch with one hand, knocking off large flecks of tree bark onto the crackling fallen leaves below as he desperately tried to latch on to the branch with his other hand. Swinzal hissed at Taukin's lack of coordination and skill, then pulled the outcast on top of the branch. All paths leading to the prison were seen and it was up in the tree that Swinzal declared, "We'll go sssouth of the prissson."

"But the Peah mounds are north of Sik Jukote, we'll be going much farther that way," said Taukin.

"There are lesssss pathsss and lesssss chanssse of being dissscovered," said Swinzal before leaning close to Taukin's face to read his expression and skin. "Why do you mention the Peah moundsss?"

Taukin's skin started morphing amber, but he controlled it with a misdirecting question. "We are on the path to the Peah mounds are we not?"

Swinzal's light gray eyes squinted with a twinge of distrust. Another flute alarm was heard coming from where they were and a dust cloud appeared heading toward them. "Keep up with me," said Swinzal as he dropped to the leafy forest floor and veered off Akaretel trail, heading North instead to the Peah mounds through the thick of the limbs and growth of the Carth forest. Running through the forest growth was much different than running along the smooth trails of the forest, tree limbs seemingly appeared out of nowhere and slapped Taukin as he ran. Light from the Eastern star had all but faded into the tree line and the forest was starting to come alive with the quiesce creatures. Taukin's chest pumped large quantities of cool, quiesce air into his strangely warm body as he ran at an absurd pace through the folds of the dark forest. Patrols of rintic soldiers had increased and the runners easily concealed themselves behind the thick of the swaul trees, but the ascending trisians would ultimately give them away if they didn't move back to the trail. Taukin's heart beat wildly, he was so nervous about being discovered with Swinzal.

"We'll take our chansssesss on the path," said Swinzal grunting at the thought. Random penetrations of moonlight guided Swinzal and Taukin through the seemingly endless array of towering trees and Taukin welcomed the feel of the smooth, cold dirt under his feet again. Around a slight turn was a rintic squad returning from their patrol along the trail, when they happened upon them. Swinzal didn't avoid the oncoming rintic, but instead ran directly at them, launching over the unsuspecting soldiers. Taukin's suvanth instincts kicked in as he jumped over the soldiers, narrowly missing the pointed tip of a long sword of a fast-reacting rintic. Bodies were but a brief moonlit blur to both the rintic and Taukin. A fierce cry came from the rintic and Taukin turned to see the rintic giving chase, but there was no catching them. A few par-tems later and a few turns down the winding shadowy path, and the sight of running rintic was but a short-lived memory. Taukin relished the feeling of empowerment over the rintic. Swinzal felt they had made it far enough away from the village and the patrol that followed behind to slow to a steady trot. Taukin welcomed the change of pace—his lungs burned as they processed the large quantities of chilled air. Aebean and Febus had moved across the blackened sky revealing the fork in the path leading to Sik Jukote. Swinzal now walked to allow Taukin to catch his breath. Taukin found a felled tree near the fork and sat upon it. He was merely winded, but still energized from the agrum.

"Wait here, I'll be back sssoon," said Swinzal, then dropped Taukin's ruck next to the felled tree and ran down the path toward the Peah mounds. Taukin, alone now, rested his hands on the interior of his pelt-covered knees and slowed his breathing, choosing slow, deep breaths over shorter shallow breaths. He created a continuous, icy white cloud that moved upward toward the moons. It was on his fifth deep breath that he heard the gentle pounding of inobi hooves against the worn dirt path. He turned and at least four inobi sled runners breached a crest in the path so quickly that he didn't have time to strap his ruck on before speeding down the path to warn Swinzal.

Taukin was sure that he had been discovered, so there was no use in remaining quiet any longer. "Swinzal!" he yelled, hoping that the suvanth would respond, but he heard nothing. Taukin's feet carried him swiftly, but he was no match for the inobi, who had promptly gained on Taukin. He had no choice but to veer off the path in hopes that he could lose the inobi in the dense maze of trees. The path cut through the side of a hill, on the left, the ground sloped downward and on the right inclined. Taukin made his move. The sled runners dismounted and began their ascent up the hill in pursuit of Taukin. He climbed upward on the steep slope of swaul trees and crumbling rocks, slipping on the dried leaves and sliding down within two spears length from the soldiers. One soldier had almost reached Taukin with his long sword, but Taukin got to his feet and climbed the hill, zigging upward and separating himself from the rintic. He moved Northwest up the slippery slope and toward the Peah mounds where his mission took him. He slowed enough to sling the heavy ruck on his back and tighten the straps, allowing for faster movement through the forest. He had easily distanced himself from the sled runners when a large, striped garwelve slithered out from behind a cluster of fallen swaul trees, warning with its loud popping sound and startling Taukin to the point that he fell on his rear.

A strong hand gripped Taukin, pulling him up to his feet, "Follow me," said Swinzal, and at an angled descent, they ran back down, slipping and sliding, to the path leading to the Peah mounds. Both Taukin and Swinzal picked up speed as they ran along the loamy trail until they encountered a squad of suvanth hidden among the tree line and waiting for Swinzal. The hair on Taukin's neck stiffened as the squad of demons rolled out from behind the trees and onto the path. Five suvanth of different shapes and sizes stood before them, covered in camouflaged pelt coverings and blended into to the black background of the forest. A squatty suvanth warrior saw Taukin and locked eyes in a gaze of wonderment. He was the reason that the squad was away from the warmth and welcomed calamity of the pit. Their mission was based upon the retrieval of this one being who was neither suvanth nor rintic.

Swinzal spoke and disrupted the visual connection, "There isss a sssquad of rintic inobi runnersss behind usss. Wait for them here, then dissspatch them. Bring up the rear and make sssure we're not followed."

A thin suvanth, who stood taller than Swinzal and Taukin, but was slightly hunched over, spoke in a deep tone, "As you command." His dialect was different from Swinzal, but the conviction was the same. Taukin's feelings tore at his heart, the desire to help his tribal brothers pulled at one vein and the criticality of his mission pulled at another. Was he even part of the tribe anymore, or an enemy of the tribe like his father? He so badly wanted to warn the sled runners of their impending doom, but he would most certainly be found out by the suvanth and would jeopardize the mission. He stood motionless, numb from the feeling of despair raging in his heart. Even though the knowledge of this treasonous act would remain with Taukin, guilt rose up from his gullet for not trying to prevent the coming massacre.

"Wait!" said Taukin and turned to Swinzal, "They don't have to die."

"We can't outrun the inobi," said Swinzal growing flustered, his skin turning yellow with dark diagonal tiled stripes.

"We don't have to. Wait here," Taukin climbed the hill and returned shortly holding a short branch with the popping garwelve draped over it. "Inobi are afraid of garwelves. If we can trap it on the trail in the moonlight, it'll stop them."

"That won't ssstop them," said Swinzal.

"It will, trust me. I just need a heavy rock." Swinzal motioned for a warrior to find a large stone and he returned with a rock about the size of a malpwa fruit. Taukin lowered the tail end of the garwelve onto the lit path and the suvanth warrior placed the rock on its wriggling tail claw, trapping it in place. Taukin lowered the stick allowing the garwelve to slide off the end and drop to the cold soil. Taukin leapt out of the way as the creature lunged for him, fangs splayed.

Swinzal faced his tribesmen, "Ssstagger about and if

thisss trick failsss, kill them all." Each of the suvanth moved back behind a large swaul tree along the path and waited. The consistent cadence of pounding hooves was getting louder and Swinzal was growing impatient with Taukin. "Let'sss go," he said to Taukin. The pace they kept was fast, and if it had not been for the large amount of agrum, Taukin would be weary and weak from the lack of rest.

Lumeren came and made the pair visible, so Swinzal decided to deviate from the path shortly before they reached the edge of the forest. Swinzal was careful to avoid any type of worn path and the pair quickly and silently traversed the dry, stone river making it to the tall grassy fields of the plains of Gadush. Traveling and staying hidden in the tall, swaying golden kulee grass was much simpler than the porous forest. The early lumeren rays triggered a desire to rest, but Swinzal wouldn't let the young outcast slow down.

"Keep moving," spouted the ash-colored spy. One could easily get lost on the way to the Peah mounds in the dense stalky grass. Their route cut across the already established paths leading south to Sik Jukote and north to Fort Benja, indicating they were close to the Peah mounds. Finally a cleared path leading to the Peah mounds appeared and Swinzal, annoyed with running through the chest-high grass, decided to move down the cleared path and take his chances with the rintic and other travelers along the path. The two quickened their pace following the cleared path, which wound around small moss-covered stones and as they did, the rocks grew larger as they made it closer to the Peah mounds.

Seven emerald, moss-covered chalky-gray monoliths encircled the Peah mounds. There was a stone for each god, a vessel by which visiting gods entered and exited the planet. However, no tribesman had ever witnessed such an event, be it rintic or suvanth. Hallowed grounds to most Onestonians, but not to Swinzal or other suvanth. Their faith in such gods waned as their desire for agrum and enmity of others grew. A fresh, clean scent, redolent of the stone courtyard leading to the caverns of the Eltepsu overcame Taukin, reminding him of his time with the sustainers and the sacredness of their domain. The same feeling of sanctity was felt after passing the massive oblong god stones.

The actual number of smaller stones that filled the mounds was unknown, but was estimated in the thousands, which many believed represented the stars and planets in the universe. Swinzal jumped high onto the first of the smaller stones that filled the mounds in a spiral pattern. Taukin followed suit thinking that this was the easiest way to traverse the confusing maze of rock and grass. Clouds descended from the Eastern side of Binesmir hovering over the mounds, making the surface moist and visibility hazy. Swinzal and Taukin leaped from rock to rock covering distant gaps and smaller gaps depending on what area of the mounds they came to. Taukin covertly opened the pouch and readied the minuscule piece of russet-colored sassa root. His skin briefly changed to gold, reflecting his nervousness, but he quickly changed it back so as not to alarm Swinzal, who was busily leading Taukin across the mounds. Taukin was correct, Swinzal jumped from his perch into an outer ring of the maze. There, a mass of rocks covered the entrance to the suvanth tunnel. Taukin followed and landed just behind Swinzal who studied the entrance closely.

"Is this…a tunnel?" asked Taukin, winded from the exhaustive pace forced upon him.

"Sssomething isss amissss. The ssstonesss are ssstacked asss expected, but not in the way a sssuvanth would choossse to do. Do you know a reassson why thisss tunnel would be compromisssed?" Taukin fought back his body's natural nervous response of reflecting his feeling through his skin. Taukin merely shook his head in response for fear that a single word would collapse his levy of protection and his skin would tell what his lips didn't. Swinzal, satisfied with Taukin's answer, stared at the tunnel entrance as if he was looking for an answer to his own question. Swinzal slightly cocked his head, focusing on something where the tunnel met the dew-laden grass. He went to his knee and reached to the bottom right edge of the tunnel. There, wedged under a head-sized rock, was a scale. Swinzal picked up the smooth, wide, whitish scale. Taukin knew exactly what it was, a scale from the underbelly of a garando.

"Cursssed rintic! They've dissscovered thisss tunnel. There isss another tunnel, near Binesssmir and before the river. We'll enter there." Taukin was troubled by this turn of events. Swinzal, without concern of discovery, decided to follow the route along Binesmir with much apathy and bravado for whoever crossed his path. The only way to direct the garandos which way to go was to leave a trail of sassa root leading out of the Peah mounds and onto the path along the mountain range. Swinzal led the way by hopping back onto the tall oblong rocks and then leapt toward the outer ring of the mounds. Taukin, clenching a handful of the root, discreetly dropped tiny fragments in a straight line starting on the ring outside of the tunnel so as not to confuse the bungling garandos. Swinzal reached the outer stones of the Peah mounds and pulled another vial of agrum from beneath his trochin coverings, the same size as the one he gave Taukin earlier, a drop vial as it was known, the smaller of the two sizes of vials. Swinzal knew Taukin's body would shut down without the jolt of agrum. He took a long swig and passed it to Taukin. "Drink," said the suvanth demon. Taukin did as commanded. The surge of sustaining fluid went to his blood-filled capillaries, making Taukin slightly dizzy from the sudden onset of energy.

With renewed strength and speed they took off, racing down the path alongside Binesmir with the steep mountain base on their left and the tall kulee grass on their right. They made it to Promisel Point before the Eastern star rose midway in the azure sky. It was shortly afterward that they came across a tribe of white fuzzy fumins close to the path, grazing in the swaying kulee grass. They spotted the unmistakable suvanth pale skin coming towards them and hunkered down into the golden field of grass for fear of death. Taukin's feet carried him so quickly he hardly had time to pay atten-tion to the frightened fumins, and the vision of them taking cover was just a brief vapor of thought. Though they ran swift, the Eastern star graciously conceded to the sister moons. Even the fleet feet of Swinzal couldn't outrun the shadow of Binesmir consuming the Plains of Gadush. They maintained their pace in the blackness of the quiesce, following the rocky path that hugged the rugged side of the mountain. Swinzal cursed the bitter chill that came with the stirless time. The path was empty of beings, be it from the cold blanket of air placed over them, or the late par-cycle in which they traveled. Now, in the deep stirless time, and without obstacles impeding their mission, Taukin's thoughts drifted but he remained vigilant in planting the root. He hadn't slept, but his mind and body seemed unphased due to the large amount of agrum consumed. He wrestled with many things on his journey, but the thoughts that bubbled up to the forefront mostly were whether or not Keel was alive, would his family ever trust him again, and could he ever trust Soyha. His anger toward her subsided and the feeling that still colored his skin came forth. He quickly renounced the feeling as just a result of the lack of sleep or due to the consumed agrum. No matter the excuse or the reasoning, Soyha lingered in his heart and he couldn't force her out. This battle of anger, care, and confusion about the General's daughter waged inside his mind through the darkness and well into the new lumeren.

Swinzal said, "We are nearing the lower Kappa River," but there was no sign from Taukin's viewpoint, only tall waving stalks of amber kulee grass until the stalks gave way to short green grass by the river. Dew from the previous quiesce had followed the paths of light laid out by the Eastern star back up into the fluffy white clouds that hung overhead. Swinzal and Taukin broke from the worn rocky path along Binesmir and moved toward the river at a slower pace through the grassy plain. The soft dirt underneath Taukin's feet was a welcomed relief from the hard cluster of stones. Swinzal suddenly stopped at the edge of the cliff, holding his rigid arm out to prevent Taukin from suffering another cliff-related incident. The lower Kappa River raged in front of them, constantly roaring as white caps broke over the rocks below. Swinzal moved cautiously down to the edge of the river, grasped a thin tree and hung over the water, scooping up handfuls in his pale, clawed hand and drinking fervently. Taukin followed suit, finding a large rock to cling to while he filled his gullet with the clear frigid water.

Swinzal moved back up the embankment with Taukin following behind a short time later. Swinzal had already uncovered most of the dead tree limbs when Taukin breached the cliff. There it was, the tunnel entrance. It was well hidden amongst dead tree limbs that had washed down shore during floods and the high kulee stalks. Swinzal looked at Taukin once an opening was made large enough for Taukin to crawl into, and said, "From thisss point on, we will be under the protection of the sssuvanth." Taukin nodded in understanding, but his gut instinct was that from this point on, his guise as traitor to the rintic had to be foolproof, and if it had not been for Swinzal's actions against Keel and Avent he might have had a harder time convincing others and himself of this case. Swinzal, still staring at Taukin, went to his knees then reached overhead and down his back underneath his pelt coverings. He slowly removed the long, tapered bone that allowed him to walk upright, a clear organic ooze stretched down from the ivory bone to the ground, and he placed it in a special holster inside his coverings alongside his ribs. Taukin reached to the back of his neck, where there was a trivial bone notch, but one that was fixed and sealed with skin. Swinzal, on hands and feet, slithered down the narrow entrance and called out from the darkness of the tunnel, "No harm will befall you, Manisssta hasss commanded thisss. Enter your true domain." The thought of running away tempted Taukin, this was his chance to escape, not just from Swinzal, but also the Carth tribe. He could meet up with Ethius and together they would find Luspa. This was his last chance to run, but it would mean that he would be labeled a traitor by the rintic and would be forever hunted by the suvanth. That life would be a dismal one, even if it were a life with his birth mother and father. Not knowing if the rintic would be able to find the tunnel where Taukin entered and if a rescue mission was even possible now, Taukin clumped together an ample amount of sassa root and tossed it in the direction of the path along Binesmir.

Taukin's skin brightened, "Can't we rest first?" Light illuminated the onyx octagonal pattern of Swinzal's pale, blue face as it slowly protruded and appeared to be floating out from the blackness of the tunnel. "You will ressst after you ssspeak with Manisssta," replied the suvanth spy, "remove your armband and come with me." Taukin pulled the powder-blue band from his sweaty coverings and stuffed it in his ruck. He faced the Eastern star, closed his eyes, and soaked in the warmth and light, then turned and slowly placed one leg in the hole and paused. "Come on, come on," said Swinzal impatiently. Taukin's face contorted into a form of a grimace as he crawled into the darkness of the tunnel and pulled his ruck down with him.

CHAPTER 7
ENTER THE PIT

A grum still flowed through Taukin and energized his sleep-deprived body and mind. Swinzal quickly led the way down the dirt tube. It was surprisingly wide and tall, with much more headroom than what Taukin had imagined, but so dark that Swinzal could only be heard and not seen. "Where are you? I can't see anything," said Taukin.

"Land dweller," spurted Swinzal and suddenly a blue trisian bulb lit the confines of the rintic-high tunnel. Swinzal took Taukin's ruck from him and turned back toward the direction of the pit and scurried off with the blue light fading quickly. At first the descent was steep and Taukin leaned back and walked with bent legs, one hand dragging along behind him in order to keep from sliding down. Taukin caught up to Swinzal when the tunnel flattened out, this was the point where the passage was beneath the raging river above, so at least Taukin thought. A sassa root shaving was driven into the dark soot as Taukin pushed his way upright against the sloped path. It wasn't long before Taukin's large eyes adjusted to the blackness, as much as they could with the lone blue bulb.

As they ran along the straight pathway, a mixture of Swinzal's sweet scent and that of freshly disturbed dirt filled the confines of the tunnel. Swinzal's ability to crawl almost as fast as he ran surprised Taukin, and it wasn't until they deviated from the main tunnel to a smaller tunnel, that Taukin understood why he crawled in the first place. Taukin's hands met the surprisingly warm soil as he crouched and there were now tentacles of a fungal system that dangled overhead and occasionally tickled his hairless crown. Swinzal switched tunnels a few more times, each one seemingly brighter and warmer than the last and after each fork Taukin inconspicuously planted sassa root.

Then, as suddenly as they were upon the tunnel, they had entered a hub. The open area was large compared to the confined space of the previous tunnel and there were at least three other tunnels that connected at this junction. Dimly lit silhouettes suddenly froze at the sight of Taukin, and Taukin's skin color unintentionally lightened, which caused a stir amongst the suvanth. Their large eyes glowed pink in the darkened tunnel. Swinzal shouted, "Make a path!" and all suvanth, subservient to the master's reconnoitre hastily scattered and crawled away down the hollows. As Taukin ran, a pattern of tunnels and hubs emerged and at each junction, Taukin's confidence that the rintic would find Cuvsor waned. The trek seemed never-ending and Taukin began to believe he was being led to the other side of Onestonia. More and more suvanth crossed paths with Taukin and some followed behind close enough for Taukin to smell their unique aroma, making it easier to plant the sassa root under their feet. At the larger hubs, torches were hung between the channels lighting the connection points allowing Taukin to see the bustling suvanth who moved past him and back toward the way from which they came. Taukin's legs began to tire, his body desperately needed rest, although agrum pumped voraciously through his circulatory system, certain physiological systems started shutting down. They made it to a hub that had some sort of rail system running along parallel tunnels. One tunnel had empty carts being pulled upward into the darkness, each by groups of burly suvanth, and the other had carts full of soil and rock traveling down speedily toward the light.

Taukin had just dropped a cut of the root when his sight blurred and his right leg gave way, causing him to stumble and nearly crash into a passing suvanth. Taukin's mind reacted to the severe physical conditions that Swinzal forced upon him and he tucked the pouch into his bottoms. Sweat from the increased heat ran down his forehead and dripped from his nose, causing him to remove his torso covering. His body was overheating. Taukin took a few more bumbling steps before completely falling prostrate against the warm soil. Swinzal grabbed Taukin and placed him on his back, holding onto Taukin's limp arms that draped over his own shoulders, and then ran behind a cart that was traveling down toward Sheol Balla. Swinzal launched onto the cart and crudely dumped Taukin and his ruck on top of the debris. Traveling by cart was slower at times than running, but the extra load brought upon by Taukin's limp body made it the most expedient method of travel. The occasional squeak of the cart's metallic wheels rubbing against the side of the metallic tracks woke Taukin, who faded in and out of consciousness. The cart passed numerous suvanth, all of which stopped in their tracks to look down on the oddity of not only a land-dwelling visitor, but one who was neither fully suvanth, nor rintic. Glowing pink eyes contrasted the top of the dark tunnels and moved swiftly above Taukin, and his mind subconsciously drifted back to when he rode on the melp and stared up at the glowing stars.

The cart entered a brightly lit and expansive hub with multiple tunnel openings from floor to ceiling, and the tracks that they followed ran parallel to a series of other tracks that led toward a large and shadowy passageway. Suvanth scrambled in and out of all openings, some carrying weapons strapped to their backs and walking upright, some galloping like a satupha chasing its prey. Swinzal quickly put Taukin's covering and ruck under one arm, and with the other, gripped the belt wrapped around Taukin's waist and pulled him up from the debris. The cart swerved and sidled brimming carts speeding toward the gaping black opening. Swinzal, with Taukin, now fully unconscious and facing upward toward the rock ceiling, arms sprawled and legs dangling, leapt from one cart to another until he reached the solid rock floor beyond the tracks. As Swinzal walked, the suvanth gathered around him to view the rarity of the one known to all suvanth, but never seen, until now. The crowd of pale blue beings formed a circle around Swinzal, a suvanth formed flauva bubble of sorts that moved with Swinzal, as if he was the center. Quiet rumblings could be heard echoing throughout the cavern. Swinzal paid no attention to his brethren, nor their inquisitive banter, his mission was his focus. He carried Taukin, feet dragging across the smooth stone floor, to the entrance that led to Manista's chamber. Two elite soldiers, known as Hannon Lite, stood upright at each side of the round portal, each with a hand on a long pointed dunion staff. Not even Swinzal knew the correct series of tunnels that led to the leader's chamber, but he did know the protocol for communicating with the leader of the suvanth. Swinzal gently lowered Taukin in front of the well-lit tunnel entrance and called for the glingus messenger. Neither guard acknowledged Swinzal, they stared straight ahead, expressionless and he was careful not to make a move that triggered the Hannon Lite. The guards had a unique purpose, in the case of an uprising or enemy attack against the leader, one Hannon Lite soldier would stand at the entrance and fend off as many of the enemy while the other would close off the other tunnels by releasing the massive cut stone that hung above the four tunnel entrances beyond the single guarded entrance.

Ahead of Swinzal, a shadow emerged against the

curved tunnel wall and continued to grow until it stretched from the tunnel crest to the floor. A glingus appeared, standing scarcely waist-high to the Hannon Lite guards. Swinzal spoke to the miniature suvanth, "Tell Manisssta I have returned with hisss prize." Glingus were proud beings, who thought their selection as personal assistants to the suvanth leader was one of positive stature, instead of a cursed enslavement, as other suvanth viewed them. Their placement above the other suvanth was done so on purpose by Manista so that they would remain loyal to the master. The squatty glingus angrily squinted at Swinzal and tsked at the command, as if his rank was higher than that of the suvanth spy, then promptly hobbled off down the curved stone corridor. While Swinzal waited, crowds gathered around the unconscious outsider and more importantly, near the entrance to Manista's chamber. As the crowd grew, the Hannon Lite guards reacted, one swiftly moved inside the tunnel, the other silently and without notification unsheathed his Anglis blade and in a single motion slayed the closest layer of suvanth onlookers. This sent a flurry of frightened suvanth scattering and spitting out blasphemes against the guard. Swinzal stood motionless; he had no conflict with the guard, and even the slightest movement toward the entrance could be perceived as a threat against the leader. Death Tenders, suvanth whose sole purpose was to deal with the deceased, ran up and claimed the eviscerated brethren by carrying them off on rolling trochin-pelt stretchers.

A multitude of hobbling glingus arrived ahead of

Manista, forming a sort of diminutive suvanth entourage. Manista, tall, upright, and gaunt for a suvanth, and wearing a long, hooded tyrian-purple robe, arrived, hands clasped together near his chest, revealing his longer than normal suvanth nails. Swinzal went to his knee and lowered his head in the presence of Manista.

Manista spoke, "Well done Swinzal, once again you have shown your capability and proved your loyalty to me. You shall be generously rewarded," his tone gentle and lingering. The leader stood over the unconscious visitor like a satupha over its conquered prey. Manista called to one of the glingus, who clumsily hobbled around Taukin and over to his master. "Swinzal shall receive an elder vial of agrum from my supply, a feast from my personal servant, and to join me in my quarters for leisure, after you've recovered from your mission," said the suvanth leader, turning to look at his loyal emissary.

Swinzal bowed his head in appreciation and followed the diminutive guide away from Taukin to collect his recompence. With his long, pointed finger, Manista motioned for the glingus to lift Taukin. Eight glingus surrounded the limp body and raised him up over their heads, nearly level with Manista's waist. Manista turned and followed the seemingly floating body of Taukin into the stone corridor. When the glingus turned fully in the torchlight at the entrance to the four tunnels, Manista noticed something peculiar.

"Wait!" Manista ordered. The glingus halted and moaned, struggling to support Taukin with their stubby arms. Manista moved in closer to Taukin's body and bent over to see what protruded from his covering that was strewn across his chest. It was the wooden carving of the Eltepsu that Lantia had given Taukin as capethica. Manista inspected the wooden Eltepsu bauble closer with his gangly fingers, all eight of them. He smirked at what he imagined was a rintic toy and Taukin's lingering adolescence and innocence until he turned it bottom up and noticed a tiny decorative marking. He pulled the trinket closer to the light and his smile disappeared as he placed the carving in a pocket in his silken robe. "Carry him to the unfound chamber," said Manista angrily. The glingus moved upward into one of the four tunnels that led to Manista's personal living quarters.

A fragrant aroma filled Taukin's head and he cracked his eyes open, taking in the dim firelight. A cool wet cloth slowly and gently ran across his forehead and down his cheek and a voice, gentle and melodic, sang.

"What lies beyond horizon crest
a place of rest and no regret
wind dancing on the swaying grass
cries through the trees until at last
we are free from our dark chain
free to run and free of pain."

She softly spoke, "You have beautiful skin." Taukin's eyes squinted and closed long, and briefly opened. Her eyes were large and blue like cerulean gems, and her skin was the color of the gray-blue moon Febus, and just as smooth and her long ebony hair laid flat against her shoulders.

Taukin was still coming to his senses when he said,

"You…have…a beautiful…," he paused briefly, "voice." She smiled, her full indigo lips revealing her fondness for Taukin. Taukin's eyes opened wider and he focused on his caretaker. "You!" said Taukin as he went to his elbows then slowly sat up on the soft bed of pillows and locked eyes with this unknown suvanth, when his eyes widened and his skin flashed a light red with minuscule blue dots. "I saw you in the Carth forest," said Taukin, his voice shaky.

Drami Sol leaned in, "Do not speak of that where ears can hear," she said in a hushed voice and her skin went violet similar to Taukin's color, but with white dots. She looked back toward the exit to see a stubby scowl-faced glingus standing watch over them.

"Who are you?" asked Taukin. She moved from Taukin's side to get a container of cool water from the stone water channel against the wall inside the chamber. Sweat ran down Taukin's neck. "It's so hot," said Taukin.

"You haven't adjusted yet, but you will. You feel the heat from the cinder tubes," she said. A lone torch lit the chamber and it was much warmer and more confined, compared to the hubs leading to the pit, with stone all around and a low soft pillowy bed near the rear of the chamber. She returned to the bed and handed him the flask as she placed her hand underneath for support. "Drink this," she said. Leaning on one arm, Taukin raised the metallic container to his parched mouth. He drank slowly, but started gulping the water as if he hadn't drunk anything in tem-cycles. "Slow down or you'll purge. You depleted your body traveling here and you will need to slowly be rehydrated. Drami Sol."

"Drami Sol? Is that where I am?" asked Taukin.

Her smile appeared at the comment and she tucked her black hair behind her ears. "My name is Drami Sol. This is Sheol Balla, or what the rintic call the pit. You are in one of the master's chambers. Taukin glanced down, his muscular chest exposed, then his skin went gold, and he quickly draped the blanket over his shoulders, stood, and searched for his cold-weather covering. "What an interesting color. What does it mean?" asked Drami Sol, lost to Taukin's colors and emotions.

"I'm not exactly sure how to represent it in a way that you would understand," said Taukin as he searched earnestly for his covering.

"Are you looking for this?" she asked as she presented his furry covering draped across both her arms.

"Thank you," he said as he gently lifted it from her. He placed the covering over his torso, causing more sweat to bead up on his forehead.

"Perhaps you should go without your covering until you've acclimated to your surroundings," she said.

"No, no, I'm quite comfortable," replied Taukin, now with drops of sweat hanging from his square jaw. Drami Sol stared as Taukin squirmed around and tried to pretend he was comfortable and that the sweat didn't bother him.

"I need to inform the master you are awake, he is anxious to meet you," and with that she slowly walked toward the exit, her thin black and gray covering clung to her body and made Taukin flutter with shyness. She called out to the glingus, who appeared to her rather quickly. She went eye level and quietly told the glingus her message all the while grinning and looking back at the captivated Taukin. Her beauty was mesmerizing and had it not been for the discomfort of something scratching him in his undercloth, he would have remained frozen with adoration. Taukin turned away from Drami Sol and reached down into his undercloth and removed the tickly object. It was a single thin wiry root. *Sassa root!* thought Taukin in alarm.

"What are you doing?" asked Drami Sol as she peeked over his shoulder.

He quickly tucked the root back in his undercloth at his waist. "Nothing. Just adjusting myself to this heat," said Taukin golden-skinned.

She leaned closer and her dark lips whispered in his brightly colored ear, "Taukin, you don't have to hide the truth from me." Taukin still facing away from Drami Sol, his eyes frantically searching for the sassa root pouch. "I'm not hiding," said Taukin with a slight quiver in his voice.

"You can tell me anything," said Drami Sol, hoping to assuage his nervousness while the glingus was away.

"Could you turn around while I put on my bottom coverings?" asked Taukin so as to diffuse the surreptitious feeling between them. Drami Sol turned and Taukin hurriedly stuffed his bare legs into his bottoms before the glingus returned with their master, all the while trying to not look at Drami Sol's silhouette. "You can turn around now," said Taukin fully clothed in his pelt coverings with beads of sweat tracing one another down his face.

Her delicate smile faded when a voice, low and firm from across the chamber penetrated the silence, "Do you know the one trait that binds all living things? Desire; the want of what we do not have. It drives us. You and I share this trait. We both desire what we do not have Taukin. Our particular situation is one of interdependence. You can help me get what I want, and I can help you get what you want." Manista, long black hair pulled back on top and covering his shoulders, stood near the chamber opening and said to Drami Sol, "Leave us." Drami Sol pulled away from Taukin and proceeded to the exit in the same unintentionally captivating way as she had done before Manista arrived. Taukin's skin blazed even brighter with the presence of Manista in the chamber.

Manista watched Taukin's eyes as he traced every step that the alluring suvanth took. Drami Sol lowered her head as she approached Manista, and he said, "Wait for me in my chamber." Then she placed her hands on the warm stone floor allowing a glingus to cover her head with a tan cloth sack, then followed the leading glingus out of the chamber. Manista smiled and approached Taukin, almost as if he floated with his feet just above the stone floor, "She is enticing, wouldn't you say?" asked Manista.

Unsure how to respond, Taukin's face contorted, "Mhmm," dribbled from his lips.

Manista paused an arm's length away and bowed his head slightly to Taukin, "I am Manista." Uncertain of the customs of the suvanth, Taukin followed suit and lowered his glabrous head. Manista continued, "I wondered if you were going to wake from your slumber. I trust that you have recovered from your difficult journey?"

"How long was I asleep?" asked Taukin unaware of the time and light above ground to gauge how long he had slept.

Manista moved closer to Taukin, looking down upon the golden outcast, he placed his pointy fingers on his shoulders, "Long enough," said Manista, baring a jagged-toothy smile. Taukin's skin maintained its bright-yellow hue. "There is no cause for unease, I assure you that the suvanth will treat you with the utmost dignity and respect. No harm will come to you." Taukin locked on Manista's onyx eyes and as difficult as it was, forced his skin to its normal hue and pattern. "Good, you understand. We have to trust one another if we are to help each other. Can I trust you Taukin?" The white sclera of Manista's eyes had almost completely succumbed to the encroaching blackness of the pupil, a rare evolutionary trait of certain suvanth, which made it impossible for Taukin to fixate upon for fear his skin would reveal the truth of the matter. Taukin's eyes looked to the side of the stone chamber for a par-tem before focusing on Manista's awaiting eyes.

Taukin's mind went to the missing sassa root pouch, but he took a chance and nodded his head, and quietly responded, "Yes my Lord."

Manista smiled, "Of course I can trust you," and he released his grip from Taukin's shoulder and pulled away. As he turned, he spoke, "We have much to discuss." The suvanth leader seemed to glide across the room to the exit, and on the way out said, "Replenish your fluids, your body needs it. I will send for you shortly. And change out of those ragged trochin pelts, you'll receive new coverings," then he left the chamber without a glingus guide.

Taukin cautiously but feverishly searched for the sassa root pouch, first in his coverings, then around the bed. There was no sign of the pouch, and the concern that his plan had already been compromised grew in his mind. The overwhelming feeling that he failed his mission for the rintic, if he was even still on his mission for the rintic, impeded his thoughts. If Manista knew of Taukin's true purpose for being there, not only was Taukin in danger, but the rintic, and even worse, the Eltepsu could be in danger. "I'm a fool! How could I have slept so long? And to lose consciousness, am I that weak?" He made his way to the water channel that was carved into the stone wall and dipped his face in the cool water, pulled up, then cupped the water over his smooth crown and rubbed it against the back of his neck. He washed away the grime that had collected on his body as well as the anxiety that had built inside him. The one thing that he couldn't rid himself of was the sharp hunger pains emanating from his belly. His stomach rumbled so loud that he never heard his visitor enter the room.

The dimly lit stone room was made brighter when his guide, a rather joyous glingus named Pecril appeared, carrying folded clothing in one hand and a lamp with his short arm that looked like more of an extension of his shoulder than it did an actual limb. The suvanth walked up to Taukin, his head at Taukin's waist, and with his long arm placed the folded clothing on the pillowed bed then hugged Taukin's leg. Taukin, confused at first, patted the suvanth on his cloth-covered back, occasionally hitting his long black ponytail and then the glingus squeezed tighter.

Smiling wildly, he pulled away from Taukin's leg. "You're a friendly fellow. I don't believe we know each other." The squatty suvanth shook his head at first, but then nodded, signifying that they did indeed know each other. "We don't, but do. I don't understand, or are you confused? What's your name?"

The glingus slapped his chest and, keeping his arm against his body, rolled his hand open.

Taukin, still confused, "Can't you speak?" His guide smirked sadly and shook his head. Taukin squatted down and looked the glingus in his large ebony eyes. "I'm sorry, I did not know. My name is Taukin." Pecril smiled and nodded his head excitedly in agreement. "You know who I am? I guess you would. There aren't many who look like me." Pecril pointed to the clothing and motioned for Taukin to change. Taukin obliged and stripped to his undercloth and slid on the more comfortable thinner clothing, which consisted of loose-fitting white trousers and matching top with a dark-blue robe and woven sandals.

Pecril motioned for Taukin to follow him toward the exit. Pecril removed a cloth sack and tugged on Taukin's robe requesting Taukin to squat once more.

Taukin obliged and Pecril rubbed Taukin's hairless head and grinned. "Another uncommon feature huh?" asked Taukin. Pecril nodded before placing the opaque covering over Taukin's head. The cloth cover, musty and scratchy, hid Taukin's eyes from the path they set out on. Taukin's hand encompassed Pecril's tiny fist and with the loss of one sense, his other senses were heightened. Pecril led Taukin up and down the humid tunnels and through numerous turns, all the while Taukin focused on the deep crevices that etched Pecril's callous skin. Taukin stumbled while traveling the narrow passageways, causing his free hand to pop up and outward scanning for any obstacles that might impede his movement, or at least to catch himself upon falling forward. The echoing sounds of shuffling feet dissipated and Taukin knew they were no longer in the tunnels.

The low, but dominating voice spoke, "Remove the cover," Pecril tugged Taukin's robe and Taukin obliged by taking a knee on the solid rock floor. Pecril pulled the hood from the top and Taukin blew off the strands of loose fabric and dust from his lips. Multiple torches illuminated the room and Taukin squinted until his eyes adjusted to the brightness. Manista made his way over to Taukin, and cradling his shoulder between his lengthy, pointy digits, helped him to his feet. Manista being a tall suvanth, stood at least a head taller than Taukin. "The practice of cloaked guidance is a necessity that all suvanth must obey," said Manista in his unique reverberating voice.

Manista motioned for Pecril to leave with his hand as if he was sweeping the dust from the air with his elongated claws. Pecril bowed his head, turned, and then scampered out. Vibrant plush pillows the size of melp shells, covered over half of the room's floor, and the dome above arched high above their heads. Torches along the wall surrounded the room, creating enough light to rival that of the Eastern star. Multiple portals lined the walls and the thought of the Eltepsu's prayer adytum came to mind, the main difference being that there was no opening from above in which light shone down. On the right a single guard stood perfectly still in the front of a vault of agrum vials that lined the walls. Taukin's eyes widened at the sight of the incredible agrum stockpile. To the left, a long wooden table stood covered with fruits from the land above, roasted meats, goblets of malpwa wine, and vials of agrum. The aroma overtook Taukin's manners and his focus went to the delicacies that lay out beside him. Manista spoke, "Taukin, you have traveled a long distance, you need victuals. Join me."

Manista's long silky tyrian-colored robe flowed along the stone surface as he passed Taukin and took his seat at the far end of the long table. "Please…sit," said Manista as he gestured open-handedly toward the opposite end of the table. In place of Manista's last two fingers were pale nubs. Taukin paused focusing on his host's missing digits before sitting in the wooden chair, which seemed to fit his body much better than any rintic chair he had ever sat in. He sat with his sandals flat on the floor and shifted his chair closer to the table and closer to the feast that olfactorily and visually called to him. He sat in front of the sworn enemy of his adoptive kin, who also happened to be the most benevolent suvanth he knew. This, the leader of the tribe that the rintic despised, that they had banished to this underground prison, sat reverently in front of Taukin, offering a bounty of food to a famished outsider. Out from behind Taukin, a female appeared, clothed with red silky coverings and a sheer cloak. Her long dark hair was braided and rolled into a spiral that rested on the side of her neck, much like the shape of a flattened doka shell. Taukin focused on the charming older suvanth who now stood next to Manista's decorative wooden chair. Her right arm rested on the high crest rail above Manista's head that ran the width of his shoulders. Her light brown eyes rested on Taukin, studying his features as if she was talking to him with just her eyes. "Prepare our meal," said Manista in a gentle tone, and the female did just that, starting with the guest's meal. "Try the malpwa wine. It is the best you will ever have," offered Manista, and his servant poured a full glass for Taukin who cradled the goblet and put the metallic rim to his nose, then against his lips. At first the taste was aromatic and sweet, but the tilt of the wine trailed close behind and addled Taukin. He raised the drink two more times before finishing off the entire vessel. Taukin's skin color bubbled with an array of all possible colors and patterns, revealing his sense of desire.

"Another?" requested Taukin.

Manista replied, "Taukin, the first taste of Malpwa wine should be done with prudence. One can grow quite fond of the drink without realizing the impact until the chase has caught the mind. Perhaps later."

Taukin received his plate full of the most delicious, cooked meats and vividly colorful fruits and looked up at his server who knowingly stared at him. His manners left him and he grabbed up the meat-covered bones and tore into them with a voracious appetite. Manista smiled at his guest's primal instincts, "Just like your brethren," said Manista.

Taukin paused and with meat-filled cheeks said, "pardon my manners my Lord."

"I expect nothing less, eat how you will," said Manista with as much politeness as he could fit into his words before Taukin continued devouring his meal. Manista sent his servant away and feasted as Taukin did, but with more reserve so as not to cause unease with Taukin. They ate until their bellies were full. "We need to discuss a matter," said Manista and continued, "Taukin, when you first arrived and were unresponsive, something fell from your coverings." Manista now held Taukin's attention captive. Taukin was certain that Manista found the sassa root and now his mission and life were in jeopardy. He tried to fight the dulling effects of the wine, but could only do so temporarily and his skin slowly changed color and pattern, but before it could fully show his fear, Manista held up the wooden Eltepsu bauble. "How is it that you came by this?" asked Manista.

Taukin felt relief that it was only the trinket, but the fear still existed and his skin remained yellow. Taukin was slow to speak and thought surely there would be no repercussions for telling the truth, and the influence of the malpwa wine reinforced this thought. "It was given to me by an Eltepsu."

Manista, needing reassurance asked, "You met an Eltepsu?"

"The Eltepsu Lantia, at their caverns."

"And do you know how this Eltepsu acquired such *an exquisite* carving?" asked Manista as he examined it closely, walking over to Taukin.

"The Eltepsu did not say who or from where it came."

"I see. Be sure to keep it secure. You wouldn't want to lose a gift from an Eltepsu again." Manista handed the bauble back to Taukin who placed it inside his robe pocket for safekeeping, allowing his skin to go violet once more.

Manista stood before Taukin, pale and tall with his dark-purple robe draped over his gaunt body like drooping skin over a skeleton. "May I ask what brought you to meet with them?" Taukin's skin started to slowly morph yellow, but Taukin forced it back to its normal hue, which was difficult given the wine's physiological control. Manista continued before Taukin could utter a sound, "It's uncommon for any Onestonian to be permitted to meet the sustainers, especially at their dwelling place. It must have been something of utmost importance?" said Manista hovering over Taukin, who couldn't look at those black eyes without changing skin color.

"I swore that I wouldn't tell any tribesman of the matters discussed with the Eltepsu. I have told you about the bauble, and I feel like that is enough. I honor my promises my Lord," said Taukin woozy and wondering if his words came out correctly and convincingly enough.

Manista stood behind Taukin and said, "You hold true to your word. I respect that Taukin. Walk with me." Taukin pushed against the arm rests to steady himself as he stood. He staggered to the right, but was able to catch himself. He had never had malpwa wine before, and even though it was a relatively trivial amount, it was potent enough to dull his senses including his sight, and Taukin's eyes widened as he blinked repeatedly to focus. Manista wrapped his long, clothed arm around Taukin to help him walk out of the chamber and into the maze of winding tunnels. They walked up and down and left and right through the lit tunnels.

Taukin and Manista walked out into the massively large opening, Manista relinquishing his grip on Taukin, allowing Taukin to control his own legs. Looking down at the smooth rocky surface, Taukin stretched his arms out and bent at his knees to steady himself. "I want to show you something, come," Manista said as he reached for Taukin's arm, and they made their way past the bustling and bowing suvanth and into a wide and spacious opening that was a portal of portals.

Across the cart tracks and far away from Manista's chambers, a deep recess cut into the vast opening, revealing two tunnels. The left tunnel was well lit, much like Manista's chamber, and was guarded by two motionless Hanon Lite guards who stood directly in front of the tall portal that Manista was leading Taukin toward. Two warrior guards holding temper staffs stood next to the tunnel on the right which was filled with a misty haze that glowed blue, and dreadful screams that seemed to narrowly escape the winding throat of the cave. Upon hearing the cries, Manista stopped and quickly made his way toward the blue mist-filled opening.

Manista led Taukin into the blue tunnel. A strange mist filled the pathway and Taukin waved it away as if he was swimming through a river of vapors. A pair of suvanth carrying a lifeless body on a stretcher rushed past them. Swirls of haze were the only thing seen, and Taukin's mind was still under the effect of the wine, but he swore the lifeless body had a rintic armband. More hushed cries came from the opposite end of the tunnel causing Taukin to slow, but Manista urged him to follow lest he be left behind. Taukin moved on, hesitating with each scream, but still curious about the cerulean light, which drew him closer. The tunnel merged into an opening the size of General Reibo's quarters, and just as tall. Surprisingly the chamber was free of the lingering fog that filled the passageway, but was colored in a bright blue glow, and was warmer than any chamber Taukin had visited. A waterfall of mist flowed down from above the tunnel entrance into the portal, a result of the mixture of underground water, minerals, gas, and heat. A large, bright blue flame shot out from the same opening, with steam rising and the thick vapor falling and following the heated air flow into the tunnel. Equipment, which looked like tools and weapons and liquid compounds in translucent containers, filled the shiny metal experiment stations that sat at various locations inside the chamber. A thin short-haired suvanth with a thin nose, dressed in a long gray cloth coat and covered with a trochin skin smock, wearing tight, thin hairless pelt-skin gloves stood over a rear-facing chair. Taukin could see a muscular red arm secured tightly to the metal arm of the chair and the crown of a being thrashing side to side. The strange suvanth turned and locked eyes with Taukin, who looked a darker shade of violet under the blue light. The slender suvanth faced Taukin and allowed his skin to change to that of Taukin's to show humility and respect. "Taukin, at last we meet. I am Beezelg, chief researcher," his tone was friendly as if he was numb to the anguish that was taking place just an arm's distance away. Taukin dipped his head, but remained speechless, his large amber eyes went back to the suffering rintic.

A cold-weather covering was draped over a metallic station and the powder-blue armband on the sleeve was that of the Carth rintic. Taukin and Manista moved around to the side of the chair where a rintic tribesman was strapped to the chair arm with his mouth gagged with a twisted piece of white cloth, wriggling, and screaming out as Beezelg scribbled down words on a tablet. "Fesenius!" shouted Taukin and he moved to free the suffering tribesman. "What are you doing to him?" asked Taukin, his tone loud and unsteady.

Beezelg spoke, "This rintic was caught setting traps in our tunnels, and now he is helping us test the effectiveness of a new weapon." The rintic tribesman briefly looked at Taukin for help before clenching his eyes shut and screaming as his body went taut against the chair.

Taukin's skin showed anger and he yelled out, "You're killing him! Release him!"

Unlike Beezelg, Manista looked dismayed. He gently shook his head and talked over the cries of pain, "How much more suffering must there be? If only the rintic and Umgara agreed to live in harmony with the suvanth, there would be no need for weapons or pain. I cannot stand this agony, give him the antidote." Beezelg obeyed and produced a glossy and elongated, black eight-legged insect that bit into the prominent arm vein of the screaming rintic. Within par-tems, the rintic calmed and his head drifted back and forth, in and out of consciousness. Manista loosened the pelt straps from the rintic's arms, removed the saliva-soaked cloth from his mouth, and placed his weakened body against his own. "Brother, we come from the same seed, yet we are considered enemies. I will change this. We will again live in peace above ground. All Onestonians," said the leader with tears rimming the edge of his eyelids. "Beezelg, have the guards help him back to his chamber and feed him. Provide him a drop vial of agrum to restore his health and once he's strong enough, release him near his home," said Manista. Beezelg walked over to a stone wall that was covered with fungal roots and ran his gloved hand over the vascular matrix releasing at the point toward the tunnel exit and spoke, "Guards come forth."

An organic electrical signal spread out as a ripple of green luminescent light, much like water does when disturbed by a foreign object, and a sound of many whispers, which repeated Beezelg's words, carried across the ceiling and down the tunnel. Beezelg took the staggering rintic from Manista and led him toward the vapor-filled tunnel.

Manista turned to Taukin, "He will survive," he said sympathetically.

"And he'll be returned to the Carth forest?" asked Taukin.

"As soon as he has recovered, I swear it," said Manista allowing his skin to show his sincerity with a flash of yellow with blue dots. Before Beezelg and Fesenius made it to the passageway, two soldiers that were standing guard at the entrance to the tunnel appeared and interlocked arms with the weakened rintic essentially carrying him as they departed. Once Fesenius was out of sight, Taukin's emotion left him and his focus went to the ceiling and what seemed to be an organic communication network. He was still gazing upward at the incredible interconnected pathways that made up the extraordinary system when Beezelg sidled him.

"It's really quite remarkable," said Beezelg in his proper tone. "One simply chooses the distance and direction the message travels. It's a proportional distance, relative to the touch. One can send communications anywhere the roots span. It's an ancient fungoid system that has been around since before the suvanth were imprisoned here. We call it the spectrum."

Taukin noticed the white opened cap that was at the base of the organic rooted network. "What is that?" asked Taukin.

"That's the Hollo pod. The open pod encapsulates an object which transmits a visual replication to another Hollo pod elsewhere in the network," replied Beezelg.

The entire system was very impressive and Taukin wanted to learn more, but Manista interrupted the conversation, "Taukin, come with me," said the suvanth leader with grief in his voice. They walked out through the swirling blue mist and Taukin was bewildered by Manista's compassion for this rintic tribesman. His entire life he was led to believe that the suvanth were heartless and cruel beings. Manista was neither of those it seemed.

Manista led Taukin to the brightly lit tunnel entrance guarded by the Hannon Lite soldiers. He spoke to the elite soldiers in an ancient tongue, one that Taukin had heard about, but never actually heard spoken. "Maractu rrrillped oltanum," said the leader and the motionless guards moved to the side of the opening, allowing Manista and Taukin past. The tunnel was less warm as the blue tunnel and the light blinded Taukin, whose eyes didn't have time to adjust, and the malpwa wine made it even more difficult to see. A multitude of torches filled the winding tunnel. Manista spoke, "Taukin, you are unfamiliar with these surroundings, and probably feel uneasy by what you just witnessed, but you should know that you can change everything between the suvanth and rintic. I need your help to restore peace and trust amongst the tribes.

Taukin replied, "What can I do? I'm neither suvanth nor rintic. I have no say in matters of importance. I am an outcast."

"You are not an outcast! Not with us," replied Manista fervently. He calmed then continued, "Will you help me? Help free the suvanth from this prison, and restore our rightful place among the tribes above ground? And in return I will give you anything you desire."

"Can you help me find my mother?"

Manista stopped and placed his gangly hands on Taukin's shoulders and looked Taukin directly in his brightly lit amber eyes.

"Taukin, I promise you will meet your mother."

Sincerity poured out of Manista like vapors from the blue flame, and although Taukin's instinct was to distrust this suvanth, the opportunity to find his mother was worth any amount of peril put before him.

"When?"

"In time, you need to prove yourself."

"My Lord Manista, I pledge to you that I will do what you need in order to help bring peace amongst the tribes."

Manista smiled, revealing his long and pointed opalescent canines. He then squeezed Taukin's shoulders. "I believe you. There is something extraordinary about you Taukin."

At the end of the tunnel, Taukin and Manista moved past another pair of Hannon Lite soldiers and into a large, dimly lit chamber, with torches scarcely lighting the corners on either side of two holding cells constructed of stone and metal bars. Hinged bar doors faced each other and Taukin couldn't see past the base of stone that grew from the floor halfway up into the rods on the side of the cell. The confines matched each other in height and space, but one difference stood out to Taukin. The cell on the right had bars that were three times as thick as the adjacent cell's bars.

Rumbling and rustling sounds, like that of a low grumble and scratching as nails against stone, could be heard as Manista and Taukin moved closer to the bars. Through the thick black bars, a massive creature, nearly white in color, huddled toward the rear of the confinement. Bulging muscles riddled its back, and Taukin couldn't discern what was locked up in this cage. He peered harder, moving his head a finger's distance away from the bars. Manista looked at Taukin to take in the reaction of the outsider.

"What is that?" asked Taukin quiet enough to not be heard in almost any setting, but in the stillness of this prison, his voice was that of a resounding horn and the creature stirred. With its back toward Taukin, the behemoth stood on two legs that resembled the girth of swaul trees and its head nearly touched the top of the stone ceiling. It turned and in two quick steps it was at the bars causing Taukin to trip over himself and fall backwards. The beast let out a loud, air-filled roar that would have quieted the fiercest of satupha. Taukin scurried backward on all fours until his hairless head hit the bars of the cell behind him. The creature wasn't a creature at all, but a suvanth. His pale powerful hands wrapped around the thick bars pulling and pushing like a strong wind blowing against a perfectly aligned row of trees. Manista found humor in Taukin's reaction and spoke through his toothy smile, "Do not be afraid, he can't touch you. He is Sagog, and in this cell, he remains until needed. He is suvanth, just like us. Blessed with the body larger than the Umgara giants but cursed with the mind of a beast, incapable of thinking like you and I." Taukin ran his hand up the thin metal bars behind him as he stood and took in the enormity of the giant Sagog, whose large black eyes contrasted his pale white skin. Taukin having examined the Umgara up close, knew that the colossal suvanth before him was larger than even General Reibo, the largest of the Umgara. Manista held his needle-like fingers out to Taukin, "Take my hand."

Taukin stepped forward and held Manista's bony digits. Sagog breathed heavily through his wide nostrils. Manista spoke, "Taukin, I only want peace and to live the way our ancestors did once before. Sagog is proof of this fact. If I had wanted to destroy the rintic, I merely need to release Sagog among the tribes. No rintic or weapon could stop him." Manista, still grasping Taukin's hand, moved toward the bars. His long, emaciated fingers gently stroked the branch-like fingers that gripped his prison door. Manista slowly moved Taukin's now-aureolin hand toward the calmed creature. Taukin's hand quivered and moved toward Sagog's finger, and he carefully rubbed the rugged bristly skin. Sagog took a knee and lowered his head closer to Taukin. His giant head and eyes moved side-to-side to piece together Taukin's face through the metal rods. His nostrils flared as he pressed them against the bars in order to sniff Taukin. Sagog inhaled Taukin's peculiar scent and processed it for a par-tem before unleashing a ferocious roar. The giant's putrid breath and drops of saliva covered Taukin as he fell backward into the waiting arms of Manista.

Just then a soft, pleasant sound filled the chamber, quiet at first, but gradually grew louder. Sagog's rage quickly subsided and Taukin stood again, wiping mucous away from his face with his robe. Manista spoke, "Now turn and see the reason the rintic and Umgara have such disdain for the suvanth." Stepping into the light at the center of the opposite cell, was a scrawny being with long clods of matted auburn hair, chanting a prayer that calmed the giant Sagog.

"Cuvsor," said Taukin reactively and under his breath.

"It saddens me that the rintic have forced this male-diction upon the Eltepsu," said Manista. He approached the thin black prison bars adjacent to Taukin. "For ulti-cycles, the suvanth have had to resort to less-than-ideal measures to come by agrum. Trading with those who were willing to trade, taking from those who weren't. Why, before we had a steady supply from this Eltepsu, some had resorted to taking the bloodlet-ting. As you know, one can survive an entire cycle on merely a drop, but when I came to rule, I decided a change was needed to our methods of acquiring the life-sustaining liquid. We needed a steady agrum source, and the only way to ensure our survival was to interrupt the normal cycle of life and take an Eltepsu for our own. Surely you understand our predicament and do not judge us for this travesty, desperation drove us to take action," and he looked at left his hand, which was missing the last two digits, "Desperation can drive us to do the detestable."

Taukin stared at Manista's nubs and absorbed everything he said, but didn't respond. He only stared at the fractured Eltepsu, who in a debilitated state mustered enough strength to praise Hobaja Vael. The Eltepsu finished the prayer, but stood motionless in the center of the cell. Tufts of dirty auburn hair hung over Cuvsor's large despondent yellow and green eyes and Taukin wished that he could help the weakened Eltepsu and at that par-tem, he also wished he hadn't failed to leave the proper trail of sassa root for the garandos to follow. Knowing that now, he alone was responsible for rescuing Cuvsor made Taukin feel hopeless and feeble, more so than any rintic ever made him feel. His sadness made his skin deep blue and he came to look more like a darkened suvanth. The Eltepsu, motionless and quiet, stared at Taukin as though he couldn't tell if he was friend or foe.

"You must free the Eltepsu," said Taukin as his pigment changed to a light orange. Manista looked at Taukin, and his ears hung on the next words. "I'll help you if I see my mother and you free the Eltepsu. It must be both conditions."

Manista stared at the shaggy Eltepsu with gentle eyes and replied, "There will be no need to imprison anymore Eltepsu, the suvanth will be free, and it shall be as you request." Taukin nodded his head in agreement. "You ask for much Taukin, but you do not yet know what I require. What if my demand is too much for you or you are unable to perform the necessary tasks?"

"I will do what it takes my Lord," replied Taukin showing conviction.

Manista smiled and said, "Then let us go see Onestonia."

CHAPTER 8
INSIGHT OF THE GODS

Taukin entered the confined offshoot where Manista had pelt maps of Onestonia strewn about and room for only one table half the size of the table in Manista's quarters. Manista searched for the map of interest and found it bundled along with others in the corner of the small space. Taukin gathered, from the musty odor, that this was not a chamber that was used very often and was only surpassed by Manista's odiferous scent. "Ah yes, here it is," said Manista as he spread the map out and pinned the corners with jade-colored statues of his likeness. "Do you recognize this region?"

Taukin responded as he pointed, "Those are the Uru mountains, which lie west of Binesmir, and to the south, Olin Fell, the largest body of water in Onestonia."

Manista pointed to the south quadrant of Olin Fell where a small onyx object protruded through the shimmering representation of the Fell. "And do you know what this is?"

"The crystal dome," answered Taukin.

"And do you know what resides inside the crystal dome?" asked Manista.

"The light cipher."

"You are not lacking in knowledge. Yes, the dome is impenetrable nionan crystal, and that is where the Basatab is located, and that is why I need you to retrieve it for me."

Taukin looked quizzically at Manista. "You want me to retrieve the Basatab?"

"You will recover it, I have no doubt," said the suvanth leader assuredly.

"How is this even possible? The waters are frigid, the distance from the shore is great, the light cipher is guarded by the Staleans, and I cannot breath underwater nor swim."

A devious grin appeared on Manista's face, and he replied, "You will learn to summon." Taukin's skin briefly pulsed before he was able to force it back to the normal shade and pattern. "In the lumeren, you begin training, and when you are ready, you must depart for Olin Fell." Manista paused to let Taukin take in what was just said, and then he continued. "Now, let's enjoy the rest of the quiesce, you are in for an awakening, a glimpse of what it is like to be a god." Manista and Taukin left the map-reading chamber, Taukin's skin wanting to burst with desire, but he held back.

A short while later, a glingus removed the sackcloth from Taukin's head and the bright light of Manista's chambers temporarily blinded him. The mysterious female that served their meal earlier had returned. "Prepare a pipe and bring us some more wine," commanded the suvanth leader. Taukin looked forward to the fragrant malpwa wine. Manista offered his smoking pipe to Taukin. Taukin, surprised to share such a personal item with the leader of the suvanth, the feared enemy of the rintic, who with each passing par-tem seemed more like a respectable and humble leader than the Carth tribe leader Hiko did. The malpwa wine was better than before, this time it was cooler and had a tinge of bitterness, which helped offset the sweetness. Taukin took the long pipe with both hands, cupping the shank and guiding the bit to his wine-laced lips. Time seemed to slow and then speed up again, and finally Taukin lost track of time all together. Other suvanth joined them while a suvanth near the chamber corner strummed a relaxing and somewhat entrancing melody on an instrument unknown to Taukin. Lifemates of Manista and other females appeared along with males of higher order, designated by the aesthetic, colorful robes they wore, each bowed to Taukin and Taukin returned the comity. Two young females approached Taukin, one delicately placed her soft hand on Taukin's shoulder and the other around his arm. Taukin's skin swirled with various colors.

Glingus came and partook of the wine, but not of the smoke. One goblet of wine was enough for their small bodies to succumb to the drink, and they would dance and be merry, and sometimes fight each other, all to the pleasure of their leader. Manista reserved his pipe for Taukin and himself only. Manista, whose tolerance for the hannes leaf and wine was great, observed Taukin and made sure he had enough to enjoy the quiesce activities, but not too much so as to affect his training. Manista's lifemates lay on the pillows next to Manista and laughed at the inane acts of the succumbed glingus. Taukin laughed as well until Drami Sol appeared from one of the entrances to the chamber. Her sudden appearance drew the attention of all in the room, even that of the wrestling glingus, as well as the ire of Manista's lifemates. Moans and hissing were heard from behind Taukin. He turned and watched as the pack of lifemates shot evil glares and offensive sounding words that were unfamiliar at the young suvanth. All except the eldest took part, which was the same suvanth that laid out his meal earlier.

Drami Sol paused at the stone fixture from which food and wine were prepared and searched the chamber for kind eyes. She stopped when she found Taukin, who smiled not only out of sympathy, but also out of interest. The drunken glingus continued their shenanigans and with wobbly legs, Taukin made his way to Drami Sol. Drami Sol grabbed Taukin's violet hand and brought him to Manista. "My Lord, may I take Taukin away from you? I won't keep him long."

Manista, feeling spirited, asked, "And what are your plans with him?"

"With your permission, I would like to show him something that cannot be seen from the surface, I would like to show him the stars of Sheol Balla."

Manista turned his head to the left and partially to the right, silencing the chamber guests with a simple motion. The room went from a joyous and jubilant celebration to one of grave silence and all attention shifted to Drami Sol and Taukin. Manista's toothy smile disappeared, and he then turned his attention to the beautiful being that stood before him. He looked suspiciously at Drami Sol, closely reading her body language and color and face for any sign of falsehood. Manista's gaze locked on Taukin whose skin wanted to blaze bright yellow for no reason other than the darkness of Manista's eyes causing his trepidation. The quiet trisian taking flight would have sounded like a terrible storm in the stillness of the chamber.

"My Lord, I have troubled you with my request?" And even though she asked in a non-threatening way, this was a bold statement and Manista's lifemates changed their hue to pure white with waves of brown stripes to signal betrayal. Manista took notice, but discounted their visual message as mere jealousy. Her beauty put others at a disadvantage and Manista was captivated by and susceptible to her. He also didn't want to be seen as insecure, for insecurity spread faster than fear and could lead to colpus, an overthrow of the suvanth leader. Manista, with a sweeping motion, waved his open hand in front of his grinning face and replied, "I see no harm in your request, and I assume you see no harm in having a glingus escort you and young Taukin to ensure that you both find your way back?"

Drami Sol closed her eyes and bowed deeply at the waist, "As you say my Lord."

Manista called for one of the sober glingus standing next to a portal to come to him. Manista leaned forward and whispered into the ear of the glingus, "Keep them close. I want them back before the next par-cycle."

The obedient glingus nodded and replied, "Understood my Lord," and moved with his jingling lantern toward the exit.

Taukin had some difficulty maneuvering through the bustling great chamber. The combination of scurrying suvanth and his delayed reaction forced Drami Sol to take his arm and lead him through. And despite the fact he had succumbed to the wine, Taukin maintained his skin color so as not to give away his attraction to her. They made their way to a discreet tunnel that led upward with the prodding glingus and his lantern close behind. The slope was steep, and Taukin occasionally lost his grip, but Drami Sol was there to catch him. They eventually moved down and came to a split in the tunnel. The area was dark with no movement, no suvanth running past, and full of silence except for the clanking of the ever-present lantern swinging close behind. Taukin stumbled and almost went into the tunnel on the left, but the glingus spoke in his gruff and inimical voice, "You wouldn't like what's down there. I suggest you stay to the right."

Taukin moved to the right tunnel and quietly asked Drami Sol, "What's down there?"

Drami Sol replied, "Corpses and those who make them. The perished are fed to the Kravaes."

"Kravaes?"

"They were suvanth a long time ago, but have mutated to something else, something that is more creature than being." Taukin cringed at these words. Drami Sol pulled Taukin along now at a faster pace and their escort was slowly being separated from them and his lantern light showed an occasional sandaled foot, and then only the tunnel floor.

"Slow down. Where are you?" cried the glingus. There was a faint scuffling of feet against the rock walkway. The lantern soon revealed another split in the tunnel, both paths leading to the location that Drami Sol led Taukin. Frustrated, the escort went left thinking it would be an easier path to traverse with his stubby legs. Drami Sol called out to the glingus but heard no response and saw no light.

Taukin's eyes widened when he saw the infinite number of multi-colored iridescent organisms that lined the high ceiling. "Amazing," he said softly as his eyes scanned the vast display of lights. There, at the edge of the opening to a chamber as large as the main chamber that the suvanth occupied, Drami Sol pulled Taukin close before he could say another word.

"Taukin, you must listen very carefully to me. I need your help. Promise me, that you will help me."

Taukin nodded his head in agreement and asked, "Help you with what?"

Drami Sol's voice heightened, "Promise to Hobaja Vael that you will help me no matter what."

Taukin's skin changed upon hearing a suvanth use Hobaja Vael's name and instantly he knew how serious the situation had become. "I promise to Hobaja Vael, that I will help you."

"Manista plans to take me as a lifemate."

Taukin turned blue and feeling defeated, said, "So you want me to help you become his lifemate?"

"That's the opposite of what I want!" said Drami

Sol, frustrated as her skin went yellow with large blue ovals as she slapped his shoulder. "I'll be imprisoned in his chamber. He'll make me his slave, like the others." Startled, Taukin pulled his face away and she continued, "I refuse to live that way, that's why I plan to escape from Manista. I need you to help me get to a safe place. A place where the suvanth cannot find me."

"Where?"

"Somewhere far from Manista's reach. The Carth forest."

"You can't stay in the Carth forest. I've lived there my entire life and I'm still considered an outsider, even with rintic blood. You are pure suvanth and would be imprisoned as soon as you were discovered."

A trace amount of light highlighted half of Drami Sol's charming face and her eye was cupped by a tear. "My heart belongs to one from your tribe. You must help me."

Taukin was shocked at her admission and the story of his mother and father came to mind. He felt compassion for her but his curiosity burned for the knowledge of who the mysterious treasonous tribesman could be.

"I saw you in the forest, why do you need my help?"

"Manista became suspicious after my last journey and won't let me leave now. I'm imprisoned already."

"I can get you to the Carth forest, but I can't help what happens to you by hands of the rintic."

"That's all I ask of you," said Drami Sol and she kissed Taukin on his smooth cheek. Taukin's skin flushed gold and his attraction to her grew, but deep inside he still had feelings for Soyha whose name he had long lifted in prayer to Hobaja Vael.

"Is the one who has captured your affection the same one that you've visited in the forest?" asked Taukin shyly.

"It is," said Drami Sol, smitten.

"It's Keel, isn't it?"

"Keel?" she said, unaware of his brother.

Taukin's face contorted and his skin morphed light red. "Who then?" asked Taukin, so consumed by her response that he leaned in close enough to pick up her sweet scent.

Before she could answer, the brusque glingus appeared from below and tugged on Taukin's dangling leg. "Get down here, both of you!" Taukin quickly dropped down from the tunnel to the stone floor of the chamber followed by Drami Sol. "What have you two been talking about?" asked the nosy and nervous glingus.

"Drami Sol was explaining this wonder of illumination above our heads."

The glingus grunted and replied, "Are you sure there was nothing else?"

"Quite sure master glingus," said Taukin convincingly.

"You've seen what you came here for, it's time to return," replied the guide. He hobbled back toward the cave entrance and picked up the lamp and moved toward the way in which he came with Taukin and Drami Sol close behind. As the glingus walked into the portal, he turned and motioned with his hand to come closer. Drami Sol and Taukin leaned in close so that the light from the lamp painted their faces orange. "Not a word of our separation to Manista, or I'll tell him that you two were plotting treason. Understand?"

"Yes," came a unified response from them both.

"Now let's get a move on and no more talking." Drami Sol led the way with the glingus in between her and Taukin so that they couldn't be separated again, and that's how they remained until they reached Manista's chamber.

The next lumeren, a loud clanging from a metal rod against the bottom of a metal lamp filled Taukin's still chamber. Taukin awoke, groggy from the previous quiesce's drink and activities. "I'm awake, you can stop making that dreadful clamoring," said Taukin loudly. Pecril pulled the pelt cover from Taukin and pulled his violet arm to sit him upright. Pecril pushed Taukin from the side with his functional arm. "I'll get up, you don't have to push," said Taukin somewhat flustered with the aggressive glingus. Pecril moved to light the torch in the room, while Taukin dressed. Taukin had only doused his head once with the cool water flowing through the stone wall before Pecril tugged at his robe. "I know, Manista is ready to see me," said Taukin, and he grabbed the cloth hood and placed it over his wet head.

The journey took longer than normal and Taukin could tell from the warm air and the humidity that he was no longer near Manista's quarters. At one point there was a steep descent and Pecril removed Taukin's hood so he could keep his footing as he went feet first and dragged his hands behind him along the gritty rock. At the bottom waited Manista in a well-lit area much larger than his quarters, but smaller than the main hub of Sheol Balla. "Leave us," said Manista in a stern manner toward Pecril. The minuscule suvanth ascended with surprising speed, and his light disappeared.

"Taukin, your life is about to change. What you will learn is a secret that only the gods and I know. This secret cannot be told to any tribesman, regardless of allegiance, for fear of misuse of this gift and certain calamity amongst all living things of Onestonia. Once you tell one being how to harness this ability, they will no longer care about you, you will have no sway over others, you will no longer be respected as you once were. It is imperative that you keep this secret between you and me. Those who you trust the most will be the first to betray you Taukin, always remember that." Taukin bowed to Manista in a slow and deliberate manner to show his concurrence.

Manista held a malpwa seed-sized object in front of Taukin and said, "Do you know what this is?"

Taukin studied its fragile black skin. "No my Lord," said Taukin.

"It is a pych pod. They grow only in the darkest most humid environments, which is why the rintic have never learned of this fungus."

"What do you do with it?"

"Consume it. The taste is quite unpleasant I assure you, but when you are hungry, starving to the point that you will eat anything," Manista paused to stare at the two nubs where his fingers once were, then continued, "they taste like the finest fruits in all of Onestonia." Unease fell over Taukin once he learned what happened to Manista's missing fingers. Manista returned from his distant stare and continued, "Inside this pych pod there is tahmill, the mineral that Seranphopids thrive on."

"Seranphopids?" replied Taukin.

"Seranphopids are the creatures created by Hobaja Vael to construct planets and stars. Onestonia was made by such creatures."

"You're a believer?"

"I wasn't…but now I am," said Manista.

"Seranphopids remain on Onestonia now?"

"On…and in Onestonia, and other worlds," said Manista.

"I have never seen such creatures."

"They are here in the air, as well as water. They are so small that we cannot see them individually; only when they come together, can we see their existence. Let me show you." And Manista crumbled the dry pych pod and placed it in his gaping mouth. His head pitched to the side, an involuntary reaction to the extreme rancidness of the fungal growth. His head rolled back, around, and back to the original upright position as he forced the pod down his pale, vein-ridden neck. Instantly his exposed skin showed light. It was the color of his skin, but was illuminated more and more with each passing par-tem. Taukin stumbled backward, nervous about what was happening.

"You see, the seranphopids cannot help but be attracted to me, to the combination of tahmill and agrum that fill my vessels. The agrum intensifies the scent and potency of tahmill. The more agrum you consume, the more seranphopids are summoned. They feed from you, giving you control over them for a short time. They will serve you as long as you possess the tahmill and it still fills their bodies." Manista loosened his robe and clothing exposing the pure white under-cloth and his slender skeletal frame draped with pale, bluish-gray skin. It was as if his deep violet robe was replaced with a glowing cloth of grayish seranphopids. Manista closed his eyes and tilted his head back and rose off the warm stone floor. Taukin stood amazed, not believing what he was seeing. Hovering at least two rintic high, Manista faced Taukin and opened his black eyes. Manista luminesced brightly against the liver-colored cavern wall. "Watch and witness the power of summoning," said Manista, and with that stones, small and large, surrounded by glowing seranphopids, simul-taneously lifted off the ground. Manista, still hovering high above Taukin, moved all rocks to one side of the cavern and then back to the opposite side and had them orbit the central nucleus of stones before lowering them back to the floor. Manista's glowing feet met the floor and he was once again level with Taukin.

Manista opened his mouth and allowed the feasting seranphopids to pour down his gullet into the deep recesses of his core. A disturbing glimmer was emitted like lamplight shining through the tunnels of Sheol Balla. Suddenly Taukin glowed the same color as Manista and he was instantly lifted up. Taukin's arms flailed and his legs wriggled and kicked and he yelled out, "I'm not ready. Set me down!" Manista obliged, after moving him back and forth as he did with the rocks par-tems before. Taukin hunkered against the grainy cavern floor and the glow left him and returned to Manista, who laughed at the folly. Taukin, still stimulated by the thrill and folly of what just happened, joined in on the laughter.

"Now you try," commanded Manista. Taukin's legs shook a bit to gain footing and he received a small onyx pych pod from Manista. Pitch black, thin-skinned, and hollow was the only way Taukin thought to describe the pod. His violet palm enveloped the nut-sized fungus, then he crushed it as Manista had done and brought it to his salivating tongue, which instantly dried upon contact. He scraped his dry tongue with his upper teeth and spit the contents out onto the cavern floor. "You must overcome the taste," said Manista. Taukin took a deep breath in an effort to counteract the gag reflex that was sure to succeed once he tried to swallow the pod. He opened his mouth and tossed the pych pod as far back as he could. He hoped it was crushed enough to avoid mastication, but soon discovered that the dry fungus required chewing so it could be ingested. Taukin lurched, and the odious taste overcame and his body ejected the crushed pych pod and the contents of its belly.

Frustrated, Manista demanded, "Try again," as he handed Taukin another pod. Taukin regained his composure and crushed another pych pod and gently placed it onto his tongue. The vile taste and involuntary reaction was the same, but instead of vomiting, Manista summoned the seranphopids to force the pych pod down Taukin's gullet. With no unpleasant taste in his mouth, Taukin swallowed hard then stumbled backward and studied his hands, which slowly luminesced a brighter version of his violet skin. And as Manista had done, Taukin removed his white cloth top to see the seranphopids swarm his skin and feast upon the fluids pulsing throughout his body. The sensation was that of a stinging compression surrounding his exposed skin, one that neither troubled nor appeased Taukin, but felt like a tight pelt swaddle that bit ever so slightly at his flesh. Manista spoke, "Now they are yours to command."

Taukin pointed to the nearest stone and spoke aloud, "Seranphopids, lift that rock." And the creatures covered the stone in purple light and lifted the stone as high as Taukin pointed. His finger traced the path that the seranphopids followed, eventually landing back on the cavern floor.

"This time do not speak, use your mind to control and your eyes to move them. They move as swiftly as your thoughts," said Manista. Taukin concentrated in order to view all visible stones in the cavern and place seranphopids around each one. Taukin envisioned the rocks being held high, close to the cavern ceiling and so it was. Manista was curious to know if one could summon seranphopids away from their controller. So Manista, without Taukin's knowledge, stepped back behind and out of Taukin's sight and summoned the creatures to him and watched as their luminescence changed from vivid violet to bright pale blue. Manista's delight grew in the gaining of this knowledge and ability, and he released the summoned creatures from his control. Unaware of Manista's action, Taukin imagined the rocks stacked largest at the bottom and smallest at the top against the far wall and the glowing rocks moved instantaneously against the wall opposite from Taukin and Manista and in the exact order he envisioned. Taukin summoned the infinitesimal creatures to return the stones to their original location and order. He stood staring at his brightly lit hands that started to dim, twisting them front and back, and then his control over them faded. Weakened by the experience, Taukin fell to his knees.

Manista clasped his elongated hands around Taukin's exposed shoulders and helped him to his feet, but Taukin was too weak to stand on his own. His hairless violet head, dull once again, hung low. Manista put his arm around Taukin and Taukin's arm over his bare bony shoulder, "Such is the effect of summoning. Your body can only offer so much to the seranphopids. Too much feeding can leave you frail. Come, let's return to our quarters to regain our strength."

Taukin awoke on his own, weakened, and slowly stood next to his bed and removed his white top in a failed attempt to summon. "Has the tahmill gone already? Was it a dream?" The residual bitter taste of tahmill lingered in his dry mouth. His dry lips gulped the water from the channel and after he had his fill he tried to summon again. There was nothing, no luminescence, and no movement of objects. The thrill of summoning overtook his thoughts and for a while he had forgotten that he was there for a mission. A lone torch flickered and grabbed his attention and he suddenly remembered the sassa root that hadn't been planted yet. The plan to help the rintic seemed like a fleeting thought compared to his experiences with the suvanth who embraced him as their own. A faint shuffling sound came from the chamber portal and Taukin quickly returned to his bed and pretended to sleep. Pecril appeared next to Taukin and using his lamp, moved up and down Taukin's covered body, examining him. Taukin wanted to peek to see what was happening, but didn't want to risk being discovered. The sweet suvanth scent was peculiarly more appealing this time. Pecril set the lamp down and placed his only functioning hand on Taukin's shoulder and shook him. Taukin pretended to awaken, acting surprised that Pecril was there. Taukin was even more surprised to see the mysterious female that had served him his food and drink in Manista's quarters. "You?" said Taukin, surprised that Manista's lifemate was in his room.

"Quiet," she said as she raised her hand and turned to listen down the tunnel for any sound of movement. She moved in closer to Taukin, her large, amber-colored eyes locked with Taukin's eyes. "My name is Valla. Pecril brought me this pouch of roots that he found here in your chamber."

Taukin's skin turned golden, and he replied, "It's not mine."

"What's the purpose of this root? This came from you," she said hurriedly.

"I've never seen it before," replied Taukin, whose skin flickered a multitude of colors. Taukin moved toward the exit, curious as to who or what was just outside the opening, but Pecril latched on to his robe, stopping him from moving. "I want to see what's out there," said Taukin insistently.

Valla quickly responded, "There's no time. We must know if we are in danger. You can trust us. This will not go beyond this chamber. Taukin we are your blood. I am sister to Luspa, your mother."

Taukin's eyes widened at the mention of his mother and his skin turned dark auburn with gentle yellow slivers, but he stepped back, leery of this meeting. His eyes glistened and he asked, "Where is she?"

Valla replied, "Luspa left Sheol Balla almost two Febus-cycles ago and she hasn't been heard from since. Taukin, I want to tell you so much about your lineage, but I am limited on time. I'll be punished if I'm discovered here. I need to know what I must do to protect my son," looking at Pecril. Taukin's eyebrows raised and his skin changed to a light red. "He cannot defend himself. I beg you tell me what this root is for," pleaded Valla, her skin violet like Taukin's normal hue expressing her fear. Taukin stood there stoic and with normal hue, completely blank.

"Come Pecril, he's like all the other rintic," she said.

"I can only tell you that when the time comes, you'll know, but you have my word that no harm will come to either of you because of it," replied Taukin, purposely avoiding a direct answer in order to test her motives.

"If you say no harm will come to us, then I believe you," replied Valla looking at Taukin with slight suspicion, her fear and Taukin's concerns of trust assuaged for the par-tem. "You can hide the pouch in this chamber until you need it. Pecril, show him and be quick about it," said Valla. Pecril waddled over to a small fissure where the stone wall and floor met, near the back of the chamber where light was scarce. Pecril moved Taukin's ruck to the side and slid the tan pouch into the crack far enough so that not a strand of root nor pouch was visible, then moved Taukin's ruck in front of the crack. "You will be requested soon. Wash up first, your smell is like that of Manista after he…" her words trailed off as a strange look came across her face. Valla's eyes squinted with awareness and then she and her son turned and shuffled toward the exit.

"Wait," said Taukin. He moved closer to them and spoke softly. "Do you recognize this?" asked Taukin as he handed the shimmering suvanth bauble to Valla.

"The bauble of baubles? How did you come by this?" she asked in a grave manner.

"It was given to me by a rintic who received it from an Unknown in the Carth forest," said Taukin.

She gently shook the bauble, bringing focus to it. "This bauble belongs in the founders vault," said Valla, her skin pulsing with confusion.

"Why would a rintic receive such a bauble?" asked Taukin.

"The answer lies in the vault. If Manista discovers you have this…" said Valla as she carefully handed the bauble back to Taukin.

"I must go to the vault," said Taukin, his desire to understand the bauble's purpose driving him.

"Only Manista can access the vault for there is a

long open vastness between the vault and the tunnel leading to it," she said.

"How can I find the vault?" asked Taukin.

"If we're discovered helping you, we would be put to death and you would too. Now we must go," said Valla as she pulled Pecril out into the blackness of the tunnel, but right before Pecril disappeared into the darkness he glanced back at Taukin with a fiery look of duty and nodded.

Taukin stood motionless as if the seranphopids held his body in place. He spoke to himself, "I have to hide the bauble!" His head twisted around the chamber knowing hiding places did not exist, except where the sassa root was now hidden. He crouched down, pressing his finger into the fissure, moving his finger around until he felt the drawstring and pulled it out. Taukin carefully tried placing the jewel-encrusted bauble into the safety of the crack, but no matter which way he turned it and twisted it, it would not fit. He paced around the dimly lit room searching for any place that could serve as a hiding place, but the fissure was the only worthy location. The tan pouch of sassa root went back into the slim crack and Taukin went to the water channel and drank its cool water. A splash of chilled water went over his hairless head and down his neck as he turned his head back and forth, rubbing his neck. His eyes went to the channel opening, which was roughly the size of his fist. A flickering light coming from the chamber opening caught his attention and his skin went yellow. Instincts kicked in and he placed the suvanth bauble into the darkness of the water channel and then went back to his bedding and raised his knees up over the side with his hands propping him up on the edge of the pillows. His hue changed back to violet right before they appeared.

Hardly a dole par-tem had passed since Valla and Pecril were there when Drami Sol's gentle voice filled the quarters with a soothing song. Taukin turned to her. "Where is Pecril?" he asked.

"The master sent me to prepare you for his presence. Again, you have rested long and you smell of rotten carcass. He wishes to visit with you in his quarters," said Drami Sol in an unusually loud and proper voice.

Confused, Taukin stood and met her at the water channel. "I've thought about your request, and I have a plan," Taukin said.

He moved in closer, and she whispered, "Careful what you say, there are listening ears nearby." Taukin looked at the portal and saw an unfamiliar glingus standing with his lamp, watching Drami Sol's every action. Drami Sol continued in her loud voice, "Sit so that I may bathe you and prepare you for Manista's honorable presence." Taukin obliged and sat on the pallet of pillows, and reluctantly removed his robe and top half. Drami Sol gently dabbed a cool wet cloth against Taukin's warm forehead and passed it around one ear to the next and across his muscular, now golden-colored back. Drami Sol then turned Taukin around so that the glingus could only see the back of Taukin's head. Drami Sol leaned closer and in her lowest voice said, "Tell me what I must do," then moved around Taukin so that the glingus wouldn't become suspicious.

Taukin, in the same spirit, spoke softly, "I have strands of root that must be planted from the confines of the Eltepsu through the tunnels that lead to where the lower Kappa River and Binesmir mountains meet. Do you know the tunnel?"

Drami Sol moved around so that Taukin's head obscured the view of the glingus and continued the cleaning. "Yes, where is the root?"

"To my right in the crack at the base of the chamber wall," replied Taukin and continued, "Plant the root after I depart for my mission. Look for rintic soldiers that infiltrate the pit in the coming tem-cycles, you can help them find Cuvsor and upon my return we'll help you escape. Tell the rintic that I sent you to help them find Cuvsor."

"How will they know they can trust me?"

"Show them the wooden Eltepsu bauble from my coverings and tell them it was given by the Eltepsu named Lantia while with Captain Avent and General Meraco at the Caverns of the Eltepsu."

"Will they trust me?"

Taukin locked with her cerulean eyes and said, "I don't even know if they trust me anymore, but you must try."

"What's taking so long?" grumbled the gravelly voiced glingus and he continued, "The master is waiting."

Drami Sol spoke, "I am done." Taukin covered himself with clean, pure-white garments and led by the minute glingus guide, they made their way through the maze of passages to Manista's quarters.

"Depart, I want to be alone with Taukin," Manista said to Drami Sol and the glingus guide, and waited until they were well away before speaking, "Taukin, I'm curious about how you feel?"

"I feel as if all strength I had has been stolen from me."

"You allowed the seranphopids to take too much of you."

"Why didn't you warn me that they could weaken me so?"

"You needed to know what they are capable of and to learn your limits. This is crucial for your mission. You must control how much of you they take."

"I can do better."

"You will…do better. Now, eat and restore your strength then try again."

Manista's patience seemed to be growing shorter with each passing tem-cycle, thought Taukin.

"Remember, tell none that you have learned to summon."

Taukin thought on this statement, and then shook his head in agreeance.

Manista called for his servant. Valla appeared and Taukin avoided eye contact with her, but he couldn't control his color and his skin lightened. Manista took notice and faced Taukin asking, "Does my servant make you nervous?"

Taukin, facing away from her, shook his head, "No my Lord."

"Look upon her face," commanded Manista. Taukin's eyes slowly traversed the chamber until locking with her large amber eyes. It was all he could do to keep his skin from lightening even more. "Does she remind you of a tribesman you know?" asked Manista, probing Taukin further.

"None my Lord," said Taukin as his skin darkened.

Manista nodded and redirected his attention to Valla, "Have you any knowledge of Taukin before now?"

"Only from earlier whilst serving him my Lord," said Valla maintaining her poise. The hushed trickling of water in the channel seemed as loud as the roar of the lower Kappa River as Manista traced the expressions of both Taukin and Valla.

"Prepare our food," said Manista as he ushered Taukin to the table. She served them meats, breads, and fruits as she had before, except no malpwa wine and Taukin obliged as his hunger had grown tremendously since his summoning lesson. Manista sent Valla away with a flick on his long fingers then said, "This tem-cycle I will teach you the most vital control. You will learn how to summon the seranphopids so that they transport you, but not completely drain you. This ability is critical to your mission. While in the waters of Olin Fell, you must summon in order to move through the Fell." Manista placed two pych pods in Taukin's hands to allow for this feat to be accomplished. "Keep these close and concealed, none shall know you have these, not even your escorts."

Escorts? thought Taukin.

"It is essential that you consume a full Elder vial of agrum and ingest one pych pod before entering the water, and one pod after you have the Basatab to make it back to shore. Failing to do so will mean death. Understand this ample amount of agrum is dangerous, not even the Umgara consume as much, but the seranphopids will drain it from you as you move to and from the crystal dome and as such, reduce the risk of harm. The distance from shore to the dome is too great to swim alone. Without performing these two acts, you cannot accomplish your task."

"How will I gain entrance to the dome?" asked Taukin.

"To the Staleans present an offering of agrum as their recompense for protecting the Basatab as is the custom between the rintic and Staleans. They should receive you as the retriever selected by the rintic and provide you a sherob creature so you can breath underwater. If the gesture fails, Swinzal will provide you a sherob and you will have to rely on your summoning ability to retrieve the Basatab before the Staleans seal the crystal dome closed."

"Seal the dome closed?" asked Taukin, a look of concern strewn about his face.

"That is why it is necessary for you to master summoning. There is another challenge that you could face, one even more challenging than the Staleans." Taukin's face grew even more distressed and he swallowed hard.

"If the Staleans feel deceived they may choose to release the beasts of the shadow waters. If this happens do not try to fight them. Your only chance of survival is to move faster than they do." Taukin's skin blazed yellow.

"Do not fear Taukin, your ability to summon will see you through. Make sure you are aware of what surrounds you at all times. Now it's time you learn your final lesson," said Manista who stood and called for a glingus to escort Taukin to the training chamber. Taukin's skin returned to its normal hue finding comfort in Manista's words, and sensing relief in the security and certainty of his newly acquired godly ability.

After the final lesson, Manista allowed Taukin to walk back with him, still blinded, through the twisting and rising and falling tunnels that led to Manista's quarters. As they walked back, Manista steered Taukin and said, "You are ready Taukin, I have no doubt that you will retrieve the Basatab."

Taukin asked, "How did you come to learn the secret of summoning?"

Manista replied, "Ahh. This is the one story that I shall keep to myself. It is a tale of deceit and pain best left untold."

"We haven't discussed when I will meet my mother or the release of the Eltepsu."

"You are correct. We haven't. I needed to see that you were capable of summoning and now that you have proven yourself, we can discuss the details of the plan. Once you retrieve the Basatab, you will return where you entered Olin Fell, by the horn of Cerona, you will be escorted to a meeting point nearby, and there you will be reunited with your mother."

"And the Eltepsu?"

"You have my word, upon your return to Sheol Balla with the Basatab, I will release the Eltepsu.

"Taukin, I know in your heart you feel compelled to return to the Carth forest, it is where you were raised and you consider it home, but know that if you return there you will be treated differently. Those that tolerated you will scorn you, and those who disliked you will have enmity for you simply because they will feel betrayed by your disappearance and the actions that took place before you left. Their distrust of you grows every tem-cycle that you are gone. You could easily rule over them since acquiring your newly found gift, but ruling by instilling fear is much more difficult than ruling by earned respect. We need not walk this path any longer," said Manista, and through the rugged cloth sack, Taukin could see the blue light emitted by the seranphopids and he and Manista quickly floated through the tunnels until they arrived at their destination.

Floating was a strange sensation, one that was uncomfortable at first, but later elicited excitement to the point where it was desired. Taukin's mind focused on how easily Manista controlled the creatures without waning and as for as long as he wished. A hint of jealousy flowed through Taukin, envious of Manista's summoning superiority. Exotic incense filled the sackcloth, they were at Manista's chamber. All bustling and talking stopped and Taukin requested the removal of his head covering. There was no reply, Taukin's curiosity grew and he reached for the sackcloth when he felt two tugs on his robe. Taukin moved his hands back down and remained blinded. Pecril took Taukin's hand and led him away and into another series of tunnels.

A feeling of warmth came over Taukin and the familiar sound of stirring suvanth came from below. Pecril brought him to Manista who was standing at the base of a point high above the main hub of the pit. The platform extended outward over the main hub of the pit like a narrow rigid tongue in a wide, cavernous mouth. The sound of thrumming voices all around him grew louder. Manista spoke, "Remove his blind." Pecril tugged on Taukin's robe and Taukin obliged by taking a knee, steadying himself with his hands against the smooth stone walkway. With his long arm, Pecril pulled the dusty cloth sack from Taukin's head. Taukin, even though balanced by his arms and legs, hunkered lower as if he was avoiding a midriff swing of a long sword. The combination of light, height, and incredible mass of gathered suvanth overwhelmed Taukin. Manista's toothy smile appeared and he said, "Rise Taukin, this is your tribe, your followers." Taukin moved his arms outward for balance as if the ground moved below him and slowly rose up. Behind him were two Hannon Lite guards posed as still as the god stones of the Peah mounds. Manista motioned for Taukin to come closer to the edge of the rocky overhang.

Manista faced the crowd and spoke loudly, "Tribe, the time has come for us to be freed from our prison!" A roar of cheers filled the cavern and rang in Taukin's ears, making him cower down once more. Manista continued, "No longer will we have to suffer this life of darkness and solitude. No longer will we have to scour the land for our provisions. Agrum will flow abundantly and be available to all suvanth! The one who will help us gain our freedom stands before you. He is Taukin, your tribal brother! Bow before him!" The legion of suvanth went to both knees and bowed repeatedly to both Taukin and their master. Taukin's fear turned to pride and it swelled inside him. And it was here in Sheol Balla, among the suvanth, that he found his reverence, the respect that he so longed for from the rintic, but never received. "Now go prepare yourself for your journey," said Manista as he motioned for Pecril to lead him back to the guest chamber.

Pecril's sweaty hand shook in Taukin's larger hand as they wound through the network of tunnels alone. Pecril paused, lowered the flame in the lamp, then hurriedly continued, pulling Taukin at almost a full-on run. Running blind felt like running behind Swinzal in the darkened tunnels when Taukin first arrived to Sheol Balla, he was cautious but without fear. A cool flow of air came over Taukin as they slowed and Pecril urged him to lower his head. When the sack was removed Taukin asked, "Where are we?" Pecril increased the flame to full brightness, illuminating the surrounding tunnel opening, then aimed the lantern toward the black void, across which was the founders vault. "Thank you," said Taukin with his hand on Pecril's shoulder. They had arrived at the large opening that seemingly had no bottom, but was covered at the same height as the tunnel in which they stood. Blackness encompassed the gulf, but Pecril's lantern revealed the distance from tunnel to vault was great. Shimmering flashes twinkled from the open vault, no doubt gifts and hoards from the suvanth conquests. Taukin removed a pych pod without Pecril taking notice and slipped it into his salivating mouth. He struggled to ingest, but with the concern of discovery by Manista increasing with every par-tem, Taukin's eyes watered as the bitter fungus traveled across his tasters and down his gullet with a quick lurch.

"I'll be quick," said Taukin. Pecril tugged on his robe and motioned as if he was taking items from the vault and placing them in his coverings. Taukin asked, "You want something from the vault?" With his long arm, Pecril motioned as if he were picking up items from the vault and placing them in his pocket, then motioned from his opposite shoulder down to this waist and shook his head. "Do not take anything, I under-stand," said Taukin as his skin began a dull violet glow. Pecril stepped back into the tunnel in fear of Taukin's luminescence. Silently, Taukin floated across the chasm with haste, knowing the minute amount of agrum coursing through his body would only quench the seranphopid's thirst for a short while. Taukin relin-quished the control over the creatures and examined the contents of the open vault. Elaborately decorated charms and goblets lined the black stone shelves, and silver-etched swords and jewel-encrusted charms were strewn about the piles of silver and golden coins about the floor. Taukin made his way into one of the many twisting coves of the stone vault and had it not been for the ambient light from Pecril's lantern, it would have been as black as the tunnels leading to the pit.

Suvanth tribesman baubles embellished with a variety of jewels and markings unknown to Taukin were neatly aligned on carved shelves all around the inlet. He traced the baubles around starting at the top right wall and noticed the minute physical evolution of the figures from the first tall, strapping rintic-colored being to the latter being, shorter with notched backs and lighter skin and the last bauble was a reflection of Manista. Taukin spoke to himself, "Suvanth leaders, the first to Manista, except I have the bauble of baubles." On the shelf, in the middle of the leader baubles, was an empty spot and this is where Taukin gathered his bauble belonged. Pecril knocked his lamp against the stone and signaled Taukin to hurry along with a rolling of his hand. At the edge of the inlet, where two coves met was an ancient text revealing the same figures as the baubles next to him. Taukin delicately placed the bauble of baubles back on the middle shelf where it belonged.

He turned just as Pecril's lantern went dark and he called out, "Pecril…Pecril, I can't see," but there was no sound coming from where Pecril stood. Taukin swallowed hard with the possibility that they had been discovered. A dull blue light illuminated the tunnel where Pecril had stood. "Manista," said Taukin under his breath. The light grew brighter until a mysterious blue glowing mist billowed from the tunnel entrance. The rolling fog made its way across the gully without hesitation. In the shadowy darkness, Taukin frantically felt his way to the edge of the vault and moved to the outer rim, his right foot slipping down into the opening, but he gripped what little hold there was in the stone face and remained hidden until the glowing haze was at the vault and in the same inlet where the baubles were.

Taukin peeked around to see the cloud hovering in place in front of the missing bauble. A firm voice, echoing as if it were coming from a faraway place, emitted from the pillar of mist, "Reveal yourself." Taukin pressed his back against the outer wall, but again the voice said, "Reveal yourself Taukin." Taukin's skin blazed yellow and he tried to summon back across the void, but he hadn't enough Tahmill nor agrum left and his yellow glow dissipated. Taukin cautiously edged his away around the wall and in front of the billowing vapor that was centered in the inlet presenting the bauble of baubles that Taukin hid in the guest chamber. "This bauble represents a suvanth, once chosen to lead the Bazwodda. The end war. Once opened, this bauble will beckon the god Cenro and destruction will follow," said the echoing voice.

"Why did you give it to Keel?" asked Taukin.

"Not I, but another messenger. Keel is now the one chosen to lead the Bazwodda."

"He's alive?"

"Lead him to the light," said the cloud then continued, "A war between gods is raging and Onestonia will have its battle, but *when* is dependent upon those who sway the balance of good and evil. Cenro, the god of darkness wants Keel to lead his army and overtake this planet but needs the suvanth to build the army for him." The bubbling cloud grew larger, nearly filling the vault. "Manista will start the Bazwodda unless you stop him. Present your hand," said the cloud.

"But I'm to help Manista, as he is to help me," said Taukin as he slowly extended his right hand, opening it palm-side up. The slow rolling haze stayed in place but extended a bubbling blue branch engulfing Taukin's hand making his body tense and his eyes widen. As quickly as the vapors covered his hand, it retreated and left in its place was an amber jewel of spectacular brilliance forcing Taukin's eyes shut.

"It is your choice Taukin. You have been presented a gift from Levic, the goddess of light. This gift can only be used once, do so wisely," said the cloud.

"How will I know when to use it?" asked Taukin.

"When it is darkest," replied the billowing mist. "Now you must return to your chamber, Manista approaches." Taukin's skin blazed golden and he turned back toward the tunnel entrance frantically pacing along the edge with no way of getting back across the gully. Without warning two pillowy hooks went under Taukin's arms and carried him across the chasm, then vanished without another sound.

Taukin entered the darkened tunnel and found Pecril asleep. He shook his guide waking him and said, "Pecril, lead me back to the chamber now, Manista is coming." A shadow from the opposite end of the tunnel receded and Pecril popped up and covered Taukin's head and with his lantern flame low, he moved as fast as his little legs would carry him with Taukin in tow away from the direction of the shadow.

They reached a junction where the left led to the guest chamber, and the right to the main hub of Sheol Balla and through the rugged cloth cover, a familiar pale blue light appeared. "Quickly," said Taukin to Pecril who took three steps, then tripped sending his lantern tumbling against the rigid stone floor causing a loud repeated CLANK, CLANK, CLANK! Taukin yanked off his cover from his sweating head and the blue light grew brighter. Taukin snatched up Pecril and the lantern and in the dimmed light ran through the tunnels with Pecril pointing the direction until they were back at the guest chamber. Taukin set Pecril down outside the chamber entrance and quickly hid the light stone under his folded coverings and went to the water channel and with his robe and top removed, doused his body with the cool water to cover up any sign of sweat and treason.

Manista appeared and scanned the room before locking eyes with Taukin. "Was it you that made that noise?"

"What noise my Lord?" replied Taukin, doing his best to keep his color static. Manista's eyes squinted with suspicion and his mouth arched at the corners as he paced around the chamber. "What is taking so long? You should have left by now," said Manista with a hint of displeasure.

"My Lord forgive me. I asked Pecril to grant me time to cleanse myself before making the long journey for I do not know when I will get another chance to do so."

"When you enter the waters of Olin Fell, that's

when," said Manista with displeasure then continued, "Dress yourself accordingly, you have already acclimated to the warmth of Sheol Balla for too long. Your body will be in shock from the cold of the Fell. It won't be long before you feel the chill of the surface air again," said Manista as he exited the chamber.

CHAPTER 9
ENTER THE FELL

Turmoil churned inside Taukin's head like the swirling waters of Denba. An Unknown planted a seed of doubt against Manista, who had been stern but benevolent toward Taukin. Was this god-play for Taukin like the suvanth had been for him, or against him like with the rintic? A gift from a god could mean favor or could be works against another god for the benefit of the gift-giving god. Near the outer tunnel of Manista's chamber, Swinzal hauled a large ruck on his shoulders. Taukin knew the ruck contained agrum as Manista said would be necessary for retrieval of the light cipher, but what else? Taukin's curiosity engaged as his loyalty to Manista wavered, and his awareness was heightened by two other suvanth that appeared from behind Swinzal.

Manista spoke, "Taukin, this is my most trusted soldier and personal protector, Nebbar." Swinzal's eyes squinted with jealousy. Manista continued, "And next to Nebbar, my eldest son. He is my pride and the future leader of the suvanth, Bitur-Udo." Taukin examined the young suvanth that shared similar physical features with

Taukin, except for his prominent backbone and dull blue skin color that flashed a display of colorful emotions before returning to its original hue. Bitur-Udo's dark eyes were hidden by his jaw-length ebony hair as he lowered his head and Taukin returned the gesture. Bitur-Udo and Taukin were similar in height, but Nebbar was slightly taller than both.

Nebbar looked unique amongst the suvanth with a single tuft of white hair streaking from front to back on his otherwise hairless head. His physique was muscular and his arms were covered with pallid scars that seemed to bubble up off his light, cobalt complexion. Taukin bowed his head, but Nebbar, his face expressionless, only stared as if Taukin was subservient or Nebbar himself was blind.

Manista smiled at the exchange and said, "Forgive Nebbar, he is of the Hannon Lite clan, which are not known for their social formalities." Manista continued, "Nebbar will accompany you and Swinzal to provide security in the event that something unexpected occurs. You understand, we must mitigate all risks."

Taukin internally questioned why there would be a need for security, but didn't reveal his uncertainty through expression of face or skin. Swinzal bowed his head in concurrence.

Manista placed his gangly arm around Bitur-Udo and turned him away from the party as he softly spoke instructions to his son. Bitur-Udo walked off, but glanced back at Taukin once more before disappearing into one of the tunnels leading to Manista's quarters with an awaiting glingus.

Taukin asked, "How long will it take to get to Olin Fell?"

"It dependsss on what troublesss we encounter," said Swinzal.

Manista returned and spoke, "Follow Swinzal's instructions, he and Nebbar will ensure your safety and success. Taukin, you will be reunited with your mother near Olin Fell and the Eltepsu will be released once you present the Basatab to me."

Taukin bowed to Manista, agreeing to the pact that was made between them. Swinzal and Nebbar turned and moved toward the exit with Taukin in tow. The trio passed through the bustling enormity of the main chamber and past the overhead perch where Manista introduced Taukin to the masses. With Nebbar leading the way, the crowd seemingly parted as if they were part of an organic seam that opened by an invisible field and sealed back closed once Taukin passed. As they neared the first tunnel leading to what Taukin imagined as the first of many hubs, he saw a faint flicker of light to his right, far enough away from the torches of the tribesman to catch his attention, high up in the dark- ened holes that aligned the wall opposite Manista's chamber opening. For a few par-tems, Taukin saw in the lamp light pure illuminated beauty that was Drami Sol. Her face was both sincere and uncertain. Taukin's heart felt she would fulfill her promise to plant the sassa root, and in turn he would fulfill his promise to help her escape to the Carth forest. Ambient light in the voluminous chamber was subdued, but Taukin tried his best to assure her by expressing a nod right before he entered the first of the portals to the outside world. Taukin was surprised at the speed the suvanth traveled upward through the tunnels, even on two legs. The number of suvanth lessened as they moved farther away from Sheol Balla. With each transition between hub and passageway, Taukin grew weaker and it wasn't until they reached a hub where stone gave way to dirt that Nebbar and Swinzal rested.

It was then that Swinzal opened the ruck that had a shaken bulb glowing in it and withdrew three drop vials of agrum, one for reward went to Swinzal, one for stamina went to Taukin, and one for dominance went to Nebbar whose veins pulsated and engorged with agrum after consuming the vial. Swinzal's head dropped back reveling in the surge of agrum. Nebbar seemed less affected by the intoxicating effects of the life liquid, perhaps his tolerance to agrum was at a higher level than most, or his mind and body had been trained to show no sign of sensation or emotion. Taukin felt the rush of agrum flow throughout his body and his heart rate increased. Though he tried to remain surreptitious in front of his guides, he couldn't fight the agrum's euphoric effects and his mauve head rolled. As his head dropped, Taukin caught a glimpse of a larger object in Swinzal's ruck. A clear film, much like the organic vials that the Eltepsu produced, encapsulated a black object and a split par-tem before Swinzal closed the flap, there was movement. It was alive and living inside a large vial inside Swinzal's ruck. A sudden sense of worry fell over Taukin, not only did he not know where he was going or what dangers lay before him, but the security that

Nebbar's company was supposed to provide was now the source of concern.

"The feeling isss unequal, yesss?" said Swinzal to Taukin.

Surprised, Taukin responded, "What?" he then took his eyes off the ruck and moved them to Swinzal's eyes.

"The agrum. Nothing comparesss. Even for the ssstolid Nebbar," said Swinzal with a twinge of mockery, but only enough to make his point while Nebbar was under the strong influence of agrum.

"It's…it's most gratifying," replied Taukin.

Swinzal laughed a raspy croak, "heeek, heeek," and repeated, "mossst gratifying indeed," then with the back of his hand slapped Nebbar's chest repeatedly. Nebbar, whose austere expression never changed, took Swinzal's hand and bent it in a way that brought Swinzal to his knees in pain. Swinzal's smile turned to anguish. "Rele-assse me!" Swinzal cried out. Nebbar released his grip and Swinzal crawled backward saying words that were unfamiliar to Taukin. Feeling less jubilant now, Swinzal stood rubbing his wrist and said, "We will make it under Binesssmir before the dark of the next quiesssce." Nebbar didn't say a word as he entered the tunnel. Swinzal, trusting the direction of Nebbar and not daring to challenge his authority, followed behind. The slope of the tunnel had flattened and the soil had cooled on his bare feet, and Taukin knew that they were getting closer to the surface.

The long portal was dark at first, too dark for Taukin to see and not having the acclimated eyes like his guides did, he slowed. "Move fassster," said Swinzal far ahead. Taukin spoke up, "I can't see where I'm going." Swinzal growled with disapproval. Suddenly a bright pink glow appeared and Taukin moved quickly toward it. It was Nebbar, who held an unhatched trisian luminescent bulb in the clasp of his shadowy fingers. Then he spoke, a gentle sound emitted from his lips as if he was a conduit for another being whose soft words channeled through the vessel of a fierce warrior, "When it dims, shake it." Taukin wasn't sure what to say, so he simply nodded his head and looped the curled top of the transparent chrysalis into the strap of his ruck against his chest. Then as if there was god-play at work, they instantly disappeared into the shadow ahead of Taukin. Taukin moved forward as fast as his agrum-filled legs would carry him. He could hear the puffs of breath from Swinzal and Nebbar just ahead of him and could feel the soft globules of dirt pelting his legs from Swinzal.

The tunnel was long and straight and the reason for helping the suvanth, the reuniting with his mother, was in the forefront of Taukin's mind. Right behind that thought was the possibility that this was all a ploy and that he would be killed as soon as the Basatab was in the hands of Nebbar. He had to take the risk.

Taukin could sense a physical difference in the tunnel, it was colder now and the soil was drier, and it seemed as if there was less pressure in the air around him. Then Taukin's legs jolted at the steep incline. They slowed and moved toward the surface, and Taukin felt a sense of relief, it had felt like a lifetime since he had seen the Eastern star and felt its warm embrace. Before they reached the exit, they were met by two sentries in a small hub not far from the opening. The guards bowed their heads upon seeing Nebbar, who still wore his Hannon Lite patch on his chest, and whom Taukin gleaned was well known and well respected amongst the suvanth. "Master Nebbar, we have the inobi sleds ready as you requested," said the larger of the two guards.

"You have done well," replied Nebbar in his soothing way. Swinzal, Nebbar, and Taukin made their way past the guards and toward the exit. Taukin thought it odd that this tunnel was simply covered by a thin sliver of wood, but soon discovered why. Above the tunnel entrance was a covering that encompassed not only the opening, but had enough room for the inobi sleds and supplies and rations. Under the cover it was dark, but it had been tem-cycles since Taukin had seen natural light and the thin rays stung his eyes as if he had just awoken. Eastern star rays traced the cracked outline of a rock-shaped door in the blackness of the cover. The cold air of the world above was new again and Taukin pulled and fastened his coverings tighter around his chest and strapped on boots, for he didn't remember it ever being this cold before, he had indeed acclimated to the warmth of the pit.

Swinzal and Nebbar covered their torsos with a soft golden pelt, which Taukin had never seen the likes of before. Swinzal then handed Taukin a golden pelt, the same as he wore and also a pair of single-slit, wooden eye covers, "Put thessse on, it will protect your eyesss from the brightnessss of the Eassstern sssstar and the debris." Taukin slid the clunky device over his eyes and pulled the strap tight against the back of his hairless head, which reduced the brightness of the shelter as well. Swinzal spoke, "Attach your ruck to the rear of the sssled. It will balanssse the weight dissstribution evenly." Taukin bent over to latch his gear to the wooden beams strapped to the top of the hairy inobi. His focus turned to his new endeavor and his hands began to sweat, nervous to take the inobi sled reigns. Steadying the anxious inobi, Taukin followed Swinzal's orders and tethered his pelt ruck to the rear net, connected to the two poles that ran across the inobi backs.

Taukin, certain that his ruck was secure, laid prostrate on top of the canvas and wood sled. "I've never steered inobi sleds before," said Taukin, now more anxious than the fidgety inobis underneath.

Swinzal responded, "You only need follow the lead sssled. Onssse moving the inobi will follow the pressseding sssled. Pull left to go left and pull right to go right. If you need to ssslow pull both sssstrapsss back easy, or firmly if you need to ssstop." Nebbar and Swinzal pulled the slit goggles down over their eyes and mounted their sleds, then motioned for one of the sentinels to open the rock-shaped door. Nebbar went first, followed by Taukin, then Swinzal who ordered the door be shut as he passed the suvanth guard.

Taukin watched as Nebbar's sled accelerated into the short grass plains of Mahala. Just as Nebbar's sled accelerated, the inobi underneath Taukin surged forward and Taukin slid to the back of the sled. If it hadn't been for Taukin wrapping the pelt straps around his wrists and his ruck impeding his dismantle, he would have easily fallen off. Taukin adjusted to the galloping, and he quickly pulled himself back to his steering position and took control of the inobi. The speed at which the creatures ran was unparalleled and Taukin wasn't sure if it was the agrum or adrenaline or both that caused him to laugh excitedly. Taukin's sled was now just behind Nebbar's sled and Taukin turned to see Swinzal only a few sled lengths behind. The Eastern star's long, incorporeal fingers reached down and touched Taukin's head and back, a welcome warmth against the cold air. Taukin inhaled the cool air into his warm lungs and appreciated the absence of smoke and dirt that had saturated Sheol Balla.

To the right and far away were the black peaks of the volcanoes of the Swata region, made gray by the distance. Never had Taukin thought he would see the fabled volcanoes for fear of journeying too far from the safety of the forest. And the cause for such fear was now leading him on the adventure that no other Carth rintic tribesman had before.

The Eastern star had already breached the midpoint of the sky and steering the inobi sled through the dry, knee-high grass had become a mundane task. Following Nebbar was simple, almost effortless, which tempted Taukin to tug on the straps to see what would happen. Taukin checked to see if Swinzal was still behind him— he was behind by a few sled lengths, so Taukin gently tugged to the right and the inobi shot right, away from the convoy. Taukin panicked and tried to readjust by pulling hard left, but overcompensated and the inobi angled directly toward Swinzal's sled. Swinzal pulled back so hard that his inobi dug their hooves into the grassy dirt propelling Swinzal and his ruck over Taukin's sled. Swinzal rolled and tumbled, losing his eye cover and was slow to get up, but once he had his wits about him, he threw off his luteous covering and sprinted toward Taukin with wrath painted on his face. Taukin dismounted to prepare for the attack.

Swinzal had nearly reached Taukin but before he was within striking distance, Nebbar stopped his sled in front of Taukin and dismounted with his anglis blade drawn prepared to strike Swinzal down. The suvanth spy stopped just shy of Nebbar's sword, breathing deeply and spitting angry suvanth words at Taukin, but he was angrier at his fellow suvanth's display of loyalty to Taukin. "Ease yourself Swinzal, we're on mission, mind the master's command," said Nebbar, his voice loud and more direct. Taukin's heart raced as fast as the inobi ran, but was relieved at Nebbar's protection of him. Swinzal was obedient to Nebbar for he knew he was no match for a Hannon Lite warrior. Swinzal secured his gear to his sled and placed the eye covering over his eyes. Taukin mounted his sled again, this time tethering his straps to the sled frame so there would be no more delays or deviations from the caravan.

As the Eastern star fell below the Western horizon, Nebbar slowed his sled. They had arrived at the foot of the Uru Mountains. Taukin took in the scenic uniqueness of Binesmir's smaller sibling. White poteau flowers, which had suffused most of the mountain face making it look like the icy caps of the highest peaks of Binesmir, flowed down in a wide ivory covering. "We will camp near the base of Uru. Swinzal, clear a spot on that ridge," said Nebbar as he pointed toward a spot surrounded by the flowers. Swinzal bowed his head in obedience and hastily wrapped his lower jaw with a cloth and took a blade to remove the anesthetic buds. Taukin watched as Swinzal made quick work of the clearing. Nebbar turned to Taukin and threw him a white cloth. "Wrap this around your face, make sure you cover your nose and mouth fully," said Nebbar through his cloth-covered mouth.

"Why?" asked Taukin.

"The poteau flower pollen induces sleep through the poisoning of blood. Too much pollen is lethal." Nebbar, nose and mouth covered, led his and Swinzal's inobi sleds up the gradient.

Taukin followed, but stopped after a few steps. "Won't the inobi be poisoned as well?"

"Inobi are immune to the effects of the poison." And Taukin witnessed this truth as the inobi to his side were eating the flowers faster than Keel ate malpwa.

In the cold blackness of the quiesce, Taukin pulled his limbs closer to his body underneath the layers of pelts supplied by Swinzal. As the bitter wind passed along the brae of the mountain, it sang a song of isolation and loneliness. Taukin thought that the song was just for him because his life had been one of such feelings.

Taukin wrapped himself completely with the thick pelt coverings so that only his eyes were exposed. And with that, the crisp gusts bit at his eyes causing them to produce tears. Occasionally he wiped them away, but it wasn't until after he gave them a good rubbing and blinked a few times that he noticed something glowing and moving in the distance. It was pairs of glowing eyes moving toward them. Taukin called for Swinzal, who had piled multiple layers of pelts upon him and fallen asleep from the exhaustive travel. "Swinzal…Swinzal… Swinzal," said Taukin, whose voice grew louder and louder each time he said his name.

Swinzal propped open his pelts in order to see Taukin. "What isss it?" asked a perturbed Swinzal.

"Over there, approaching us, do you see their eyes?" asked Taukin. Swinzal swung his makeshift hood in the direction of Olin Fell. "Yesss, I sssee. They are sssat-upha." Taukin started to rise, but Swinzal caught his arm and stopped him, "We are sssafe here. Sssatupha cannot breach the flower field. Now sssleep, we will be at Olin Fell next tem-sssycle." With the bright white light that Aebean and Febus provided, Taukin watched as the satupha paced along the edge of the poteau flow-ers, careful not to stir the poisonous pollen. Their glowing eyes occasionally disappeared then reappeared, and there was enough light for Taukin to witness them licking the drool from the edge of their mouths. Taukin wanted to throw stones in hopes that the four-legged predators would scatter and he could sleep peacefully, but he conceded to Swinzal's command and laid down, covering up with the layers of pelts as Nebbar and Swinzal did. No matter how tired he was, the feeling of being watched by the satupha with nothing between them and himself but a field of flowers was unsettling.

It felt as if he had just fallen asleep when Swinzal

woke Taukin, whose mind and achy body begged for more rest. "Pack up. It'sss time to depart for Olin Fell," said Swinzal as he tossed Taukin a cloth-wrapped package of dried meat, bread, and some exotic green melon that Taukin had never seen before. Taukin drank from his pelt canteen and hurriedly ate his meal. After his eyes adjusted to the lumeren's brightness, Taukin looked out searching for the satupha, but the beasts had retreated. What he did see was Olin Fell and its awesome expansiveness out into the horizon. Taukin's eyes were fixed on the enormity of the body of water. Seeing the Fell from above the plains, it was even more impressive than all the stories he had heard from the rintic.

"You mussst be ready to go in," said Swinzal in a sarcastic tone. Taukin broke his gaze and sneered at Swinzal, but was still entranced by Olin Fell. Taukin rolled up his makeshift pelt pallet and fixed it to his ruck. He looked right and noticed the inobi were huddled together, their heads tucked into the adjacent inobi's belly. Nebbar grabbed the first by its brown, hairy nape and carried the immobile creature, legs splayed, to his sled and fastened the rugged straps underneath the inobi. Swinzal followed suit and ordered Taukin to do the same. The group put on their gear to protect their eyes and skin against the elements and with their faces and heads wrapped, led their inobi sleds back down to the grassy plains where there were no signs of satupha. And as they had caravanned before, did so again with Nebbar leading the pack with Taukin and Swinzal following behind respectively. Taukin, stomach to sled, could touch the cool Onestonian ground and would occasionally float his hand at the top of the grass blades feeling the tickle of the grass heads as the inobi drove him across the plains.

It wasn't long before they were near Olin Fell, but Nebbar continued around the body of water so that they never quite reached the water's edge, but instead kept their distance so that they remained out of sight from any shore-dwelling Onestonians. The Eastern star had passed directly overhead and began its trek toward the western horizon. Monotony set in and Taukin chose to lay his head down on the wooden sled crossarm and face the Fell since the inobi essentially steered the sled without Taukin's assistance. A rhythmic motion ensued and Taukin's vision of the Fell gently rocking back and forth lulled him to sleep.

An extremely loud, piercing screech woke Taukin and a shadow was cast that covered Taukin's sled and Nebbar's sled just ahead of him. It was a straxan, a vicious flying creature, the ruler of the skies, and whose fabled tales had become instant reality. From below, the straxan's scaly white belly blended with the clouds and its bright red talons were as wide as a rintic hut. Nebbar knew what was upon them and it was then that he slowed to allow Taukin and Swinzal to catch up. Nebbar shouted, "Take Taukin with you to the destination point!" And with that Nebbar's sled shot away from the other sleds toward the volcanoes of the Swata region in an effort to lead the straxan away from Taukin.

Swinzal pulled alongside Taukin and yelled, "Ssstay along ssside me until I tell you to move!" Taukin nodded his head and followed Swinzal's command, staying near Swinzal's sled as the inobi pounded their hooves faster than before. Taukin turned and looked back, Nebbar's sled growing smaller by the par-tem. The straxan swooped down to attack Nebbar, but he was able to steer his sled out of reach and avoid the red talons of the beast. Taukin turned his jolting head to check his distance from Swinzal, he was close enough. There was no cover, no place to take shelter from the scourge overhead. Taukin realized that their survival depended solely on Nebbar's sacrifice to satisfy the creature's hunger. A deafening and terrifying shrill unlike anything he had ever heard before blasted the plains. It was the straxan, and it was a far distance off, but both his and Swinzal's inobi sleds slowed to witness the event. The pair looked toward the direction of the shriek as the straxan swooped down viciously. It was too far off to tell what happened to Nebbar, but the gray head of the straxan dipped up and down and the creature was grounded long enough for Swinzal to know they did not need to wait around to find out. Swinzal popped the sled straps to speed up the inobi and Taukin's sled sped up as well.

Fear of the straxan swooping down on Taukin made him periodically turn his googles toward the ever-darkening sky. Taukin's anxiety grew with the thought of the straxan and satupha seeking them out in the light and dark periods. The stirless time was near and the inobi would need to rest, but there was no safe shelter, no poteau flowers to protect them from the predators of the quiesce. Swinzal slowed his sled and dismounted.

"We will ressst here for the quiesssce," said the suvanth spy. Taukin looked around and could see Olin Fell nearby to his left and to his right the wide-open grassy expanse with the dead trees of the Bulkus region not far off.

"Isn't it dangerous to sleep in the open?" asked a confused Taukin.

Swinzal tossed Taukin a metallic spade. "Dig," replied Swinzal.

For every scoop of dirt that Taukin managed to dig with his digging tool, Swinzal dug three with his clawed hands. Taukin dug feverishly and his face was pelted with tiny granules of dry gritty soil. Swinzal went deeper into the burrow while Taukin moved the dirt that Swinzal dug out of the hole. A reflection of the sister moons softly danced on Olin Fell and if not for their light, the sky and the plains of Mahala would have merged into one. Swinzal instructed Taukin to unstrap the inobi from the sleds and corral them into the deep burrow. Taukin had one last inobi to unfasten when he saw the glowing eyes approaching at a rapid pace. Taukin hurried and pulled the pelt strap through the loop and worked it up over the metal prong. He looked up and could see more pink eyes closing in on him, the satupha were within a kracklin's throw now.

Swinzal called out from the burrow, "Get in now!" Taukin freed the inobi and dove headfirst into the hole, with the inobi following behind, but before the inobi's hind legs made it in, a satupha reached in with its long curved claws and pulled the squealing creature out and snapped its neck with one powerful bite, silencing the innocent prey. Taukin scrambled all the way inside out of reach of the bloodthirsty beasts. Swinzal stacked the two rucks in front of the long narrow opening that led to the deep burrow, in order to keep the inobi in and other creatures out. "Cursssed beassstsss. They're an abomination," said Swinzal still breathing hard. He then leaned against the packs for extra security and shook a blue luminescent bulb, lighting the tight enclosure. Taukin's heart beat faster than when the first surge of agrum hit his blood stream. The blue light turned Taukin into a green being until his fear subsided and his skin turned violet again. The seven inobi huddled together at the rear of the hole with their heads tucked away from sight.

Taukin spoke, "Can we make it out of this hole alive?"

Swinzal replied, "We will make it out alive. We only need wait until the lumeren before checking the exit."

"How do we safely check the exit?"

"Sssend an inobi out, if it squeals and doesn't return, or if it quickly returnsss it'sss not sssafe."

"We're already short an inobi, can we really spare another?"

"We will connect our sssleds together with the remaining inobi."

Taukin nodded in agreement. "What about Nebbar?"

"What about Nebbar?" repeated Swinzal sarcastically.

"Do we need to wait for him?"

Swinzal laughed, "Thisss will be our grave. Not even the mighty Nebbar isss a match for the Ssstraxan."

The reality sunk in and Taukin wasn't sure if he should feel relieved or bothered by the loss of Nebbar. Time passed in the blue hole and Taukin continued thinking about the possible problems that would or wouldn't occur now that Nebbar was no longer with them. He had felt more secure when the fierce suvanth warrior was still around, but the concern he felt with the uncertainty of what was to come after he retrieved the Basatab was lessened now that Nebbar was gone.

An occasional growl and muffled tapping of debris rolling against the rucks let Taukin and Swinzal know that the cursed four-legged creatures were waiting for them to make the mistake of breaching the burrow. Taukin tried sleeping, but the discomfort of the odd-shaped dusty hole, close confinement with the foul-smelling inobi, and thought that this could be his final resting place made it impossible to sleep longer than a few par-cycles at a time.

Taukin's body shook, Swinzal's foot rocking the young tribesman back and forth in his fetal position. Slivers of light infiltrated the makeshift shelter. Taukin woke in a panic, throwing his pelt coverings off and trying to stand but was instantly stopped by the inability to even get to his knees. Dust filled the confined enclosure and inobi started squealing and Taukin pulled away the rucks to escape.

Swinzal yelled, "Calm yourself!" repeatedly, but it was of no use. Swinzal seized Taukin by the arms and held him still against the side of the dirt burrow until his wits were about him again. "We are down here until I sssay we can leave," said Swinzal in a direct tone so that Taukin understood the situation. Swinzal grabbed an inobi by its dusty nape and prodded it up the slanted burrow opening. At the exit, the inobi stopped for a par-tem, and then jaunted out. Swinzal sent another inobi out and neither returned and there was no sound of fear, so he slowly crawled up the narrow opening. At the exit, he quickly poked his head out, with firm grasps of the sides of the opening, prepared to slither back down the opening if necessary. There were no satupha to be seen, but Swinzal waited to see if the inobi would lure them out in case they were in waiting. Once satisfied, Swinzal crawled back down and retrieved his ruck and ordered Taukin to send out the rest of the inobi and to exit the burrow.

Taukin cautiously exited much like the inobi did before him, stopping at the exit and breaching the hole with his eyes only. The brightness forced Taukin to don his slit goggles before helping Swinzal connect the sleds together and strapping the sled to the seven inobi. Swinzal steered the elongated sled and once again they journeyed toward their destination at Olin Fell, this time just two of them, seven inobi, and one sled.

Riding secondary on a linked sled was almost as miserable as being stuck in a burrow surrounded by satupha. A constant stench wafted up from the lead inobi from under Swinzal. Taukin covered his nose and mouth with the cloth as before and laid his head down on the sled and faced Olin Fell. Rest had not come easy during the quiesce and Taukin once again fell asleep on the sled, which had been easier to do as a passenger. He must have slept for par-cycles and woke once the Eastern star had cast its light against their backs and reflected off the large body of water. Taukin raised his head to see a large, rocky formation straight ahead and knew that they were getting close to their final destination. Taukin pulled his cloth from his mouth and spoke loudly, "What's that landmark ahead of us?"

Swinzal turned his head back and shouted, "Quasssa butte."

When they arrived at the butte, Taukin looked out on the horizon, the Eastern star had colored the sky indigo much like Taukin's natural skin color and the reflection cast upon the Fell was breathtaking. Swinzal tethered the unstrapped inobi to the elongated wooden sled near the base of the hill. They rested for a short time and Swinzal reviewed his master's plan for Taukin. "Remember when you addresssss the Ssstaleansss, presssent yourssself assss the rintic retriever of the basssatab and offer thessse elder vialsss of agrum assss payment for their ssservice. If they believe you, they will presssent to you a sherob and will guide you to the cryssstal dome. Once inssside do not wassste time, take the basssatab and plassse it inssside thisss pouch then ssseal it and come back here to the butte."

Taukin responded, "Understood." He continued, "But what if the Staleans don't believe that I'm the retriever?"

Swinzal unfastened his ruck and spread it open to reveal what Taukin had wondered about since they left Sheol Balla. "You will go it alone with thisss sherob."

Just then the sherob spun around in its translucent bubble with its flat wings at the rear of its body, to face upward. Its eyes were as black as the richest soil in the Carth forest, and its skin was a strong gray on top and bright white underneath its curled body with dangling gray probes protruding from its sides. Taukin stared at the unique creature and for a par-tem it stared back, almost as if it knew Taukin was just as unique as it was. Swinzal removed the agrum and closed the ruck then instructed Taukin to take the seven Elder vials with him to the horn of Cerona and call for the Staleans.

Taukin said, "I would like to lift up a prayer to Hobaja Vael before I enter the Fell." Swinzal looked at Taukin as if he thought the remark was in jest, however Taukin's stoic expression told Swinzal the opposite.

The suvanth spy replied, "Make it quick," then turned and walked back to the inobi sleds to give Taukin the time he needed for his supplications.

"Father of all be with me now in this time of uncertainty. Guide my thoughts and my actions so that I glorify you. Allow me to outmaneuver those who wish me harm. Allow me to outwit my enemies. I thank you for everything in my life, for the trials and wisdom only you can provide. I ask that you continue to bless me in all that I do." And Taukin turned away from Swinzal so that he couldn't see Taukin choke down his only remaining pych pod. His body bucked at the putrid taste, but after a brief pause, he was able to swallow the bitter fungus.

Swinzal silently crept up to Taukin's back. "It isss time," said Swinzal and Taukin jumped at the words and removed his coverings, leaving only his undercloth around his waist. Taukin removed the Elder agrum vial from his ruck then punctured a finger-sized hole in the bottom of the clear cell and squeezed the contents into his awaiting mouth. With each gulp he squeezed the vial tighter and drank faster as if he was famished. He threw the flattened vial down and grabbed the sack of vial offerings for the Staleans and moved toward the edge of the Fell as if he was a god. As the agrum over-took Taukin, he wanted to dig into his chest and pull his skin apart, but he kept moving forward. He knew he would have to summon soon before the agrum killed him. His mauve skin perspired which was unnatural in such cold air, and his mind became consumed with thoughts of being discovered in his deception. He made it to the Horn of Cerona, the calling horn, and seized the somewhat corroded wheel with both of his pulsating hands. His strength amplified, he twisted the wheel free, emitting a loud screech in the process. With each full rotation of the metal helm, the whining noise faded and a deeper, muffled tone grew louder from the submerged horn. The call from the horn emitted a wave of sound, reminiscent of Itil's voice, echoing from underwater and it pulsed through Taukin's body.

Shortly thereafter, wet silhouettes appeared dark against the setting Eastern star, at least ten, to see who called them to the surface. Looking upward, the sister moons Aebean and Febus were nearing alignment, which signified the retrieval of the Basatab. They awkwardly approached as if something was keeping their legs stationary while trying to move. Their white and golden, streamlined upper torsos breached the surface and periodically dipped back underneath. One particular Stalean, which Taukin determined to be the male leader of the group, had decorative, symmetrical black markings on his smooth white chest, like that of the fabled Ank tribal warrior tattoos, and he staggered in front of the others. Taukin thought the Stalean must be a warrior as well and as the warrior's body came further out of the Fell, the retriever's sherob flailed around in his webbed hands. Taukin approached cautiously, observing how the warrior and his sherob were as one being. His sherob wrapped its cephalic gills around the neck of the Stalean, with the tapering appendages disappearing into the sides of his mouth and down his throat. Taukin's head swirled, filled with the lethal amount of agrum and his thoughts became cloudy. He wondered if the sherob's black eyes, which rested on the back of the Stalean's white face, golden ear holes, and black head, somehow transferred sight information to the Stalean.

Taukin stepped into the freezing Fell, but the agrum dulled his sense of the frigid waters. The Stalean moved closer to the shore and once the water was too shallow to tread, the leader leaned on the floating sherob and raised his conjoined legs. In a movement that could only be described as disjoining, the Stalean slowly pulled his tail apart down the middle, and as each staggered suction cup stretched and popped, his large, webbed feet wiggled looser and splashed droplets of water all around. With his wobbly legs completely separated, the Stalean crawled on his knees until his waist was exposed and with one wide-webbed hand, he motioned for Taukin to come closer. Taukin did so and he offered the seven elder vials of agrum to the Stalean, who examined the gift before accepting it and throwing the vials to one of the other surfaced Staleans behind him. Another Stalean, whose smooth skin sagged over the sherob's wrapped appendages, communicated to the leader through a series of loud clicking sounds. The Stalean leader turned to listen and without a sound, quickly turned back to Taukin, moving close enough for Taukin to smell the Stalean's briny breath. Sweat now poured from Taukin's hairless head and ran down his exposed torso.

Another round of clicking noises caused the Stalean to lean his head and look past Taukin toward Quasa Butte. His head moved side-to-side scoping the land until he paused and focused on a particular spot, the spot where Swinzal had tried to remain out of sight. The warrior leader's dark eyes filled with suspicion and went back to Taukin, whose body began to quiver, not from fear of being discovered, but from the deadly amount of agrum he ingested. Taukin's amber eyes rolled back and the blood red color that filled the thin capillaries of his eyes was replaced with agrum green. More clicks from the pod of Staleans filled the air and the leader, who was so trusting with the sherob offering, pulled the sherob close to his white chest and fell backwards and in one fluid movement joined his legs together and spread his webbed feet to form one massive fin.

"No! Wait!" yelled Taukin, but there was no sign of the beings, only faint ripples where their bodies once were. Taukin focused his eyes on the Fell, his shroud of deceit had been shed, and the Staleans would surely do what they could to protect the Basatab. Swinzal tucked away his doka shell and snapped the straps on his inobi sled with a direct path to Taukin.

Swinzal spoke, "There isss little time to acclimate to the sssherob, but you mussst get the basssatab before the dome isss sssealed!" Taukin's skin began to glow violet, his pulsating spotted pattern was mesmerizing and before Swinzal could remove the sherob from his ruck, the sherob glowed the same luminescent hue as Taukin's skin and was already on his head.

"You're wrong, there's no time for acclimation," said Taukin as he opened his mouth wide, emitting a bright light from his esophagus until the sherob's long slimy probes plunged down and quelled the light. In an instant, Taukin's radiant body disappeared under the water's surface and shot toward the opaque crystal dome.

Translation through the sherob under the influence of agrum had no effect on Taukin. His mind focused on his mission and neither breathing in the murky water, nor the opposing Staleans could impede his effort. Seranphopids were fully under Taukin's control and they pushed his glowing body through the shadowy water faster than a Straxan's steep dive from high above. Taukin passed the pod of Staleans and they were but a brief blur. It seemed like a dream, as if he was floating, fluid with no resistance, yet with each passing par-tem as the agrum drained from his body, the chill of the water brought him back to reality. Reality was now before him. A long crystal tube, a product of the reformation of igneous crystal from a volcanic eruption, extruded downward from the floating dome above and at the narrow entrance were two ellipses of swirling drawns, creatures with two large eyes and whose bodies were covered with glimmering scales and short, paralyzing tentacles and a wide flat tail. Taukin looked closer and could see that in the middle of the cyclone of drawns were Stalean sentries posed and ready to engage Taukin with their dual-tipped cluster spears. Taukin moved toward the dome's entrance and with a noticeable clicking command by the Stalean guards, the drawns sped toward Taukin. Taukin envisioned the drawn's tentacles wrapped together rendering them immobile and after a brief violet lustrous flash, it was so. The Staleans witnessed this act of fascination and knew they alone were no match for Taukin. One of the guards twisted and quickly swam off toward the middle of the Fell, while the other guard centered himself in front of the dome's entrance. Taukin wasted no time in summoning the seranphopids to wrap the Stalean's staff around the sentry, taking care to not drive the barbs on either end into his delicate skin. The lone guard, with his slimy arms bound tightly, wiggled his linked legs and fanned feet away from Taukin. Taukin shot up the tube, knocking against the random bumps of crystal on the way up. He surfaced under the dome and the blackness was that of the darkest tunnels of Sheol Balla. The once brightly illuminated seranphopids now provided a trivial source of fading light. He pulled the sherob from his head, surprised by how long the breathing tubes stretched as the seranphopids drained the Tahmill from his body, but Taukin still felt the agrum filling his muscles and the coming of the cold against his skin. He climbed onto the mushy ground and pulled the trisian bulb from his undercoverings and shook it until it lit up the immediate area. He waved the bulb in front of him, scanning the entire dome for the light cipher. As he moved the bulb, a reflection of pink light shot in multiple directions and briefly added light to the gloom of the damp chamber. Taukin climbed the steep incline up to the highest point under the dome, paying no attention to what was under foot.

There it was, he found it, the light cipher dazzled with beams of pink light as the luminated bulb passed over its crystalline face. Taukin shook the trisian pupa before placing it on the cylindrical stone pedestal behind the light cipher. With the entire dome now illuminated, which was similar in size to Manista's personal chamber, he could see his surroundings clearer, albeit under the trisian's pinkish hue. Nowhere else on Onestonia could offer such seclusion, such quiet, such peace, such calm, and no worries of war, or belonging, or deception, or hurt, or hate, or…love, would ever penetrate its dark nionan shell. He moved the cylindrical cipher to the cloth sack tied to his waist, diminishing the rays of light from the trisian bulb.

CHAPTER 10
WHERE LOYALTIES LIE

Taukin knew that this was his turning point. There was no guarantee he could make it back with the remaining agrum and if he did, once he gave Manista the light cipher, it at once severed his ties to the rintic and sealed his loyalty to the suvanth. A loud echoing clank came from below and filled the compact dome, it was the banging of submerged crystal against crystal. He underestimated the speed of the Staleans and now was sealed in a tomb of darkness. He summoned the sherob from the edge of the water entrance to his body then dove in the freezing water, lighting the way. Taukin squeezed his way down the long narrow tube to where the exit once was and pushed against the crystal with all his given strength. The crystal seal was resolute, immovable. Time was running out, and by now Taukin imagined what awaited him on the other side of the crystal was nothing less than an army of Staleans. Taukin tried turning around to swim back up, but the tight space of the tube wouldn't allow for it. He summoned his way back up the tube, feet first, then summoned as many of the creatures possible. Doing so, however, would mean he wouldn't make it back to shore, but there was no other option, he must escape. Taukin then shot down the tube, fists first, shearing and chipping the protruding crystal edges until his glowing fists met the thick crystal seal at the bottom. Shards of black crystal shot through the water and an underwater shockwave sent clusters of Staleans tumbling through the Fell. Taukin sped through the water like a blazing fireball through the darkest quiesce sky. He moved through the water as easily as falling from the clouds until his body was suddenly subdued as if he had run into the rocky face of Binesmir, sending his sherob tumbling ahead of him and out of arm's reach. A multitude of white wiry tentacles wrapped around Taukin's right leg like long wet fibers clinging to a dry branch. Shocked by the attack, Taukin turned to see what had seized him. A formidable beast with large iridescent eyes, and long lengthy tubular extremities which shot out more fine appendages and pulled him closer. Taukin's air supply rapidly dwindled and he turned back to summon his sherob. Instantly, hair-like tentacles encapsulated his body forming something like a soft malleable shell with only a minimal number of tentacles securing his leg, so that he no longer could see his sherob and summon it to him. He tried to blindly summon the sherob, but without being able to see the creature, it was a wasted effort. Water rapidly flowed across his body in the opposite direction of Quasa Butte and the sensation of cold returned to his formerly numb sensory system. His agrum was being drained too fast. Taukin summoned   to   tear   through   the   lithe appendages, but with each bundle he tore apart, a multitude more replaced them, sealing the fissures and quelling the light poking through the sinewy capsule. His body spun in the water, completely confusing his sense of direction.

His air supply depleted, Taukin stopped struggling. He understood this to be his doom, his thoughts drifted to Soyha, Larnhi, and Luspa and how he had failed them, but loved them most of all. His eyes fixated as if he could see Luspa in front of him, envisioning Valla's face, his hand reached out to her. All of what he did was for his mother who would never appreciate the trials he endured to find her. He would never see her expression when they met for the first time after their long separation. He would never feel the warm, loving embrace of his mother. His eyes closed and his body went limp and the remaining seranphopids left him, darkening the tubulous confine. Suddenly, Taukin's body forcefully shifted downward and water poured from Taukin's mouth, forcing him to choke and gasp for air. Air, fresh air, cool and inviting to his weakened lungs came in spurts until every drop of the Fell was expelled, then Taukin inhaled, deeply expanding his lungs to their full extent. A cool breeze perforated the beast's white, wormlike appendages. Reflections of Febus and Aebean glimmered on the Fell below, but which direction he was moving and how was still unknown. Taukin's senses returned to him and he pulled open the thatched tentacles to find himself in the slimy clutch of a dead beast of the shadow waters, being carried off by an ascending straxan toward an unknown destination. From the rear, only flatland could be seen in the light of the sister moons, but ahead, against the star-filled quiesce sky, was the outline of the Uru mountains. Taukin summoned any seranphopids he could with the remaining agrum that was present in his body and like a brilliant star streaking amongst its kind, Taukin shot from the creatures toward Quasa Butte. And it wasn't long before, like a star falling from the heavens, Taukin's light died out and he dropped to the frigid water below. His body skipped across the calm surface of the Fell as if he was a flat stone thrown by an Umgara. Lacking agrum and without the ability to summon, Taukin felt the icy chill of the Fell and shock instantly set in. His skin flickered with light as the seranphopids left his weakened body and his arms flapped as he tried to keep his head above the Fell.

Out of the shadows of Quasa Butte, a voice, unfamiliar and muffled at first, yelled out. "Taukin! Keep moving! Come to me!" said the voice, but the water was dangerously cold, too cold to swim and Taukin was on his own. He gasped for air and in a random motion slapped his arms against the water to get to the shore. He swam close enough to feel the silt and sand with the tips of his toes when he made out a lone figure standing at the edge of the Fell. Taukin tried calling out, but his quivering jaw would not allow it. He mustered all his strength to push on, but knee deep in Olin Fell, he collapsed. "Taukin, no!" She dropped her cover as she ran out to him and pulled him up from the water, dragging him to shore.

The icy water slowed her legs, but she placed the

thick pelt cover over his shivering, gray, frozen skin and helped him from Olin Fell. "Soy…Soy"

"Don't speak, your body is too cold, you must get somewhere warm. Come with me." She pulled Taukin to his feet, still covered with the pelt; he staggered forward, struggling to place one foot in front of the other.

"You must move faster, we're at risk out here in the open," she said. With each step, Taukin's muscles warmed, but his strength waned. Near the base of the butte, Taukin's knees gave way and his face crashed against the cold hard ground.

"Taukin, wake up, we must climb." There was neither response nor movement. "I cannot carry you, get up." Just then a brief sound of metal scraping against stone came from the base of the butte not far from where they were. She shook Taukin's limp body and talked in a hushed tone. "We need to conceal ourselves." Taukin's mind awoke and he struggled to push himself to his knees. She helped him up and together they moved part way up the butte and took shelter behind a cluster of thorny wildebush. Through the wiry branches, she could see a shadow of a being down below examining the spot where they had been just par-tems ago. The being looked at the wet patch on the ground and followed the trail out toward the Fell. A moist path was cut through the short grass, highlighted by the sister moons. The silhouette then looked up the butte for signs of traversal, but in the coarse terrain of rocks and plants, the moons revealed nothing. Then the being moved on along the base of the butte, disappearing out of sight. She breathed a sigh of relief. Taukin, already on his knees, went to his hands, the shock of Olin Fell had not yet released its grip. "You need warmth, come with me, but be quiet" she said as she helped Taukin to his feet.

Up high on the butte and by the fire, she ladled a serving of warm broth into a wooden bowl and carefully poured a spoonful into Taukin's mouth and continued until he finished the entire bowl. The heat from the fire and layers of fur cover brought Taukin's body temperature up enough so he was able to think coherently. She was tending the fire with her back to Taukin when she heard a soft voice say, "Mother." Tears filled her eyes. The word she was uncertain she would ever hear from her son.

Taukin, weak and crushed with emotion, reached out for her. She turned, tears tracing the prior tears' path down her now-green face. They embraced, and cried on each other's shoulders for a period of time, both too overwhelmed to speak. Luspa pulled back and wiped Taukin's green cheeks dry. "I have missed you," said Luspa. She ran her hands down to his sturdy shoulders. "You are such a handsome tribesman and strong just like your father," she continued.

Taukin smiled. "I have so many questions," said Taukin, "Where have you been? How did you find me?" Taukin blurted a flurry of questions faster than she could respond.

Luspa smiled, "Gather your strength. Here let me get you more broth and I'll tell you everything," she said, then took the empty bowl and filled it, placing a piece of leavened bread in the broth for more sustenance. Luspa turned back to Taukin and handed him the bowl. "I know you have questions for me, and I have questions for you, but there are those who might be nearby seeking you or me, first tell me, how is it that you came to be in the Fell?" asked Luspa.

Taukin swallowed his bite and started to respond, but was interrupted by a voice outside of the camp. "I can tell you."

Luspa's body went cold, and trying to delay a possible attack, she asked out loud, "Who's there?" and she reached for a short sabre hidden under a satchel next to Taukin.

Taukin grabbed her wrist and said, "I need agrum."

She leaned toward her son and whispered, "I have none. Arm yourself," and she pushed the blade to Taukin. The voice seemed to encircle them.

"I am here, but who am I you asssk? I am the one who movesss as the wind through the treesss. He who catches trisiansss in flight. The one who ssseesss all, yet who isss unssseen, who ssstalksss asss a sssatupha."

The wretched voice was painfully recognizable to Luspa. "Swinzal," said Luspa and her dark stripes went diagonal across her skin.

"You remember..." replied Swinzal. "It hasss been many cyclesss, but I sssee your beauty hasss not left you."

Luspa spoke, "And your wickedness, as vile as ever."

A hissing laugh came from the other side of the camp. Swinzal continued. "Tell me thisss. Which isss more wicked? Pain of truth or comfort of lie?"

"Your words are full of deceit," said Luspa.

"And the wordsss of your ssson? They are jussst asss mine," replied Swinzal.

"What do you mean?" asked Luspa.

"He ssstole the basssatab for Manisssta."

Luspa looked at Taukin as if he plunged the dagger deep into her heart.

"That's not true, I couldn't retrieve it," said Taukin, his voice cracking with anger.

Taukin's face was guilt-stricken and his skin was a deep violet, and Luspa asked, "You did this for Manista?" shocked by his skin's admission.

Swinzal laughed his gasping laugh at the displeasure he caused.

Taukin leaned in close to Luspa and with utmost sincerity said, "I *did* this for you." Luspa followed Taukin's firelit eyes as he steered hers to the cloth sack tied to his waist. Luspa's eyes widened and her skin morphed a flurry of colors.

Swinzal replied, "Not only are you the pooressst of thievesss, but a pathetic liar asss well." Swinzal's tone turned sarcastic. "Poor Taukin, alone and wanted by none, weaker than the rintic, and ssslower than the sssuvanth, thisss isss why our tribesss are sssplit. The mixing of rintic and sssuvanth blood createsss inferior beingsss."

Taukin's skin turned as orange as the fire and the wavy stripes on his skin flickered like flames as he went to his feet. "Look at my skin you demon! I have no fear of you! Show yourself!"

Swinzal continued, "In time…thessse revelationsss are ssso sssatisssfying. And asss we sssspeak Manisssta is preparing a trap for your Captain and his sssoldiersss. They'll be tortured and killed."

Taukin spoke up, "We have a pact. He wouldn't hurt Avent. Manista will have you put to death if you harm me."

Swinzal laughed his wretched hissing laugh. "Your father'sss foolish tendensssiesss were passsssed on to you," said Swinzal.

"You know nothing of my father!" said Taukin.

"I remember your father. He wassss a sssimple-minded tribesssman, clumsssy and credulousss. Sssuch isss the rintic way, though among hisss rintic peersss, he wasss consssidered too cowardly to be a ssscout, and too weak to be a warrior, he wasss the leassst of thessse. Hisss underssstanding of trussst and pactsss between the rintic and sssuvanth wasss pathetic, and that isss why it wasss ssso easssy to convinssse the rintic that he wasss ressssponsssible for the Eltepsssu abduction."

Taukin looked at Luspa who was equally shocked. "How did you…?" stumbled Taukin.

"After Lussspa disssappeared I convinsssed your feeble father that she had been captured by the sssuvanth, and that I could deliver her to him if he would tell me about the Eltepsssu. He followed through and brought a map showing the detailsss of their trek, but he tried to trick me with a map that would lead the sssuvanth amisss. He had no intention of giving over sssuch vital information. Only he wasssn't the only one capable of sssuch trickery. We lured him from the protection of the Norody foressst, which wasss crawling with rintic.

"When the rintic caught up to Ethiusss it looked asss if he sssimply handed over the map to the sssuvanth in an act of treassson. We essscaped with what appeared to be covert information. Manisssta eventually learned which path the Eltepsssu would follow through torture and other meansss and then captured the lone Eltepsssu."

Swinzal's voice continued to surround them in a sporadic and faster manner. "Manisssta usssed you to obtain the basssatab. You were the only one acclimated enough to manage the frigid watersss of Olin Fell and foolish enough to believe in the wordsss Manisssta planted in your head. He no longer hasss a need for you and I've wasssted enough time on you and your sssseditiousss mother."

"You'll never touch the light cipher."

"You're even more foolish than your father!" said Swinzal as he suddenly appeared holding his long sword pointed toward Luspa and Taukin.

"Now I finish what Nebbar couldn't." And with that, Swinzal raised the sword overhead. Taukin readied for the attack with his short sabre in hand and Luspa let out a scream that carried the distance of the butte and beyond. Just then the tip of a red, blood-covered blade emerged from Swinzal's chest. Swinzal slowly dropped his head to see a swirl of blood and reflection of firelight protruding from his pulsing chest. A dark, crimson-colored hand peeled away Swinzal's blade from his weakened fingers still overhead.

A voice eerily familiar said, "I was young and lacked direction, but given time, I learned to be quick-minded and stealthy as you have now witnessed." With this statement, the blade slowly pushed through further. "Your pride led you to believe Taukin is the lesser of the two tribes when in fact he is stronger than the suvanth and quicker than any rintic, and much more clever and wise than you or I will ever be." The blade pushed through further. Taukin moved to the side away from the fire to see Ethius, skin darkened with rage, standing behind Swinzal. Ethius grit his teeth and said, "Long I have waited for our paths to cross again, causer of my tribulations. You are he who has no stride. Whose body and words fail him. He who was not stealthy enough to escape my blade." The blade pushed through until the crossguard met Swinzal's spine. Swinzal raised his head and spit out a gurgling hiss as blood poured from his lips and then his head dropped forward, lifeless.

Ethius pulled Swinzal's body back toward a steep slope facing Olin Fell. He grabbed the protruding bone from the base of Swinzal's neck and with one foot, pushed Swinzal off his sword and down the butte's face. The fractured osseous weapon remained in Ethius's hand until his disgust grew to a point that he reared back and launched the bone past the base of the butte and out of sight, into the blackness of the quiesce.

"There could be others," said Ethius who was wary of suvanth roaming the butte and held his guard.

He scanned the base of the butte then Taukin spoke, "It was Swinzal and I, we came alone." Ethius's eyes swept the side of the butte before making eye contact with Luspa, who looked on in disbelief.

Luspa ran to Ethius and they embraced, a grasp so

strong that not even seranphopids could separate them. Ethius cupped Luspa's neck and his thumbs stroked her trembling jaw and pronounced cheek bones, "I've searched all of Onestonia for you and a flash across the quiesce sky brings me to you."

Luspa replied, "The same light brought me to Taukin, it's a sign. We are reunited by Hobaja Vael." Ethius's face passed her pious comment off with a gentle smile, but their lips met and their skin, highlighted by Aebean and Febus's brilliant white light, flashed multitudes of colors and patterns in an uncontrollable display of emotion and affection.

Taukin slowly approached his blood father and mother who were tangled up in each other's arms. Ethius and Luspa welcomed their son into their embrace and they held each other firm and wept. Ethius pulled loose, "Why were you with Swinzal?" he asked.

Taukin replied, "I was on a mission to retrieve this." He removed the crystalline Basatab from his inner covering pocket and presented it to Ethius and Luspa, who examined the light cipher by holding it up to Aebean and witnessing its delicate detail etched in the crystal tumblers. Taukin then continued, "Manista recruited me to do so and in return he would reunite me with you and release Cuvsor the Eltepsu."

"Taukin you have been reunited with me," said Luspa.

"Was it by Manista's doing?" asked Taukin.

"Partly his and partly yours." Luspa uncupped her fingers revealing the ivory stone charm that she had given Taukin when he was born. "It was time to find you."

Taukin's eyes widened, "You…you were with the Eltepsu?" then his left leg collapsed, still reeling from the complete drain of energy from the events at Olin Fell. Ethius and Luspa helped him to his feet. They made their way back to the fire and again covered Taukin and fed him more broth. Taukin tried to speak, but his words were garbled and incoherent. The seranphopids had indeed taken too much of Taukin.

Luspa hushed Taukin and said, "Rest now son, you're safe." Taukin's wide eyes slowly closed and he slept.

A soft voice called out, "Taukin, it's time to depart." Luspa's loving face smiled as she ran her hand back and forth over his hairless head. There was a glow outlining her head, god-like, what Taukin imagined the gods that Hobaja Vael created looked like. Taukin stood, legs a bit wobbly, but still secure. Her black hair fell midway down her chest and she had Valla's face. Across the plains, Binesmir was traced with the golden lining of the lumeren sky. At the base of the butte, Ethius tended his timid Flauva, which was tethered to a thick leafless tree.

Taukin followed Luspa around the camp asking, "Where are we going? How were you allowed to be with the Eltepsu?

Luspa smiled, "We'll talk on the way to Fort Binesmir," said Luspa as she rolled her pelts and attached them to her ruck.

"Fort Binesmir?"

"We're bringing the Basatab to the Umgara."

"If we go to Binesmir we'll be handed over to the rintic and imprisoned."

"Taukin, the decegen cycle cannot be broken…a new Eltepsu must be born, all of Onestonia depends on the agrum supply, and the Eltepsu are less by one."

"There has to be another way to get the light cipher to the Umgara without risk of our separation."

"There's no time for diversions, we must go directly to the Umgara."

Ethius appeared and smirked when he saw Luspa and Taukin together. Taukin's face spewed forth concern, "How can you lose her again?" asked Taukin.

Baffled by the comment, Ethius said, "I can deliver the Basatab to the Umgara and then return to your mother. You both will remain on the outskirts of Fort Binesmir. I'll tell them I bought it from the Pugotals."

Luspa spoke, "Do not be concerned about what will happen in the coming tem-cycles, focus on this tem-cycle for it has enough trouble of its own." Ethius shot a look of agreement to Luspa's words toward Taukin, rubbing Taukin's smooth head before pulling Luspa close to himself briefly for a firm embrace, then grabbed Luspa's ruck from the dusty ground. They wound their way down around the thorny wildebush and past the rocks to the waiting Flauva.

Despite carrying the weight of extra gear and passengers, the Flauva moved swiftly across the grassy land toward the jutting leg of Binesmir. Early lumeren was the safest time to travel to avoid the satupha that roamed the plains on either side of the butte. The rhythmic canter across the plains of Nasant induced drowsiness for both Luspa and Ethius. Taukin's mind, on the other hand, pulsed with questions that clawed to get out of his mouth.

"Why did you leave us?" asked Taukin. Ethius shot a scornful look at Taukin who was at the front.

"All that matters is that we're together again. Leave the past be," said Ethius with a flattened mouth.

"It's a fair question, and one that you both need answered," replied Luspa who held on to the saddle horn at the back of Taukin, which was the smoothest area to sit on the Flauva's furry back.

"I never wanted to leave you, but your life was in danger as well as your father's as long as we were together. Manista would stop at nothing to get me back to Sheol Balla. I couldn't risk harm befalling either of you."

"The ivory charm…how did you get it?"

Luspa produced the bauble and placed it in Taukin's hand and closed his fingers over it. "I survived in the lower recesses of the caverns of the Eltepsu. That is where I stayed so that you may live a life without fear, without the constant feeling of being hunted by the suvanth."

Ethius spoke, "The Eltepsu were not aware of your presence?"

Luspa replied, "Only one. The gentlest and most kind being in all of Onestonia. Lantia provided sustenance and companionship for me." Tears ran down her pale face, "It's been a challenging life of solitude, but one that was necessary I felt, until now."

Ethius placed his worn hand on her shoulder and gently comforted her.

Taukin responded, "If I had only known where you were…I would have saved you from your prison."

Luspa replied, "Taukin you did save me, when you came to the caverns. You are the reason I left. I never would have had the courage to leave if you hadn't had the courage to meet with the Eltepsu and to…" Luspa lowered her head and continued, "Lantia informed me of your mission. Rescuing Cuvsor is certain death. You can't go back to Sheol Balla."

"I made a promise to a friend that I would return and help her escape from the pit," said Taukin uncertainly.

Luspa's pattern went yellow with large blue ovals as she spoke, "Your intention is noble, but if you return to the pit, Manista will kill you Taukin. He is ruthless and cunning and only desires power and abilities beyond our understanding. He'll stop at nothing. You are simply a path stone on his quest for ultimate power."

Taukin's color fluctuated with the mixture of emotions. He so badly wanted to tell them about his ability to summon, that he himself has the same godly ability, but knew now was not the time to do so. "I can rescue your sister and her son too. They were there."

"Their fate is with the suvanth, you cannot change that. I can't lose you again Taukin."

"I will return to you, I promise." Taukin was as stubborn as she was and there was no changing her son's mind.

They all rode without speaking and with their skin reflecting frustration, love, and uncertainty.

Ethius spoke to break the uncomfortable silence, "When we're close to Fort Binesmir you both will take shelter along the base of the mountains. How the Umgara will react to me presenting the Basatab I cannot be sure."

Taukin replied, "Let me deliver the light cipher to the Umgara alone. There is no need for you to be involved. I'll tell the Umgara the truth, that I was retrieving the Basatab so that Cuvsor would be released. I fulfilled my rintic mission as promised, but deviated from the plan in order to save lives and accomplish the mission. If any judgement is handed out for these actions, it should be on me for disobeying my orders and should not come to either of you."

Luspa spoke, "Your father will deliver the Basatab as planned."

In the distance, a dark splotch amongst the field of ochre-colored grass appeared to be approaching. Ethius pulled his translucent doka shell from his side pouch and halted the Flauva to get a clear view. "The Basatab retriever and Umgara escort approach," said Ethius. "There's no way for us to avoid the rintic now, we will face punishment."

"This is Hobaja Vael's will," said Luspa.

Taukin twisted around to Ethius and Luspa and said, "Let me go alone, turn and go back."

"You'll stay on this Flauva with us. This is not your burden to bear alone," said Luspa, but Ethius's scowl said otherwise.

Taukin hopped down to the grassy plains and started toward the oncoming caravan.

"Taukin wait!" said Luspa right as the brown dart entered her chest.

Luspa gasped and pulled the poinjin dart from her bosom, but it was too late, its poison had been delivered. She stared at the blackened tip in disbelief and waned until Ethius caught her.

"No!" yelled Ethius and he frantically scanned the field for the culprit. Taukin had spotted him and was in a full-on stride toward his mother's attacker. Ethius then saw him…

"Nebbar," said Ethius faintly. "Taukin, stop!" Taukin blocked out everything, including his father's plea, killing Nebbar was his sole purpose. He moved swiftly through the chest-high grass toward the awaiting assassin. Ethius laid Luspa across the flauva's back and chased after Taukin. Nebbar poised his anglis blade overhead and pointed the tip at Taukin. Taukin drew his short sabre, oblivious to the certain peril he was about to encounter. Nebbar sidestepped Taukin and sliced him across his hip, separating the cloth sack and painting his blade's tip red. Taukin lurched sideways and fell, the tall grain providing temporary concealment. Nebbar quickly searched for Taukin in the grass and found him squirming on the ground, holding his wound. Nebbar tore at the cloth sack in search of the Basatab but found a stone inside. Ethius was upon them and Nebbar swung his sword horizontal to counter Ethius's attack. Their blades clanked and screeched and sparked in a flurry of attacks and counterattacks.

Nebbar drove Ethius away from Taukin, disarming Ethius in the process.

Ethius stood there weaponless, prepared to feel the sting of the suvanth's blade, when a deep, penetrating voice broke the silence drawing Nebbar's attention. Ethius frantically went to the ground, hands feeling for his sword amongst the mesh of grain, keeping a watchful eye on Nebbar. Nebbar recognized the booming voice of his foe and ran back to Taukin for the light cipher. Nebbar ripped and removed pieces of Taukin's coverings in search of the light cipher, forcing Taukin to roll over and over in the process. "Where is it?" asked Nebbar in a more frantic tone, feeling the pressure of his enemies closing in on him. Then in a final tug of the coverings that rendered Taukin's torso bare, the crystalline cipher fell from his inner pocket to the grassy turf. Nebbar ran his hands through the tall grass searching for the Basatab. He grasped the light cipher just as a large Umgara blade came down, separating his hand from his arm. His face and white hair went red with a splatter of blood as he narrowly escaped the blow that was aimed to remove his head.

The blood-soaked sword was General Reibo's and Nebbar crouched to avoid another swipe of the blade. In shock and with a single swoop, he clenched his loosened hand that firmly clutched the Basatab, turned and with unmatched suvanth speed, ran to his awaiting inobi sled. Nebbar yelped and the sled took off before the Umgara, rintic, or their weapons were able to reach him. The tall grass bent as the inobi swung wide and headed North toward the Uru mountains.

General Reibo's powerful voice could be felt on their skin, "Retrieve the Basatab!" Three Umgara ran after Nebbar, but even with their great might, they were no match for the speed of the inobi. Two rintic scouts mounted one of their inobi sleds and sped off after the suvanth assassin. Reibo mounted his melp and watched as the two paths of bending grass merged together and abruptly ended. Reibo pointed and shouted to his Umgara soldiers, "They have stopped. Quickly, toward the Uru mountains!" All three Umgara soldiers continued the path of broken and bent grass, but halfway there a hollowed path started toward the Uru mountains and Reibo's eyes dropped slightly, and defeat stole his spirit.

Ethius growled at Nebbar's escape, but his focus returned to Luspa, whose pale skin couldn't hide the black poison tracing through her veins. Ethius's life partner was fading in and out of consciousness. Soyha came to Taukin's side to tend to his wound. She clenched his tensed shoulder and said, "Lie still, I can't administer healing salve if you keep moving." Soyha steadied Taukin, and before placing the saturated silk, said, "This will sting, prepare yourself," and then pressed the white webbing against the splayed violet skin and thin strip of exposed muscle. Taukin snarled in pain.

Ethius appeared next to Taukin, "How severe is the wound?"

Soyha replied, "He needs attention, but he'll live." Satisfied that Taukin would survive, he ran back to Luspa, who lay motionless over the flauva opposite the direction of General Reibo. Syonis appeared standing next to Soyha, curious of Taukin's agony.

Taukin grit his teeth and opened his eyes and asked, "Mother? Where is she?"

Soyha responded, "She is there, on the flauva. Okos is tending to her, but her health is fading." Taukin pushed to his elbow in an attempt to see Luspa as a gurgle of blood seeped through the webbing.

"I need something to stop the bleeding," said Soyha.

Syonis replied passively, "Look around, there's only grass and dirt. He's going to bleed out." Soyha's look pierced Syonis and he took a half step back to distance himself, but his curiosity drew him back to Taukin's discomfort. Soyha noticed a corner of a blue piece of cloth protruding from Syonis's coverings and yanked it out and pressed it on Taukin's wound before Syonis could react. Blood soaked through the cloth as though it had fallen into Olin Fell.

Syonis barked, "How dare you take from me!"

Soyha quipped, "His life outweighs your precious garb."

Syonis replied, "It's tainted with suvanth blood, destroy it, I command this!" Taukin glared at Syonis through the pain.

Soyha spoke to Taukin, "Keep pressure on your wound."

Syonis, angered over the disastrous situation, turned back to General Reibo, "What do we do now? Wait here to see if your soldiers return with the light cipher?" Ethius walked his Flauva past Taukin and toward General Reibo's melp.

As the Flauva plodded toward the retrieval party, Ethius shouted, "She's dying! She needs to go to Fort Binesmir!"

Syonis, confused, asked, "Okos? Why are you here?"

Ethius yelled, "She needs help, now!" Tears streamed down his face and disappeared in his thick black beard.

"Ethius!" said Syonis as he stepped in between General Reibo and Ethius, then he continued, "It all makes sense now. Taukin stole the light cipher for Manista. All three of them are in league with the suvanth! They cannot be trusted," said Syonis.

General Reibo asked, "How did Taukin come to possess the Basatab?"

Ethius pleaded to General Reibo, "General, the loss of the light cipher is calamitous, and I take responsibility for Taukin's actions and mine, but they urgently need to see the Umgara healers. Will you help?"

The General spoke, "Sled runners, take them to Fort Binesmir and inform them of what took place here and that General Reibo orders for Luspa and Taukin to be cared for. Tell the rintic that I will ensure Soyha and Syonis return to Fort Binesmir safely." Ethius turned and helped strap Luspa to the inobi sled.

Syonis went to General Reibo, "This will not stand, Taukin and Ethius are enemies to the rintic and should be imprisoned for their treasonous acts!" General Reibo's large gray and speckled face scowled and moved in close to Syonis, making him step backwards in fear.

"Taukin and Ethius will be dealt with in time. The primary task at hand is retrieving the Basatab." Syonis shrank down and away at the penetrating words of General Reibo. Ethius and Soyha hauled Taukin to the awaiting inobi sled, which was linked to a lead inobi sled just like Luspa's sled was fashioned. Reibo spoke again, to the rintic scouts, "Get word to Lord Hiko, the retrieval of the Basatab from the suvanth is now Captain Avent's primary mission."

Taukin's eyes opened upon these words and he said, "Avent musn't go to the pit. He'll be killed."

General Reibo looked down upon Taukin, "Are you indeed in league with the suvanth?"

"Never. But Manista is aware of the Eltepsu rescue plan and has a trap waiting for Captain Avent."

"We will have to launch an attack on the suvanth," said General Reibo.

"General there is another way. I can retrieve the light cipher. Let me go back to the pit," said Taukin wincing and wriggling.

Syonis appeared again and spoke up, "He plans to join the suvanth. We'll never see him or the light cipher again!" Taukin tried to counter, but the pain took hold of him and put him flat against the inobi sled.

General Reibo turned to the scouts waiting on the sleds, "The Umgara will meet with the rintic and plan the new mission."

Both rintic scouts nodded in concurrence and were about to depart when Taukin raised his head, "Wait." General Reibo put up his head-sized forward-facing hand, halting the scouts. "The new mission…A war? Captain Avent must stay above ground," said Taukin, with all the energy he could muster.

General Reibo kneeled next to Taukin and leaned in close, his voice low, "I tell you this…Captain Avent has already breached the tunnels by now."

Taukin's head fell back against the inobi sled. "Then it's too late," said Taukin, now numb from the knowledge given.

Soyha's skin tanned and branched black, and her eyes gleamed with tears as she looked down on Taukin and she said, "What have you done?"

Taukin could only close his eyes to hide his shame, but his blue hue revealed his transgressions. General Reibo stood and lowered his goliath hand as he gave the order, "Move out," and the inobi sled runners sped off with Luspa and Taukin in tow. Ethius and Soyha shrank with each stride of the inobi until they disappeared behind the tall strands of swaying grass.

CHAPTER 11
WANDERING SPIRITS

The jostling of the inobi's rhythmic gallop combined with the loss of blood made Taukin drift in and out of consciousness and the light that had blinded him early on had been replaced by the quiesce. When he awoke, there was a tall, but slender and slightly hunched Umgara dressed in tattered coverings and covered in dark swirled markings standing over him. "Hobaja Vael watches over you," he said, his voice low and ancient, he then limped past a small fire set in a metal drum that crackled and burned in the middle of the dimly lit tent over to where Luspa lay suspended from the tent perch by healing wraps and surrounded by a cloud of smoke.

Taukin followed the Umgara with his eyes, "Mother," said Taukin as he went to his feet with no pain at his side.

Over the sound of colossal marching soldiers, the elder Umgara spoke, "She can't hear you."

"Is she…alive?" asked Taukin, his voice trembled.

"Her spirit is not with her body, it roams."

"Where?"

"Other lands…other worlds, the kingdom. Places far from here."

"Will her spirit return?" asked Taukin now by her side noticing his own wound was nearly healed.

"I cannot say. Some spirits continue to roam and there are those who return as if they never left, but other spirits…they return and are forever changed."

Dangling metal containers burning penetrating aromatic oils surrounded her body. Her restful face protruded through the wet, white cloth strips.

Taukin's eyes pooled and he squeezed her cloth-wrapped hand. "I'm so sorry. If I had stayed on the Flauva, it would have been me lying here instead of you. Please come back. Ethius needs you. I need you," said Taukin, his skin as blue as Drami Sol's eyes with his tears adding to the liquid dripping from the wraps.

The Umgara appeared with a metal bucket and a metal handle protruding from a dark liquid.

"What is that?" asked Taukin as the elder Umgara's worn hand poured a large ladle full of a viscous brown liquid onto her wraps from her feet to her neck. "Ohwnby sap, to draw out the toxin," said the Umgara, then limped back to his wooden chair at the far end of the tent.

Frustation grew inside Taukin so he pushed back the tent opening and left the warmth of the healing tent for the cold of the valley of the Umgara. Taukin came face to face with single-armed Colonel Pella, "Come with us," said Pella who, along with three other rintic soldiers, surrounded Taukin and moved him to an awaiting inobi prisoner sled donned with straps.

"Where are you taking me?" asked Taukin as he fought to wrestle his arms free from their grasps.

"By order of Lord Hiko, you are to go straight to Akaretel where you will be imprisoned for the act of treason for theft and loss of the Basatab and conspiring with the suvanth," said the Colonel.

"No! No! My mother, she needs me!" said Taukin as he pushed one guard to the ground and shook loose from the other and ran back toward the healing tent. Taukin pulled back the tent opening just as a dart entered the back of his neck. Taukin reached for Luspa, took two steps, and fell limp against the wooden floor.

CHAPTER 12
FOUND TRUTH

"Taukin," said a blurred voice as if it was calling out through the waters of Olin Fell. Taukin slowly lifted his head off the stone floor, but his body felt like stakes were driven through his hands and feet as he was unable to move his body at all. His head sunk back to the floor. "Taukin, can you hear me? It's Ethius. Are you awake?" Taukin nodded his head, but no words were generated. "Taukin, wake!" Taukin rolled to his side and vomited, a side effect of the paralyzing compound used by the rintic soldiers.

"I hear you," said Taukin, groggy and sick.

"Are you healed?" asked Ethius.

"Healed enough…to be here," said Taukin wiping his mouth with his forearm.

"Your mother?"

Taukin paused, "As before." Ethius growled in anger. Taukin pushed his torso up and sat against the stone wall, his back toward Ethius's cell. "I stepped out from the Umgara's healing tent and I was taken by Colonel Pella and his soldiers, she was wrapped and covered by the healing cloud of the Umgara."

Ethius, frustrated, spoke aloud, "I'm confined here while she's there dying. If I ever get my chance, I'll inflict the pain she suffers onto Syonis seven times over."

Hiko appeared in front of the cells, "After all this time, you still hold bitter enmity toward your brethren?"

Ethius replied with distaste growing in his voice. "Your son is not my brethren."

Hiko shook his head, "Ethius, Ethius…the rest of your life will be spent here along with *your* son. You can make up for lost time," replied Hiko as he moved over to Taukin's cell. Hiko looked down at Taukin and shook his head. His color and pattern went maroon with yellow dashes, reflecting his anger, "I knew the first time I saw you, that you were not to be trusted. If not for Jusha pleading to allow you to live in the forest, you would have been out on your own. Because of you the Basatab is in the hands of my enemy and the decegen process will fail. This is what you wanted, yes? To destroy the natural order of Onestonia?"

Taukin's emotions came over him and his skin and voice showed this, "I wanted to be accepted, to be treated as those around me."

"All of the trouble you've caused, for what? A feeling? A want to be as the rest of the tribe around you? You have never been Carth rintic. Now I must go explain to the tribe why the light cipher is gone and why there will be an all-out war with the suvanth."

"My Lord, wait," Taukin stood, grimacing, and gripped the vertical bars moving his face close to the opening. "There is no need for a war, I can retrieve the light cipher. You only need release us."

Hiko laughed, "I release you and your father and the light cipher will be returned?"

"We just need agrum and weapons," said Taukin changing his tone.

"Ah, I see, Manista will simply trade the light cipher to you for agrum?" Hiko's lighthearted expression darkened along with his skin. "You take me as a fool. I would never see you or the Basatab again," said Hiko as he turned to leave.

Taukin's skin turned auburn, "My Lord your life is in danger," said Taukin, his voice drawing Hiko back to the bars.

Hiko's skin went white with flowing blue lines at the importance of what he was about to be told, showing Taukin he was ready to listen. "This must be said in confidence," said Taukin. Hiko motioned for his guards to move to the exit. He turned and walked to the far side of the cell where Taukin awaited, giving them the most privacy allowed by the confines.

"Do not waste your words."

Taukin's skin lightened and he produced the blood-stained armband used to stop his bleeding after Nebbar's attack and handed it to Hiko.

"A blood-ridden band of Avent's house?"

"The other side," replied Taukin.

The crest of Hiko's house was sewn into the opposite side of the armband, causing Hiko to stumble backward.

"Betrayal," announced Hiko. "You have taken it upon yourself to accuse me of treason?"

"No my Lord, not you."

"Then who?"

"This band belongs to Syonis," said Taukin with intensity for fear that any hint of uncertainty would cause doubt.

Hiko's maroon skin crawled with anger. "Son of a traitor and suvanth! You've hated my son all your life and now you seek your vengeance!"

"My Lord, I don't know what's happening but there is god-play at work and Syonis is in league with the suvanth. Soyha pulled this band from Syonis's coverings."

Hiko's eyes watered with fury and he moved to strike Taukin through the black bars, but pulled back before reaching his face. Taukin lurched backwards and Hiko turned and left with his guards in tow. Taukin gripped the metal bars and slid to his knees in defeat.

"What did he say?" asked Ethius loudly.

Realizing that his life would forever be spent in the confines of Akaretel, "It doesn't matter," replied Taukin as he stared off through the bars where the tunnel stairs led to freedom, while he slid against the back stone wall of the cell. "We'll live out our lives here in this prison won't we?" asked Taukin. "Losing the light cipher to the suvanth means we will be here for a long time." Taukin lowered his head. "It's my fault that you're not with mother."

"It's not your doing that I'm here, I let my emotions reveal my identity. I was careless," replied Ethius.

"We're getting out of here," said Taukin assuredly. Taukin went into deep thought.

Ethius spoke, "Unless you convince Hiko that we're not traitors, this is where we'll die."

Taukin kept thinking and began pacing around the edge of the cell that was the size of his and Keel's room at Avent's hut.

Ethius spoke again, "When I met your mother," a hint of emotion came out from the otherwise stoic Ethius who chuckled, "there was never any doubt that she was to be my lifemate. So beautiful and kind, unlike any from my tribe." Ethius paused and his voice became grittier as he said, "They better not…"

Taukin felt the guilt come over him and his skin went blue as his forehead pressed against the bars and he spoke, "She'll recover. She has to and you can't give up." Ethius's head perked to this response, but no words were spoken for the rest of the quiesce. Firelight from the torches along the stone hallway warmed the cells and the gentle crackling of the fire lured Ethius and Taukin to a deep slumber.

Taukin awoke to a faint clinking noise and then guards dragging Ethius from his cell. Ethius kicked and yelled out, "Where are you taking me?" But the guards were silent as they dragged him up the stairs by his wrist shackles and out of sight. "What's happening?" yelled Taukin, but he could only stare through his metal bars as Ethius was taken away. A voice from an area outside of Taukin's view said, "None shall enter."

"Yes my Lord," replied the guard.

"No harm will come to him…yet," Syonis appeared

in front Taukin's cell. His smug red face made Taukin's skin go dark orange.

"What do you want?" asked Taukin.

"Where is she?" replied Syonis.

"Who?"

"Drami Sol," spouted Syonis, whose dark skin contrasted the sand-colored prison.

Taukin, shocked, replied, "It wasn't Keel, it was you. You want her for a lifemate."

Taukin paused as Syonis's guileful grin grew larger, but disappeared altogether with the following comment… "You won't have her, she's with Manista," said Taukin.

"Curse you! I should have known better than to suggest you for the rescue mission."

"What do you mean?"

Syonis shook his head slightly, "You have no idea do you? The plan to rescue the Eltepsu from the pit, I was the one that suggested it and that you be sent. It wasn't difficult convincing my father that you were the perfect one to send for such a ridiculous mission to plant sassa root."

"Because I'm part suvanth," said Taukin, thinking out loud.

"That, but if the suvanth decided to kill you, the tribe wouldn't lose one of their own, just you."

"What was the plan to find Cuvsor if I had been killed?"

"Do you really think I care about the Eltepsu? Drami Sol was the real reason you went to the pit. You had the best chance of reaching her. I told Drami Sol to find you to help her escape, but you couldn't even do that. Instead you deviated from the mission and stole the light cipher. You were supposed to deliver her to me."

"Even if I were able to get Drami Sol away from Manista and deliver her to you, you couldn't stay in the Carth forest. Hiko would never allow it. It would spark an uprising."

"It would only as long as Hiko was ruler over the Carth." Syonis paused, then continued, "But if I was the leader, I could change the law…"

Taukin paused for a par-tem, letting Syonis's words sink in and his skin turned light red with blue dots, his voice lowered, "You would overthrow your father? Because of her?"

"I would do anything to have her. I've never seen such beauty. I know you've become captivated by her charms as well." Taukin looked down so as to break the strong gaze that Syonis threw at him; his skin went deep violet with guilt. Syonis nodded at Taukin's admission. "That's why I must have her."

"What would happen to Lord Hiko?"

"I couldn't simply ask him to step down and let his son rule over him. He's too proud for that. Manista and I had an agreement he would get Hiko when I had Drami Sol, but you ruined that deal when you stole the light cipher and created this chaos. He doesn't need Hiko now, he has what he wanted…the light cipher."

"You're dealing with Manista?" asked Taukin, whose face and skin looked as if he had faced Dhevna, the quencher of life herself.

"How do you think Swinzal was able to reach you in the forest? We sent the patrols away so he could recruit you and hid him while others travelled the forest paths. The chances of you going to the pit were greater if you were pressured by both sides."

"We?"

"I *will* have Drami Sol alongside me in the Carth forest. As long as Hiko is around that won't happen and the future leader of the Carth can't kill his own like the suvanth do," said Syonis rather flippantly.

Taukin shook his head in disgust, "Evil."

"Seize him!" a voice, firm and familiar came from the stairs.

"Father!" said Syonis as his legs buckled and his skin went pale green, his body's response to the danger coming toward him. He ran off down the winding tunnel only to find it was sealed off shortly before the four guards tackled and bound him. Hiko stood watching his only son being dragged along the stone floor toward the cells. With each step the guards took toward Ethius's empty cell, the future of the Carth rintic tribe grew more uncertain.

"Father! Stop them! My Lord, please!" The bars clanked shut and Syonis gripped them with his bloody hands, trying his best to shake them loose. "Father, why are you doing this?"

Hiko's skin was darker than the quiesce sky and he growled, "You are no son of mine! Another Eltepsu has been abducted by the suvanth and innocent blood is being shed because of you and your wanton desire," said Hiko.

"No my Lord, there is war because of Taukin's misdeeds," pleaded Syonis. Taukin's skin went golden with the news of war.

Hiko shuffled around the bars to Syonis's cell with his fingers curling toward his face, "I thought Taukin was recruited by Manista, but Taukin was recruited by you through me and others. If it weren't Taukin, it would have been some other tribesman that you chose to destroy. You were so convincing and I was foolish."

Hiko stepped closer to Syonis, his light blue and yellow skin reflecting his disappointment, he spoke, "My life has been wasted on you. A disgrace to our house…to me and your mother, to our *tribe*. I didn't want to believe Taukin, but after seeing this, I needed the truth," said Hiko as he held up the bloody armband that belonged to Syonis. "No tribesman would dare stitch the house of Hiko on their band. Only your armband could have been altered. You killed the Needlesmith. Everything you wanted you were given, and now I see the error of my ways. Being the future leader of the Carth wasn't enough for you. You desire to break the laws and system that have been in place for ulti-cycles for your own selfish reasons. And…you would have me killed?" Hiko's eyes filled with tears at this painful truth and he shook his head.

"Father, no, that's not…"

"SILENCE!" shouted Lord Hiko so loud that Syonis fell backward. Hiko's skin blazed blood red. "I will no longer listen to your lies and deceit. I will have you placed in crosschains if you even set eyes upon me again." Syonis turned and cowered in fear.

Hiko approached Taukin and with fierce eyes and skin said, "Our times are dire. Total suvanth domination is certain if you cannot retrieve the Basatab."

"My Lord I must confess to you," said Taukin.

"If it means you cannot deliver the Basatab at Lithica then speak, otherwise there's no time," said Hiko, more vulnerable than Taukin had seen before.

"I will not fail you my Lord," replied Taukin whose eyes blazed with a wild intensity.

"Guard, release Taukin." The same guard that was to prevent entry to any tribesman, unlocked Taukin's cell and swung the door fully open.

"And Ethius?" asked Taukin.

"Outside you will find two scout escorts and a sled for you and Ethius. On the sleds are two vials of agrum and a short sabre and long blade for each of you."

"My Lord, grant him allowance to be with Luspa, he can be of no help once inside the pit," said Taukin.

"So be it." Hiko gripped Taukin's sturdy arm and said, "I am putting my trust in you, do not fail me. The fate of the rintic and all of Onestonia depends on you stopping Manista and retrieving the Basatab. Take the Basatab directly to Lithica. With great speed go!" Taukin nodded and ran up the stairs with the guards escorting him and Ethius out of the prison.

Outside the prison, the frigid pre-lumeren air was cold enough to darken their skin and they donned their cold-weather coverings that had been taken earlier and equipped themselves with the blades and agrum. "Father, go be with mother, Lord Hiko has granted this."

Ethius grabbed Taukin and pulled him close to his chest and in his ear said, "Come back to us." Taukin, surprised by the concern, hugged him back. Ethius mounted his inobi sled and along with another sled runner, jetted off toward Fort Binesmir.

Dyant appeared, "It's good to see you friend."

Taukin nodded, "You as well."

"Are you ready for this?" Dyant asked.

Taukin downed a quarter of the vial of agrum then mounted his sled and along with Dyant's sled in the lead said, "Let's go," and they took off for Sik Jukote.

White light from the sister moons faded and the Eastern star painted the path between Akaretel and Sik Jukote orange. Each turn and hill that Dyant's sled made was followed exactly by the inobis under Taukin as if they communicated without being heard. All along the way Dyant sounded his warning whistle and both sleds dodged carts of wounded and dead rintic soldiers being brought to Fort Carth. The wounded soldiers increased in number as the sled runners approached Sik Jukote.

In the open field at Sik Jukote the inobi sleds turned north toward the Peah mounds and sped forward through the rear platoons of rintic awaiting their chance to battle the suvanth. Rintic soldiers spread wide across the field marching north, one line of soldiers moved left of the Peah mounds at the base of the Binesmir mountains. Taukin pointed toward the lone platoon and Dyant followed Taukin's direction. Shadows cast from the god stones blackened their path as they passed the mammoth mounds. Just as the inobis followed each other's path, so did the rintic soldiers, all except one who fell out right as Taukin met him. Taukin's sled hit the soldier with such force that the soldier flipped over Taukin and his ruck flew into the mounds. Taukin's inobis, freed from the collision, scattered amongst the mounds and disappeared.

Taukin moved to the soldier, "Are you hurt?"

Dazed and with his eyes cinched shut the soldier said, "My leg, I can't move it," then opened his eyes to see Taukin gripping his shoulder.

"Suvanth!" shouted the soldier. Four of the marching soldiers came rushing toward Taukin.

Right as one of soldiers swung his blade to strike Taukin, Dyant's dagger met the sword with a spark. "Pull back! Lord Hiko has granted Taukin freedom," said Dyant.

The soldier, a sergeant, lowered his sword and stared at Taukin in disbelief. "He might be free, but he's still not one of ours," said the hardened soldier and he helped the injured soldier to his feet and over to the empty inobi sled.

Dyant turned to Taukin and said, "Lord Hiko's orders were that you do not delay. Your sled is destroyed, take mine. I'll handle what happened here."

Taukin turned back to the injured soldier now sitting on the remaining sled and said, "I need this sled."

The angry sergeant spoke up, "Stay where you are soldier, Taukin can march like the rest of us."

Dyant walked up behind the injured soldier and yanked him off like a ruck off the shelf. "Taukin, go!"

The sergeant moved to strike Dyant and a brawl broke out, but Taukin quickly mounted the sled and sped off. Taukin rapidly approached Promisel Point, the largest jut of Binesmir on the eastern side of the range. As Taukin rounded the point, great flashes of light lit the ground and fires burned from the mountains all the way to the Norody Forest. Taukin had reached the crux of the war.

Platoons of rintic soldiers marched toward the oncoming waves of suvanth, some running and some galloping, all with weapons at the ready. Farther away Taukin could see the outlines of soldiers tangled like the leggy insects scattered on the field. He steered the inobi sled as close to the base of Binesmir as possible so as to avoid the raging battle. Taukin was almost to the lower Kappa River when he happened upon a squad of rintic soldiers running across his path toward Binesmir in order to escape the slew of suvanth coming at them. "Brickels! Watch your step!" yelled one of the rintic as they ran past. Taukin weaved the sled through the soldiers the best he could until the front of the sled, as if one of the gods had placed a fallen tree in front of him, slammed to a halt launching Taukin up and forward onto the rocky field. Taukin laid still but heard the inobi squealing from the chaos and he turned his head to the right to see that the suvanth were upon him. His instincts kicked in and he pretended to be dead as suvanth galloped over him to get to the rintic that were escaping. After the last of the suvanth ran past, Taukin turned his head back to the left to see three rintic soldiers upright with their legs rooted to the ground by brickels, stabbed through by their enemy's bony saber.

Taukin closed his eyes, angry with himself that he didn't try to help the rintic soldiers. A faint grunting sound pulled him back from his self-loathing. Taukin turned to the right, then the forward direction. He saw a suvanth with one arm, crawling ever so weakly toward the lower Kappa River. Taukin followed suit scraping his face against the abrasive land and pausing only to see if he had been discovered by either the rintic or suvanth. He was at the feet of the crawling suvanth when he saw a fallen warrior nearby. Taukin scrambled to the lifeless body and yanked off the healing wraps from his head and neck then sat up and feverishly wrapped them around his head and before wrapping his neck and shoulder, placed the partially empty vial of agrum at the back of his neck to mimic the protruding neck bone of a suvanth. "Come on now," said Taukin as he helped the crawling suvanth to his feet, but the suvanth's body was mostly limp and he was near death. Taukin draped the warrior's remaining arm over his shoulder and dragged the dying suvanth to the tunnel near the river where hordes of suvanth were pouring out and allowing only the wounded in. As they approached, Taukin forced his skin color and pattern to match that of the warrior's skin, then together they entered the black hole that had been widened seven times over.

Taukin placed one hand on the packed loam and with the other held on tightly to the suvanth as they descended down the steep tunnel so as not to draw attention to himself. Once the tunnel flattened Taukin picked up his pace, only through the surge of agrum was he able to carry another body this far without collapsing himself. Suvanth warriors stepped through the tunnels and the hubs past Taukin and his newly found comrade. The sweet aroma produced by the suvanth was overwhelming in the confines of the tunnel. Taukin did his best not to make eye contact with those marching by, but couldn't resist the urge to gauge whether or not the suvanth had seen past his disguise. Death Tenders carrying other wounded warriors on pelt stretchers skirted past Taukin as if he was trapped in place by a brickel. These periodic distractions of the suvanth runners afforded Taukin the opportunity to make it to a larger hub, but the mumblings from the marching suvanth increased causing his pace to increase.

As Taukin made it closer to the pit, the warmth of the air and tension caused Taukin to perspire and unbeknownst to Taukin, the wrappings around his neck loosened, revealing the translucent vial with the unmistakable green liquid contained therein. It was in the next large hub that Taukin found refuge in the form of a rail system leading closer to the pit. Taukin dragged the suvanth to an awaiting cart, where other suvanth were loading the wounded and dead. A lead suvanth warrior, squatty and ill-tempered asked, "What's his condition?"

Taukin thought it to be obvious, but responded nonetheless, "He lost his arm and can no longer walk, he's weak," said Taukin in his best suvanth accent.

"Load him up," said the suvanth. Taukin carried the

warrior to the cart and carefully removed his remaining arm from around his neck, but as he was doing so, in the bright light of the hub, the wounded warrior saw Taukin's face as the wrap began to loosen.

"Taaauu….Taaauuk" dribbled from the warrior's lips, not strong enough to say Taukin's name.

"What did he say?" asked the suvanth in charge.

Taukin continued to look down into the cart as he tightened the wrappings. "He said 'talk,' he's too weak to speak," said Taukin and he pushed the injured suvanth over the side of the cart and into the pile of others. Taukin put one leg up on the cart to get in, but was stopped by the lead suvanth.

"You can walk like the others, get out," said the suvanth to Taukin. Taukin, not wanting to draw any more attention obliged and began his exit from the cart teeming with the wounded and dead. Taukin's feet hit the stone floor and turned to continue his trek to the pit when a firm grip was placed upon his wrapped shoulder. Taukin half turned, avoiding eye contact. "Your shoulder is healed?" asked the lead suvanth.

"It still pains me," said Taukin as he started to walk again.

"Wait, what's that on your neck?" ask the lead suvanth, focusing on the partially exposed vial of agrum.

Taukin replied, "Healing wraps," as he clandestinely moved toward the front of the cart where the release lever was engaged.

"Come here," said the overseer to Taukin, but Taukin slowly kept moving toward the cart front.

The wounded warrior that Taukin carried from the battle zone pulled himself up to the cart side and said, "Tauuu…kinnn."

The lead suvanth yelled, "Stop him!" and the marching soldiers moved in to secure Taukin, but Taukin had already pulled the release letting the cart roll forward. As it gained momentum, Taukin ran along the side of the cart opposite the soldiers preventing them from reaching him until at the last par-tem, he grabbed the tubular metal edge of the cart and slung himself in on top of the pile of lethargic suvanth. A lone suvanth warrior was able to make it in the front of the cart, his blade at the ready, as they both did their best move to amongst the mixture of dead and moribund. A hand grabbed Taukin's leg distracting him long enough to feel the thin break of air from the suvanth's sword as it swung past Taukin's nose, a narrow miss. Taukin's long blade clanked against the suvanth's sword and they awkwardly moved back and forth and side to side through the cart and over the moaning bodies.

The cart sped into a turn and tilted to the left enough to make Taukin lose his balance as well as his blade, but he and his enemy jumped to the right and added counterbalance, forcing the cart back on four wheels with a spark. The warrior quickly got to his feet and struck at Taukin who had hardly rolled out of the way of the blade before it sparked against the cart's edge. Arms and legs of the wounded covered Taukin's entire body like roots pinning him down. The warrior stood over him, blade raised overhead ready to eviscerate Taukin. A sudden dip of the cart and the suvanth warrior and his blade were gone. Taukin wrestled with his captives until his agrum-fueled strength beat out their dying frailty. Taukin turned to see what happened to his enemy, but the cart had dipped and turned through the torchlit tunnels too many times to see.

Taukin shot up a quick prayer of praise to Hobaja Vael and sliced across the fungal spectrum overhead, then ducked down and kicked at the arms of the suvanth reaching for him. He guzzled more agrum to renew his strength and reapplied his disguise by tightening his wrappings with a wadded piece of suvanth coverings underneath on the back of his neck. The wounded warrior grabbed at Taukin's leg garnering his attention.

"You…arr…noooot…my…….bro..ther," said the wounded warrior and grimaced at Taukin one last time before his eyes went lifeless. Taukin turned his attention to the tracks that the cart was now speeding down making the marching suvanth look as if they were standing still. Taukin crawled to the front of the cart to work the brake and slow the cart through the sharpest curves, while keeping great momentum. Tunnels grew in number and the number of marching warriors thinned as he approached the pit. Taukin passed through the last hub before the pit and it was there that the cart slowed as the tunnels flattened, and in some cases ascended ever so slightly. The sudden open feeling of expanse covered Taukin and he knew he had made it to Sheol Balla.

Taukin remained crouched in the slow rolling cart, watching suvanth workers scurry around the firelit pit carrying supplies and weapons as they prepared to load the cart in which he rode. A suvanth standing near the stockpile engaged the brake, forcing the cart to screech as the wheels clamped still upon the smooth metal tracks. Some of the wounded experienced emesis, losing the contents of their stomach due to the sudden change in momentum. Taukin crawled out the backside and froze for a par-tem when he saw the giant suvanth Sagog walking toward him. With each step his large metal collar clanked against the chains used to keep him bound. Sagog sniffed the air and detected Taukin's scent, but Taukin walked away quickly to distance himself from Sagog and the still living, knowing that if it wasn't them or Sagog that gave him away, it would be word that came down from the tunnels above. The pit was abuzz with firelight and gleaming metal and the sweet scent of suvanth and warmth unmatched. He blended into the busy crowd of suvanth and moved toward the quarters of Manista.

Taukin turned back to see if any commotion had stirred, nothing yet, and he sighed. He then looked to the north side toward the tunnel where Avent and his squad were to enter the pit, but there was stillness, even at the entrance to Drami Sol's quarters, that entire area of the pit was dormant. Taukin could see Manista's chambers ahead, and turned back again to see a multitude of suvanth clamoring about moving toward Manista's chambers. At the entrance to the chamber, Hannon Lite guards stood at attention with their dunion staffs upright and motionless as if Taukin could walk right past, but he knew it would mean instant death. A glingus waddled to the entrance of the chamber and Taukin called to him, the Hannon Lite guards readied their staffs at Taukin.

Taukin raised his hands and took a step backwards, "I have a message for Bitur-Udo from the rintic General Meraco, who spared me so that I could deliver this message." The glingus, a particularly grim looking one, staved off the guards and moved into Taukin's space. Taukin took a knee to speak face to face with the glingus, whose nose angled down and came to a point near his upper lip and whose ears were large and scarred with bite marks.

"Speak," growled the glingus.

"It's only to be spoken to Bitur-Udo from me," replied Taukin.

The glingus's brow furrowed and he said, "Hmph," then turned and waddled down the portal to find Bitur-Udo. Taukin turned back again to see the ruckus moving closer to Manista's chamber.

Taukin yelled out to the glingus, "It's an urgent matter, make haste!" One Hannon Lite drew his anglis blade and moved closer to Taukin. Taukin stepped back further and kept his limbs as still as branches and from that point on was cautious in his movements so as to assuage any sense of threat the Hannon Lite might perceive from him.

Bitur-Udo appeared right ahead of the riotous mob. "Guards eliminate any from the crowd if they get too close. What is the message you have for me?" asked Bitur-Udo.

Taukin limped toward Bitur-Udo and responded in

his best suvanth accent, "My Lord, I am weak, come closer before this angry mob deafens us. This message is for your ears only." Bitur-Udo walked past the posed guard and up to Taukin, who he did not recognize with his skin changed and cloth wrappings applied. "Lean in my lord for my voice is fading and the crowd descends upon us," said Taukin. Bitur-Udo stepped closer and placed his pale hand on Taukin's pale shoulder, then moved his ear close to Taukin's lips. Taukin whispered, "I'm sorry, but I have no choice," then placed the silver blade against the now violet throat of Bitur-Udo. Wailing and shouting echoed throughout the pit as Taukin, with his back toward the stone wall, pulled Bitur-Udo with him. Taukin yelled, "Move back, all of you get back!" and nervously checked behind him as they assiduously moved toward the Eltepsu's holding area. Instead of the Hannon Lite guards trying to stop Taukin, they took action upon the suvanth, one slicing at those that came within their circle of safety and the other prepared to seal Manista's chamber. Suvanth hissed and spat at Taukin, but none came within two rintic of him, and it was when the wall behind him opened to the nether realm below, that the ferocity of the mass quieted.

A blue-gray glimmer covered the suvanth crowd closest to Taukin. He and Bitur-Udo turned halfway around to see Avent, Drami Sol and five rintic soldiers, one of which was Fesenius, floating above the black abyss, glowing and flailing around as if they could run through the humid air. Bitur-Udo struggled to get loose from Taukin's firm grip around his chest, but Taukin tightened his restraint and repositioned his short sabre. Taukin's disguise loosened and dangled from his shoulders.

A voice, singular and unique amongst the multitude, spoke loudly, "Taukin your presence here is most unexpected. Had I known you were bringing others I would have prepared a more inviting welcome. You have what I want and I you, so let's trade and go about our doings," said Manista, glowing from his perch high above the cavern floor below.

"Release them all, the rintic and Eltepsu, and give me the light cipher," said Taukin loud enough for Manista to hear. Manista's body was a shadow outlined by a gray glowing ring and it floated down upon the mass of suvanth as they cleared away.

"Taukin lower your blade, Bitur-Udo has done no wrong against you," said Manista.

Taukin replied, "He's who you treasure most, free them all, give me the light cipher and he will live, I swear it," his hands began to sweat with the humidity and fear.

"Taukin, you can't harm him," Manista summoned Avent and the other rintic to the edge of the pit next to Taukin and released his control of them, both they and he abandoned their gray aura. Manista looked to Avent, "Don't move," said Manista, then focused on Taukin. One rintic soldier felt the pull of the openness behind him and advanced forward only the slightest bit. Manista noticed and summoned him up and launched him into the abyss.

Avent yelled, "No!" Manista summoned Avent up as

well and he said to his remaining squad, "Squad, be completely still." A roar came from below, a combined echoing sound like that of chattering teeth followed by a sound of screaming and screeching woven together. The sound raised the hair on Taukin's neck.

"Put him down!" demanded Taukin as he pressed the blade into Bitur-Udo's neck, letting a trickle of blood down the silver sabre. Manista returned Avent next to Taukin and Bitur-Udo. "Give me the light cipher," said Taukin.

"Ease your blade. Here is the Basatab," said Manista empathically as he moved closer to his son and Taukin, with the light cipher wrapped by his thin gangly fingers like vines around a trunk.

"Do not test me. Let them go now," said Taukin as he reached for the crystalline cipher.

"Taukin you would never forgive yourself," pleaded Manista, who reached to hand the light cipher to Taukin.

"I'll open his throat if I must," said Taukin fearlessly.

"You wouldn't kill your brother by blood," replied Manista with as much sincerity as he could muster.

Taukin breathed deeply and as he exhaled said, "I know," and he lowered his blade from Bitur-Udo.

Avent yelled out, "No!" but Bitur-Udo took advantage and knocked the sabre away and kicked Taukin back, sending him over the edge of the dropoff. Drami Sol ran to the bluff and found Taukin holding onto a sliver of an edge, his skin blazing gold. No sooner had Drami Sol reached out for Taukin than all of them,

Drami Sol, Taukin, Avent, Fesenius, and the remaining rintic soldiers were luminesced and hovering over the deep dark hole.

Manista cackled out a laugh and then spoke, "You're not a killer Taukin. But I am. I wanted to tear you into a thousand pieces each time you were in my presence, but I needed you. You were the ideal one to retrieve the Basatab, no suvanth could survive the trials of Olin Fell, and no other surface dweller could be trusted with the secrets that I taught you. I will say that you have tremendous fortitude and will. I wasn't sure if you could retrieve the Basatab, but you surprised me. And to find out your and Bitur-Udo's mother was with the Eltepsu all this time. Luspa had avoided me for so long, but once I saw her mark on the bottom of the bauble you carry, you, in your bibulous state, confirmed my suspicion that she was with the Eltepsu. I sent Lantia an honor offering with a hidden message for Luspa making her aware of your journey to Olin Fell to draw her out."

A ruckus brewed down below, that of chattering and a chilling shriek that went straight to Taukin's bones. Manista read the panic on Taukin's face and skin and said, "Ah the Kravaes are anxiously awaiting their meal. They first eat the skin off of the living, and then pull away the muscle tissue until they reach the vital organs. I assure you it is the most horrific death you could experience."

"My Lord, please do not drop us down there, I beg you," pleaded Drami Sol.

"Drami Sol, I had sincerely hoped not to involve you, but you played an important role in convincing that rintic fool Syonis to help Swinzal recruit Taukin. Unfortunately, you also showed your true allegiance when you helped Captain Avent access the Eltepsu," said Manista, then his brow furrowed and he continued, "Your recreant ways are about to come to an end as are your beloved rintic," replied Manista.

Taukin spoke, "I did everything you asked. And now I ask you to let the others go. I'm the only one that poses a threat to you, and you know that. I beg that you let them go from here unharmed."

Manista smiled his toothy smile and said, "They know the intricacies of Sheol Balla, how to gain access, our inner workings…they've witnessed my power and now they're a threat to my goal of taking over Onestonia. Once I possess all the Eltepsu, I'll become a god."

Taukin shook his head, "You'll destroy Onestonia!"

Before any more words could be exchanged, Manista summoned his captives over the mass of suvanth, and back over the inner edge of the dark hole. Manista relinquished his vicarious grasp on Taukin and the others and they instantly dropped down into the void. A chorus of cries echoed from the nether realm as Taukin and his group tumbled down the slope toward their demise. Taukin tried to steady himself, but the momentum was too much to overcome. A hollow rattling sound was emitted as they crashed into each other upon landing in the darkened tomb.

Dazed, Avent spoke up, "To your feet quickly and form a perimeter with your backs to the embankment!"

"I can't see anything!" yelled one of the soldiers.

"Hold your place and strike at anything that's a threat," said Avent.

Taukin, whose wits came back, looked back above to see a faint glimmer of light the size of a bayphea pod and spoke, "I can get us to safety."

"You're the reason we'll die here," said Avent. Those words stung like a blade had been thrust into Taukin's side.

"I ask your forgiveness," said Taukin.

"Ask Keel for forgiveness," said Avent.

"Listen…do you hear it?" asked one of the soldiers. Taukin pulled the green luminescent bulb from his coverings, already glowing at full brightness from the tumbling revealing the white bones and skulls scattered amongst the floor ahead of them.

"Kravaes," said Drami Sol, whose bleeding skin turned deep purple with fear in the darkness. Taukin raised the bulb outward to reveal saggy, translucent-skinned creatures on hands and feet, their long, pointed teeth chattering, and thin, skin-covered sockets where eyes once were. Their heads moved in a circular motion as if they were trying to locate something with their large, webbed ears. "Do not move," whispered Drami Sol. Taukin carefully reached for the vial of agrum, but his pocket only contained the ivory charm and the jewel from the Unknown.

Taukin grew frantic, "Where is it? Do you see the agrum vial?"

"There are so many bones," said a soldier next to Avent. A single kravae nearest the group shrieked loudly and in unison the kravaes' heads leveled and focused on

Taukin. In unison, the kravaes rocked forward, snapping their chattering teeth at the farthest extent of the lurch and with each movement they advanced closer. Taukin swung the light of the trisian bulb around, scanning the field of bones for the agrum vial. A faint green glint to the right of the group and under the kravaes on the stone floor caught Taukin's eye. Taukin reached down and picked up a bone shard, then threw it to the left side of the pack of kravaes. The kravaes swiftly turned and moved on the cracking noise and began their chattering and orbital head movements while Taukin cautiously made his way to the agrum vial. Taukin carefully stepped in any opening between the scattered remains with his bulb casting a green hue on the ivory bones and scarce stone floor. The others stayed in their circle, motionless except for one soldier who was missing from the circle.

"Where is Fesenius?" whispered Avent. Taukin moved the glowing bulb around from his new location. Between him and Fesenius were the Kravaes who were moving in Fesenius's direction. Taukin's eyes widened with each lurch that the Kravaes took and he started making his way to help Fesenius. Fesenius was grasping his leg with one hand and waving for Taukin to leave him be. Fesenius tried balancing on his good leg but tumbled over into the pool of bones, drawing the attention of the kravaes with even more aggressiveness. Fesenius scurried back, pushing with one leg and struck at the chattering beasts with a suvanth back bone, knocking one unconscious and into other kravaes. Weakness among the mutants meant death, and the motionless kravae was quickly made into a meal by the ravenous creatures who dragged him away into the black pitch.

Taukin guzzled down the rest of the vial and let the trisian bulb light fade. Fesenius howled when his foot caught a thin stone ridge and pulled his broken leg further apart. Sensing his presence, the kravaes were on top of him and began to drag him off, but an immense brightness, like that of the Eastern star lit the nether realm. Drami Sol, Avent, Fesenius and the three rintic soldiers shielded their eyes from the intense light. A change in pressure pushed through like a wave, sending the eerily white, glowing kravaes back to the deep recesses, and there was no longer a sound of chattering, nor of shrieking, the region was void of sound for a par-tem. Fesenius was now back with Avent, and Taukin revealed himself to his tribesmen and Drami Sol.

Avent, shocked by the event stuttered, "How? How do you have the same ability as Manista?"

"We have to leave this forsaken place now," said Taukin.

Fesenius spoke, "I'll only slow you down, leave me to die an honorable death."

Avent put his arm around Fesenius. "Can you get us past Manista?" asked Avent.

Taukin said, "I can, but not for long," and he shrouded the group in a violet aura and summoned them upward over the ledge and landed with a blast that sent all suvanth, including Manista, tumbling back-wards. Taukin pointed to the tunnel where he entered the pit, "Fight your way through that tunnel and keep moving upward!" said Taukin as he summoned them over the bewildered suvanth and to the weapons depot by the tunnel that led to the lower Kappa River. Manista summoned himself upright above the crowd of suvanth and met Taukin mid-air, high above the cavern floor, their skin ablaze with a turbulent mix of blinding violet and gray light as they tried to summon one another.

"Impossible! You had two pych pods," said Manista as he swung Taukin around and gripped his coverings with his gangly fingers. Taukin swung Manista back around and pushed him against the stone ceiling nearly impaling him on a hanging spike. "The crystal dome," said Manista, stupefied. Taukin's eyes were now replaced with violet beacons of light and when he spoke, light poured forth from his mouth.

Manista growled, "Such power!...I'll have some," then he summoned seranphopids from Taukin, who didn't know how to prevent the extraction, and with his extra control, slammed Taukin against the floor, sending debris flying in a circular cloud. Suvanth piled on top of Taukin, one after another, growing into a mountain of beings reaching the height of two Umgara. Manista walked over to the fleshy entanglement, satisfied that Taukin was subdued, and halted further piling. He peeled back the suvanth to get to his traitorous pupil. Rapidly, one suvanth after another was summoned up and thrown to the side, but the pace slowed as the mound dwindled. A pile of five remained and Manista carefully pulled them off and set them to the side.

When the last suvanth was moved, Taukin was nowhere to be found.

Manista roared in anger, his aura now yellow. "Where is he?" shouted Manista, angry that he had been tricked by what he considered a lesser life form. Manista swung his head around, frantically searching for Taukin, but it was a Fell of suvanth that surrounded him. Manista flew to the ledge of the nether realm and looked down for a sign of Taukin, but there was only darkness.

"Father! Behind you!" yelled Bitur-Udo. Manista turned and stopped the blade Taukin held from penetrating beyond the royal robe he wore. Taukin was frozen still, surrounded by a white aura, which moved him to the edge of the nether realm. Manista's fury grew, as did his glow, and he summoned Taukin onto the floor of the pit again and with each push of his hands, Taukin's body fractured the stone floor around him. Taukin glowed with his seranphopid control, but it wasn't enough to overcome Manista who continued to take from Taukin. White light from Manista illuminated the pit and blinded all who were exposed.

"This is your end," said Manista as he lowered himself to the cavern floor and pushed Taukin further into the stone, shattering the rock around him. Taukin's effulgence slowly faded just as Manista's glow disappeared and the pit was absent of light. The intense pressure upon Taukin lifted and his eyes opened to the dark. Fires were stoked brighter, and the new dimmer light revealed a being with slit goggles standing behind Manista, holding a blood-stained sword. Taukin watched as Manista's pale head fell from his gaunt shoulders and rolled past him and down into the dark abyss below. His gangly body collapsed to the trough of the pit and the crystalline light cipher clanked against the floor and rolled over the edge, but Taukin summoned it back and placed it in the interior pocket of his coverings. The slit goggles were removed to reveal Bitur-Udo standing over Taukin.

From the background, a suvanth turned back toward the legion and yelled out, "Behold our leader Bitur-Udo!" and an eruption of approbation ensued. Taukin winced as he propped himself up on his hands, with Bitur-Udo near his feet.

Subtly shaking his head Taukin spoke, "You saved me."

"I sealed my place amongst the gods," replied Bitur-Udo.

"What have you done?" asked Taukin scurrying backwards on hands and feet while facing his brother. "You stole your ability from the gods. I earned mine." Beads of sweat formed on Bitur-Udo's forehead and as if he was never there, Bitur-Udo vanished right before Taukin. A loud gasp from the suvanth resonated around the pit and Taukin scanned around looking for his brother.

Taukin felt a presence behind him and turned as Bitur-Udo's sword came swiftly, but was halted now glowing violet. Bitur-Udo pushed harder, but the sword wouldn't move. Suddenly the glow disappeared, then just as fast, reappeared allowing the blade closer to Taukin's neck. Taukin summoned Bitur-Udo back into the swarm of suvanth and then Taukin summoned himself up and to the Eltepsu. The glowing bars spread apart and both Cuvsor and Lantia, now glowing violet, hovered with Taukin through the tunnel from which he came. Taukin turned in time to see Valla and Pecril running toward the tunnel and he ushered them on, summoning them part way before their glow disappeared.

Taukin felt the drain of the seranphopids on his weakened body and stumbled to the tunnel wall, "No," said Taukin woefully, knowing that their future was uncertain now that Bitur-Udo was their leader.

"Stop them! Release Sagog!" screamed Bitur-Udo and with a loud clank of metal, the giant was released. Sagog's giant frame filled Taukin's view, blocking Valla and Pecril and he knew he had to save the Eltepsu with his remaining ability, so he, Lantia, and Cuvsor summoned upward through the maze of tunnels past the living and dying suvanth, periodically falling to the tunnel floor. It was just past the third hub from the pit, that they met Avent and his soldiers and Drami Sol fighting their way up the tunnel. Sparks flashed as their swords met the suvanth blades with great force.

"We can't continue, our strength is waning," said Avent. Taukin used the battling suvanth as a summoned ram to push through to the next hub. A roar, like that of ten satupha, filled the tunnel and the suvanth fighting against Taukin turned and ran toward the surface so fast that Taukin could only see them when his summoning allowed them to catch up. Cuvsor and Lantia ran as fast as Taukin and Drami Sol, but Avent and his soldiers lagged behind carrying injured Fesenius. Sagog's presence was sensed by the rintic and Avent yelled, "The beast is right behind us!"

Taukin slowed the Eltepsu to let the rintic catch up. Deep grunting and screams of the suvanth crushed by Sagog poured through the tunnel. A mixture of appealing sweetness and repulsive bodily stench swept through the tunnel; Sagog was upon them. His massive hand swiped at them, narrowly missing a rintic soldier who fell backwards to avoid the colossus's fist. Taukin focused and surrounded the group and summoned them closer to the lower Kappa River. The last of the seranphopids left them, and the Eltepsu, rintic, Taukin, and Drami Sol reached the last hub before breaching the surface. With each hub passed, the empty tunnels reduced in size and Sagog was now crawling, not slow like a rintic does on his belly, but fast like a suvanth does on all fours even with his backbone in place. A haze of misty soil showed beams of light just ahead in the empty tunnel and Taukin halted the Eltepsu until Avent and the others were there to protect them once they made it to the surface.

Avent yelled, "Move!" and the group rushed up from the darkness of the soil tunnel into the brightness of the cold visage of the surface. Knowing Sagog was right behind, the group continued forward swinging their blades and pushing past the suvanth who donned their slit goggles and were thick near the tunnel exit. An eruption of dirt and rock preceded Sagog's appearance and alarmed those engaged in battle, halting the fighting. Some suvanth, which kept near the safety of the tunnel, were now running toward the rintic and away from Sagog. Paralyzed by the beaming rays of the Eastern star, the beast held his massive arm up over his blinded eyes, for it had never been exposed to such brightness. Avent called for more troop support and two squads abandoned their fighting positions to assist their captain, cutting down the fleeing suvanth in the process. Sagog let out a fierce roar, stopping the rintic soldiers briefly, and started his charge after Taukin and the others who were now running Northeast toward Lithica.

Taukin tried to summon the group away, but had no ability to do so, and Sagog swung his free arm wide, knocking Avent and his soldiers across the battlefield. A loud cheer from the suvanth spread across the bloodied field. It was for Sagog, a beast among the suvanth, but foe to the rintic more so. Rintic soldiers charged Sagog, their blades ready to strike the beast down. Sagog's mighty hand came down to crush a soldier, but when the rintic sword pierced the pale flesh of Sagog he let out an even louder wail of pain and angst. Sagog gripped the weaponless rintic soldier and in a series of powerful strokes, swung him at the other rintic, knocking them back into the fold of the rintic army. Sagog tossed the lifeless soldier to the bloodied grass at his feet and turned his attention to Taukin and the fleeing rintic. Sagog burst through the rintic ranks as if he was harvesting kulee stalks. No rintic weapon could slow the mammoth creature and the suvanth let their battle cries out and followed the beast into the battle. Sagog was upon the fleeing foes and his roar paralyzed his prey. A loan Umgara scout named Caliben came charging toward Sagog and they interlocked arms and wrestled around, clearing out both tribes. Sagog's size was unmatched and he was at least half a rintic higher than the Umgara. Raw strength from Sagog was channeled into his bulging arms which compressed Caliben's shoulders until Caliben delivered a kick to Sagog's midsection, knocking the giant on his back. Caliben ran to Sagog with flailing punches from the front toward the giant's head and repeatedly spun and delivered body shots with his backward facing arms, which popped like kracklins hitting their target over and over. Blood flowed from Sagog's face and Caliben delivered a blow that knocked Sagog, face down, to the cold surface.

The rintic bellowed their war cry boosting the confidence of their tribe and Caliben. Sagog rolled over and got to his knee, then was up on his feet again and roared with pain and anger, a sound that filled all within earshot with unease. Caliben ran at Sagog and this time, the seemingly mindless beast sidestepped and latched on to the rear facing arms of the Umgara. Sagog's powerful arms pulled as Caliben's arm muscles splayed. Caliben was helpless. Sagog growled as he placed his large grimy foot against the back of Caliben and pulled at both arms while forcefully kicking against the Umgara's back. Caliben yelled out in such a way that you couldn't hear his arms rip apart from his back, but the red blood splattered across the green grass and gurgled down the back of his legs. Caliben spun around and swung at Sagog who caught his fist and used Caliben's own arm to beat him down. Sagog's mouth foamed as he repetitively struck the Umgara until he no longer moved, and the suvanth giant dropped the Umgara appendage that was roughly the size of a rintic youth on top of his foe. A beast entranced and enraged is the only way to describe the event that unfolded before the tribes. Gasps and murmurings went out amongst the rintic before the suvanth filled the plains with their war cry. Sagog turned back and slobber and angst poured from the beast, covering his pale chest as he strutted toward Taukin with enmity in his blackened eyes. Avent yelled for support and rintic soldiers surrounded the Eltepsu as they made their way through the crowd of soldiers, and a barrier was made between them and an incensed Sagog. A few brave rintic swung their long swords at Sagog who received some shallow cuts, but it was Sagog who wielded a lifeless rintic soldier and thrashed at those who dared face him. Bodies flew all around as Sagog gained ground on Taukin and the Eltepsu, and once he caught them they turned to face their fate. The Eltepsu, Taukin, and Drami Sol all faced Sagog, fearing that their fate was about to be dealt by the lethal hand of the giant. Their trembling legs stumbled backwards not knowing what was behind them.

A mysterious hooded being, whose face was covered with a dull green cloth leaving his piercing gray eyes visible, stood in the midst of the now-empty battlefield, between Sagog and those seeking safety. He wore no armband, no markings, and none knew if he was friend or foe until he locked eyes with Taukin and spoke in a calm but resolute voice, "Go." Taukin's skin morphed as bright as the Eastern star, not because he was afraid, but because this masked being had no fear of Sagog. Taukin slowly backed away, captivated by this warrior's presence. Sagog's head twisted to the side slightly and he examined the being, not knowing what type of creature dared challenge him, before letting out a fierce roar of intimidation; only the mysterious one wasn't stirred. He slowly moved to a slight crouching stance, unsheathing his sword—which peculiarly was an anglis blade inscribed with dark writing unfamiliar to Taukin—and positioned the blade overhead with the tip pointed at Sagog.

Infuriated, Sagog charged at the hooded adversary. Taukin witnessed speed unlike any other. ***Is it godly ability?*** thought Taukin. The hooded figure ran toward Sagog, jumping higher than the giant to draw the Sagog's focus upward, blinding the creature, and with quickness slid underneath, sticking his blade into Sagog's rear upper leg propelling himself up to the giant's massive shoulders. Sagog danced around, flailing his arms overhead in an attempt to reach the warrior, but was unsuccessful. His anglis blade plunged deep into Sagog's spine, right above his knot, quieting the giant and dropping him to his knees before his large face met the cool Onestonian ground with a thud. The hooded being rode the beast down to the ground and stepped off his lifeless skull, slinging the excess blood into the grassy field.

Sagog's defeat breathed new life to the rintic, and the soldiers' cheers turned into aggression against the suvanth. Swords and shields clanked and sparked, energizing Taukin and the others. Suvanth exited the Kappa

River tunnel like insects fleeing their nest and swarmed the masked warrior. Avent and his rescue squad made it back to Taukin and the Eltepsu. Fesenius was propped up by his two fellow rescuers and they all started toward the Norody forest, seeing that the path to the Carth Forest past the kulee fields was all but sealed off by the suvanth. Rintic formed protective perimeters around the Eltepsu and Taukin, even Drami Sol per Avent's orders as they moved through the battle. Flauva balls rapidly rolled by, trapping suvanth to their sticky exterior and adding to their rolling mass as they bounced through the waving kulee fields. More and more rintic soldiers poured out from the Norody forest, offering protection to the Eltepsu and a welcomed relief to those at the battlefield front. Kracklins whirred past, thudding into the unsuspecting suvanth warriors, knocking them off their feet and tearing into their flesh. A platoon of suvanth charged after the group, but a brave squad of rintic took hold and set up their fighting position awaiting the attack. In a clever move, the suvanth launched brickels over Taukin and the Eltepsu, slowing them down and forcing them to veer to the East, but not before trapping two screaming rintic soldiers, rooting their legs to the frosty field. Rintic hacked away at the sprawling black roots that regrew each time they were cut, the fear in their voice urged the soldiers to keep cutting away.

Looking back, Taukin saw the squad of rintic overtaken by the suvanth. "They're closing in!" yelled Taukin. The two soldiers propping Fesenius slowed as their energy waned.

Avent called for two scouts mounted on inobi sleds. In full stride, Avent yelled out, "Tell your commanding officer… Captain Avent requests…reinforcements from Fort Benja. Send word to…the Umgara…we have the Eltepsu…and the Basatab…we're being overrun…make haste!" With great urgency, the scouts steered their inobi sleds Northeast and darted off toward the Norody Forest. Taukin and Avent relieved the two soldiers and held up Fesenius, whose face was a permanent grimace and who could only hop along with one leg during their run. Avent yelled out, "Keep moving to Lithica!" As their distance from the Carth forest grew, their numbers declined and the number of suvanth increased. Suvanth poured out toward Taukin and the Eltepsu as if waves from Olin Fell were overtaking the land and the rintic.

In their run, Taukin turned to Avent, "There's too many…we won't make it…I can stop them…I need agrum," said Taukin.

"No!" replied Avent. Lantia, weakened and unaccustomed to the arduous activity stumbled and fell. Drami Sol pulled Lantia back up and helped the Eltepsu move ahead.

"The Eltepsu need to rest," said Drami Sol with her hand on Lantia's hairy back.

Avent spied a platoon of rintic forming a fighting position up ahead. "There, not far, the barricade, keep moving!" Drami Sol pulled Lantia to her and Lantia leaned on her while they ran ahead, slower than before. Rintic soldiers continued to pour in and tried to establish a barrier between the suvanth and Eltepsu, but just as fast as they arrived, the soldiers were dispatched by the deadly suvanth. This sacrificial pattern continued until they entered the barricade, which was a crossed stack of stripped swaul branches positioned in a jutting pattern and set up four wide, with platoons of rintic flanking each side. Fesenius's skin darkened and he grimaced when his protruding leg bone was bumped by a passing soldier, as Taukin and Avent carefully lowered him to the pelt stretcher.

One soldier on each end of Fesenius's body raised the stretcher when Avent nodded and looked to some bright-eyed subordinate soldiers, "You three get him to Fort Benja."

Fesenius grabbed Taukin's arm and said, "Protect the Eltepsu." Taukin's skin's pattern was violet once again, feeling a temporary sense of peace as platoons made a path for Fesenius, but his gaze shook loose and he took up arms to allow the Eltepsu time to recover.

Avent yelled out, "Protect the Eltepsu!" as he swung his long sword and beheaded a suvanth warrior who climbed up the barricade. Rintic launched hundreds of bashams over the barricade with a sling large enough to hold a rintic tribesman. The palm-sized creatures' plump brown sacks and green slender legs made their way onto the suvanth's chests and backs before bursting and spilling their green acidic fluid on their victims, causing tremendous pain and death. More rintic appeared from the Norody forest, and they had almost made it to the Eltepsu when the suvanth overran the barricades. "We have to move. Soldiers fall in behind the Eltepsu!" said Avent as they hurriedly made their way to the Norody forest. The suvanth grew in number and the rintic from the Norody and Carth forests were dwindling.

A suvanth yelled out, "Taukin has the Basatab, come brothers!"

As they ran, Taukin turned to Avent, "We won't make it…I must do something."

Avent knew Taukin was right and conceded. "Do what you must," replied Avent.

"Who has agrum?" yelled out Taukin desperately. With focus on the battle, every rintic's eyes were on the multiplying suvanth.

"I have agrum," came the squeaky voice of Lantia. Taukin smiled graciously and approached his friend.

"Run your hand along my side," said Lantia exhausted and frail and Taukin did as he was told. The most diminutive of pale brown hands protruded the tufts of dark brown hair holding an elder vial of green agrum. Taukin's eyes widened at this, but he had no time to process or ask questions. He grabbed up the vial and reached for the pych pods kept safe in his inner pocket, but they were gone. He checked other holdings in his coverings, but they contained the charm, luminescence bulb, jewel, and light cipher. Somewhere between Sheol Balla and the Northern plains of gadush, the pych pods were lost.

"No…No…" growled Taukin, "I can't!"

Surprised, Avent asked, "Why not?"

"I lost them," said Taukin. Taukin's skin brightened to gold, and he said, "It ends here."

Suvanth battled their way closer to the Eltepsu, who now were wearied and moved as slow as dokas. "Take up arms, all of you, fight!" yelled Avent. Drami Sol unsheathed her curved and hooked kalarmy blade and readied herself. Taukin forced his skin to an intimidating white with pulsating brown spots to match his fellow rintic and picked up a fallen warrior's sword. Suvanth warriors closed off the line of rintic soldiers from the Norody forest encircling the Eltepsu in a vicious trap. Taukin was caught between two suvanth, one upright and one with his backbone removed. He lunged at the one on all fours and lobbed off an ear, sending the suvanth into a frenzy. The other suvanth swung his sword at Taukin's neck, but Taukin, fast and precise, blocked the suvanth blade with his long blade. Taukin kicked back at his attacker knocking him backward and at the same time swung his sword downward at the crawling suvanth who pounced at Taukin. Blood spilled from the crawling creature's split skull, painting the ochre field red as he fell over lifeless. The lone suvanth ran at Taukin, who in defense formed a cross with his blades, blocking the forward attack, and used the suvanth's momentum to fall backward and kick the suvanth overhead into the raging battle.

Drami Sol stabbed and ripped open the chest of her attacker and yelled, "Avent behind you!" as a suvanth backbone came directly at his back, but was cut in two by Taukin's blade. Avent and Taukin locked eyes briefly, each understanding the gravity of the situation, Avent nodded and they returned to the fight. No sooner had Taukin rid himself of the two suvanth, when four more appeared, their covered eyes fixed upon Taukin. Taukin's skin went violet and his pattern went back to its normal speckled white spots, knowing that the skin color and pattern at the time of death is the color it would remain after death. He wanted to be remembered as he was—not rintic, not suvanth, but both. His head dropped back and his focus went to the sister moons moving toward alignment, then remembered the jewel in his coverings pocket. Hope was gone and he reached in and carefully removed the amber-colored stone which shone brightly even in the blinding light from the Eastern star. Just as the suvanth moved in, Taukin raised the jewel overhead to break it against the rock at his feet, but below him was a pych pod, black as the quiesce. Taukin forced the pod down his gullet and tore into the elder vial, guzzling as much as possible as it spilled out the sides of his mouth. Suvanth blades came hurling down upon Taukin and froze at his face with a violet glow, scarcely seen in the brightness of the star overhead. All suvanth near Taukin looked on as he cried out, throwing his arms outward tossing those he could see back into the mass of oncoming suvanth. Taukin summoned up the bag of kracklins next to him and ran into the Fell of the enemy slinging kracklins at all he could see, tearing into them systematically and so quickly it was a metallic blur. A glowing violet push from Taukin kept the suvanth from getting within two rintic of him. Their focus was on the Basatab and therefore on Taukin and as he went so did they. Taukin moved through the suvanth with great speed and with kracklins whirring all around like stinging whits to its victim. Taukin led them away from the Eltepsu and back toward the tunnel from which they came. He then leapt high, seeing the suvanth from above as crawling insects on the plains of Gadush. A platoon of rintic were cut off from their company and surrounded by suvanth outside of the Carth forest. Taukin summoned the largest Swaul tree from the edge of the forest and with it horizontal, leveled the suvanth all around the rintic platoon in a sweeping circular motion before landing next to the rintic. Fear was read on the suvanth and rintic alike, not for each other, but of Taukin. A mixture of relief and gratitude and shock poured forth from the rintic—all but two that approached Taukin with purpose.

"Soyha!" yelled Taukin as he moved to embrace her, but as Taukin moved in close her fist met his face with enough force to cock his head to the side and draw blood from his lip, forcing his skin yellow. Taukin ran his fingers over his busted lip and turned back to see Soyha standing next to Keel.

"You stole my legacy!" she said, fiery-eyed and skin darkened. "I trained my entire life for this! I was to retrieve the light cipher." Taukin replied, "I was selfish. I'm so sorry. I never meant for any of this to happen."

"Your brother could have died!" screamed Soyha.

"Forgive me, both of you," conceded Taukin. Keel stepped up to Taukin who stood steady, ready for a second blow, but his brother paused and stared at Taukin for what seemed like a tem-cycle. "Go ahead," said Taukin, expecting to feel the brunt of his brother's strength. Keel squeezed him and Taukin hugged him back in a firm embrace.

"Best you let that hit be from the both of us," said

Keel and pulled back, tears swallowed their eyes and they laughed. Soyha shook her head and joined them in the embrace and for a par-tem it felt like the war was over and life was the way it was before they were soldiers. No sooner had they released than a lone suvanth appeared before them upright, and his back toward Taukin in the now-barren field. Taukin summoned this being to him and twisted his body around so that they were eye to eye.

Bitur-Udo held the opened suvanth bauble with a knowing look smeared across his face, his skin bright blue with pulsing red stars. "What have you done?" asked Taukin and released his seranphopidal grip on his brother. Bitur-Udo vanished and a stream of blackness roared down from the sky to the Peah mounds, followed by a deafening sound as if a mountain fell from sky. A blast of cool air went through the plains in an ominous wave. A god was upon them.

CHAPTER 13

REVELATIONS

Overhead the sky was blackening as if quiesce overtook the planet but at a rapid pace. Soon it was dark, similar to the quiesce, but in a surreal way knowing that just a few par-tems ago it was warmer and as bright as the Eastern star would allow during the late-cycle, and not as dark as pure quiesce. An aura of ambient light surrounded the plains, but it was just enough to allow the suvanth to remove their slit goggles and not be affected.

From the direction of the Peah mounds, a swirling buzzing black haze that seemed to orbit itself, with multiple bands of darkness, approached Taukin. It was as wide as seven huts and as tall as the walls of Fort Carth. Blasts of air spouted from the enormity of the cloud, sending the dead and splintered kulee and tree fragments away from it while emitting a noise like grinding stones. A wicked face, part being, part beast protruded from the black cloud. Its dark-gray, pointed nose and protruding cheek bones along with its completely blackened eyes made most of the suvanth's skin purple with fear while the rintic put forth a false skin of intimidation, white with brown pulses.

It spoke loud and fierce as if many beings and many beasts spoke in unison and with a blistering chill from its mouth, "Ruler of nations bow before me." When it spoke, it's long ivory teeth like that of a satupha, contrasted the darkness, making the mass of nearby suvanth run in fear. Taukin appeared using his left forearm as a shield to block the debris from hitting his tilted face, his skin violet and glistening with sweat. All suvanth cowered far behind and away from the god.

"My Lord, the time has come for Bazwodda, the final battle," said Bitur-Udo, who appeared near Taukin and on his knee in front of the gusts of the god.

The echoing voice spoke, "It is forbidden to possess a godly ability without recompense."

"My Lord, my debt has been paid," pleaded Bitur-Udo.

"Sacrifice is required," echoed Cenro as his eyes focused on Taukin.

"Who are you to demand of me?" asked Taukin, insolent and arrogant fueled by the agrum that colored his eyes green.

Just then the cloud grew massive as if it was a newly formed peak in the middle of the plains right before it shrank to the size of a rintic hut, then kept shrinking slower as a pallid foot materialized and another and the form of a being, gray and ashen as a burnt tribesman appeared before them swallowing the buzzing black cloud with his head tilted back until it was completely consumed, then looked directly at Taukin with his full ebony eyes.

"You know who I am."

"The bringer of darkness evokes no fear in me," replied Taukin, his hands quivering with a need for release.

"Fear me and live."

"Fear is reserved for those with equal," said Taukin firmly.

Cenro pointed his open palm at Taukin and twisted his palm skyward and with that, Taukin flew upward, his body outlined by darkened seranphopids and his arms and legs pulled back with his torso stretching toward Cenro as he grunted, face skyward, eyes closed, and teeth exposed in a wretched agony.

From the interior edge of rintic came the high priest Kuxain leading his Warriors of Light, a platoon of dark-robed priests and tribesmen of the cloth carrying staffs tipped with chromatic crystals. "Let the light repel you!" screamed the hairless priest and started a chant that the other warriors channeled with their voices and aimed their crystals at the darkened god. Words as old as the planet itself poured from their mouths and grew louder, but this only managed to anger Cenro and he summoned their hoods over their faces and with a closing of hand destroyed their staffs completely. Kuxain and the other Warriors fell back into the safety of the Carth forest.

Cenro's focus went back to Taukin and a slight closing of hand led to dreadful screams from Taukin. Keel went to move toward Cenro but Soyha grabbed him, "Don't," Keel shook loose and ran at the ashen god with his long sword drawn and Cenro, with his right hand, raised Keel up alongside Taukin but in a fashion free of pain, attentive to Cenro's words, "The true bringer of Bazwodda, yet this planet is not ready as you are not ready."

Cenro turned toward Taukin and said, "Remit."

Taukin fought to push his head level in order to see Cenro, but only managed to move his head slightly toward the god and his eyes remained skyward toward the eclipse. "How?" The word struggled out of Taukin's clenched jaw.

"A life worthy."

"Take me," grunted Keel, breathless.

Cenro's focus went to Keel and he spoke to the rintic, "You will unite the tribes and rule this planet."

Bitur-Udo cried out, "I have learned your ways, I shall rule!" But Cenro's focus was on sacrifice, and the words of Bitur-Udo were as the fleeting embers from the battlefield.

Cenro scanned the opening of the field and only Soyha remained amongst the random rintic soldiers. "You," declared Cenro.

Soyha's skin went pale green and she shook her head in disbelief as Taukin roared, "Not her!" Cenro fixated on Soyha and her body darkened with seranphopids and she cried out in agony but Taukin, strengthened with resolve, took advantage of Cenro's neglect. He forced his head and eyes downward enough so that he could see Cenro, and his eyes glowed orange with anger and his light burst forth and with all the seranphopids he could summon, he surrounded Cenro the bringer of dark with an orange aura and summoned the god skyward, piercing the black cloud and flying toward the Eastern star until Taukin could no longer distinguish between his glow and the great star's glow.

Wind rustled the shards of kulee and splinters of swaul tree around the trio, and the darkened haze that covered the sky was lifted revealing the warmth of the Eastern star. Keel lay upon the cold forest floor processing the words of Cenro, and Taukin lowered his hands and fell to his knees, weary from the unseen creatures. On hands and knees Taukin crawled to Soyha who lay motionless.

Taukin cupped her fragile head in his violet hands, "Soyha, no," he said but there was no response. Taukin lowered his head to her pale green forehead and prayed quietly to Hobaja Vael. Keel went to his feet and staggered to Taukin and Soyha.

"Is she?" asked Keel with watery eyes.

Soyha gasped a deep breath and her eyes went wide, "He's here," she said, wide awake, looking skyward at the black object speeding toward them. As if a blanket of pitch fell over the planet, the sky darkened as before, where there was scarce enough light to see, but enough darkness to feel the enormity of coming events.

A gray bolt with yellow and orange slivers crackled down from the sky striking the ground before Taukin, knocking them back onto the cold surface and leaving a small crater and a frigid blast of air flowing in waves through the plains. Amongst the smell of burning soil, Cenro stood and grew tall and wide, the size of a god stone, with shifting cracks of molten materials, before speaking in a voice that penetrated like that of forty Umgara, "Your impudence will be rewarded with death." Cenro raised his arms toward the sky and a funnel of darkness swirled overhead, the tip of the funnel drifting downward to Cenro's awaiting ashen arms.

Taukin quickly went to his feet and scarcely floated above the crater, glowing less bright than before, and with focus on Cenro, he summoned the seranphopids upon the god; but as Cenro began to glow violet, the glowing field collapsed into the shadow that was once a god and Cenro was nowhere to be found. Taukin raised his arms outward and rose higher than the towering swaul trees in an attempt to find Cenro, but there were a multitude of shadows moving among shadows along the field of the dead. High above Taukin, the tip of the black funnel spiraled downward.

"Taukin, move!" shouted Keel from below just as the uprooted swaul tree slammed into Taukin, sending him flailing into the thick of the battlefield tumbling about the bloody bodies until he stopped, limp and unconscious. Keel ran to aid Taukin, but just as he did, Cenro's bulky body again collapsed into a legion of shadows and scattered as they moved about the bodies toward Taukin. It was a race to Taukin and Keel couldn't match the speed of darkness through the maze of the dead.

Taukin stirred and made out a blurry being moving toward him. With wobbly legs, Taukin went to his feet and a voice yelled out to him, "Taukin, run!" which came through as though he was speaking to him from a great distance. Taukin shook his head and his senses adjusted to the dim world. "Run!" came through clearly and Taukin heeded these words as the shadows lurched at him and with great suvanth speed, Taukin ran, clearing piles of fallen soldiers on his way back to Keel. Taukin reached into his inner pocket and removed the shimmering, amber light stone as he ran to his brother, which shown in amber rays among the open field. A shadow-raised mound of dirt tripped Taukin, sending the shimmering light stone rolling and bouncing to Keel who lifted the stone and examined its brilliance with wonder.

A horrendous sound like that of a thousand straxan whooshing their wings overhead penetrated the sky and the tip of the swirling funnel neared them. Taukin yelled out to Keel, "Shield your eyes and break the jewel!" Keel continued to examine the sparkling jewel, blocking out all that was happening around him as if mesmerized and looked at Taukin, but couldn't make out his words over the spinning torrent above. "We're all going to die! Break it!" said Taukin, whose view of Keel was blocked by a quivering haze of stacked shadows in the form of Cenro, a form without matter, yet through the shadow, the amber glow of the stone shone through. A pull like the beasts of the shadow waters dragged him toward the funnel as it neared them, even louder than before and with more ferocity.

Suvanth warriors and rintic soldiers alike tumbled toward the funnel in an act of obedience, an unnatural force upon the natural world. Crawling creatures were not immune to the draw of the funnel and they scrambled and slithered and jumped, only to be pulled back by the invisible force. Taukin gripped a rock no larger than his fist and it loosened from the soil but it didn't move, as only living objects were the under influence of the funnel's pull. Keel stabbed the field with his long blade and Soyha reached for Keel's hand but was sucked past him adjacent to Cenro's shadow and into Taukin's view. Soyha latched onto a loose bloody suvanth backbone and used the funnel's pull to wedge the pointed bone into the dirt, holding on desperately as it twisted her completely around.

Tribesmen's screams rivaled that of the Kravae's shrills. Their fingers dug into the dark soot, but there was nothing to grip or grab onto and despite their best efforts, they were dragged toward the epicenter of the funnel. A violent, blackened, viscous swirl of debris and dirt was cast out from the base of the funnel as it made landfall on the trail. Taukin tried summoning the tribesmen away, but the force of the black twisting funnel was great upon the Onestonians and his summoning ability waned. A lone rintic soldier was pulled up into the deadly twisting funnel and his body was tangled and torn by the sheer force of the storm as he went up and disappeared into the blackness. There was nothing of Cenro to summon, not the vestige of a god standing right in front of him, and not the light stone for its form was obscured. Taukin was pulled within five rintic of the deadly cyclone when he shouted again, "Break the jewel!" Taukin looked behind to see rintic soldiers getting pulled up, unable to escape the powerful suction.

Soyha's legs had just lifted off the ground when she yelled, "Give me the jewel!" and Keel tossed her the light stone and she held it so Taukin could see it clearly and said, "Strike it!" and she threw the jewel at Taukin, who used his remaining ability to summon the fist-sized rock directly at the light stone. A brilliant explosion forced Taukin to plant his face into the cold dirt as an incredibly intense display of light penetrated through Cenro and the black funnel and darkness overhead. A bone-chilling roar that sounded like a beast's echo receding down a hole went out and returned to its source before it went silent.

Warmth coated Taukin's hairless head and when it dissipated, he lay motionless, listening intently. The sound of a crawling insect shuffling globules of soil filled Taukin's violet ear and he slowly raised his dirt-clad face, spitting out loam in the process. Light from the Eastern star filled the plains once again and Soyha and Keel went to Taukin. "Cenro?" asked Keel, dazed by the explosion.

"The darkness has gone and Cenro with it," replied Taukin still somewhat shocked by the events and gazing upon the towering god stone that now stood tall and isolated in the middle of the plains of Gadush. Keel ran his trembling hand along the smooth gray stone surface, knowing just par-tems before a dark god stood in its place.

As the sky cleared Soyha spoke, "Aebean and Febus are nearing alignment."

"Lithica!" said Taukin, starting a trot on his way toward the Norody forest.

"You *do* have the Basatab?" asked Soyha, flustered as she sidled alongside him and Keel.

Taukin held open his coverings and reached in his inner pocket and pulled the light cipher up enough to know, but not show others "It's here," retorted Taukin as he patted his coverings for their reassurance.

Keel looked back and said, "They haven't given up, look!" Suvanth poured out of the tunnel near the lower Kappa River and flooded the fields taking up weapons from the fallen and charging at Taukin. Soyha, Keel and Taukin ran full out toward the Norody forest in what seemed a cleared path lined with the dead, but their pace was no match for the spry suvanth who caught up to them after five dole par-tems. Surrounded, the trio sensed defeat and their skin color and pattern went through the emotions, but their resolve remained intact.

"The forest stands firm," shouted Soyha encouraging Taukin and Keel as they steadied their blades and replied, "The forest stands firm!"

Keel quipped to Taukin, "Do something…move us from here!"

"It's not that simple," said Taukin as they circled, backs toward each other, and closed the gap between them and the suvanth who squeezed ever closer.

"Then we cut our way to Lithica!" said Soyha as she lashed out with her long blade, ripping open the chest of the nearest suvanth, killing him instantly. Suvanth collapsed on them when a horn blew, loud and far-reaching from the North. A battle cry from the Umgara echoed across the plains and the suvanth took notice. Umgara soldiers, two hundred strong, faces striped red and white wielding axes, blades, and clubs of swaul wood, emerged from the Norody forest and rushed as fast as they could toward the trio. Most suvanth turned squealing toward Sheol Balla, but others remained, willing to test their mettle in order to keep their steady flow of agrum intact. Soyha, Keel, and Taukin fought, their blades stabbing and slicing in a flurry at the suvanth, whose numbers dwindled with the sense of impending doom moving their way. When the Umgara arrived, they tore into the suvanth, ripping them apart with their powerful arms, spilling their viscera and throwing limbs and torsos about. Umgara blades grew insatiable for blood and sliced open the suvanth as they tried to fight the protectors. Small packs of suvanth banded together to confuse the Umgara, attacking from all angles with immense speed managing to seriously wound or kill some protectors. As one Umgara fell another appeared to inflict justice on the grievous suvanth. An Umgara soldier with two blades, a heavy axe, and a lumpy club tore across a squad of suvanth, cutting them down in a single blow. Umgara kept on the move pushing through like a sweeping wave of annihilation, leaving behind a sanguine trail of demise. A majority of Umgara, with the help of the Norody and Carth rintic, continued to push the suvanth back to Sheol Balla, while a group formed a circle of protection around Taukin, Soyha, and Keel.

"Young Taukin, where is the Basatab?" said a deep

and familiar voice. Taukin looked up to see the Umgara Itil standing over him.

Taukin checked to ensure he had not lost the one thing his future and the future of Onestonia depended on—the light cipher was nestled snug against his chest. "Here," said Taukin as he held the white crystalline cipher up toward Itil before securing it back in his inner pocket.

"Come with me," replied Itil as he extended a hand from his back toward Taukin.

"I've never heard better words," said Taukin as he smiled with relief and grasped Itil's pommel-sized finger, launching himself onto Itil's muscular back.

"We must make it to Lithica before the effergy," said Itil. Soyha and Keel were picked up by the Umgara and rested against their pelt-covered backs, held securely by their backward facing arms as they rushed away toward Lithica with only rintic and Umgara along their flanks.

CHAPTER 14
THE DOME OF ROCK

A row of green, feathery ealtapa trees guarded the entrance into the Norody forest. Taukin ducked his head down behind Itil's head to avoid the lashing of the branches. A dark loamy trail appeared that Itil quickly went to and continued down at a pace that rivaled Swinzal's speed. To Taukin, the forest was a mix of new foliage and creatures, and smelled of a crisp scent like that of a green swaul tree split open to its roots. Giant swaul trees and shorter ealtapa trees lined the trail and covered the forest floor. Further into the dense forest, long, slender emerald- and tan-colored trees bridged the gap in height between ealtapa and swaul. Black creatures with bright orange heads and small dark eyes, stretched their bodies from one slender tree to another, never touching the ground below. The extent at which their bodies stretched seemed boundless as they covered distances of over five rintic in length.

"How much farther to Lithica?"

"Far enough…that we might…trail Aebean's beam," no sooner had Itil finished his words than Taukin witnessed one of the slender trees open its trunk, capture the creature and encapsulate it completely within its bark. Taukin didn't understand what he just witnessed nor Itil's words. Fading beams of light penetrated through the dense foliage of the Norody forest lighting the path to Fort Benja.

"Make way!" shouted the Captain of the marching Norody rintic with their white and red armbands, they stared at the giants carrying their eclectic group of passengers as they ran past them. A yellow trisian ascended marking the beginning of the stirless time, still the Eastern star scarcely peeked through the forest trees. Rows of brightly lit tethered trisians lined the trail to Fort Benja. Taukin spotted the rintic scouts sent to fetch the Umgara standing right outside Fort Benja's walls, which stood fifteen rintic or so high, but was smaller than Fort Carth. There were rocks mortared around the wooden walls and guards paced the tops of the fort by torchlight.

Taukin spoke up, "The Eastern star is alive, can we stop for a drink?"

"There's no time…before Aebean…eclipses Febus," said Itil as he ran past Fort Benja and on toward Lithica. In the darkened quiesce sky, the large moon Aebean was on its path to engulf its smaller sister Febus. The sister moons now lit the thinning forest and large rocks replaced the trees the closer they got to Lithica. Aebean and Febus were a guiding light for the Umgara whose pace never waned, as if their blood was pure agrum. All light from Fort Benja had disappeared and the trails wound around boulders the size of Sagog. Soyha was carried right behind Taukin, and Keel behind Soyha. Even with the moon's white illumination and Taukin's ability to see in the darkest of places, Soyha and Keel could not be seen between the hills and rockfaces that made up the trail. Up ahead, through the rocks and trees, was a clearing with a rounded gray stone dome the height of ealtapa trees planted in the middle, and surrounded by Umgara and rintic.

Taukin turned to Soyha, "This is yours," and he carefully handed the crystalline cylinder to Soyha whose skin went white with wavering blue lines before cracking a hint of a smile.

General Reibo appeared through the wall of Umgara and approached Itil and the others as they dismounted. Lantia and Cuvsor joined their kind. "Where is the Basatab?" asked Reibo in his reverberating voice.

"General Reibo," responded Soyha, as she held up the light cipher and bowed toward the Umgara. General Reibo's massive hand dwarfed the crystalline and stone cylinder.

General Reibo spoke to Soyha, "The Umgara are indebted to you." General Reibo turned to Taukin, "My trust in you has been justified." Avent and Drami Sol appeared next to Taukin, Soyha, and Keel and they all followed Reibo through the Umgara and rintic, ignoring the stares and whispers, to get to the awaiting Eltepsu.

Aebean united with Febus and the combined light from the sister moons formed an intense pure beam of white light that slowly drew a path from the edge of the clearing toward Lithica. As was the custom, the responsibility to initiate the opening of Lithica fell to the second eldest Eltepsu. Arbmere, who cradled the light cipher with all six fingers and both narrow palms, carefully placed the Basatab level into an opening of a thin, brown metallic crescent, which was rooted by a sturdy rock base, connecting one side of the crescent to the other. Arbmere's delicate tan hands twisted the five crystalline rings to align the proper order of symbols, each ring containing seven markings each. Only the Eltepsu knew the correct pattern of the five symbols which changed every twelfth cycle, and only with the correct sequence of markings would Lithica open its portal. Arbmere carefully examined the order of the crystals with the bright beam of light nearing the stone base, then stepped back away from the Basatab. Ten Eltepsu formed a tight circle around Taliph and the seventh eldest, Nuban, who looked wider than the other Eltepsu. Ten hands, one from each Eltepsu, were tenderly placed on Taliph and Nuban and the Eltepsu's round eyes closed; all twelve faced upward as their harmonious voices sang praise to Hobaja Vael. Just then the radiant beam touched the light cipher like a brilliant finger extended from Aebean. Five rays of white light shot out from the Basatab, extending to the side of Lithica's smooth curved surface. On the side of the gray curved rock, five recesses appeared, one for each of the beams of light and glowed the shape of the cipher's markings. A loud grinding sound of stone against stone resonated from Lithica as it opened from the top center with each half disappearing into the ground, exposing a flowing stream unknown to Taukin. One after another, the Eltepsu moved into the open chamber, drenching their brown shaggy hair from their waist down.

Taliph and Nuban embraced in the center of the stream while the other Eltepsu formed a circle around them. Aebean and Febus's light had moved directly over the Eltepsu, showering them in a brilliant cloak of pure white illumination. Suddenly Taliph's hair changed from brown to white and Taliph's large round eyes locked with Nuban's eyes. Taliph's head slowly lowered, but kept falling further until Taliph disappeared. Taukin looked around frantically trying to find a sign of Taliph, but Taliph was no longer. Taukin's skin went deep blue and his tears reflected the bright glow of the moons above. A large pale hand embraced Taukin's shoulder, it was the hand of Subian, who smiled gently at Taukin and pointed his attention back to the circle of Eltepsu.

From the flowing stream within the ring of Eltepsu, a small white-haired Eltepsu newborn was held up by Nuban, who had given birth. "This Eltepsu shall be named Eyf Onda, for the tribulations of the Eltepsu before birth," said Nuban, whose large eyes were full of tears of sadness and joy. Cheers erupted throughout the crowd, except for Taukin. His skin was full of mixed emotions.

Subian spoke, "This is the decegen process. One life given for another taken. It has been this way since Hobaja Vael breathed life into the Eltepsu." Taukin watched as Febus separated from Aebean and their combined moonbeam dissipated and with it, the small Eltepsu's white hair turned brown, like its older kin.

As they stepped out from the waters, the Eltepsu

shook their long-haired bodies casting droplets all around to prevent freezing during the journey back to Binesmir. They were placed on massive melps by the Umgara before climbing up themselves to join the Eltepsu. Eyf Onda, who could not walk, nor talk yet, was swaddled, tan face protruding from the white cloth, and carefully carried to the caravan of melps by Nuban, the birthing Eltepsu. Arbmere removed the light cipher and the grinding noise was heard once more, until a dull thud signified that Lithica's decegen waters were well protected again.

A battle-scarred Umgara Colonel, whose insignia on his golden chest plate was partially covered in blood, appeared in front of the Gosin-Tare and General Reibo, "My Lord…General, the suvanth have been pushed back into Sheol Balla and our troops have closed off the tunnel entrance by the lower Kappa River. Our company of soldiers will remain near Promisel Point until such time as you call for their return. Our scouts have cleared the path back to the Carth Forest through Munda Ber," said the Colonel.

General Reibo looked to Gosin-Tare, "My Lord, we should leave. There's a chance the suvanth could make another advance."

Gosin-Tare turned to the crowd and spoke, "The time to depart is now, ensure the safety of the Eltepsu at all costs." A battalion of Norody and Carth rintic and a company of Umgara formed four lines that surrounded the Eltepsu. A squad of Umgara steered the melps with their scouts leading the way, the rintic battalions followed.

Gosin-Tare turned to Taukin who had reunited with Avent and Drami Sol. "Who is this suvanth among us?" asked Gosin-Tare.

Taukin replied, "My Lord, she is Drami Sol, ally to the rintic. She helped rescue Cuvsor and Lantia." Gosin-Tare nodded with concurrence.

The Umgara leader continued, "And she is to be trusted?"

"I trust her with my life," said Taukin, his skin as serious as could be.

Gosin-Tare looked at Taukin knowingly and said, "Trust is hardest to find once lost." Taukin knew the words were meant for him and his amber eyes and blue face dropped with shame. "Nevertheless, once found, it's nearly impossible to lose again," said Gosin-Tare and he gave a gentle smile to Taukin who nodded with concurrence, lightening his hue. Gosin-Tare turned to Avent, "I look forward to hearing your chronicle Captain Avent," said Gosin-Tare with his deep utterance, then he climbed up and held out his hand for his mate Subian who followed behind. Her long, white fur-laden pelt dragged the rocky ground as she stepped up onto the inverted shell of the melp. Subian turned her torso back to Taukin and pressed her large pale hands together and gave a bow to Taukin out of respect. Taukin returned the gesture with a deeper bow. "To Binesmir," said Gosin-Tare, and his driver shook the pelt reigns moving the large beast forward.

Taukin turned to Avent, "I need to see my mother."

"Speak with Lord Hiko first. He must know what transpired," said Avent.

Taukin's color morphed from yellow to orange as his head shook. "I can't lose her, not after all this…all that I've done for my tribe."

Avent grasped Taukin's shoulder, "I will do what I can to get you to Luspa," said Avent. Taukin paused for a par-tem then nodded.

Drami Sol stepped to Taukin, "I've never seen such an event; did you see the newborn Eltepsu?" asked Drami Sol, her skin green full of emotion. Soyha and Keel appeared and Taukin made the introductions. Soyha sized up Drami Sol, who seemed oblivious to the jealous glare of the taller and now gray and black-dotted rintic.

"Why is there a suvanth here?" asked Keel with as much ignorance as could be afforded.

"Drami Sol helped us in battle above and below ground. She is friend to the rintic, there's no need to worry," said Avent sincerely.

The air went still and the silence slowed Taukin's mind and body until it was penetrated by a low, vibrating voice, "Ride with me," said General Reibo who appeared alone on a melp.

"It is much appreciated General. Our tribulations have worn us to our bones," said Captain Avent as they all climbed up the thick scaly legs onto the inverted shell. Reibo cracked the reigns, driving the creature forward. Drami Sol fell backward, but Taukin caught her before she fell off the melp and pulled her close enough to make her skin go orange and pulse with clusters of colorful spots. Taukin smiled a nervous smile and Drami Sol kissed his cheek, sending his skin bursting with every color and pattern he ever felt. Keel's eyes opened wide and Soyha's eyes squinted.

"Taukin stay alert, we must be wary of an attack," said Avent breaking up the affectionate bond between them.

"But the suvanth have been driven away," said Taukin but Avent's stare said all he needed to know. Taukin pulled back and scanned the tall, dark tree silhouettes for suvanth hiding in the trees or moving swiftly on the leafy forest floor. In the darkness Drami Sol could see just as well if not better than Taukin, so she followed Taukin's lead, searching for any signs of suvanth but occasionally General Reibo's colossal frame stole her eyes. Avent and Keel held out luminescence lamps lighting the tree line in search of suspicious signs and activity. Soyha took her place next to General Reibo and faced any direction as long as it was opposite Drami Sol. The rapid pace held by the melps was faster than what Taukin experienced during his trip to Binesmir. At this hastened rate the rintic didn't last long, some soldiers fell out in the Norody forest and others disappeared in the savory-scented kulee fields of the Gadush plains, but the caravan didn't slow its pace. It was near Kiosip Fell that the company of Carth rintic met the Norody rintic and they relieved their northern brethren with the new lumeren.

A pink and violet sky grew until the arms of the Eastern star reached out, quashing the tranquil colors and covering Onestonia in its warm embrace. All four columns of Norody rintic peeled off in a rear march and began their journey back through the tall kulee grass to

Fort Benja. Avent's fellow Captain gave the order for the Carth soldiers to flank the Eltepsu. Drami Sol and Keel slept through this changing of soldiers, and the breaching of the Eastern star forced Drami Sol to dawn her eye protection while Taukin's eyes were closed due to sheer exhaustion. Even Avent had difficulty keeping his wits about him and his eyes open.

"Hold tight," said General Reibo to the passengers and their eyes and minds awoke as they began to slide down the shell.

The caravan moved down the short cliff which led to the smooth gray stones that covered the dried Orlang riverbed, and up the other side was the awaiting path to Munda Ber inside the Carth forest. The familiar swaul trees and leaf-covered forest floor which marked the entrance to his home, was inviting. Passing into the Carth forest was a major milestone for Taukin, who couldn't keep a lone tear from streaming down his violet cheek.

Under the shadow of the forest canopy, Drami Sol removed her eye protection and said, "It's cold, but feels comforting…safe."

"You'll acclimate to life outside the pit. You can share my warmth," replied Taukin.

Soyha's skin remained gray and she rolled her eyes and said, "***It's not that cold.***"

Keel's eyes widened, witnessing the uncharacteristic acts of Soyha. "She's not used to surface cold," said Taukin, defending the suvanth's actions.

Drami Sol lowered her shoulder and Taukin draped his arm around her. "You helped me be free of Manista and now I'm here in this wonderous forest," said Drami Sol who nestled closer to Taukin.

Taukin's skin morphed to a dark-blue color when he said in a hushed tone, "You left the pit for Syonis, but…he's gone." Taukin paused to carefully watch Drami Sol's skin.

"Gone? To where?" asked Drami Sol.

"He's a prisoner at Akaretel," said Taukin.

Drami Sol moved away from Taukin to face him directly. "Upon what accusation is he imprisoned?" she asked.

"Conspiring against Lord Hiko. You were to be given to Syonis and in exchange Syonis would deliver Lord Hiko to Manista."

Drami Sol's skin morphed yellow with diagonal tiled darkened stripes, "Then I was to be a slave here as well."

"What will you do now?" asked Taukin. Avent heard the question and moved up next to General Reibo out of earshot of Taukin and Drami Sol, but Soyha and Keel listened intently.

She paused briefly before responding.

With one hand, Drami Sol softly cupped Taukin's square jaw and said, "There is another who has captured my affection."

Before Taukin's skin could change, Avent spoke up, "Munda Ber, we've made it." Waiting for the caravan were more rintic soldiers, among them was a Colonel all too familiar to Taukin.

The caravan slowed to a crawl then stopped once General Reibo's powerful voice shouted, "Halt!" making the sumoguls take flight and break the beams of light from the Eastern star.

"General Reibo," said Colonel Pella as he lowered his head down.

Reibo returned the gesture and replied, "Colonel," breaking the silence of the forest.

"I counted twelve Eltepsu. Praise and respect General, neither suvanth nor The Bringer of Dark can stop the Umgara's mission," said the Colonel standing in his pelt-based battle dress uniform with one sleeve empty.

"It wasn't the Umgara's doing," said General Reibo, moving aside to reveal Taukin and the others.

"Captain Avent, you made it," said Colonel Pella in a surprised tone.

Avent nodded at his superior, "Not just me Colonel, all of us," and Avent pointed to Keel, Taukin, Drami Sol, who quickly stood in Colonel Pella's presence, and Soyha.

"You've captured a suvanth? Well done," said Colonel Pella.

Taukin spoke up, "Colonel, her name is Drami Sol, and she helped the rintic and Eltepsu escape from Sheol Balla."

Soyha scanned the pathway and said, "Colonel Pella, where's my father?" and continued, "*He* should be greeting the caravan."

"Captain Avent, a word," said the decorated Colonel, stoic and rigid as if Soyha hadn't just spoke to him.

"Suvanth cannot remain in the Carth forest. You're aware of this," replied Pella.

Captain Avent interceded, "Colonel she will be under my supervision until Lord Hiko decides her fate."

"She will be under your supervision, by whose orders?" asked Pella pointedly.

"Colonel, if not for her my squad would have died in Sheol Balla."

Colonel Pella's brow furrowed, "No Captain, she will go with me, guarded under *my* supervision, but not as a collaborator, not while there is a war underway."

Taukin leaped from the melp, "The suvanth have been forced underground, the war is over."

Avent held up his hand to steady Taukin and spoke up, "Colonel Pella, with respect I say this, she fought alongside us at Gadush. I witnessed her slay her own kind to protect the Eltepsu. This must count for something?"

Colonel Pella's anger grew at the insolence cast at him by his subordinates and responded, "It counts enough for me that during a war with the suvanth, I spare her life while she stands in front of me here on the soil of my ancestors." Pella motioned for his guards to restrain her. Taukin moved to stop the guards, but Avent pressed his arm across Taukin's chest, stopping him from interfering. The guards assisted Drami Sol down from the melp, then tied her hands against her lower back.

"Don't touch her!" shouted Taukin, his skin dark as Olin Fell.

Avent pressed hard against Taukin's chest with both hands, "Let it go Taukin."

Drami Sol turned to Taukin and said, "What did I do wrong?"

Taukin, infuriated, said, "You're a suvanth. It seems that's all it takes," as he gave a look of disgust toward Colonel Pella.

Tears streamed from Drami Sol's round, cerulean eyes and her body quivered, "Taukin I'm scared. What do I do?"

Taukin roared with fury, his skin blazing orange and stripes wavering vertically, "Let her go!"

Colonel Pella spoke, "Captain, you better secure him before he makes the journey to Akaretel,"

Captain Avent said, "Calm yourself Taukin, this'll be sorted. Be patient."

Colonel Pella spoke again, but this time with contempt in his voice, "Captain Avent you are relieved, go home, your briefing will be in the lumeren at my quarters, understood?"

Captain Avent replied, "Your quarters?"

"Yes Captain, my quarters at Fort Carth."

"You mean General Meraco's quarters?"

"I'm acting-General. From now on address me as General Pella."

"What happened to General Meraco?" asked a stunned Avent.

"He had a soldier's death, his last breath was on the battlefield," said Colonel Pella, matter-of-factly.

Soyha screamed out, "No! No! He can't be gone!" as she jumped down from the melp, running to Pella when

Avent grabbed her and pulled her back to Taukin. Soyha's darkened skin turned tan with sorrow and her head collapsed on Taukin's shoulder, soaking his pelt with her tears.

General Reibo's voice perforated the emotions that filled the space, "General Pella, the Eltepsu need to make their way to Byrre Syra."

"Of course General," Pella said with a bow of his head, and turned to make the trek to Akaretel prison without delay along with Drami Sol, surrounded by a squad of rintic soldiers including three garandos and their handlers. The Umgara General parked his melp into the green growth of the waking forest and waved the caravan forward.

Drami Sol cried and stumbled as she was taken away and with heavy hearts, Taukin and Soyha turned back to pay homage to the Eltepsu as they passed by, riding high on the plodding black and tan melps.

Keel turned to Avent, "It's not right father." Avent assuaged Keel with a nod of concurrence. Taukin's skin turned blue, but morphed as the different Eltepsu went by and when Nuban and Eyf Onda appeared, a brief joy overcame Taukin again and Lantia looked on at Taukin who smiled at the sustainer. The last of the Eltepsu and trailing rintic soldiers passed, following the trail leading to Fort Carth and disappeared in a light-filled swirl of dust. Taukin unsheathed his short sabre and sunk it into the thick, barky trunk of a lone swaul tree and let out a yell so loud that it made a nearby nide of sumoguls take flight.

Taukin spoke out, "This is what we get for serving

our tribe, for risking our lives for them! Our allies are imprisoned for looking different!"

Avent held out his hands in a gesture of ease to Taukin, "I understand your frustration Taukin."

Taukin shot back facetiously, "Oh you do? You've been an outcast before?"

Avent's skin went blood red, showing his irritation to Taukin, which was a rare event.

Taukin's skin morphed to violet at Avent's display. "Colonel Pella delights in the pain of others," said Taukin.

Avent spoke again, "You're tired, and deservedly frustrated. We've wasted time here. We'll talk with the counsel and Lord Hiko when we get back to Byrre Syra."

General Reibo's penetrating voice broke the silence, "The caravan is far ahead. I suggest we move." As the melp trotted down the dark loamy path, Taukin slowly lost sight of Drami Sol, who appeared then disappeared in between the sparse malpwa trees.

General Reibo shook the reigns connected to the melp's bridle, driving the creature faster than Taukin knew was possible for the plodding beast. Staggering soldiers traveled the sides of the path staying clear of the thudding melp. The brunt of the freezing wind struck Taukin's face forcing him to crouch behind General Reibo. Avent stood with Reibo, but Keel, Taukin, and Soyha sat on the rigid melp shell. A crushing feeling of defeat covered Taukin like a cloak of anguish, but his heart went to Soyha whose skin and tears begged for his touch. Soyha leaned on

Taukin as Drami Sol had done earlier and he embraced her as they both rested their weary eyes. Keel went prone and succumbed to the rhythmic trance of the melp's movement. Occasional noises woke Taukin, but stress and exhaustion had their grip on Taukin's mind and body and wouldn't relinquish control until the caravan arrived at Byrre Syra and eagerness took over.

Taukin rose up as the Eastern star sunk down past the tree line and Soyha followed suit. Waiting at the center of Byrre Syra, among a cheering crowd of rintic, were Larnhi and Nelkum. Torches lit the path that the melps trod with the Eltepsu in the center of the procession. The caravan halted and Avent, Keel, and Taukin jumped from the melp and ran to their family. Nelkum was the first to meet Avent who raised his son's small frame against his pelt-covered chest and hugged him tight. Next was Larnhi, who squeezed Avent and Keel as tight as a Straxan grips its prey. They embraced each other close while Taukin and Soyha stood by watching. Larnhi pulled her tear-stained face from Avent's chest and reached her arm out for her son. Taukin slowly made his way to his family only to be pulled into the middle by Avent and they formed a circle of affection around Taukin.

"Solea, solea, solea, praise Hobaja Vael you're safe," said Larnhi, overwhelmed, and her skin pulsed with emotion.

Nelkum pulled back far enough to ask, "Where have you been?"

"Everywhere," said Taukin, his smile as wide as a

crescent Aebean and he rubbed the black hair on Nelkum's head.

"Tell me all about your adventures," said Nelkum. Taukin nodded. Larnhi hugged Taukin again before breaking up the circle and wiping her face. Behind Avent and Larnhi, stood Soyha. Her face was strewn with pain. Larnhi pulled her close and Soyha let her mold her as she wanted as she cried so hard she could hardly catch her breath. With her hands, Larnhi formed circles on Soyha's back trying her best to calm her. Quiesce conquered the forest and the stirless time was upon them, and if it wasn't for the sparse firelight and the waning sister moons lighting the paths, all beings would be pitch silhouettes.

Hiko and Jusha and a crowd of rintic approached, the torchlight revealing their joy as well as Taukin's discontent. Jusha smiled at Taukin, "All Eltepsu are safe with the Umgara, you and Captain Avent are home with your family, why are you downcast?"

"General Meraco is gone, my mother is dying, and my ally is imprisoned by order of General Pella." Hiko's face contorted with puzzlement at Taukin's comment.

Hushed silence fell among the crowd as the focus shifted to General Reibo, Itil, Gosin-Tare and Subian as they escorted all twelve Eltepsu to Avent and Taukin, who stood there immobilized by the assemblage of nobility standing before them. Had it not been for their tan faces being lit by the torchlight, the Eltepsu would have been unseen. Avent and family, Soyha, Jusha, and Hiko went to their knees.

Arbmere walked to Avent and said, "Captain Avent,

the bravery of you and your tribesman will be forever sung in our caverns. The Eltepsu thank you for the return of Cuvsor and Lantia." Avent bowed in respect to the sustainer. Arbmere walked over to Taukin and said, "Taukin, you are special among all Onestonians. You will take many paths in life but those paths do not make you who you are, the destination determines that. Stay true to Hobaja Vael's will and your life will be full of virtue and blessings. The Eltepsu are indebted to you." Taukin bowed in respect to Arbmere and the other Eltepsu. "You are friends of the Eltepsu and are most welcomed to Binesmir," said Arbmere, then returned to the other Eltepsu.

"The Carth soldiers will continue their security escort for the Eltepsu to Binesmir if you wish it Lord Gosin-Tare," said Hiko.

"We appreciate such an offer, but our pace will only increase between Byrre Syra and Binesmir," replied Gosin-Tare, his deep voice reaching the captain of the rintic who shouted, "Company, fall out," to his soldiers.

"Lord Gosin-Tare...If I may, I have a request. Taukin's mother Luspa, she is being treated at Binesmir by your healers."

"I am aware of her situation," said Gosin-Tare.

Hiko continued, "Will you allow young Taukin to ride with the Umgara to Binesmir to stay beside her while she heals?"

"I see no need for Taukin to make a journey that would only delay his reuniting with his mother," reverberated Gosin-Tare.

Hiko's face twisted in confusion and Taukin's skin

morphed from blue to his normal violet, uncertain of what to make of the Umgara's response.

Gosin-Tare and Subian moved to the side, followed by Itil and Reibo who parted to the opposite side from the Umgara leader, leaving a void large enough for Luspa, who had an arm across Ethius's shoulders and his arm around her side, to walk through.

"Mother!" shouted Taukin who ran to Luspa and wrapped his arms around her allowing Ethius to withdraw as Taukin became her foundation.

"My son," whispered Luspa, still weakened by the lingering effects of the poison on her body.

"How do you feel?" asked Taukin, surprised by her appearance.

"Weak, but happy to see you."

"You're here. You and Father, all of us, even the Eltepsu," said Taukin, his eyes glistening, looking at Ethius and Luspa.

Lantia, now the third youngest Eltepsu, went to Taukin and Luspa and said in a squeaky voice, "Come with me." As Luspa leaned on Taukin, they walked over to the edge of the trail and out of earshot from the others. Lantia said, "Hobaja Vael has reunited you." An emotional grin formed on Luspa's face. Lantia continued, "If we do not see each other again, I need to ask, Taukin, do you have the capethica I gave you?"

Taukin paused, and his eyes widened, "I lost the wooden bauble in the pit," said Taukin.

Lantia's small mouth formed a smile and Lantia took Taukin's hand and said, "That was Hobaja Vael's will. Capethica is given to bring one back to another, and that is what has happened." Taukin grinned at the Eltepsu's words. Luspa let go of Taukin to wrap her arms around the matted tufts of hair on Lantia's neck. She then reached back for Taukin's support releasing the Eltepsu. The other Eltepsu made their way back to the awaiting melps.

"I must go," said Lantia. "Perhaps our paths will cross again." Tears traced Luspa's face and she grabbed Lantia's soft hand.

"I am indebted to you forever," said Luspa. Lantia's shaggy brown head dipped down and Luspa bowed her head in return, then Lantia turned and with thin legs scurried off to catch up with the other Eltepsu.

Luspa focused on Taukin, "I won't let anything keep me from you again," said Luspa, her smile slowly fading due to the exhaustion and her skin color wavered. Ethius came to her other side, placing his arm around Luspa's back providing support as they walked back to the others.

Hiko spoke, "Luspa needs rest and healing still. Take her to the healer."

"This is allowed?" asked Taukin with confusion spelled across his face.

"By my word," said Hiko.

"And Drami Sol?" asked Taukin fervidly.

"Your friend of the rintic will be freed before the lumeren's light," vowed Hiko. He then turned to Ethius, "Ethius, when you reach the healer, tell him to treat her as one from the house of Hiko."

A look of disbelief covered Ethius's face, but still

nodded in appreciation of Hiko's offer. "Taukin, help me carry your mother," said Ethius.

Both Gosin-Tare and Subian nodded in concurrence of Hiko's act. A gentle smile drew across Subian's face at the unspoken reconciliation between Ethius and Hiko, and the reunification of Luspa's family. Subian's prodigious hand grasped Gosin-Tare's shoulder, letting him know it was time to leave. "They are waiting," said Subian in her comforting tone.

Gosin-Tare spoke, "Lord Hiko, rintic…and suvanth who are allies to the rintic, it is through Hobaja Vael's will and your incredible courageous feats that we leave here with all Eltepsu under protection of the Umgara and their lineage unbroken. The safekeeping of the Eltepsu is the Umgara's purpose and we will work with the Carth rintic and other Onestonians in the coming cycles to combat threats upon the Eltepsu and their allies. As was said before, judgement will be handed out to the suvanth and their punishment will be just and swift and the Umgara will not hold back, nor have pity, nor relent." The powerful tone of Gosin-Tare cut through the crowd and skin lightened uncontrollably at the fearsome words. Gosin-Tare's harsh stare conceded to a grateful look and he said, "Carth rintic, your assistance in battling the suvanth and rescuing Cuvsor and Lantia will be rewarded. Now we must leave your forest to ensure the safe return of the Eltepsu to Binesmir."

Hiko stepped up and looked upward to Gosin-Tare, whose large head blocked the light from Aebean and said, "The Carth rintic will continue to be of service to the Eltepsu and Umgara anytime the need arises. May Hobaja Vael carry you and the Eltepsu on your journey home. Solea my Lord, my Lady."

The rintic collectively lowered their heads in respect to the Eltepsu and protectors as they passed by. With each long Umgara stride the vibration could be felt through the ground. From the front, Itil turned his torso completely around and called for all Umgara drivers to move forward. Slowly at first, the caravan moved until they established their set distance, but gained speed as they moved past the cheering crowd that lined the trail of Byrre Syra. Taukin watched as the last of the bright luminescence bulbs, which swung from melp shells, disappeared over the hills and past the darkened forest trees.

Luspa's legs went limp and she sunk down, forcing Taukin and Ethius to keep her upright. "Let's go," said Ethius.

"This way," said Taukin as he steered his mother and father toward the healer's hut.

Avent looked to Nelkum, "Run and tell the healer to prepare for Luspa." Nelkum ran ahead and disappeared into the darkness. Not far away, the Carth healer stood outside his hut wearing only tan-colored undercloths with a torch in hand.

"You never said she was a suvanth," said the old tribesman to Nelkum.

Ethius spoke, "You'll treat her as Carth."

"I'm not opposed, healing is healing regardless of tribe, I'm just surprised is all. I've never seen a living suvanth before," replied the slender gray-haired healer, who rubbed the back of his neck while speaking.

"Come, lay her down here on the open cot," said the healer while Larnhi held the pelt door back allowing the group inside the wooden hut. Ethius and Taukin carefully laid Luspa down on the pelt cot. "What happened to her?" asked the fragile-looking healer.

"She was struck by a poinjin dart. She was treated by the Umgara and traveled here from Binesmir," said Ethius. The healer went to his knees and said, "Poinjin eh? Whooff, that's deadly toxin," and put his bearded face next to her mouth and nose. He felt of her neck and pressed down around her waist, moving up below her chest.

"What are you doing?" demanded Ethius.

"I'm checking for ruptures," said the healer, oblivious to Ethius's frustration. "She's breathing fine," said the healer and continued, "She just needs rest and nourishment. A good quiesce slumber will serve her well." The healer covered her with a pelt blanket and placed his hand on the cot to help his scrawny legs support his frail body as he stood up and said, "Come, let her sleep and when she stirs, she'll need to eat."

"I'm staying with her," said Taukin who sat on the wooden floor and rested his arm on the side of Luspa's leg.

"As am I," said Ethius, who sat across from Taukin, but near Luspa's head, so that he could listen for her words.

"That's your choice. I won't say no," said the old tribesman as he placed another piece of wood in the stone fireplace across from Luspa's covered body, stoking the flames with a metal rod.

Larnhi placed her hand on Taukin's shoulder and said, "If you need us, we'll come…at any time." Larnhi turned, her face revealing her heart's battle for her son whose heart was with his birth mother. Avent held the pelt door open for Larnhi, who was slow to exit. Avent paused before exiting and nodded his head at Ethius who returned the gesture. Avent stepped out and the hanging pelt brushed the wooden floor, sealing off the cold forest air.

The elder healer scuttled back to his preparatory area and shortly returned with three wooden bowls. "Take these," said the healer, putting out two steaming bowls of trochin broth. Taukin and Ethius each took a bowl, steam rolling off the top, but not the third bowl. The third bowl was set down on a stool next to Taukin and it was half-full of green paste and not steaming. "That's for her. When she opens her eyes, feed her this. Just a little at a time, it's agrum mush, you don't want to overdo it. I'm going to my room to rest now. You should rest as well," said the old tribesman, then turned and retreated to his room.

Ethius's hand ran along Luspa's cheek and across her long black hair. "I've never known another who was so full of love," said Ethius as he stared at his lifemate, lying there in deep slumber.

Taukin's skin lightened slightly as he spoke, "I want to live with you both…here in the forest."

Ethius replied, "Taukin, you are not a youth anymore. I realize that you have grown without me or your mother in your life, but Larnhi and Avent have raised you into a fine tribesman. It's time you establish the house of Taukin. Besides, there are two potential lifemates that have interest in you." Taukin's refutation was overtaken by a yellow suffuse of embarrassment transforming his skin. Taukin turned his head away, embarrassed by the statement from his father.

Ethius smirked, "You should be glad that you have them vying for your affection. We're both fortunate, I'm with my lifemate and yours is right in front of you. You just need to decide who she is." Suddenly Luspa's hand moved and Ethius was quick to caress it. A moan emitted from her closed mouth and Ethius spoke to her, "Can you hear me?" Luspa squeezed Ethius's weathered hand and moaned out. "You need to eat," said Ethius. "Can you raise up?" Luspa tried to lift her head, but Ethius was quick to place his hand underneath her neck to provide support. Luspa pushed against the cot and Taukin pulled her shoulders and neck forward. Once upright, Taukin grabbed the bowl of agrum mush and spooned a bite of the green gruel into her restricted mouth. She grimaced at first, but with the onset of the agrum, chewed the mush and swallowed. "That's good, keep eating," said Ethius, then asked, "Are you pain?" Luspa shook her head slightly.

"Now *I'm* taking care of *you*," said Taukin with a smile. He scooped another small amount of the green paste into Luspa's mouth. Luspa's amber eyes opened. They were gentle and loving toward Taukin but toward Ethius, knowing.

Ethius smiled at her and squeezed her hand and

said, "This is temporary." Her fluttering eyes went to Taukin, "The lumeren holds great things for us," she said in a weakened voice, and ran her hand over Taukin's glabrous head and rubbed the nape of his neck. Ethius lowered her head back to the cot and her eyes closed once more. Taukin fluffed up his pelt covering and formed a makeshift pillow in which he placed his heavy head. Ethius kept his arm next to his lifemate to sense her stirring and rested his cheek against his arm for the quiesce. The warmth of the room and calm crackle of the fire lured them to sleep.

A loud hiss woke Taukin, whose wits left him and he sprang up ready for battle. "No harm here, collect yourself. I was just putting out the fire," said the old healer, holding an empty wooden bucket next to the wet smoking coals. Shards of light penetrated the wooden hut and Taukin looked to the cot where Luspa had laid, but she was gone. Ethius was also gone.

"Where are they?" asked Taukin, still confused.

"Outside drinking herba linka," said the healer. Taukin pushed open the hanging pelt to receive a cold blast of air and blinding light. Luspa was covered with pelts sitting in a wooden chair next to Ethius, who was in a similar chair. Their words and the herba linka formed swirls of white clouds that twisted upward.

Taukin said, "You look much better."

Luspa took Taukin's hand inside hers and replied, "Quite. I've never had a better lumeren." Taukin smiled and took in the quiet and peace of the Carth forest. It was early enough that only pairs of soldiers walked the side trails near the healer's hut, and the sumoguls stayed perched in their nests. The Eastern star stretched its arms out and painted gold the landscape between the trees as well as Luspa's face. Her eyes closed and she said, "I want it to stay just like this and never leave."

Ethius replied, "To some I'm still a traitor, and to most you're an enemy."

Luspa's hand covered Taukin's hand, "Let's enjoy it until we no longer can," said Luspa and smiled at Taukin.

"It looks like that time has come," said Ethius as a rintic soldier, tall, decorated, and well kempt, made her way to Taukin, Ethius, and Luspa.

Taukin went to attention.

"As you were," said the Lieutenant Colonel Zelzik.

"Lieutenant Colonel?" asked Taukin.

"Taukin, I have been sent by Lord Hiko to make sure you are prepared for your recognition," said the Lieutenant Colonel. Gleaming medals and colorful ribbons covered the chest of her uniform, telling the story of the battles she fought and accomplishments during her life as a soldier.

Taukin's face contorted, "Recognition…for what?"

"I wasn't made privy to why. What I do know is that you are to go to Captain Avent's hut for further details. The ceremony takes place this mid-cycle. Finish up here and go to Captain Avent's hut without delay," said Zelzik as she took two steps past Taukin toward the main trail leading to Fort Carth. Taukin quickly went to attention. The Lieutenant Colonel paused with her back towards Taukin before turning back and scanning

Taukin's tattered pelt coverings, "Make sure you're presentable soldier."

"Yes Lieutenant Colonel," said Taukin, looking straight ahead past Zelzik, who then walked away allowing Taukin to be at ease.

Luspa spoke, "You go, I'll be fine." Taukin wrapped his arms around her neck and gently squeezed. Taukin ran away from the Eastern star and the direction of Fort Carth back toward his home.

Running down the golden-colored path brought Taukin back to before his adventures began, making him realize how simple his life had been before. As Taukin ran, rintic tribesmen appeared along the trail and greeted him and some even gave him praise as he ran by, drawing a smile upon his violet face. He gripped the swaul sapling at the corner of the trail whose bark had been worn smooth from the passing tribesmen, using the tree to slow his momentum. There before him was Avent's humble wooden hut, Taukin's home. He paused to take in the scene. Smoke billowed from the stone hearth and Taukin picked up the delectable aroma floating in the air, making his stomach growl. He had not had a decent meal since the one at Manista's table. The east side of the hut was blanketed with warm light and never had it looked so inviting...and never had it felt so distant now that Luspa and Ethius were part of Taukin's life, and the uncomfortable sense of betrayal still lingered over Taukin like an invisible cloud.

Taukin entered Avent's hut quietly at first, but purposely made a rustling sound while hanging his coverings up on his hook to make his presence known.

Just as Taukin suspected, an aroma, savory and full of spice filled the hut's space. Larnhi appeared and rushed over to Taukin, "What state is Lus…how is your mother?" she asked with her skin showing concern.

Those words struck Taukin as peculiar, but direct and his skin alternated between blue and yellow. "Much better. She slept a deep sleep and when she woke, she had agrum mush," said Taukin quietly, then his amber eyes faced the worn wooden floor.

"Praise Hobaja Vael," replied Larnhi with a soft smile, her skin returning to its coquelicot hue. Larnhi read Taukin's skin and delicately clasped his chin with her hand, pulling it up so that their eyes were locked and said, "Taukin, I will always think of you as my son. I raised you since you before you could crawl, but if your heart tells you that Luspa is who you should call mother, then you must listen to it. A mother's heart is strong and stable. Even though mine will hurt, it will heal because I know the love she has for you is unending just like my love for you is unending." Taukin grinned a thankful smirk and wrapped his arms around Larnhi's neck, and Larnhi wrapped her arms around Taukin's back and both their skins were green with love.

"This is for you," said Avent as he appeared holding Taukin's proper uniform. Taukin's skin changed to a dark auburn with a yellow crescent pattern, expressing his excitement. His teeth seemed to glow against his darkened skin. Taukin snatched the light blue uniform and moved toward his and Keel's room to change.

"Wait!" said Larnhi. Taukin stopped. "Eat before you dress. You don't want a single flaw on that new uniform. I'll wake your brothers," said Larnhi. Taukin held the cloth material up, inspecting the fine handicraft of the soldier's uniform. His violet thumb ran across the light blue and yellow Carth patch sewn on the right sleeve and his eyes focused on the patch of Avent's house on the left sleeve, both outlined in white. Taukin would have examined every perfect stitch if time allowed. His pride swelled inside.

"Fill your gut," said Avent as he reached for Taukin's uniform. Taukin watched the uniform taken from his hands and placed on the back of the wooden chair by the hearth, still fixated as if it was the light cipher itself.

Keel and Nelkum walked in and sat at the smooth wooden table. "Taukin, come sit by me," said Nelkum, yellow-skinned and rubbing his eyes incessantly. A steaming bowl of trochin broth was placed before each of the sons and Avent, with a plate of gray spice-filled gelatinous trochin noses placed in the center by Larnhi before sitting next to Avent.

Taukin turned to Avent, "At the Plains of Gadush, there was a masked warrior who came to our aid and slayed Sagog the mighty. He moved swiftly, more so than any I've seen, with precision, and carried the same blade as the suvanth Hannon Lite warriors. We also saw him early lumeren at Fort Carth before the rescue mission. Who was he?"

"Was?" asked Keel. "You saw his demise?"

"He was left behind, swarmed by the suvanth," said Taukin.

Avent replied, "I've heard of a tribe separate from our own. The Ank tribe, who live on the outer edge of the Carth forest, near the Thrysal cliffs, but do not interact with any but their own kind. They are relatives of the ancient suvanth tribe, one that had separated before the suvanth exile to the pit. It's possible he was from this tribe."

Nelkum was in awe of his father's words, and Taukin nodded his head as he pondered this new knowledge and added, "I'd like to seek out his tribe to tell of the warrior's great feat, assuming his tribe is still near the Thrysal cliffs."

"Save these stories for later, you mustn't be late," said Larnhi, followed by a period of squishing of noses between the grinding teeth and slurping of broth which drowned the hut before Larnhi broke the verbal reticence, "You should dress now."

Avent nodded in agreeance, "Alright, all of you, let's go, don't delay, you too Nelkum," said Avent back to his Captain form.

"Grab your cover," said Avent, whose proper uniform displayed numerous ribbons and medals and just as much varied chroma. Taukin stepped outside into the mid-cycle light and covered his violet glabrescent head with the tan-colored cloth hat, cupping the hat to form a ridge over his right eye as Avent and Keel did. Avent led the way down the brightly lit narrow trail between the overlooking swaul trees with Larnhi and Nelkum on the side of him. Larnhi's hand reached for Avent's hand as they walked along the loamy path. All but Nelkum were careful to keep their pelt foot coverings clean as they walked the dirt path to the telling place.

As they walked, Nelkum danced around Keel and Taukin tossing questions at them, but Taukin's mind wandered and he took notice of new things that had always been, like the crisp scent of the swaul trees and the peace he felt as he walked into and out of the tree's shadows down the forest trails. These were things he had missed about his home, but hadn't particularly noticed before, and his heart grew fonder of the Carth forest.

Taukin's arm jerked, bringing him back to his brothers, it was Nelkum tugging Taukin's hand. "How did you do it?" asked Nelkum for the third time.

"How did I do what?" replied Taukin oblivious to the question.

"How did you escape from the pit?" Taukin's focus shifted to the crowd of rintic weaving in and out of the smooth stumps around the wooden platform at the center of the telling place and the Eastern star was near its midpoint in the indigo sky. Taukin replied, "By Hobaja Vael's will."

CHAPTER 15
RECOGNITION

All of the Carth rintic were seemingly spread about the telling place, even populating the tree line surrounding the stumps and down the paths leading away to the far places of the forest. Such was the way at the time of agrum distribution, no tribesman would go without their share of the life-sustaining liquid. Soldiers were decorated in their proper uniforms and others were dressed in vibrant colored garments, which blazed in the rays of the Eastern star, a mix of every color possible against the dullness of the brown and green forest.

The tribesmen moved about finding their seat among the circular maze of stumps and as the crowd thinned, Taukin saw her. Soyha's skin turned a tawny shade upon making eye contact with Taukin. He went to her trying to keep his smile and skin from giving away his joy upon seeing her. Her blue ceremonial gown was covered with a proper pelt shoulder covering and her braided hair was pulled up into a tight spiral that sat at the cap of her head. "Solea," said Taukin admiring Soyha's elegance.

"Solea," replied Soyha who stared at Taukin in his uniformed refinement.

"Will you sit beside me?" asked Soyha, before acting-General Pella appeared and took his seat on the left of Soyha.

Taukin's eyes met Pella's and the acting General said, "This row is reserved for ranked officers and their family. Perhaps you should sit with your family."

Taukin's skin started to turn, but he forced it back violet. "Captain Avent's family belongs on this row just as much as yours," said Taukin not backing down.

"I wasn't talking about Captain Avent's family," replied Pella and looked and nodded behind Taukin's right shoulder. Taukin turned to see Luspa, still wearing the pelt wrap and hanging onto an unfamiliar rintic soldier. They slowly walked to a row near the back of the rotunda.

Taukin turned to Soyha, "I'll be back," he said and rushed over to Luspa and her escort and said, "Mother, you don't have to sit here in the back. Come closer to the stage."

Taukin glanced at the tribesman helping Luspa to her stump then stared quizzically at him, his short kempt black hair and hairless face seemed familiar and it wasn't until he turned that the revelatory scars on his carnelian neck appeared. "Father…you're unrecognizable! And wearing your proper uniform," said Taukin.

"That's the striking face I remember from long ago," replied Luspa with a delicate smile. Rintic shot ignominious looks at Ethius and Luspa and avoided sitting on the immediate stumps near them. Luspa replied, "Taukin, where we are is where we should be."

Taukin grew frustrated at the onlookers, "Look upon yourselves, there you'll find who should concern you."

Ethius replied, "Judgement is a heavy lift once it's been placed on you." Right then, a hand gently squeezed Taukin's shoulder.

"Taukin," said Drami Sol, her sultry eyes ensnaring Taukin's attention, who was accompanied by two rintic guards. Drami Sol placed her pelt-covered arms around Taukin's back and pulled him close to her.

"Lord Hiko held true to his word on your release," replied Taukin with a wide smile.

"But…Hiko still doesn't trust her?" asked Ethius peering at the rintic guards.

"These guards are with me for my protection," said Drami Sol. Ethius smirked at her comment as if it were oblivious fallacy. Drami Sol sat next to Luspa and pulled Taukin's hand to sit next to her. Taukin obliged and his skin lightened when Drami Sol placed her head on his pelt-covered shoulder.

Taukin scanned the crowd and locked in on a rintic whose furrowed brow and dark-red skin stood out amongst the lighter-skin tribesmen. It was Soyha and her display told Taukin she was not pleased with Drami Sol's affection towards him. Soyha stood and approached from the opposite side of Ethius and Luspa and with each step towards Taukin, his level of anxiety increased. Soyha forced her skin to its normal reddish-orange hue as she neared Taukin and Drami Sol.

"I've decided to join you back here," said Soyha as she sidled up to Taukin, tugging on his free arm. Taukin grinned nervously as Soyha, subtly at first, but gradually more firmly, pulled him closer to her, resulting in a separation of Drami Sol's head from his shoulder. Drami Sol's skin turned bright yellow with contrasting wavering stripes, showing her frustration, which if it had not been for the anger shown in her large blue eyes, would have been lost on Soyha.

Soyha quickly stood and opened her mouth to berate Drami Sol when Hiko took the stage and the entire tribe stood applauding their leader. Hiko, wearing his yellow and blue robe and crowned with a metallic band, raised his right hand, motioning for the tribe to sit. Soyha furiously sat back down grabbing Taukin's right hand and Drami Sol's frustration was felt as she squeezed Taukin's left hand. Taukin's amber eyes grew large from the battle for his attention, but he tried to distract them by saying, "Lord Hiko is speaking."

Ethius and Luspa grinned to each other at the affection and affliction shown to their son. All attention turned to Hiko on the stage who spoke loud enough for all to hear. "Fellow rintic, the recent events have been unsettling and many changes have happened and will happen between our tribe and other Onestonians. There are changes that will happen solely within our tribe as well. My only son Syonis, who was to become our tribe's leader, has betrayed us and will spend his life imprisoned for his crimes." Mumbling and gasps spread among the crowd, as most were unaware of Syonis's actions. Hiko spoke again to capture their attention, "As for the future, when it is time for me to cede my role as the leader of the Carth rintic, I will be selecting a leader amongst our tribesmen, a leader who exemplifies the traits and wisdom necessary to govern our great tribe. This is all I will say about this matter. As of this lumeren, I received word that the suvanth have retreated back into the deep hollows of Sheol Balla." Loud cheers and warbling sounds came from the crowd. Hiko allowed the crowd to react then raised his hand again to settle the rambunctious crowd. "Yes, yes, now, I want us to pause a dole par-tem to remember the brave rintic tribesmen who lost their lives while battling against the evil that plotted to abduct another Eltepsu, let us be silent."

The tribe lowered their heads and complete silence befell the crowd. About forty par-tems passed and during this time emotions grew and some in the crowd wept for their fallen. Hiko spoke, "For the courageous rintic tribesmen who survived this attack, I want to honor them by giving them recognition through our tribe's unified voice, join me." Hiko raised his clenched fists shoulder-level and with a warbling tongue, gave a warrior's yell. A stifling unified cry filled the rotunda, raising Drami Sol's fear, drawing her closer to Taukin and making Soyha's skin darken. Hiko continued, "Among these honorable warriors is Soyha, Keel, the rescue team led by Captain Avent, and Taukin. Soldiers, come up to the stage."

Taukin fidgeted his way up and away from Drami Sol's grasp then hurried with Soyha to join the other soldiers on the stage. As he passed the crowd, those who never left the forest scowled at the sight of Taukin, but those who witnessed the powerful summoning event by Taukin revered him out of fear, all except General Pella who glared at the outcast. "These soldiers which stand before you and beside Captain Avent, and who with great courage, faced tremendous danger by infiltrating the tunnels of Sheol Balla to rescue the Eltepsu, and Fesenius our own Carth soldier. They are presented the distinguished golden band of the Carth tribe." Hiko approached each soldier, handing them a shimmering gold band and cupping each soldier's left shoulder. Taukin was last in line and Soyha was next to him. Hiko smiled and nodded, but didn't hand either a golden armband. Hiko turned from Soyha and Taukin and faced the tribe, his face solemn and his skin white with downward moving blue lines. "Carth rintic, there is one among you who has dedicated her life to performing a mission that only occurs every twelve cycles and that is possibly the most challenging and dangerous mission that any tribesman could undertake. Soyha, from the house of Meraco, step forward. The retrieval of the Basatab, known to some as the light cipher, requires cycles of training and mental and physical preparation. Soyha was ready for the task, but unexpected events unfolded and quelled her quest. But this does not negate the fact that Soyha not only helped in the ultimate securing of the light cipher, but also in the abolishment of the bringer of the dark. She truly is the daughter of our late, great General Meraco. These events that have unfolded over the past few tem-cycles have caused Onestonians great concern, but knowing that

Soyha has the strength and wisdom to succeed where most cannot, brings me comfort as it should you. Because of her heroic actions, she is presented the Nionan Star. The second in her family to receive the most distinguished honor!"

All tribesmen went to their feet warbling and cheering and Soyha's eyes glistened with joy and sadness for the thought of her father and how proud he would be of her. Hiko cheered and honored Soyha and eventually the crowd sat, and a hush came across the forest. "Tribe, I turn now to a soldier who is responsible for a key component in the rescue of the missing Eltepsu and our fellow tribesman Fesenius. From the house of Avent, Taukin, step forward." Taukin took one step forward, and did what he could to maintain his dull violet hue, but the weight of his guilt overcame him and his skin morphed a deep violet color. Hiko continued, "Taukin, because of your courage Fesenius is home and the Eltepsu have been reunited, thus allowing the decegen to occur as well as the continuity of our tribe's safety and security. Battling a god has never been witnessed by Onestonians since the time of written word. Onestonians hope that such an event will never be experienced again, for the death and destruction experienced will take many cycles to forget. The Carth tribe, as well as all of Onestonia is indebted to you. On behalf of the Carth rintic, we present you the Nionan Star."

A boisterous roar came from the crowd and the tribe went to their feet in appreciation and recognition of Taukin's deeds. Taukin smiled as big as the moon Febus, and tried to keep his skin color intact, but the dark violet hue showed through. Taukin examined the badge, which was identical to Soyha and General Meraco's medal. Taukin closed his eyes briefly, but it felt like a tem-cycle had passed as he battled against his conviction.

Taukin said, "Lord Hiko, this medal doesn't belong to me. What you think happened did not, and what did happen is not known to you." Luspa looked as if Onestonia's existence could end depending on what Taukin said next. Taukin spoke loud enough for all to hear, "It's true that I made it to the inner chambers of Sheol Balla and did what was requested of me by my superiors, but I was able to make it there because I was expected by the suvanth." Grumblings were heard among the crowd and confusion was splattered across Hiko's crimson face.

Taukin continued, "Carth tribe, I fulfilled my part of the rescue mission for our tribe, this is true, but before I volunteered for this mission, I was recruited by the suvanth with no knowledge as to why, only that I could be reunited with my birth mother. My entire life, I have been scorned, and alienated, and here was an invitation to live a life free of persecution. I thought the only being that could show me love no matter the color or pattern of my skin, would be my mother. Now we're reunited, and I have realized that I have always been loved by those closest to me and that those who treated me with contempt only made me stronger. I cannot accept this medal."

Taukin stepped back in line next to Avent and faced

the wooden planks of the stage, shame covered his face and his skin turned white. Louder grumblings came from the audience and an elderly zealous tribesman stood and yelled out, "Imprison the traitor! He's like his father! Imprison them all!" Other anti-suvanth supporters stood and shouted out in support of the proposition. Luspa drew close to Ethius and Drami Sol leaned toward Luspa for security.

Hiko scanned the crowd of protestors and waited a few par-tems to let the commotion die down before speaking, "Carth tribe, hear what I say. Have you not dealt with anger toward you? Have you not felt as if you didn't belong at times? This is all he has ever known. Would you then blame Taukin for his actions? Hobaja Vael forgives us of our trespasses, and we should forgive Taukin as well. Taukin could have abandoned his rintic beliefs and joined ranks with the suvanth, but he didn't. He chose to remain a Carth tribesman. His works prevented the death of our planet."

Hiko waved Taukin to him. With his head hunkered, Taukin approached Hiko and stood next to him. Hiko had a slight height advantage and he draped his robed arm around Taukin to show support to the tribe. "Carth rintic, Taukin has spoken the truth of alienation and persecution. In the past, there were times that I felt as others did about Taukin, but that time has come to an end, as it should for all who live inside our sacred forest." Hiko faced Taukin, "Taukin, the rintic values ring truer in you than they do in me and if it were not for you, I would not be standing here now presenting you with an award that you most assuredly deserve."

A lone soldier still wearing a sling on his left arm, four rows back, stood and yelled out for all to hear, "He fought for our tribe and helped rescue Fesenius! He looks different, but his heart is like that of my brothers."

Dyant stood and yelled out, "Taukin is Carth rintic!" Some in the audience supported the comments and the anti-Taukin murmurings died down and were replaced by encouraging words. About the crowd were mixed colors and expressions and Luspa, Ethius, and Drami Sol, who vicariously shared Taukin's pain and joy. Larnhi and Avent's pride of Taukin poured out almost as if they were yelling without moving their lips. Light and heat from the Eastern star shone down unobstructed by the trees, and Hiko turned to Taukin and said, "Accept this medal on my behalf and on behalf of the Carth rintic tribe."

A radiant glimmer emitted from the nionan crystal and shone on the crowd, drawing Taukin's attention to the tribesmen he didn't know and he examined their faces to see a change, like that of relief and understanding. Taukin stepped away from Hiko and his skin turned violet as he spoke loud to the crowd, "Carth tribe, I have lived among you all my life, but as unequal." Taukin briefly flashed a rintic red hue and pattern before returning to violet. Some tribesmen showed their shame as Taukin continued, "I tried to look like you and act like you, but I know who I am and I have proven my allegiance to my tribe. If you believe in me now, if you can accept me, then I accept the Nionan Star!" The crowd was driven into a frenzy of praise and cheers loud enough to be heard throughout the forest. Hiko smiled and watched as the crowd was won over by Taukin. Tribesmen opened their covers and flashed their skin violet in approval of Taukin and his words.

When the roar lessened, Hiko approached Taukin and spoke out in front of him, "Ethius approach the stage."

Ethius looked at Luspa, surprised by the order, but stood as directed and made his way past the murmuring words of the tribe up on the platform in between Taukin and Hiko. Hiko turned Ethius around to face the crowd and brought him to the forefront of the stage, "Ethius has been considered a traitor all these cycles, but this was in error. He was made to look as if he betrayed our tribe by the suvanth, and their evil deed was realized. For too long we have held on to this misplaced anger and hatred against our brother for no reason. I tell you now, that there is to be no disdain toward Ethius from this tem-cycle forward." A solemn hush captured the crowd, the truth and their contrition clamped down upon them. Hiko patted Ethius below his shoulder and with his open hand directed him to stand next to Taukin.

"The last matter I intend to address before we celebrate is one of acceptance. I speak of acceptance of all Onestonians by the rintic, regardless of tribe, regardless of color or pattern, and regardless of their beliefs. For far too long, our tribe has cast a dark shadow on those who do not look like us, act like us, or believe what we believe. This mindset will no longer stand. The simple truth is that there is good and evil throughout our world and beyond, even in our beloved tribe, as recent events have proven.

Good and evil are not based on what a being looks like, or what they believe, but it is rooted in their actions. This is a lesson that I learned through difficult trials." Hiko waived for Drami Sol. She looked at Hiko and then Luspa with uncertainty. "Drami Sol, approach the stage." Drami Sol cautiously stood, and pulled her pelt cover tight against her frame, offering a false sense of security. Murmurs from the crowd drew her attention as she slowly shuffled toward Hiko with the two guards in tow. Hiko continued as Drami Sol approached, "If it were not for the bravery of Drami Sol, the suvanth you see before you, the Eltepsu rescue attempt would have failed. Drami Sol helped Captain Avent and his soldiers while in the depths of Sheol Balla and the on the battle-field." Drami Sol took the steps up on stage and was greeted by Hiko's welcoming arms. Hiko placed his hand on her shoulder and continued. "When her actions were found out by the suvanth, she received the same fate as Captain Avent, a death sentence. She has witnessed the evil that some are capable of and has chosen to live in the ways of the rintic, here in the forest. Carth rintic let us continue to be virtuous! Let's recognize her for the pivotal aid given to Captain Avent and his soldiers."

Another loud rumble burst out, cheers mixed with jeers, and then Hiko continued, "The Carth rintic are proud Onestonians and should remain that way, but only if our pride is related to our understanding and acceptance of those who are not native to our tribe as long as their actions prove worthy of our acceptance. I issue this decree that tribesmen from outside our tribe will be permitted to live inside the forest with approval by the council of elders. They shall be treated as equals as long as they follow the Carth ways."

The clamorous sound of cheers and warbles mixed with harsh moans and hisses forming a separation between those who pursued change and those who resisted it. For some in the crowd the words meant a gain of freedom, while to others the decree meant a loss of self-identity. Drami Sol's smile seemed to illuminate the stage and Taukin held back his emotions as joyful tears ran from Luspa's amber eyes.

Hiko spoke, "Carth rintic, I have spoken enough, let us give now praise to Hobaja Vael for our safety, the return of our tribesmen, and the sustainers of Onestonia, the Eltepsu and their gift of agrum. It is now time for the agrum distribution!" And Hiko held up an illuminated green Elder vial of agrum, secured with both hands, high overhead. All in the crowd stood and lifted their praise to Hobaja Vael in the form of song and dance. Luspa stood, raising her hands, palms out and gave specific praise for Lantia and Hobaja Vael for their protection of her, Ethius, and Taukin. Hiko respectfully motioned for Captain Avent's squad, Soyha, Ethius, and Drami Sol to return to their loved ones offstage. Single file, they made their way to the steps leading down to the cool forest floor. Waiting for them was a soldier who expeditiously handed each of them an

Elder vial of agrum as they stepped onto the dark forest skin.

Drami Sol was surprised by the size of the vial, requiring both hands to hold and even more surprised by the fact that she would receive such a gift from the rintic. "I've never seen an Elder vial up close. It's bigger than I imagined. The words of Lord Hiko have made me happy. I can stay in the forest with you," said Drami Sol and she bumped her hip into Taukin in a sign of affection and joy. Taukin grinned but couldn't help acknowledging the peering presence of Soyha not far from them, who remained near the stage as a line formed for the agrum distribution. Unfamiliar tribesmen, in line for their share of the agrum, approached Taukin, their skin a blazing array of various colors, verbally and visually praising him for his works.

Fesenius limped his way with the use of a wooden crutch under his right arm to Taukin and the others, "You could have left me so many times, but you didn't. I don't know how I can thank you."

Avent spoke, "Brothers take care of one another." Ethius smiled at Avent for those were his words to Avent many cycles ago. Encouragement from the rintic replaced dread but was just as overwhelming, for Taukin had never known such a feeling.

The last vial of agrum was handed out just as the low-burning fire that circled the stage was lit and the Eastern star had receded behind the forest horizon. Tables covered with leaf-wrapped kulee mush, succulent meats and colorful fruits from all over Onestonia were located at the side of the telling circle. Music rang out and families danced together, raising and lowering their hands in praise and appreciation. Torches scattered near stumps were burning and Hiko took to the center of the wooden platform. "Carth tribe, raise your vials in celebration and drink with me." All heads of houses raised their green vials overhead then punctured the vial with a thin metal needle to allow the agrum to flow out when squeezed, but not otherwise. Each member of their own house squeezed some drops into their mouths and ingested the energizing fluid, instantly feeling the stimulating sensation. Hiko stood silent, watching the rite be fulfilled in the new post-effergy quiesce of the moons, reveling in his tribe's accomplishment to supply their tribe with the sustaining substance.

Both of Taukin's families and Drami Sol were huddled together near the main trail, but still nearby the telling place. Avent spoke, "Taukin, just because you've received the Nionan Star doesn't mean that you will be treated any different than before. I haven't forgotten about you disobeying my orders to stay here when we were searching for the suvanth in the forest. The inobi stables need a good scrubbing." Ethius and the others laughed at such a comment.

Keel had wandered from the group and Taukin found him alone and along the edge of the tree line watching the celebration. "A lot has happened," said Taukin.

Keel just stared at the flames and spoke, "A god said I'd rule this planet. That can't be true?"

"You have a choice," said Taukin.

"The bauble was a trick, if I had opened it…"

"You didn't."

"What if I do something worse?"

"We don't know what'll happen from one cycle to the next. Not even Cenro knows. Come on, let's get back," replied Taukin.

Keel and Taukin made their way back to their families and moved through the jubilant crowd toward the telling place.

When all houses were done taking part in the ritual, Hiko announced, "Carth tribe, we will celebrate late into the quiesce, and our jubilation will continue with the telling of a tale, far beyond what we have ever known. I welcome our respected speaker to the stage. Taukin, if you would honor us by coming to the stage to recount your heroic quest to our tribe and…leave no detail unaccounted for." Hiko stepped over to Taukin, "It's time you tell your story."

The music died down and the Carth rintic tribe faced the former pariah and their jubilation was replaced with silent bows of reverence as Taukin made his way to the break in the fire and up the stage to where Hiko stood just par-tems before. The gaze of the tribe upon Taukin felt like being wrapped in hundreds of constricting slings and the respect given him was more than he could take. Taukin's voice choked up as he tried to speak, "Car…" Taukin turned his head to the side and cleared his throat and took a deep breath and let his skin return to normal. His family, rintic and suvanth alike, sat at the front by the ring of fire and watched as their son and brother and friend stood among them as a leader of the rintic. Taukin breathed slowly and began, "Carth tribe, my tribe, this story begins on a cold quiesce, not long ago and much like this one when I traveled alone into the darkness of our majestic forest."

THE END.

ABOUT THE AUTHOR

Emory Frost is a Science Fiction writer from Bryant, Arkansas. He is a Veteran and has a bachelor's in Electrical Engineering with Computer Science. He currently resides in Arkansas, where he writes and likes to explore. Onestonia Pursuit of the Light Cipher is his first novel.

www.ingramcontent.com/pod-product-compliance
Lightning Source LLC
Chambersburg PA
CBHW022020300726
48970CB00003B/972